The Urbana Free Library

To renew materials call
217-367-4057

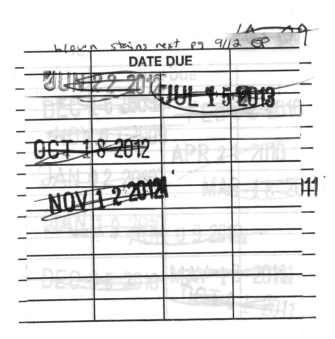

SENRID

Sherwood Smith

Copyright © 2007 by Sherwood Smith

Cover Design Copyright © 2007 by Vera Nazarian

ISBN-13: 978-1-934169-63-6
ISBN-10: 1-934169-63-3

Second Edition

Trade Paperback Edition

September 1, 2007

A Publication of
Norilana Books
P. O. Box 2188
Winnetka, CA 91396
www.norilana.com

Printed in the United States of America

SENRID

YA Angst

an imprint of
Norilana Books

www.norilana.com

ೲ Acknowledgements ೫ಐ

My heartfelt thanks to:

Elizabeth Parks for her expertise in manuscript preparation

To Athanarel gang for their enthusiastic support

Vera Nazarian, for taking a chance on me.

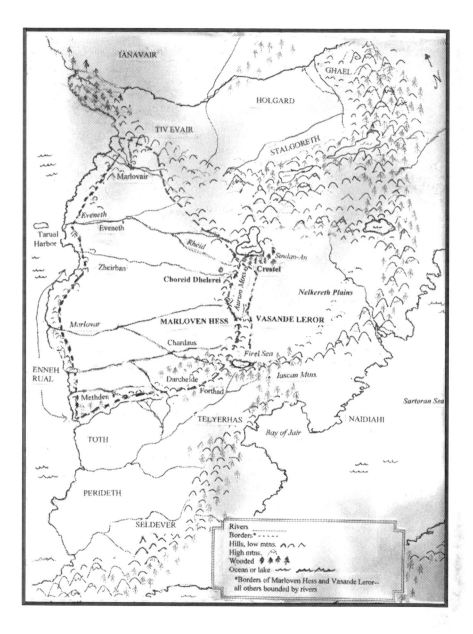

IANAVAIR

GHAEL

HOLGARD

TIV EVAIR

STALGORETH

Marlovair

Eveneth

Eveneth

Rheid

Tarual
Harbor

Sindan-An

Zheirban

Crestel

Choreid Dhelerei

Nelkereth Plains

Aurun Mnns

MARLOVEN HESS

VASANDE LEROR

Marlovar

Chardaus

Firel Sea

ENNEH
RUAL

Darchelde

Iascan Mtns.

Sartoran Sea

Methden

Forthad

TELYERHAS

NAIDIAHI

TOTH

Bay of Jair

PERIDETH

SELDEVER

Rivers ....
Borders* - - - - - -
Hills, low mtns. ∧∧ ∧
High mtns. ⋀
Wooded ♠ ♠♠ ♣
Ocean or lake ~~~ ~~~~
*Borders of Marloven Hess and Vasande Leror—
all others bounded by rivers

You don't cross their kings and live...

"Well, none of us knew at the time that that king is Senrid. He's king in name, but not in power. His uncle is the regent, and he doesn't want to give up the throne any time soon, from everything we've learned."

"So where does Faline come in? And executions?"

"Don't you see? She messed up Senrid's plan, so he's got to make good—make bad?—well anyway, he's got to correct the 'mistakes' by killing everyone who thwarted him, according to Marloven custom."

"That's a custom?"

Leander said grimly, "To the Marlovens. More of a law: You don't cross their kings and live."

Senrid

SHERWOOD SMITH

PART ONE

ONE

In a tiny, rural kingdom called Vasande Leror, the new ruler and his stepsister were busy with books. The castle where they lived was small, built stolidly of gray, unadorned rock, and mostly empty. The ruler, Leander Tlennen-Hess, sat in his library working hard at magic studies; down the hall in her suite of rooms, Princess Kyale Marlonen lay curled up on a couch reading, two cats nestled against her and one stretched along the headrest. Kyale's mind galloped through the pages of a historical record written by a long-ago princess not much older than she, whose life had been fraught with danger.

She'd sunk so deeply into the past that she failed to see the face peering in at her through the window.

Tap! Tap! Tap! came the sound of knuckles on glass.

Kyale jerked her attention from the book to the window, where a round, freckled face peered in.

"Yagh!" Kyale shrieked, flinging up her hands, and the book sprang into the air.

So did the cats. Before the ancient book (and the three cats) hit the rug Kyale had already dashed out the door. She ran straight to Leander's study.

He looked up, hating to be distracted; when he saw his stepsister's frightened face, he vaguely remembered hearing a scream.

Wondering if the horrible ex-queen Mara Jinea had come back from Norsunder to threaten them again, he set down his book. "Kitty? What is it?"

Kyale pointed back toward her room. "She—a girl—my window—"

Leander ran out, followed by Kyale. He arrived at Kyale's room at the same time as her governess, Llhei, an older woman of comfortable size and demeanor. Leander bent out of habit, carefully picking up the hand-copied history book.

Then all of them stared at the girl outside the window. This astonishing visitor stared back in at them, laughing; they could just hear her as she chuckled at the sight of the stout woman, the tall dark-haired boy, and the tiny, silvery-blond girl in the pretty dress, all with identical expressions of surprise.

The laugh was an infectious one, a friendly one. Leander and Llhei were the first to notice that the girl's expression was good-humored, and not at all frightening. Kyale just stared.

Leander set the book down. He flung open the casement of the window next to the one the girl peered into. "Who are you? What are you doing here?"

"Holding onto the ivy," the girl exclaimed, still chortling. "If you'll just listen—"

"Push her back down," Kyale demanded, frightened.

"Will you fleebs listen?" the girl yelled. "And let me in," she added meekly, peeking down at the courtyard below.

"First you can explain why you didn't come to the door," Leander began, squarely blocking the window, his mind full of the wicked former queen, Mara Jinea, and the cost in lives to get rid of her. He did not like any situation that he couldn't understand—the memory was too painful and recent, the sense of threat too near.

At that moment some of the ivy gave, and the red-haired girl dropped lower. "Ulp!"

Her nose was now barely level with the windowsill as she turned her gaze to Kyale. "Tell that kid with eyes the color of pond-scum to stop lip-flappin' and listen!" she pleaded through the glass.

Kyale didn't bother telling Leander what he obviously heard as clearly as she did; still in the grip of the written history, with its dangers and heroism, she bustled to the second casement and swung it open.

The girl surged up in a great rustling of ivy, flung herself over the sill and tumbled into Kyale's room. Then she stood up and dusted herself off. She was short—Kyale's height—but where Kyale was shaped like a reed, this girl was sturdy. Her bright red hair was confined into two stiff braids from which tight curls aggressively tried to escape.

Leander pointed out wryly, "*Your* eyes are the color of frogs."

The girl's laugh was warm and humorous, and not the least bit threatening. Then she said, "Would you believe froggies can help EEEE-mensely?"

"Help?" Leander and Kyale said together.

"I mean what I say. So park yer duff, and I'll take a turn at lip-flappin'. Hoo! This is the very first time it's been *me*— and not the gang at home—who's having an adventure." The girl tipped her head. Her hosts seemed even more confused. "Never mind that. I climbed up the window because everything but this window was dark, and you didn't have anyone waiting around like you usually find at castles. I tried knocking below but no one answered. Though I didn't knock loud because that thick wood hurts." She showed them reddish knuckles.

Kyale glanced at her brother, her nose lifting. "Well, we don't really have enough servants, and our few were busy elsewhere—"

"Kitty," Leander began.

"Though that's not *my* fault," Kyale said. "But do go on."

"All right. You've got this big country west of here, right? Marloven Hess? Full of warriors, seems to me."

"That's Marloven Hess," Leander said grimly.

"And the rulers use magic. Not just the rulers, either," the girl added. "Because I was a prisoner there. Of a magician, I mean, name o' Latvian. I made friends with his daughter Hibern. Fern's what she likes to be called."

"Fern?" Kyale repeated.

"Yes. She's fifteen, and wow, is she smart! See, her father had made some sort o' nasty plan to marry her to the Marloven king some day—"

"Eeeuw!" Kyale exclaimed.

"Well, she thought so too! So she pretended to be crazy. And lame. So her father locked Fern in a tower, where she studies magic without any interruption, and I'm here to tell you she knows plen-teee!"

Leander whistled.

"Go on," Kyale said, thinking Fern already sounded dull. Too much like Leander—studying and working all the time— and not enough like an adventurous hero ought to be.

"Well, so I also made friends with one of the guards, who was bored with guard duty, and we talked through the tower window a lot, and he was bragging about how smart their king is, and he's going to launch this plan soon, about taking over here. Reclaiming is what they call it."

The two Lerorans reacted typically: Leander worried about what this possible threat meant to the kingdom, and Kyale what it meant personally. Both were scared, so Kyale tried to disbelieve it.

"Huh," she said, wrinkling her nose. "If you got it from a mere foot-warrior, it can't be anything real. I mean, we haven't done anything to *them*."

Leander frowned at the girl. Could she be part of this plot? "Why did you come to tell us?"

The girl's eyes were wide and earnest. "Because we kids have to stick together, that's what Clair would say. Especially when there are kid rulers, like us. Well, like Clair. I'm not a ruler, and let me add, I'm grateful for that!" The girl paused, looked at them, sighed. "I see I'm not making any sense. Again. See, Clair's thirteen—another kid—"

"Kid," Kyale repeated, liking the sound of the word— which was the English word, and not the Leroran word for baby goat.

"It means people our age! We got the word from this world called Earth, after—augh! There I go again! Clair's our queen, and I know she'd want me to do what I did. So I did." The girl now grimaced comically, adding, "Did do. Do did?"

Kyale snickered.

"So what're your names?"

"I'm Princess Kyale Marlonen of Vasande Leror," Kyale enunciated with pride. "He's Leander Tlennen-Hess, the king."

The red-haired visitor drew herself up and executed a bow. "Well, Your Greenness and Your Shortness, I—" She smacked her chest proudly. "—am My Lamejokeness, Faline Sherwood of Mearsies Heili!" She pronounced her name *Fah-LINN-eh*.

"Never heard of Mearsies Heili," Kyale stated.

"Well, I never hear o' you gnackles either, till ol' 713 spilled that plan," Faline retorted in a reasonable voice.

"If you've never heard of us, how do you speak our language so well?" Kyale demanded. "I mean, you don't make any mistakes, only that accent."

"It's this spell Clair found and put on us, makes us hear other languages in Mearsiean, and when we speak, it comes out right for you. 'cept for words that you don't have, then you hear them real. Like 'kid'."

Leander began to relax inside. Adults, in his recent experience, rarely told the truth, and were mostly motivated by selfish or incomprehensible desires. He knew he couldn't judge their trustworthiness by word or expression, but someone his own age he found far easier to trust.

"I've heard of that spell, and wish I could find it," he said. "Of course you haven't heard of us. We're not exactly famous here. Where lies Mearsies Heili?"

"On the other side of Enneh Rual, over the ocean."

"That's not all that far," Leander said. "I haven't yet had time to study the map of the Toaran continent, but I know it lies just across the sea from us here on Halia..." He saw Kyale's impatience, and Faline's confusion, and added in haste, "But all that can wait. What's the plan, exactly?"

"To bring a mage with a bunch o' splatbrains—uh, warriors—up to some famous pass at your western border, and break the old spells that guard the pass. And while you're busy with magic trying to fix the spells and get rid of the mage, they'll have already brought another gang o' slobs around that way." Faline pointed north. "Meantime, smasho!" She clapped her hands together. "They bucket in and klunk you all."

"Bucket," Kyale repeated, delighted.

Faline grinned. "That's from CJ, too. Er, Princess Cherene Jennet. Like 'kid', 'bucket' is slang from Earth. CJ first came from that world, y'see. She had a terrible life on Earth. But Clair rescued her. Brought her to our world. Now she's our princess, since Clair doesn't have any brothers or sisters. Only a cousin, and he said if she tried to make him an heir, he'd—there I go again! *Any*way, CJ likes funny words. Remind me to tell you about pocalubing, our rule for the proper insulting of villains."

Leander sighed, not really listening to Faline's story about people he didn't know. He was worried about his ignorance of the enormous kingdom over the mountains to the west.

He had tried to find some records of Marloven Hess's recent history, but Queen Mara Jinea seemed to have destroyed them. All he knew was that they'd mostly been fighting one another for the past few centuries or so, when they weren't fighting their larger neighbors in order to regain access to the sea. So he'd given up the search. It wasn't as if he didn't already have too much to do, like repairing Mara Jinea's damage to Vasande Leror during her years of rule—and he needed to learn as fast as he could how to be a king.

So far, no one over there had bothered with little Vasande Leror. Obviously that was about to change. "When, do you know?"

Faline flapped her hands in a circle. "Soon, that was what I gathered. Soon like days away. They were marching these fellows here and there when I escaped from Latvian's." She twiddled her fingers back and forth. "Which lies not far from the border straight that-away, or I'd still be runnin' and hidin'!" She flapped a freckled hand westward.

Leander rubbed his hands down his face.

"How can we stop them?" Kyale asked, looking worried.

Faline glanced from one to the other. "I don't pretend to know anything about military junk, because I don't. Why, during this horrible adventure we got stuck with a year or so back, in this real military camp, where the bucketbrain in charge was planning a *really big* takeover—"

Leander whistled. "Insane."

"Well, he was that, too, but anyhoo, guess what I got stuck with? Supplies! Some of the other girls had better jobs, though we didn't have to do it—oh, I'm getting all tangled up again. I can see that this adventuring stuff would be *much* easier if the villains would let us know one involving us is coming, so we could send CJ's records on ahead to the people on our side, so they could read them and know us first." Faline grinned, rocking back and forth from heels to toes.

"Would you send them to the villains, too?" Kyale asked, snickering.

"Only the insults," Faline assured her. "And CJ always puts plenty of those in when she writes up what happened. Anyhow, seems to me with this plan your problem is, you have to be in two places at once, and you don't have any army, right?"

Leander sighed. "Right. It'd take days to raise the locals in a militia—everyone's busy with summer planting."

"Your group from the forest," Kyale began.

Leander gave her an impatient look. "What can thirty people do against an army?"

"They can look like an army, if you've got your magic," Faline said.

Leander leaned forward. "Keep talking."

Faline turned as red as her hair. "You mean it's a good idea? Well, it ought to be, because Clair used it first, see, when we squelched that insanitic I was talking about. But somehow, if an idea comes from me, it's gotta turn ridiculous—" Faline tipped her head to one side, and laughed. "Never mind! I'm not used to bein' the one in the adventure. I usually follow along."

"Adventures?" Kyale asked. "You keep saying that. Girls?"

"Yes! See, there are nine of us altogether. I'm one of eight friends of Clair, the queen, like I told you, and we always seem to get into these big splats. But we have lots of fun."

"Uhhh," Kyale sighed, in sudden and intense envy.

"Anyway," Leander prompted.

Faline's face turned redder as she stared fixedly at the bedknob. "I don't like to talk about this in the ordinary way, but you see, I happen to be an Yxubarec. I'm pretty sure that's why Kwenz of the Chwahir snaffled me and sent me over to Latvian in the first place." She sidled a quick peek at the two Lerorans.

Kyale looked blank; Leander grimaced, and then smoothed his expression.

But not quick enough. Faline pointed at him. "See? That's how everybody feels about Yxubarecs. Well, I hate being one, too."

"Being what? What is it?" Kyale asked, eying Faline, who looked ordinary, if rather scruffy. "And who is Kwenz of the Chwahir?"

"Easiest first," Leander told Kyale. "The Chwahir are another kingdom who really like conquering. They've been a threat at the other end of the continent for centuries, but there's a colony over on Toar, where they've been trying to invade and expand. Their rulers are pretty wicked, from anything I've heard."

"You've heard right," Faline said, holding her nose and waving her hand. "Kwenz is pretty bad, but his brother Shnit, who rules their homeland, is far, far worse."

"As for the Yxubarecs, they are shape-changers," Leander went on. "Read about 'em. Caused trouble elsewhere in the world, until some mage exiled them to a kind of cloud-city so they couldn't copy the forms of ordinary humans and get rid of the originals."

He paused, gripped again by doubt. He dismissed it again. In his experience, adults were not to be trusted, but people his age were. Also, if Faline were evil like her ancestors, would she have admitted to what she was? In the books, the Yxubarecs always kept their abilities secret.

To Faline he said, "So if Latvian enchanted you, you could be used against someone over there—taking the person's shape."

Faline nodded, her round, cheery face now somber. "See, I ran away when I was little. I didn't like copying people and killing the person so I could take their life for as long as it was fun. I don't like using my shape-changing talent because it reminds me of *them*. But here's an idea." Her freckled brow puckered in question. "I could, um, copy you, and go to the north border, and you could magic a bunch of fake warriors. Long's they don't actually attack, see, I can try to hold the villains off—being you—and you can scare off the real magician on the west border."

"I don't think I can face down an accomplished mage," Leander said, fingering the history book lying on the table. "I haven't been able to study like I should—"

"You study all the time," Kyale said fiercely.

Leander shook his head. "What does that matter, against some mage who's got dark magic—which is stronger in destructive power—and decades of learning behind it?"

"But it won't be Latvian," Faline said. "He was mad at someone else. I don't know all the details, just some. You'll be up against someone from the capital who isn't as good as he thinks he is. If that's what 'He should confine himself to military matters, the thing he knows best' means. So you throw in a bunch of extra spells and things, that's what Clair would do. So he smacks into more trouble than he expected."

Leander nodded slowly, his mind racing through possibilities, some very recently learned—others hinted at farther along in the books. But maybe with some fast study...

He said to Faline, "What about you in the north? I don't quite get it."

"Here," Faline said. "I'll show you. Got some of your duds you could lend me?" She gave Leander an acute, narrow-eyed scrutiny that fascinated Kyale and made Leander feel uncomfortable.

Leander closed his eyes, muttered, and with a soft *paff!* of displaced air some neatly folded clothes appeared, smelling of the rosewood trunk where they'd been stored.

Faline grabbed them and vanished into Kyale's dressing room. She came back a few moments later, and both kids were startled to see Leander's twin appear in the doorway. "Convincing?" she asked. The voice wasn't quite the same: it was a teenage boy's voice, but the intonations weren't Leander's.

However, it would do.

Leander let his breath out in a whoosh. "What this means is, we've got hope. All right. I've got to send some people out to locate these Marlovens, and we'll use your plan. It sounds better than anything I'd come up with. And thanks."

"Well, thank Clair, if you ever meet her," Faline said, clearly embarrassed. "Was her idea. I just pinched it."

Kyale snickered at the sight of this copy of Leander who spoke in such an un-Leander-like tone.

Faline whisked herself back into the dressing room, and returned a bit later as herself. She dumped Leander's clothes into his lap, and sat down cross-legged on one of Kyale's satin hassocks.

Leander got up, thrust his clothes under his arm, and said, "Kitty, you stay here and entertain our guest. Arel and Portan should be in the stable, but where's Lisaeth?" He opened the door and stampeded out, his mutters diminishing rapidly.

Kyale sighed, then turned to her guest, wondering where to begin. Faline was hardly dressed like one would expect of a member of a royal court, but hadn't she been a prisoner? Maybe she'd stolen that ugly tunic and those old kneebreeches from some peasant during her escape.

She'd listened carefully when Faline described being friends with a queen and a princess who were also girls. She hadn't once used titles; Kyale veered between introducing herself as Princess Kitty, to maintain proper rank, and—"You can call me Kitty, if you like," she offered, watching Faline anxiously.

Perhaps Faline would suggest the proper ranking herself.

Faline said, "Kitty! That's a great nickname! Diana would like it—she likes animals. So does Seshemerria."

No *Maybe I ought to call you Princess Kitty*. But at least she hadn't rolled her eyes, like the Mayor's daughter had, or worse, sneer, like that girl had who'd come with the duchess from Telyerhas, the big kingdom to the south, when Kyale had tried to get them to call her 'Princess Kitty' as a friendly compromise between informality and proper decorum.

"My best friends are animals," Kyale said. It was the truth. She had had no success finding local friends—either they were too lowborn for her to bother with, or else they were, like that duchess, used to a proper court and fine things, and they looked down on her even though she was a princess. "How many friends does your queen have?"

"There are nine of us, all told."

"And all of royal birth—or noble?"

Faline snickered. "Only Clair. I think. I dunno, never asked. Clair adopted us all, and some talk about their past and some don't. But we don't have any nobles in Mearsies Heili," Faline added cheerily, without the slightest vestige of embarrassment or apology. "It's mostly farms and mountains and forest—we're too small, I guess. Why, you can cross most of our kingdom in a week's ride!"

Kitty stared at her, thinking, *Vasande Leror is much smaller than that.*

But Faline went on to describe the girls' underground hideout, magically protected, all cozy and decorated by the girls, where they had endless fun—no adults allowed—and when they wanted they ran around in the woodland above their hideaway and played day-long games. They also had duties, such as guarding against the Kwenz's teenage heir and his friends, who kept trying to discover the underground hideout.

Kitty listened in fascination, her emotions swinging between dismay at the utter lack of the protocol and etiquette that she had always thought was essential to one's status, and envy at all their fun.

It wasn't until Faline had yawned several times, her vivid blue-green eyes bleary, that Kitty realized she might be tired and hungry.

When she suggested a meal, Faline agreed with fervent gratitude. She ate with enthusiasm, but her yawns came more frequently, and after a short time back in Kitty's rooms, she reluctantly suggested a rest.

"Oh, that would be nice," Faline said, her relief plain.

"Llhei will show you to a suitable room." Kitty reached for her summons bell.

"L—ya—lya—how do you say her name?"

"Ll-yeh-AY-ee, but you run it all together," Kitty said. "She comes from Sartor, or somewhere far away like that. Sartoran has all those funny l's and yuh sounds, Leander says."

"Really?" Faline asked. "How did she end up all the way here? Must be a good story!"

Kitty said, "She's only my maid."

"Oh." Faline looked surprised, a subdued sort of surprise, and Kitty wondered if she'd said something wrong.

Llhei opened the door. "I trust you are going to let your visitor rest now?" she said, beckoning to Faline, who jumped up. "She had a very long day."

"Of course," Kitty said, hoping to impress Faline. "That's why I rang. I'll see you in the morning," she added as the two left the room.

Hopefully those idiot Marlovens wouldn't try any tricks for a while, and in the meantime, Kitty would have this entertaining girl all to herself.

TWO

"The horrid thing is," Kitty said the next day, "that Leander doesn't know the least thing about being a king. It's not his fault," she added quickly. "I mean, his father was king—the Tlennen-Hess family is *very old*—but my mother, the wicked Queen Mara Jinea, did away with his mother when Leander was really small, and used magic to enchant the king, which is how she got to be queen. Alaxandar sneaked Leander away to keep him safe—Alaxandar was the captain of guards—and they lived in the forest. So that's why we usually eat in the kitchen, and there aren't enough servants, and Leander wears old clothes when he ought to dress like a king. He's used to living in a forest camp, not in a castle."

She sidled a peek at her guest. Faline was listening with a polite, friendly expression on her face.

Kitty rushed on, "So you see, if you mentioned to Leander that your queen always observes proper protocol when interviewing people of lower rank—so everyone knows where they belong, and how to behave—it might help him to see how we should do that here."

Faline reached to stroke the closest cat, her lips pursed. Finally she said, "Well, I don't know if I'm the best person for that kind o' thing. Fact is, we don't really have any protocol, at home. Or at least not much. I guess Clair has some when she meets with people who have petitions and things, or gets advice from the grown-up governors, but we girls usually stay out o' that kafuffle. And except for CJ, we don't have titles or anything."

Kitty gave up, and changed the subject. "How did you
end up with Latvian, since you live on a different continent?"

"Kwenz of the Chwahir is a friend of Latvian's. He
needed someone to experiment on with these spells. Latvian
tried it first on his son, and made him crazy, so the long and
short of it is, old Kwenz and his heir, Jilo, scouted me out, on
account of my being an Yxubarec, and they wanted to get back
at Clair for—well, never mind that. Anyway, I bumbled into
Jilo's stupid trap. Next thing I knew, I was in Latvian's house."

"Ugh!"

"It almost worked, too. Clair has no idea where I am. If
Fern hadn't been been studying light magic—she's the real hero,
not me—and I didn't happen to be able to shape-change, I'd
probably be as crazy with wicked enchantments as poor Stefan,
Fern's brother, who set fire to Latvian's house one day, after he
saw my red hair!"

"No," Kitty exclaimed—less envious and more
frightened. Oh, sure, she wanted to have adventures. But
nothing creepy or really, really dangerous!

"It was pretty weird. But Fern is fun, and she knows a
lot of stories about magic history. And it was fun talking to 713
through the window. The warriors give up their names when
they join, and they only get numbers, which change when they
get promoted. I always thought guards and the like would all be
creeps and bullies. Well, a couple of them were. But ol' '3 was
funny! He even liked my jokes!"

Kitty thought about Alaxandar, Leander's most trusted
liegeman during the bad old days, and shuddered. "Some are
definitely bullies," she said, but didn't explain. After all,
Alaxandar was loyal to Leander, and if he'd thought Kitty was
like her mother at first, well, she had to admit she couldn't really
blame him.

Faline shrugged. "So that's my story. How about
yours?"

"Oh, it's probably not as interesting as yours," Kitty said,
hoping to be prompted. Faline's life was interesting, all right;
but Kitty wanted desperately for someone to think her own life
interesting.

Faline laughed. "Evil queens and outlaws—boring? Try another one!"

Relieved, Kitty smiled. "There isn't a lot to tell. I didn't really do much. See, I didn't know my mother was horrible, that she used her magic against people, so she could get to be queen. I thought she was very beautiful—which she was—and I never saw her do bad things because mostly I lived in Tannantaun, a day's ride south, all alone except for servants. Sometimes I went to court, and everyone smiled at me, and I got to wear pretty clothes. Then Leander's people kidnapped me, and took me to their hideout in Sindan-An—that's the forest north of here..."

Kitty didn't tell her story well. She kept jumping back and forth in time, and it was very hard to make herself the hero of actions she'd only peripherally witnessed or understood, but she tried.

"... and my mother didn't trust any of her courtiers, not really, so I was never permitted to see other children. Just once a year, on my birthday. They didn't like me, and I didn't like them. So I made friends with the local cats."

Faline nodded, understanding a lot better now. This girl was about as pretty as any girl Faline had ever seen, with her silvery eyes and silvery hair and her beautiful dresses, but it was really obvious she had no other girls to talk to.

"All of these cats I see here?" Faline asked, looking around at the cat-loaves on the bed, the couch, and the cushions. There must have been at least a dozen of them, all resting contentedly, their eyes slitted.

"Oh, these aren't the only ones," Kyale said. "I have six friends among the big felines, and my favorites are Meta, who's a leopard, and Conrad, who's a lion. But they don't like to come inside."

"A lion!" Faline exclaimed, her eyes round. Wow!"

"He understands me—he really does," Kitty said. "Le— other people don't believe it, but I *know* he does. Watches out for me, too. Meta and Conrad both. I think animals know a lot more than we think they do—or some of them, anyway. Horses, well, I think they're stupid."

"Two of my friends will agree with you about animals and understanding," Faline said. "Though maybe not about horses. But I think it's great about those cats!"

Kitty talked on about her experiences with her pets, and some of the stories she'd made up during her days alone in the garden at Tannantaun. Faline listened with obvious sympathy and interest, and by the time the two parted for sleep that night (there having been scarce sign of Leander all day) Kitty was determined to lure Faline into staying as her own special friend. Surely that thirteen-year-old queen Clair, who had seven other friends, wouldn't miss just one, and anyway, if she had magic, she could go find another replacement, couldn't she?

‽CℤΩcs

A knock on Kitty's door brought her out of sleep.

"Huh?" she sat up, then thrashed her way out of the blankets. "Who's there?"

"I am." Leander opened the door, and snapped a zaplight into being. In its mild blue glow Leander looked as tired as he felt.

Kitty stared at him in worry.

He said, "Would you give these to Faline? I don't want to embarrass her by waking her up, but we need to hurry." He thrust a bundle of clothes into Kitty's arms, a heavy bundle that *chinged* faintly. When Kitty began to frown he said in haste, "The Marlovens have been sighted. The plan Faline overheard seems to be happening. Have her dress and meet us downstairs."

He ran back down the hall to his next task, and his magic light winked out. Kitty's initial annoyance at being asked to do a servant's job vanished. Adventure beckoned, and she did not want to be left behind.

Excitement thrilled through her. She ran down the hall to Faline's door and opened it. "Faline! The Marlovens are coming!"

The girl sat up, snorting, her wild red hair barely visible in the weak pre-dawn light.

"Here—put this stuff on, and come down at once!"

She dropped the clothes onto the bed, and backed to the door, realizing that if she were to join whatever was to happen, she had to get dressed as well.

When Kitty emerged from her room, she thought she saw Leander—except he was stamping oddly about in the hallway. "Is—which one are you?" she asked, and then giggled from sheer nerves.

The supposed Leander looked up, and grinned back, a grin that was characteristic of Faline even though it used Leander's features. "It's this stuff," Faline said plaintively. "Heavy clothes—I'm not used to these quilted vest thingies, much less a mail-shirt, and these klunking boots. I feel like I'm wearing a house!"

Kitty could make out the sky blue with gold and red trim on the battle tunic—Vasande Leror's colors. Below the tunic were quilted long trousers that tucked into high blackweave riding boots with iron on the heels. Faline stamped about, saying over her shoulder, "I gotta get used to these clodhoppers."

"Get used to them going downstairs," Kitty said, gesturing. "We ought to hurry."

Faline groaned. "How do people *wear* this stuff? No wonder the Chwahir are such sour-pies..."

Kitty smothered laughter as Faline muttered on in a voice somewhat like Leander's yet not, mixing insults with how scared she was.

They stopped in the morning room, where Leander was waiting in an outfit twin to Faline's. Unsmiling, he handed her yet more weight—a sword and dagger—and she rolled her eyes.

"I don't know how to put these on," she said, and then looked around. The expression of dismay on her face, and the servants' reactions, caused Kitty to cram her fingers in her mouth to keep from laughing.

Lisaeth and Arel, servants who had been with Leander during the forest days, all stared from the real Leander to the fake Leander, their faces aghast, their heads jerking back and forth, back and forth. Kitty's eyes watered with her efforts not to give in to giggles.

"This is why I hate changing so much," Faline whispered to Kitty. "People don't trust me."

"Are you really a boy?" Kitty whispered, almost too soft for Faline to hear.

Faline gave her a surprised glance. "Of course. Shape changing is shape changing."

Kyale laughed and backed away again.

"Here," Arel said awkwardly, holding out the sword and belt. "I'll help you put them on."

Faline obligingly held up her arms, but she said to Leander, "If there's to be a duel to the death, be sure to tell Clair what happened. I never even held a sword before, and I only use knives to cut my food!"

Leander felt a weird flutter of laughter inside him. He knew it was nerves, but the absurdity of this twin standing there next to tall, capable Arel, making faces and whispering words like *gnarg* and *fazoo*, made him want to sit down and howl.

A glimpse of Arel's anxious face doused the laughter.

"You don't have to use the weapons," Leander said to Faline. "This'll work, if it's going to work at all, if you look the part and stay silent. Alaxandar will do all the talking."

"I'm going too," Kitty stated, crossing her arms. "Don't say it's too dangerous. If we lose, I'm in danger anyway."

"Oh, let her come," Faline begged, which surprised and delighted Kitty. "If she hides?"

"I'll hide and watch," Kitty stated.

"All right," Leander said, feeling that the situation was sliding beyond his control already. There was no use in keeping Kitty out, even though she did not know the first thing about self defense. She was right about danger. If the plan failed and the kingdom was overrun by enemies they were finished anyway, and so he lined them up for transfer.

Alaxandar came in, a tall, grizzled man who stared at Faline in frank disbelief. Kitty had no time to react—though she felt laughter bubbling up inside again—before the weirdness of transfer magic seized them.

They appeared on a little hill with great pines at their backs. Fighting against the dizziness and inward wrench of magic-residue, Kitty followed Faline and Alaxandar through the trees to the edge of a long, sloping bluff. Below, bisecting the summer-green meadowlands, snaked a long, neat formation of warriors, some mounted, more on foot.

They had come to a halt, their black and gold banners glinting in the dawn light.

As Kitty's vision cleared, she felt magic all around her; the edges of her vision glittered and blurred. She ducked behind a huge maple tree directly behind Alaxandar and Faline.

"Why do my eyes think I'm inside a bubble?" she asked.

Alaxandar said, "Leander has a ghost army up here, an illusion spell. What the Marlovens see are helms and swords gleaming among the trees. Supposed to look like a couple thousand—more than twice the numbers we see here."

Faline sighed. "Oh, good. What now?"

"If they break their march formation and line up for the charge anyway, we're in for trouble. Ah! They've definitely seen the illusions—" Alaxandar broke off, pointed a callused finger. "They've spotted us. Comes their galloper."

Two horsemen had detached from the Marloven army and rode directly up the bluff. Alaxandar stood, his hand on his sword hilt, waiting in silence; Faline waited next to him. After a moment she put her hand on her sword hilt as well. Faline's profile was tense and unsmiling—in fact, to Alaxander and Kitty both, she looked exactly like Leander now.

The two horsemen reined in a spear's throw from Alaxandar and the fake king of Vasande Leror.

Kitty peeked between leaves at the two men, one maybe twenty, the other much older. Both had light hair sticking out from under helms with horsetails streaming from the tops.

The younger one carried a banner. The older one opened his mouth, but Alaxandar said before he could speak, "His Majesty Leander Tlennen-Hess of Vasande Leror requires you to withdraw from our border. We will wait the space of one glass after you rejoin your commander, and if we don't hear the retreat, we will defend our borders as is our right." He held up a small sandglass, ready to be turned.

The older one leaned on his saddle-horn, as his horse bent its head and cropped at the long, sweet summer grass all dotted with clover. The other horse tossed its head—its mane was as yellow as the rider's hair, Kitty noticed—and danced.

"Well, now," the older warrior said, his Leroran very accented. "What brought you out here today? Morning maneuvers?" He shifted his attention from the boy-king to the tough old fellow who obviously had some military training. Despite rumors...

Faline just stood there, frowning at the Marloven warriors.

That Marloven villain is stalling, Kitty thought. Faline was right about the plan!

Alaxandar's mouth deepened slightly at the corners, but otherwise he did not react. "Perhaps," he said. "Morning maneuvers on our western border as well, along the old pass at the Aurum Hills. Only there, we've got the king's favorite magician all ready to practice some spells. Mage-maneuvers, you might say. Turning the chance passing army into tree stumps, or something like."

From her vantage, Kitty saw surprise widen the two pairs of eyes before them.

A quick exchange full of military talk ensued. Under the belligerence, it was clear that the Marlovens were trying to find out if their plan had been revealed. Faline and Kitty were amazed at how skillfully the gruff Alaxandar hinted that it had been known—somehow—since its inception, that the Leroran army was eager for a fight, and furthermore their magician was eager to see how his border protections would work.

All three points made an impression, the girls could clearly see in the sidways glances the Marlovens exchanged, and in the covert sign the old one made to the young one with his gloved hand.

Faline saw that the Marlovens were now looking her way, as if for a sign.

So she turned to Alaxander, who held up the glass. That was it! She was a king, so she was supposed to give the command! She dipped her chin down in what she hoped was a kingly nod.

Alaxandar gave a grim smile. "It's time." He raised his sword in the air, made a circle, then lowered it. And then he turned the glass upside down. Sand began running through.

Abruptly the two wheeled their horses and rode back down the hill.

Hand on sword, Alaxandar let out a long, slow breath. "I believe we've won," he said in an undertone, without moving his head—almost without moving his lips. "We'll know in a moment."

And sure enough, scarcely five breaths after they reached their commander, the trumpets below sounded a fall of notes that echoed against the hills and back.

"That's the retreat," Alaxandar said, his face still grim. But he chuckled deep in his chest.

The horsemen below galloped around, changing their formation, not for attack, but for retreat, and the long column of marchers wheeled left and started the long march home.

"How'd you find them?" Faline asked, also without moving, since Alaxandar still stood motionless and alert, hand on his sword.

"Our runners spotted their camps night before last. Leander spent the day and most of the night setting up the magic here, and in the pass. He's there, where the magic battle is supposed to take place. We wait here for him to return—or for us to be overrun," he added grimly. He tipped his head a fraction toward the forest behind them. "If they do charge, a few of my old band are stationed in Sindan-An behind us, and will make it hot for them along the road into Crestel. We know every tree and shrub in Sindan-An. A big army would be a big target before they dealt with the last of us."

Kitty, who had never heard such a long speech from Alaxandar, realized he was talking to Faline the way he'd talk to the real Leander, and inwardly she shuddered at the implied slaughter, glad that at least this army was going back home.

She decided it was time to join the coversation, but as she stepped up, Alaxandar stopped speaking.

Faline muttered out of the side of her mouth to Kitty, "This adventure has got my guts a-moilin' and a-boilin'. I think in the future I'd as soon leave it to CJ, if the villains will cooperate."

Kitty snickered. Alaxandar—if he even heard—just watched the retreating line.

The three waited, mostly in silence, for what seemed an endless time. The sun was peeping through a different group of branches when the dazzle and wind of transfer magic startled them all; once again Alaxandar put his hand on his sword, but dropped it away again when Leander appeared.

"It's over," Leander said, smiling, though his face looked grayish with exhaustion. "Back home. Touch hands! Transfers are getting rough," he added.

They all took hands, and he did the magic to get them back to Crestel.

೫⎯⏀⏁⎯ೞ

"Leander, tell her your magic doesn't work," Kitty said, pulling on his sleeve a short time later.

"What?" Leander looked down. The edges of Kyale's face were blurry. He blinked, weary, longing for rest. "Kitty. I have the strength—I think—for one more spell. She saved us, and wants to go home. Don't you think that's an easy enough reward for us to provide? We owe her a lot more than that."

"That's it," Kitty whispered, looking over her shoulder at her dressing room door. "Don't send her. I want her to stay! I like her so much—"

"But she wants to go home."

"Well, why can't she make her home here? You heard her tell us both she wasn't born in Mearsies Heili, and that girl-queen has lots of other friends. Offer her money, or anything she wants!"

Leander forced his eyes to focus as he looked down at Kitty's unhappy face. He chewed his lip, trying to think, but trying for clear thought was too much like grabbing at butterflies. "I can't offer her money, it's an insult," he said. "Kitty, it's her *home*. Didn't you listen to her the other night? Every other word out of her mouth was about what CJ says or

Clair thinks. Those other girls are her family. She won't want to leave them—"

The dressing room door opened. Faline emerged, once again a short, stocky, smiling figure wearing a worn old tunic, trousers, her feet bare, her bristly red curls escaping two fat braids.

"Here's your duds back," she said, handing Leander a bundle. "I put 'em through the cleaning frame since I sweated 'em up something fierce. Was I scared! But I'm glad we did it. Now I'm ready fer home. Wow, is Clair gonna be amazed! And CJ will want to know all the details, because she writes up our records. I hope I can remember all the jokes I make up for ol '3, so those can go in, too!"

Kitty ran forward. "Please stay. You can have any room you want, any *thing* you want..." She stopped when she saw Faline's eyes widen, not in pleasure, but in fear.

In fear. She didn't want to stay—that much was clear.

Kitty forced herself to laugh, to back up. "Or if not, how about visiting again some time? And bring your friends!"

Now Faline's relief was unmistakable.

Kitty managed a nonchalant smile. "Thanks again!"

Leander felt the wrench of grief, because he read in Kyale's loneliness his own inadequacy as a brother.

He'd never had a sibling. Except for those very early years, only dimly remembered, his whole life had been a struggle for survival, but at least he'd been surrounded by friends in his forest camp—friends and laughter and fun. Kitty had never had any of that.

Resolving that each day he'd find time for Kitty and her interests, no matter what, he summoned the last of his strength, and did the transfer magic to send Faline safely home.

THREE

"Kitty."

They had just sat down to breakfast, and already the weather was hot.

The summer had been long, and balmy, and recently the heat had intensified, as if the season was reluctant to make way for fall.

Leander tried to look fierce, but it was such a false expression that Kitty giggled.

"I have what I consider a reasonable request," he stated, his tone mock-serious. "That you either confine those felines of yours at mealtimes, or else train them not to invade my rooms."

Kitty gasped. "I could never lock them up," she declared, wavering between silliness and seriousness. "They need freedom! Especially now, when it's so hot. Why, the big ones are never even around."

"It's the small ones who climb on my desk, and who put cat hair all over my papers." Leander added in an even more doleful tone, "And I resent the 'freedom' with which they leap upon the table and flavor my soup with yet more cat hairs, and help themselves to the cream—usually by spilling it first, for better access. Three books, now. Three." He solemnly held up three fingers. "Have cream stains."

Kitty snickered. "Well, don't put your books on the table, or your soup where it's in reach!"

Leander covered his eyes with his hands. "I ought to throw you all into the river. Except then you'd come back to haunt me."

"You're sooooo right. Especially since you promised to teach me to swim."

"So I did," he said, and mentally did a swift review. So much to do, so much to do, but he remembered his internal promise earlier in the summer, when Faline Sherwood had been with them so briefly.

He grinned at her. "I know how to do it." He pushed his plate away and sat back. "We'll go back into Sindan to the old hideout, and we'll get up on the bridge above the stream. You remember that stream, don't you?"

Kitty nodded, her eyes round. "It'll be a river at this time of year."

"Right. Plenty of water. You'll sit in the middle of the bridge rail and I'll push you off. If you make it to the side, you'll know how to swim!"

"And if I don't make it?" she asked, trying to sound ominous, but her silvery eyes were round with delight.

Leander shrugged. "Oh, we'll say that I'm a very bad teacher and remember it for future reference."

Kyale choked on a laugh, then flipped a bite of potato at him.

"Arrrh! I just took a bath!" he snarled, and Kitty ran shrieking from the room.

He chased her all over the palace until she collapsed, breathless with laughter, on the cool marble floor of the otherwise unused throne room. Then they played a game of hide and seek, which was always her favorite, because in this game she was as good as anyone else—if not better.

She would happily have played all day, but finally he said he had to get back to work. She'd learned that when his eyes started going distant, and she had to recall his attention by repeating herself several times, that he wasn't going to be any fun anyway, and that he would soon disappear behind his study door.

She sighed, wishing she could close out the world like he did. Not that he was having fun when he did it. She knew that. But still.

She wandered down the halls, then paused at a window and looked out at the jumble of rooftops of Crestel, the little city down the road from the castle gates. It was wonderful being a princess, but not when she was alone. Why couldn't she make friends?

She'd gone to the midsummer festival always held on the great square in the middle of Crestel, and she'd especially looked for girls her age. There had been lots of them, but mostly just farm girls or merchants' daughters. The landowners rarely came any more.

Kitty knew it was because she and Leander didn't keep court, and the old midsummer balls and parties were only boring stories in the memories of old folks. The estate-owners celebrated on their own land, or with each other. Or with relatives. Neither she nor Leander had any relatives—that she counted, anyway. Leander was descended from kings, but the great Tlennens and Sindans were long gone, leaving only crumbling castles and territory names on the map. The rest of his family had dwindled into farmers and the like.

She groaned as she looked at the slate roofs gleaming in the bright sun. She didn't want balls and adult parties, with a lot of romance and disgusting stuff going on. She wanted games and fun, or parties where she had the prettiest dress in the room. If only there was a way to have the old festivals but only with kids!

She'd have to talk to Leander about that.

And she knew what he'd say, that his time needed to go into protecting the country, that they couldn't afford the expense, that he was worried that Marloven Hess would try something new, hoola-loola, hoola-loola.

Kitty ran up the last, narrow stairway, and emerged on the castle wall. She looked at the green hills lining the western horizon, beyond which lay Marloven Hess. All she knew about them was that they liked fighting, and they were apparently ruled by a creepy sorcerer-king. Leander had been trying to find out more about them, for he hadn't known anything, he said, before Faline came. But nobody communicated with them—so far, anyone sent over the border never returned. Faline was that rarity, someone who had successfully crossed the border, but that was only because she had employed her powers during her escape. Meanwhile the few historical records they had about

Marloven Hess mostly dealt with the Marlovens in ancient times—when Vasande Leror was actually part of the Marloven empire.

Kitty turned her back on the west and trailed along the northern wall, looking out at the distant greenish line of Sindan-An, and beyond. The morning was already hot, and haze made it difficult to see too far.

Closer to home, the road was almost empty. Farmers coming to town had mostly come in at dawn, or even before. They'd wait until sunset to go back, and then the road would be clogged with people.

Wait. Was that someone on the road? Small—barely visible, but as she watched, the figure gained detail.

A lone walker—a kid! Someone's apprentice? A messenger? No, those usually rode.

She expected him to turn off down the main road into Crestel, but instead the boy seemed to hesitate, then marched on down the shrub-lined road leading to the castle!

Someone coming to visit? Or just lost?

Kitty felt the sting of the sun on her arms, and her neck was sweaty under her hair, so she decided it was time to go inside. If the kid arrived, she could get a closer look, and if not—well, she could always watch the road later.

She ran down to get another breakfast cake to munch, and then up to her room. She pawed restlessly through the books she'd pulled out of the library, but she'd already read them all, and none of them looked interesting enough to reread.

Besides, if that kid was going to arrive at the castle, it would be about now. She peeked out her window as the lone figure entered the empty courtyard. She squinted against the glare of sun off the crystal dots in the gravel scattered over the old flagstones. The boy looked like he was about her size and age. He had a round face and yellow hair, and was dressed in a white shirt and dark trousers and walking mocs. Plain clothing, but not poor: the shirt well-cut fine linen, with carved buttons instead of the usual laces down the front of a one-size-for-all cotton. But he wore no tunic, or any ornaments, and had no carriage or even a horse, so he couldn't possibly be anyone important—of rank.

His head lifted and he scanned the windows. She jerked back, embarrassed at the idea of being caught staring. It was one thing to watch people, but she hated the thought of being watched while watching!

She leaned forward and peeked—in time to see the blond head pass beneath, toward the big double doors.

Probably somebody lost, or wanting a job or something. Not that Leander would ever hire more servants, badly needed as Kitty thought they were.

She flopped down on her pillows and settled for one of her favorite histories, about a princess from hundreds of years ago, who'd gotten into all kinds of adventures, fighting pirates...

"Kitty? It's time for lunch." Llhei's familiar voice punctured the long-ago time and far-away place of Princess Sharend.

Kyale looked up, surprised. "Already?"

Llhei nodded, wiping a strand of gray hair back. "Your brother wants to know if you'll join them."

"Them?"

"He's got a guest—"

"A boy? Yellow hair?"

Llhei smiled slightly. "You've been spying?"

"Just saw him in the courtyard," Kyale said defensively.

Llhei shrugged, and busied herself straightening the room. Kyale watched, sighed, got up.

No use in asking more—Llhei had a short way with what she considered nosy questions. She was the only part left of Kyale's life with her mother. Llhei had consented to stay with Kitty, but there'd been compromise: no titles, no curtseying. "I'm too old and creaky for that," Llhei had said.

Kitty had agreed, not wanting her to leave. It was Leander who recognized that Llhei had been more of a mother to Kyale than Mara Jinea had ever been, despite the constant flow of pretty dresses and princess crowns.

She ran downstairs to the dining room.

In obvious relief Leander said, "Come on in, Kitty. This is—uh, what was it again?"

"Senrid," said the boy. He had a pleasant voice and a sunny smile.

"Yes, that was it. I'm sorry, I need them repeated a few times before I remember. My own included." Leander grinned and the boy grinned back. "This is Kyale—"

"*Princess* Kyale Marlonen," Kitty corrected.

"—but we call her Kitty."

She repressed a sigh. Now it would be awkward if she insisted on a proper bow, and to be called Princess Kitty. Really, when would Leander ever learn?

Senrid gave Kitty a cheery smile, and she sat down. Up close, Senrid looked her age, his smoky-blue eyes friendly.

"What put you on the road in this hot weather?" Leander asked.

Kitty added, "I saw you from the wall. You can see the whole region from up there."

Senrid had just taken a big bite of his bread-and-cheese. He swallowed it hastily down, blinked, then said, "At the border somebody told me you people here are kindly disposed toward travelers."

"You speak our language perfectly," Kitty observed. "Though you seem to have an accent."

"I happened to encounter a mage," Senrid said. "Universal Language Spell."

Leander whistled. "I've been trying to track it down. Or at least learn how it works. Why can we hear the words in our language, but in your own accent?"

Senrid flicked his fingers outward, almost lost his sandwich, and hastily lowered his hand. "The mage told me you hear the meaning for the words, the magic doesn't change how you speak."

Leander said, "And off-world words don't seem to translate at all. Odd. So you're seeking your fortune?"

"Yes." Senrid's smile intensified to a grin before he bent his head and took another bite of sandwich.

Kitty wondered what was funny about Leander's question; her brother said, "Did I make a joke?"

Senrid said, "When you consider that almost nobody who goes out on the road ever finds a fortune, but we seem to like using the phrase. Maybe it's a metaphor, for seeking one's goals. Do you think? If so, I hope I find my fortune," he added.

Metaphor, Kitty thought. Even Leander didn't talk like that. "But when you have it, life can still be boring." Kitty sighed.

Senrid said, "I take it you don't have many visitors."

"No." Kitty grinned. "Though we did have a great one, not long ago. She came all the way from Mearsies Heili, and what adventures she's had! She was lots of fun, but she went home."

"Did she find adventure here?" Senrid looked interested.

"Yes! See, she—uh, Faline Sherwood was her name—well, she'd escaped from those rock-heads to the west of us. Seemed they'd gotten the idea that what is ours belonged to them, and she overheard a plan, and came straight along to tell us, even though she didn't even know us. And helped us squelch it," Kitty added. "I wish she could have stayed."

"Rock-heads?" Senrid asked.

"Marloven Hess," Kitty said, holding her nose and waving her hand as if someone had made a terrible smell. "A land of fatwits and murderers."

Leander said, "Are you interested in Marloven Hess?"

Senrid flicked his hand up. "I'm interested in staying out of trouble. So you don't advise I travel west, then?"

"Not unless you want to be killed or something," Kitty said.

Leander tossed his napkin down. "I'm done, and should get back to work. If you like, I can give you a tour of the castle," he offered. He didn't say *before you go*, but it was obvious he thought Senrid would be on his way after the meal.

Senrid flicked a glance from him to Kyale, then said politely, "You seem busy. Kyale, I would like to see what it looks like from the walls."

Leander nodded. "Too hot for me up there. I'll be in the study if anyone needs me." And he left.

Senrid gave Kitty his cheery smile. He seemed younger when he smiled, like someone's little brother. "It's very kind of you to show me around."

"Oh, nothing else to do," Kitty said, trying not to preen. Even though he was only a boy, she couldn't help feeling pleased that he'd picked her company over Leander's. "I'm not like Leander—work, work, work. Boring life! This way." And as they started out, she added, "Your name is unusual. Which you'd expect from someone not around here. But I keep thinking I've heard it before."

"Really?" Senrid asked, still cheery. "When? Do you remember?"

"No, I don't. Must have been ages ago. Here's the stairway to the wall." She ran up the narrow stair. Senrid was right behind her.

They stepped out, and Senrid walked along the edge, apparently untroubled by the long drop.

"This is my favorite thinking spot." Kitty gestured. "You can see in all directions. Much better if it's a clear day. I think this little hill Crestel is built on is the highest place in the country, except for the Aurum Hills."

They looked westward. Then Senrid turned slowly around, scanning in all four directions.

Kitty, who'd seen the view many times, blinked against the noonday sun, and flipped her damp hair off her neck. "Whew! How about we come out later? It's much too hot to be here now."

"No one else is up here?" Senrid asked.

Kitty shrugged. "Not unless it's us. In my mother's day there were guards all over, but not now."

"Where'd they all go?"

"Leander took the enchantment off them. Most went off to do other things, some left. Some went to Norsunder with my mother."

Senrid grimaced. "Norsunder." He repeated the terrible name in a flat voice.

Kitty felt the back of her neck twitch, almost a chill, despite the heat. No one liked to think about Norsunder lurking somewhere just outside the world, beyond time and measurable space. They said those who had caused the fall of Old Sartor still dwelled there.

"Did your mother's followers choose to go to Norsunder?"

Kitty's shoulders hunched up under her ears. "My mother had to go," she whispered. "She'd made a bargain with them, for power. They—they *came* for her, when I broke the spell. I mean this crack in the air opened. We all could see darkness beyond it. She got pulled inside it. It was the only time I have ever seen her afraid, before she vanished."

Kitty no longer saw the heat-shimmering, dusty countryside, or even Senrid, as she stared back into the terrible events of the year before. When she looked up, she was so startled by the change in Senrid's face the memories snapped away.

Senrid's eyes were angry, his mouth pressed in a white line—he looked older. Leander's age, even. But when he saw her expression he grinned, that wide toothy grin, and he was twelve again. "Norsunder," he said. "We all know it's bad language to call someone a soul-sucker, but I've always wondered if there even is such a thing. Sounds like they can suck an entire person beyond the world, though, doesn't it?"

Kitty shuddered. "I don't want to think about it."

"Why not?" Senrid rubbed his hands over one of the stone crenellations, then gave Kitty a wry look. "You know that your mother could come back. The real horror of Norsunder is not only that they own you if you bargain with them, but they lie beyond time. They could send her back, if they choose."

"Leander is afraid of just that. That's why he studies so much, and—well, I don't want to talk about it."

Senrid opened a hand. "So no one guards your country against attack?"

"Well, we do. Or Leander does." The heat was oppressive; she started toward the tower and the stairway down.

Senrid's brows rose. "One defender? Your brother must be formidable."

Formidable? Kitty crossed her arms. "If you think he's not very good, guess again." Delighted with this chance to impress someone, she added loftily, "He got rid of those stupid Marlovens earlier this season, and he didn't have any army. Only Arel, Alaxander, and some magic. And Faline. He says he doesn't know enough magic, but personally, if you ask me, I think he knows plenty, and a person can really study too much."

"What should he be doing instead?" Senrid asked as they passed through the archway into the tower, where the air was still and musty but somewhat cooler.

It was also dark after the bright glare, so Kitty couldn't see her guest. "Oh, learning to act like a king. He's—" She stopped, realizing that she oughtn't to criticize Leander in front of a total stranger. "Well, there are plenty of things. Including having fun," she added, laughing.

෴ལ෨༄

The afternoon passed swiftly. Though Kitty would never have picked a boy as a companion, Senrid turned out to be a good listener. Everything she said he seemed to find interesting.

Kitty was delighted. She showed him over the nicer parts of the castle; he seemed interested in Leander's magic study, but she shooed him away. "Leander hates anyone going near his books," she said. "And anyway he's probably in there working. Hates to be disturbed."

Senrid obediently turned away, and Kitty was relieved. She felt a twinge of guilt at having exaggerated a little, but he was such a good audience, and anyway Leander *did* have a lot of work to do, and Kitty had nothing. It was too hot to play in the garden, so talking fit her mood.

With very little prompting she told the whole story of Leander's accession to the throne and the defeat of her mother, but she told it from her perspective. Senrid put a few questions about things she left out, but those events—having to do with adults, and politics, and magic—held very little interest or importance for her.

So she firmly brought the subject back to what did interest her: her own experiences. Her kidnapping by Alaxandar, and meeting Leander and his outlaws; how horrid it was living in the forest; how difficult it was to keep pretty gowns clean when you live outdoors where there are no cleaning frames. Senrid asked a question or two that brought her to the final confrontation with Mara Jinea.

"She'd enchanted people, you see," Kitty said. "They couldn't really think for themselves."

"Enchanted? How?" Senrid bent forward, listening intently.

He really was a good audience, Kitty thought, pleased to be regarded as interesting, her words worth listening to. That didn't happen very often! "It was strange, because I'd gotten used to Mother's guards, and her servants, and her nobles, all acting so obedient and quiet when she didn't need them. Smiling—always smiling at me, telling me how clever I was, and how pretty I looked. It turned out that she had put enchantment on them, and it all turned on *me*."

"How did it work?" Senrid asked, leaning his elbows on his knees.

They sat on hassocks in Kitty's rarely used parlor. She adored having a parlor of her own—but she rarely got to use it for guests.

Kitty smiled. "Well, see, she and I wore these black crowns. Obsidian. Leander thought there was magic put on them. Anyway, they kidnapped me because Leander thought I should have a choice between her way of life and ours—well, his, then—then Mother got her people to find us, and there was a fight, but Leander's people were outnumbered. We got taken back. And she was going to kill Leander, but by then I knew she'd lied to me. Everything she had blamed him for she'd actually done—it was all turned around, all of it. But by then I'd learned that people who use dark magic are selfish, only interested in being cruel and having power. Dark magic, or black magic as some say, it means that magic gets burned up or spent, so it goes out of the world and takes a long time to come back. Like candles going out. Light magic, which is also called white magic, stays in balance, so it doesn't get spent out of the world."

"Leander told you that?"

"He studies magic, so he knows these things. Light magic mages are good, and protect each other. Black magic mages are evil. Anyway, so I threw down my crown, and that broke the enchantment. It wasn't the crown, see—I had two or three of them, actually—it was *me* doing it that was important."

Senrid whistled. "So whoever held you held the country."

"Yes," Kitty said, trying very hard to sound careless. "Of course Leander didn't want those enchantments. He said people deserve freedom of choice."

"What if they hadn't chosen him as king?" Senrid asked, his round face bland, and his eyes steady and interested.

"He said then we'd travel all around the world and see things. Like you're doing! But he'd leave behind people free to live the way they wanted, and he'd consider it a good job."

Senrid's lip curled faintly.

"It's true," Kitty protested. "It's weird, but he was really serious. But then he liked his life as an outlaw. *I* like being a princess. It was a relief when everyone agreed he was the best to take his father's place. Even though he's fifteen, which some think young for a king, he has been learning magic, and he's *responsible*." She sighed. "I think he's too responsible, but no one asks me."

"I don't think it's too young to be a king," Senrid said. "But I can see that adults would." He gave her a strange, rather sardonic smile.

She enjoyed the crack against adults, but only mildly so. Mostly she was tired of talking about Leander—having to be diplomatic—and she wanted to get back to her own heroism in standing up to her mother. It was all too rare that someone found her interesting instead of Leander.

"Would you like to spend the night?" she offered, as a bell donged twice in the distance. "I mean, we have lots of empty rooms. And I can show you so much more tomorrow. Unless you're eager to get back to the road again."

"Too hot for that," Senrid said. "And everything here is so interesting. I'd like to stay. Thanks."

"Good. That was the bell for supper. Go down that hall, take the stairs, and turn right, then right again. I'd show you, but I need to order a room prepared for you, and all that," she said grandly.

He turned his palm up in what Kitty took as agreement. Then walked down the hall.

Kitty raced down by a shortcut, wanting to make certain that the meal would be served in the dining room. Leander was too prone to eat in the kitchen, which Kitty had gotten used to—but not with guests. It would lower their prestige.

Having spotted the table set and ready, she galloped back up to Leander's study, and not surprisingly found him there, surrounded by books.

"Dinner," she said, when he looked up, his eyes so distant she wasn't sure he even saw her.

"Oh. Thanks," he said. "I'll be down anon."

"Huh," she retorted. "Shall I have something sent up?"

"That would be nice," he said. Then he blinked, adding, "Did Serand continue on his journey?"

"Senrid."

Leander smiled briefly. "Oh. Just as well, I guess; I looked his name up, and I was right, it's close to the word for buffoon in the Old Language."

"But it's not Serand," Kitty reminded him.

Leander frowned slightly. "Senrid. Senrid? I've heard that one before, haven't I? Why do I think it has connotations?"

"Well, if it meant something rotten in that stupid Old Language, don't go blabbing it," she scolded. "Not everyone has your weird hobby about history and old words, and it could lose you friends before you even make any."

His gaze wandered over his books, and Kitty sighed and left, knowing he was already distant in thought.

Senrid was in the dining room, politely waiting for her to join him. Wherever he'd come from, he had very nice manners.

"Tell me about your home," she asked as they helped themselves to rice and a tasty fish sauce filled with chopped vegetables.

He shrugged. "So little to tell. Parents are dead, no siblings. So I decided to travel."

"It's horrid, being an orphan, isn't it?" Kitty exclaimed. "Not that I really want Mara Jinea back, because she was horrid in a different way. And no siblings either—it's so lonely. I do have Leander," she amended in haste. "But I always wanted a sister."

"Oh?" he asked politely.

"Yes," she said, and continued on to describe, in detail, the sister she had imagined for herself. This sweet, pretty little sister would have adored Kitty, and would want to play all Kitty's favorite games all day long, and would admire all her favorite gowns.

Senrid listened without speaking, his round face blandly friendly as they worked their way through dinner and dessert. She took that as interest, and so was in great charity with him when they rose at last.

"I walked a long way today," he said. "Would you mind if I retired?"

"Of course not," Kitty said, though she was disappointed. She'd looked forward to a long evening of talk, all about her favorite games and stories. But then, she reflected as she showed him upstairs, she had all the next day to look forward to.

And so she left him in the very best guest suite down the hall from Leander's and her suites, and then ran downstairs again.

She reached the kitchen and stopped when she saw her brother there, along with a couple of his old outlaw friends.

"Oh! I was going to have a tray sent up," Kitty said. "I almost forgot."

"Thanks," Leander said. "Pertar's here. Just got back from his ride along the border." Leander had set up regular scouting trips after the invasion scare.

"Oh," Kitty said, losing interest. It had nothing to do with her, so she shrugged and left, thinking that at least Senrid wouldn't see the king eating in the kitchen with his servants.

෴ఇ෨ఴ

She retired early, but woke when the vines outside her open windows rustled. She sat up, hearing the rush and moan of a great wind.

A moment later rain thrummed against her windows.

The weather had changed—quite suddenly.

Wondering if her guest was all right, Kitty clapped her glowglobes on, flung a silken robe round her, and padded down the hall to Senrid's room. Light glowed under the door. Was he scared? Did he want company?

A gentle knock produced no answer.

She hesitated, then shrugged. If he was asleep, he'd never know she'd peeked in, and she could clap out the lights. If he was awake, he might like company during the storm.

She eased the door open, tiptoed through the sitting room, and stared into the bedroom. Though the glow-globes all gave light, the rooms were both empty.

FOUR

Where could he have gone?

Kyale wondered if he'd changed his mind about sleeping
and had found his way to the study to talk with Leander.
Disappointment propelled her down the hallway as thunder
rumbled through the stone around her.

She saw faint blue light glowing under Leander's study
door. She was right. Was she missing anything fun?

She opened the door, and stared. Leander wasn't there.
Senrid was, all right, but he'd fallen asleep in a chair, with one
of Leander's books in his lap, and over his shoulder casting its
glow one of those tiny, cold blue zaplights that magic-workers
made. Had Leander just left, then? In the faint light Senrid
looked more than ever like a nice little brother, sitting there so
peacefully with the open book, one hand on the page.

She pulled the book from his hands and put it on the
table, and almost at once he stirred, then opened his eyes.

For a moment they stared at one another, Kitty in blank
surprise. His gaze was wary, and cold, and narrowed; that and
the smudges under his eyes made him look Leander's age again.

But as she watched his face smoothed into friendliness
again—a round-cheeked boy her age.

She didn't know what to think—except that Leander
couldn't have left him alone. He had never left anyone in the
study since she'd known him. "Leander doesn't like anyone in
here unless he's here. I told you that," she said.

Senrid's brow puckered, and he looked very apologetic.
"I'm sorry," he replied. "I couldn't sleep. And I really, really

wanted to see a magic book, so I thought it wouldn't harm anything if I was very careful and didn't disturb anything."

Kitty was largely mollified. "Oh, it's all right, I've done the same, truth to tell."

"Really? He won't teach you magic?"

"Oh, he would. He'd be happy to. But he insists I learn the basics. They are so boring! I only want to know a couple of spells—like how to make my gown clean without having to go upstairs and walk through my cleaning frame. Or the transport spell, when I don't want to walk."

Senrid gave her an absent smile, but as soon as they were out the door, he said, "Please don't tell Leander. I won't go in there unless he takes me, you can be sure of that."

"I won't," Kitty said reassuringly. "Since you were asleep, I guess the storm isn't bothering you, so I'll see you in the morning."

Senrid half-raised a hand, then trod down the hall to his room.

∞ C⅜∞ℭ

The next morning the weather was cold, heralding at last the end of summer. Kyale bounded out of bed and dressed hastily, running upstairs to the castle wall so she could feel the delicious coolness after days of hot stuffiness. The wind fingered through her hair, and she grinned up at the long bands of departing gray clouds.

A short time later she became aware of Senrid at her side, the wind snapping his shirtsleeves and blowing his hair about wildly.

"Llhei said I could find you up here," he said. "You like this weather too?"

"Yes! It's my favorite," Kitty said.

"Say." Senrid sat down on a stone crenellation, dangling his legs over the sheer drop and looking very much at home. "While we watch the weather change, tell me the story of your friend Faline."

"Oh, Faline," Kitty said, feeling that inward wrench of longing and envy. "She was so funny!"

"Did she talk about her kingdom?"

The envy soured into jealousy, and Kitty remembered something Leander had said. "Did she! Every other word was about the greatness of CJ and Clair—their princess and queen—and how smart they are and how much magic they know."

"Well, tell me what happened when Faline came. I like your stories. And I envy you getting to live through such adventure." He gave her his cheery smile.

Kitty's jealousy winkled away, like a candle snuffed out. She settled onto the next crenellation, her feet resting inward on firm stone. She felt pleased and proud. "Where shall I begin? I was reading a history, oh, it was so exciting, all about..."

Senrid once again was a good listener, paying close attention to everything she said. He only interrupted once. "What was the guard's number? His riding or wing?"

"I forget. And what's a 'riding-or-wing'?" Kitty saw disappointment in Senrid's face, so she exerted herself to be more descriptive of those things she did remember: what she was wearing that day; Faline's wildly curling hair; her funny talk; she was about to describe Faline's shape-changing, but hesitated, remembering how much Faline hated that part of her background. So she said vaguely, "There was magic, and it was so weird to see two Leanders."

After she finished with several gloating comments about how stupid the Marlovens were to be fooled so easily, Senrid said, "That was a great story. How did Leander manage to get rid of the evil mages at the pass?"

"I don't know. That's all boring magic talk."

"I think I'll ask him," Senrid said, swinging his legs around.

"Oh, don't bother him now." Kitty waved her hands. "He'll be busy with morning boredom."

"Well, maybe company will make it less boring," Senrid pointed out.

Kitty crossed her arms. "Have fun," she said, and she turned around to face into the wind.

She hoped he'd apologize, or at least wait there until she turned, but after the silence had gone on too long for that, she flung her hair back and sneaked a peek, to find that she was alone.

Well, huh. She'd stay there and wait. After all, maybe Senrid would find Leander so boring with his everlasting blather about magic, and history, and *what if?*s that he'd be glad to come back and hear more stories from someone with a real imagination.

And maybe Leander would find him a mere interruption, and send him away.

⟡⟡⟡⟡⟡

Leander was in the kitchen, trying to wake himself up with something hot to drink.

The door opened and Senrid came in, his face pleasant and friendly. "Mind company?"

Leander shrugged. "Help yourself." Truth be told, he'd rather Senrid kept Kitty happy, so he could catch up on what he'd meant to work on the night before. But he'd gotten distracted talking to Alaxandar and Arel and a few of the old guard about how to go about protecting a country that was—at best—the size of a duchy, and a small one at that, against a huge warrior kingdom like Marloven Hess.

We can patrol the hills from now until the dawn of the next world, but what if they come over with an army we can't fool? Pertar had asked.

If we even see them first! We don't have enough people to cover all the ancient roads as well as the pass—they could come in south of us when we're north, or north when we're busy patrolling south, Arel had added.

Leander had no answer.

The clink of silver brought his attention back.

He was not being a good host. Even though he didn't really know how to entertain a kid Kitty's age whose interests had to be completely different from hers, he had to try.

When he looked up, Senrid said, "Kyale tells me you study history."

Leander shook his head. "I'd like to study history," he amended. "Right now about all I have time for is trying to correct my ignorance on this or that thing. I've begun some reading about the old kingdom, of which Vasande was once a province—" He waved a hand, realized he still had some bread in it, and dropped the bread on his plate. "Never mind. Kitty says I go on about that boring stuff too much."

"I don't find it boring," Senrid said. "Old kingdom as in Iasca Leror? Or not so old, as in Marloven Hess?"

"So you know something about our history?"

Senrid flexed his hands, his gaze on his plate. "I hear things. And remember them."

Leander sighed. "I wish I had a better memory. Well, I do have a good enough one, but I suspect I try to do too many things at once. I like reading history when I can. By which I mean not just getting the time, but access to books. They are costly, and we have a lot of repair ahead before I can replace what Mara Jinea burned."

"She burned history books?" Senrid asked, plainly disgusted.

Leander was relieved to find that the kid and he had something in common to talk about; the polite banter of a court was not a skill he'd ever learned. In fact, talking to others his age and younger had been a rarity after Mara Jinea made certain that his first few friends among leading families, back when he was seven or eight, all mysteriously disappeared, either sent away to study—or exile.

"You know your recent history," Senrid pointed out. "Kyale told me about it yesterday. Mara Jinea, obsidian crowns—it was exciting!"

Leander laughed. "Exciting to live through, too."

"What I wondered was, how did you figure out that Kyale had the enchantments keyed on her?"

"You know something about magic?" Leander countered, surprised.

Senrid shrugged. "Only what I hear. Like, someone told me that enchantments have to be keyed to something, usually an object, though sometimes on people."

"Most don't know that much. Think it's all random spells. Kitty herself—well, anyway, no, I didn't figure that out. To tell you the truth, it was completely by accident that we found out. I almost destroyed everything by rescuing Kitty from her mother. My purpose was just to give her a chance at a real life, and don't think some of my own people weren't annoyed."

"You'd had no idea, then?"

"I'd thought Mara Jinea's obsidian crown was the key. She kept it locked up and guarded. Looking back, her reasoning is clear, and cold as frostbite. She keyed the enchantments on Kyale because she didn't think we'd ever guess they'd be on a person—" He paused, looking a question.

Senrid said, "I was told that keying enchantments on a person is dangerous since the easiest way to break a key is to destroy it."

"Yes. I'll add to that you can only force a person to be a key with dark magic. White magic won't do it, takes more power than mages are willing to spend, even if there was no danger."

Senrid said, "So Mara Jinea keyed her spells on Kyale."

"She thought the risk small because she controlled Kitty, and because she didn't think her daughter had any importance to anyone. People didn't, to Mara Jinea, except as channels to power. I guess that's common to dark magic mages, from what I've read. That's why white magic has more safeguards, to protect people. But it does take longer to do small things. Anyway, seems like dark magic learning selects for the power-grabbing sort of mage."

"Interesting," Senrid said. "So you'd throw away power if you could?"

"No—yes—I don't know. Power for power's sake, that holds no appeal. I do what I was raised to do. If someone better comes along, I think I could hand it all over and not look back." Leander looked up at the windows. Just then the light streaming in was muted as a cloud obscured the sun. "I think I could, but I don't know if I'd as easily give up my home. And I know Kitty couldn't." He shrugged. "Does that answer your question 'too much'?"

Senrid gave a quick grin. "Kyale might think so, but I don't."

"In that case come along, if you like. I've got to get through some work today, and I can pull down some records relating to use of light magic you might like to look through."

"Sure."

Leander led the way out. In the hallway, he saw a golden streak flash by him, and then he was stunned to see Senrid pressed against the wall, a growling young lion standing before him.

"Conrad," Leander said sharply.

The animal's ears twitched, but the yellow eyes stayed focused on Senrid, who did not move. The sight of those long white teeth made Leander back up to the kitchen, slam open the door, and yell, "Get Kyale!"

For a protracted stretch of time no one moved, neither animal nor human. Leander watched in dismay, after trying futilely to distract the lion, who until now had seemed uncannily prescient.

Of all Kyale's pets, he was the one who seemed to 'hear' humans. Kitty certainly thought he did; Leander was ambivalent. Now he knew that having a lion as a pet was, in fact, a very bad idea, and that Conrad might for some reason like Kitty, and tolerate everyone else, but nothing would change the truth: he was a wild animal. One who didn't like strangers.

Kitty finally appeared, breathing hard.

"Conrad!" She flung herself on the lion.

Leander winced as the wedge-shaped head jerked, sharp teeth showing, but then, miraculously, the hackled fur laid itself flat, and Conrad's growl turned into a long, moaning yeowl.

"Bad kitty," Kyale said, hands on her hips. "That's not the way we treat people." Kyale shot fulminating glances at both Leander and Senrid, and Leander wondered if his stepsister had sicced the beast onto the poor kid. It was obvious that she was irritated with Senrid. For deserting her company for Leander's? Probably.

Leander sighed as Kyale clapped her hands sharply. "Come, Conrad. We'll go somewhere else."

The lion padded after the girl, and Senrid let out a long, shaky breath. "Well, that was one way to wake up."

"I'm sorry," Leander said, wondering if he ought to explain about Kyale's likely jealousy. He decided he would only if the kid demanded an explanation.

Senrid wiped his hair back, shook his head, then said, "Do they do that often?" He gave a lopsided smile. "Or just when Kyale gets miffed with someone?"

So Kitty was obvious even to a stranger. Leander felt his annoyance switch from Kitty to Senrid, and he berated himself for being unreasonable. It was no more than the truth—but he didn't like anyone saying it out loud. "Never done it before," Leander said slowly, choosing his words.

But Senrid seemed satisfied with that. "How about a look at those records?"

Relieved, Leander said, "Come this way."

They walked up to the library first—the old Tlennen-Hess library, with its comfortable furniture for reading.

"I don't have many books," he said apologetically. "Like I said, Mara Jinea destroyed anything to do with recent history, and all her magic books. I have my father's, thanks to Alaxandar, which I keep in my own study. The ones in here are old histories. A few local. Most are the old ones about Sartor everyone learns, and a few copies of personal records."

Senrid ran his finger along the titles hand-written in gold ink on the spines of the books.

He made a couple choices, and then Leander said, "I usually work in my study next door." Senrid followed.

Leander opened the door, and glanced at his guest, who scanned around with interest—and focused, for a brief moment, on the desk.

Then Senrid looked up, saw Leander watching, and grinned. "A real magic library," he said. "I always wanted to see one. I meant to ask Kyale about it last night, when I saw her here, but I was too tired."

Kyale had been in his study? Why? "You can see it now.
Grab a chair anywhere, while I dig into this pile I should have
finished off last night."

Senrid dropped into a chair.

Leander sat down at his desk, assessing his piles. His
thoughts whirled away like fireflies winking out when he noticed
the slim blue volume lying on the edge of the desk.

Leander frowned. He knew he hadn't gotten any of those
particular books down, not for some weeks. Which one was it?
The old blue ones his father had inherited from his grandmother.

He slid the book over, and looked down at the title.

Perimeters, Boundaries, and Wards

FIVE

So had Kitty been nosing again?

But why would she be interested in protective wards?

Deciding to ask her at dinner, Leander shoved the matter from his mind and picked up the top paper from the pile awaiting his attention.

Senrid read quietly while Leander worked—and from the sound of rustling pages, he read very fast. When he'd finished his two books he returned them to the library and came back with two more. He never glanced once at the books on Leander's magic library shelves.

As usual, the sun setting took Leander by surprise, but at least this time he felt he'd gotten caught up with the most pressing demands. How grateful he was that being a king in a tiny kingdom like Vasande precluded tiresome agony like keeping court! The Guildhouse in Crestel, and the Mayor, were all the 'court' Leander needed; his responsibilities with respect to trade, and law, extended to interviewing them twice a week, once he'd gone over these stacks of reports they scrupulously sent.

Magic was entirely his responsibility.

And defense, alas.

When he suggested dinner, Senrid closed his book and rose politely. They ran downstairs, and Leander felt his appetite waken when he smelled braised onions and baked redspice chicken.

"Hoo," he said. And, with an apologetic glance at his guest, "If you'd wanted lunch, I wish you'd spoken up. I tend to forget things like meals."

"I'm used to that," Senrid said, grinning.

Leander glanced at Senrid, seeing for the first time that he was not just short but thin. He laughed. "Two of a kind," he said.

They reached the dining room, to find that they were alone. "Is Kitty around?" he asked the cook's daughter, Nelyas.

"Llhei says she's sick," the girl responded. "I'm taking a tray up soon's you have what you want here."

Sick, or sulking? Leander frowned, but said nothing more about Kitty. He turned to Senrid. "So what were you reading?"

Senrid heaped chicken over braised potato as he said, "History of your split from the empire. Why did Mara Jinea destroy recent records?"

"Um," Leander said. "I wasn't familiar with the library before she got to it. The few that Mara Jinea did not throw in the fire all had to do with ancient treaties. I don't know what she was trying to hide."

"What makes you think she was hiding anything?"

"Why else destroy knowledge except to keep it from anyone else? She wasn't born here, but suddenly appeared at court. I strongly suspect that she was sent by the old monster next door." Leander jerked his thumb westward. "There might even be some kind of twisted family connection, or some underhanded secret deal she didn't want anyone finding out. I'm almost certain that she was planning some dirty-work with the Marloven king concerning our shared border-mountains, which the Marlovens supposedly want for ore mining."

"Vasande Leror belonged to Marloven Hess at one time," Senrid said. "According to one of those histories," he added quickly. "Maybe the old monster next door thought in terms of retrieving what was once his."

"But allegiance has to go two ways," Leander retorted. "According to my own family records—the few I managed to save—the Marloven crown requires heavy payment in harvest and in human terms: each family had to send their best for military service, and also half their harvest, or work in the mines for ore to be forged for their never-ending demand for weapons. The supplies for a huge army have to come from somewhere. But for what? For supposed protection? Except no one ever attacks them. That is, from outside, but the old stories about the First Lancers make it clear that they had been far worse than any mere outlaws or brigands ever could have been. Some protection!"

"So you did away with an army entirely?"

Leander sighed. "How can I raise one? It has to be supported somehow, and it's going to take us years to recover from Mara Jinea's greed and bad governing, especially if we can't get the silk trade going again and re-establish our trade relations down south. Mara Jinea destroyed half the mulberry groves in the southern border mountains against that mine business I mentioned. Anyway, I've been hoping that the struggle to recover would make us less appealing as a target."

"Well, you're not defenseless," Senrid said, smiling. "Kyale says that you ousted two Marloven detachments as well as a mage with the help of a foreigner and a couple of easy magic tricks."

"'Easy,'" Leander repeated, and groaned. "Kitty would think so, because she didn't have to spend all night repeating the illusion spell a thousand times in the north, and laying wards and traps and illusions all over the pass in the west. It took me the better part of a day and night to set it all up."

"That's not easy, it's clever," Senrid said.

"And I can't expect it to work again." Leander twirled his fork. "Much as I'd love to join Kitty in believing the Marlovens are stupid, I can't, really. They have to have figured it out by now. And next time—if there is a next time—they'll be ready for that one. If only I had the time to master the kind of magic I need! But white magic isn't geared toward warfare, and thinking up ways to employ it to ward black magic, which is, eats up an enormous amount of time I'd rather spend finding ways to reestablish harmony in the places Mara Jinea destroyed."

Senrid flexed his hands once, then closed them around his cup. "Do you see that as a weakness inherent in white magic, the lack of defensive capabilities?"

"Only when you think in terms of war," Leander said. "A subject I don't know as much about as I ought, I guess. White magic is strongest at improving—maintaining—the quality of life." He studied his guest. Interesting, that a boy of eleven or twelve could think of asking about defensive capabilities. Kyale probably didn't even know the words—and Leander was trying to master the concept of defense, under Alaxander's patient coaching, at twelve. "These are good questions. Have you an interest in the problems inherent in ruling?"

Senrid turned the cup around and around in his fingers. "I have an interest in everything." Then he looked back, smiling cheerily. "That's why I am traveling!"

"Ah."

"I also have an interest in what might be for dessert," Senrid offered, still grinning.

"So have I," Leander said. "And since my sister isn't here to get miffed at my lack of manners, why don't we go into the kitchen and find out?"

"Lead on." Senrid rose and pushed in his chair.

They made their way to the baking kitchen, where they found peach tartlets being pulled from the ovens. As they each snagged a hot pastry they stood around and talked with the cook and her daughter about peaches, harvest, baking, and the upcoming harvest festival.

Leander realized that the Senrid's round, smiling face rarely altered expression; during the entire discussion, Senrid was exactly as bland and friendly discussing peaches as he had been while the subject was black magic enchantments and keys.

Well, so he looked bland. At least he was fun to talk to. Leander hadn't had any company quite like him in his entire life. Tiredness pulled at mind and eyes and he suggested retiring for the night, but he looked forward to the next day.

On his way upstairs he stopped by Kitty's room—to be thwarted by Llhei.

"She's asleep, poor thing," Llhei said.

"Then she really is sick?" Leander asked.

Llhei nodded, lips pursed. "Silly child sat out on the wall half the morning—that has to be what did the damage. She's made herself ill from being chilled once or twice before."

"How's she sick?"

"Fever. Headache. She sat in that cold wind until it leached out her strength." Llhei shook her head.

Leander sighed. He'd only known Llhei as long as he had Kitty, but he could talk frankly to her. "Not sure whether to be sorry or glad. I thought she was sulking."

"She was," Llhei said, nodding. "I don't know if the one led to the other, or the reverse."

Leander glanced up the hall, which was empty; the door to the guest suite remained closed. "Because of Senrid?"

Llhei nodded again. "She liked the company. He was a good audience. She didn't like it when he wanted to talk to you."

Leander felt guilty at once. "If she's not better by morning, we should have the healer in."

Llhei nodded. "I think she'll be fine. She drank down all of my listerblossom and willowbark infusion, and she's sleeping well. This has happened before, she's usually fine in a day."

"Good."

Leander retreated to his room, and stood for a while at his window, looking out at the departing rain. Had he possibly found a friend near his age? Someone Mara Jinea couldn't make vanish? Instinct said that it was much too easy.

So he'd have to arrange an experiment.

Meanwhile, the endless routine of tasks awaited him, so he set to work.

℠⟮ℛℰ⟯ﻭ

At dawn he was in the kitchen finishing up his orders to Pertar's twin brother Portan, who ran the stables and served as relay to the border scouts, when Senrid appeared.

"Early riser?" Leander asked.

Senrid flicked a hand palm up. "When you travel, you get used to being up with the sun."

"Speaking of travel," Leander said. "I have always wanted to, but there wasn't much chance. So once in a while I get out of here and go camping. My old lair. Interested?"

Senrid hesitated, then nodded. "Sure."

"Good. Let's go."

Senrid followed him out to the stable, where Portan had finished saddling two horses.

"Can you ride?" Leander asked, mounting one.

Senrid waved a hand as he mounted the other, his movements quick and practiced.

They rode out side-by-side, sedate at first. Leander kept the pace slow as they left the castle gates and started down the road. Senrid matched his pace, looking about with interest. His hand on the reins, his seat, were excellent.

The morning was balmy, and promised warmth later; Leander knew that today would be a good harvest day.

"Up to a gallop?"

Senrid turned his palm up.

Leander lightly touched his mount's sides, and she frisked, tossing her head, then began to gallop. The second mare followed.

Side by side they raced down the road, veering north at the fork. Leaping streams and shrubs, they traversed the meadowlands below Sindan-An—'An' being the old word for 'forest'.

The light had bent westward, sending shafts of glowing gold between the branches of the trees that Leander had lived among for so long, when they reached the site of his old camp, tucked up against a rocky hill down which tumbled a stream to feed the river snaking past.

Leander said, "I am unused enough to castle comfort that I keep this place well stocked. You never know when we might need it again."

Senrid looked around appraisingly. "This is where you hid out?"

"This was the main camp, but we had hidey-holes all over Sindan-An. I like this one because of the waterfall over there, and the cave. Nice place to hole up when the weather's bad, and it's got plenty of stores. We fished off the bridge downstream there—you can see it through those two maples."

Senrid squinted. "That's a nice-looking bridge. But there's no road."

"Strange thing to find out in the middle of nowhere, isn't it?" Leander grinned. "We use it for fishing. It was built by my friend Arel, and his father. Arel was trying to do his 'prentice work despite the fact that he had no home. Lots of wood around, though." Leander opened his hands, and Senrid snorted a laugh. "Hungry?"

Senrid turned his palm up.

"Well, I am."

"You stock food?" Senrid asked, brows askance.

"No—but the forest is full of it. You can catch us a couple trout, and I'll dig up some taters and greens. There's probably some garlic and spice left over. But first let's get a fire going. Would you do that while I see to the horses?"

"I'm better with horses. Never fished," Senrid admitted.

Leander nodded. "All right, then, we'll switch jobs. You'll find what you need in the cave there. Should be fodder all the way in the back."

It was true. Senrid knew how to care for horses. He worked with the same ease with which he'd ridden, but he was distracted by Leander's actions as he set up a fire with wood and a sparker, then banked it to burn slowly within their old cooking stones.

Leander left to forage. He found plenty of potatoes, and some wild onions, and succulent purple grapes from the vines that one of his old friends had tended so carefully, and a few herbs. Last a handful of carrots, and he headed back.

Leander said, "You wash these in the river and I'll catch us some fish. I know where the best ones hide."

Senrid looked down at the vegetables that Leander indicated, and opened his hand, palm upward. Leander found the gesture curious; it could have meant anything.

Senrid carried the root vegetables down to the river's edge; as Leander watched from the periphery of his vision, Senrid splashed them about in the water, rubbing them with his fingers. He did his best to get the soil off, but it was clear he'd never done such a chore before.

Leander had caught and prepared a couple of fish before Senrid was done.

When they retreated to the cave, the light was already blue, the shadows having melded and deepened. Leander said casually, "Have a knife? If the two of us chop, we'll eat the faster."

"No weapons," Senrid said, hands out.

Weapons. Interesting that a traveler would regard a knife only as a weapon. Interesting—but not entertaining. Leander felt a sharp twinge of regret.

"Well, we've a few stashed here." Leander got one out and tossed it so that it landed point down near Senrid's foot. Senrid didn't flinch or jump. He yanked it free and wiped it on his sleeve without any of the reluctance of those who seldom touch steel. His fingers were deft as he angled the knife for chopping—but the actual chopping was slow and uneven.

Leander found a few withered olives left from the last trip someone had made to the cave, and crushed them into the pan, which he set on the glowing stones. They worked, and talked more history: Sindan-An and the old plains-riding families. Senrid seemed to know more about local history than Leander did—though his knowledge was centuries old.

When he got the food sizzling, Leander sat back. "This used to be our storytelling time," he said. "Or we'd make music. But I confess I liked best the old stories, about the morvende, and hervithe, and Geres, and other magic races. I wish they lived around here—I'd like to see them once."

Senrid looked up politely. The fire leaped and snapped, twin flames, in his steady gaze. His face, lit by the ruddy glow, was exactly as bland as ever as he said, "Unlikely, as you say. The morvende live deep down under the oldest mountains, the hervithe are only found far in the northlands. And the Geres limit themselves to the belt of mountains round the world."

"True. Have you a favorite tale about Old Sartor, or the non-humans on the world?" Leander asked, leaning forward to give the food a vigorous stir.

"I like everything I hear," Senrid said. "But I confess I prefer tales about the times and places I'm in, rather than those far away."

"Why don't you tell one you know? I've talked enough."

Senrid looked out at the whispering trees.

Leander glanced out as well. The smells from the sizzling pan had overcome the familiar scents of the huge silver maples rising into the sky, surrounded by cottonwood and willow and elm and white oak, all ready to change to autumn brilliance amid the dark evergreens. One more cold storm would alter the entire forest—its own kind of magic, and art. Whatever happened with Senrid, he was glad he had come.

The lengthening silence brought his attention back to the food, which he gave a practiced stir, and then to his guest.

Senrid said apologetically, "I guess I can't think of anything that wouldn't be boring. Or silly."

Leander snorted. "Silly. You mean romantic? First thing when we defeated Mara Jinea, I sought out and used the no-growth spell, and 'romantic' is one of the reasons why. I had to watch adults acting like idiots—and dying for it—from the time I was small. Including my own parents."

"You can do that in—" Senrid stopped, looking slightly confused. "I mean, I heard that if you take the spell away, or someone does, if people had it on them long enough they wither and die like that." He snapped his fingers.

"That's black magic. You can use it at any age in black magic, but that does happen. In white, the spell won't work once you're fully grown. It only prolongs youth. But when you take it away, you just continue. Apparently our ancestors could do it by will—taking longer to reach adulthood if they needed it. I need it. Or maybe what I don't need is the foolishness of adulthood," Leander finished, sitting back and staring out at the stars. "Anyway, you won't bore me, as long as it's not a story about romance. I had enough of Mara Jinea's intrigues to last a lifetime."

He breathed deeply. His annoyance at the reminder of the former queen died away as he thought about how much he'd always loved the complex scents of the forest. To him, the smell of loam, and water, and hidden herbs, and pine would always remind him of freedom.

"You do like this place, don't you," Senrid observed.

Leander laughed. "Didn't I say so?"

"True." Senrid's tone made it clear that he hadn't believed it. Then he said, "A story. Not sure I remember any! What I heard or read latest tends to shove out what I read before." He added, "I used to make up stories for my cousin when we were little, but that was funny stuff."

"Well, you can do that now. Kyale loves that kind of story," Leander said.

"But she's not here."

"I like 'em too, I'm just not good at making them up."

Senrid embarked on a fast-paced, witty story about a duel between a pair of arrogant, eccentric magicians. It was funny, and heartless—as funny stories often are—and Leander noticed even while laughing that Senrid gauged what prompted the laughter and effortlessly bent the story in that direction.

The story, as a story, revealed nothing about Senrid, except that he was quick, but that Leander already knew. His manner of telling it made it clear that Senrid was remarkably adept at telling people what they wanted to hear.

He finished as the food did. They ate with good appetites. The grapes ended the meal, and then Leander washed the cookware and stowed it all away.

When he suggested they get some sleep, Senrid agreed immediately. Leander dug out the old quilts, which smelled slightly of dust and mildew; he'd have to put them out in the sun, or better, construct and enable a cleaning frame.

He pitched a quilt at Senrid, who rolled up in it, close to the fire. Leander made up his bed on the other side of the fire, thinking as he settled down how familiar this was—and how much better he seemed to sleep out under the stars than shut up in a castle, even with the windows wide open.

When he woke up, the light was blue. The sun was not up yet, but he heard splashes and the gasps of someone enduring a cold water bath.

He rolled out of his warm quilt to see Senrid down in the river bathing—with his clothes on. Now, why would he do that?

In Leander's experience, people bathed with their clothes on
when either they were in mixed company or they were wary of
attack at all times, waking and sleeping.

Why not test his theory?

Leander could move soundlessly when he wanted to—
another benefit of years in this environment.

He came up behind Senrid, waited, and when the kid was
stepping over a rock, he gave him a gentle push.

Senrid's arms flailed—splash!

Leander snorted a laugh. Or he started to. A foot
hooked round his ankle and yanked, and the trees and sky
whirled past as he toppled backwards, making an even bigger
splash.

Then everything changed. The splashes didn't lead to
one of those wrestle games he'd played with his old gang,
dunking one another and laughing. The kid fought hard, with
trained strength and unnervingly fast reflexes—and he fought to
win. Block, strike, block; by the time Leander's body caught up
with his mind, it was already too late, and he sank down,
whooping for breath as water closed over his head.

Klunk. His skull thumped against one of the round flat
rocks along the shallow stream bed—but he couldn't get up.
Senrid held him in a grip he couldn't break.

Through the rippling water he made out a round kid-face,
yellow hair, and staring dark gray eyes.

One last violent effort—nothing.

Leander relaxed, staring up at those eyes through the
clear water, as bubbles escaped from his nose, and then his
vision started to fade.

His mind registered that this, after all, was his end, and
surprise and regret suffused him.

Then the hands shifted their grip, and hauled him out of
the water.

SIX

For a time Leander couldn't say anything—couldn't even think. He coughed, spluttered, gasped, shaking his head in an effort to get all the water out. His nose burned, and his lungs hurt.

But finally his vision cleared again, and he blinked at Senrid, now perched on a rock within arm's reach, his bland, smiling face exactly the same as ever, right to the steady gaze.

That had been a near thing. Leander thought back on those fading images. Senrid could have drowned him and no one would have known. But he'd changed his mind.

Leander could ask, but he knew with sudden conviction that he would not get the truth. That would have to be arrived at some other way.

"Well I'm awake," he said. "And clean. And cold. Let's cook up something hot to drink before we ride on back."

"Tell me what to do," Senrid said. If he was relieved, it was impossible to discern.

Senrid was the most self-possessed kid of his age Leander had ever seen. For that matter, how old *was* he, anyway?

"Scout out some grub, maybe? I'll have to run about and visit all the herb stashes again since we used everything I found last night."

"You didn't grow them here?" Senrid looked down at the loamy soil.

Leander said, "We were outlaws. All Mara Jinea would have needed was a single warrior raised on a farm, and an herb garden would be as good as a signpost: *We're right here!*"

Senrid laughed. "Well, I don't know anything about farms."

Leander nodded. "I didn't either, until I lived here. Anyway, we've got steeped leaf and coffee beans in the cave. Alaxandar and his cronies in the old guard all like coffee. I'll get the fire going. While I'm gone, you could saddle up the horses."

Everything progressed as Leander had outlined. He roasted and ground the coffee beans, from lack of practice making it rather strong, but the kid drank it down without a complaint or even a shudder. Coffee. The army drink, Alaxandar had once called it, Leander reflected.

They ate a breakfast of fish and potatoes-with-onions, plus the late berries Leander had found along the riverbanks. By the time the gear was clean and stowed the horses were ready— groomed better and quicker than Leander could have. They mounted up and started on the way back.

Leander's mind raced ahead, considering what needed to be done, what ought to be done—and what couldn't be done.

Senrid rode beside him, apparently content to look about him, his profile giving, as usual, no clue to his thoughts.

ೲ☾♫☽ೞ

Kitty woke up slowly. Her head no longer hurt, and the dizziness was gone. She sat up cautiously. Other than her limbs feeling heavy, she didn't feel badly enough to stay in bed.

She got up, and found that Llhei had made a nice hot bath for her, with rose petals floating on the water.

She climbed in, soaking in the warmth and aromatic steam; presently she became aware of Llhei moving about the room, and opened her eyes.

"I'm hungry," she said.

Llhei smiled, her lined face looking younger. "You're feeling better, then, child?"

"Much," Kitty pronounced. "Not that Leander would care! Where is he?"

"He checked on you last night, but you were asleep."

"I suppose he's off with that creep kid?"

"Kitty." Llhei stopped, crossing her arms.

"I don't care," Kyale said. "I don't care if it's not fair. I wasn't dreaming, I was *thinking*. He's not friendly, he pretends to be. He kept asking nosy questions. I didn't realize it until he ran out of them, and then he just—"

"Just wanted to talk to someone else? Another boy, maybe?" Llhei suggested in a gentle voice.

Kitty sighed. She could tell that no one was going to believe her. "Oh, never mind. Let me get dressed, and eat something, and I'll tell Leander myself. With or without Little Sunny-face."

"Leander," Llhei said, "is not here. He rode off for a day in the woods—and about time, too."

Kitty frowned. "Why couldn't he do it with me?"

Llhei laughed. "When you decide you like dirt and camping on the ground in cold weather?"

"Oh, never mind."

"Do you feel strong enough to come downstairs, or would you prefer a tray up here?"

"Tray," Kitty grumped.

She ate with good appetite, feeling much better when she was done. So she walked to the library, and this time not seeking entertainment, but facts. Only where should she look?

She moved to a shelf she'd ignored hitherto, Leander having said once, *These are the ones Mara Jinea didn't destroy, I guess because they were too boring.* Choosing several books, she tucked them under her arm and retreated to her room and her warm bed, rising only when she heard horsehooves in the courtyard.

The time was mid-afternoon. She got up and ran to her window, looking out in time to see a dark head and a blond one as they rode past the wall leading to the stable. A short while later they crossed the courtyard on foot, talking and laughing, and passed inside.

Kitty made her way downstairs. The boys were not in the study, or the library, or the dining room. She descended last to the kitchens and there they were.

When she saw Senrid's round, friendly face, her suspicions wavered. He really didn't look like any creep—and she wondered if being jealous made her imagine things.

Maybe a talk with Leander would help her straighten out her thinking.

"Feeling better?" Leander asked.

Senrid smiled in welcome.

"Very much so," Kitty said. "In fact, I'm hungry again."

"Here comes some chicken pie, fresh from the oven."

They sat round the far end of the preparation table and ate. Kitty listened as the boys talked, mostly about horses. Kitty listened intermittently, trying to curb her impatience. When Leander stated that other types of horses might look better, or pull more, for speed there was no horse faster than those of the Nelkereth Plains, Senrid readily agreed.

Who cares about horses? Kitty fought a yawn. She was soon done, but she sat quietly until the boys had finished eating, and rose when they did.

Leander proposed a game of cards-and-shards. Kitty loathed that game—as she loathed any game that required speed and memory and what Leander called 'strategy'—but she was willing to sit and wait until she could get Leander aside.

But before they reached the stairs, he turned around.

"Kitty? You don't like cards. Why don't you—"

She interrupted. "I want to talk to you."

"I'm afraid we're not being very polite," Leander countered.

Kitty sighed, sneaking a look at Senrid. He watched, smiling like always. "Look, I just want to *talk* to you."

"How about later?"

Kitty sighed again, more loudly. "When?"

"When we both find the time."

Kitty struggled with rage, recalling some of Faline's favorite curses. "You algae-eyed clod-nosed flapdoodle—"

"You can insult me later," Leander stated, also smiling, but his gaze was uncomfortably direct. "Try to keep your pets away for now."

He turned away, and Senrid followed.

Kitty stamped her bare foot, whirled around, and retreated to her room to finish her reading.

What she found surprised her so much she felt she should double-check by reading on, but the closely written pages listing trade deals and treaties was indeed dull, and she was more tired than she'd thought she would be, after having had fever the day before. She fell asleep without meaning to, and woke briefly when Llhei covered her with a quilt.

When morning came, she was determined to have her talk with Leander no matter what. But when she reached the dining room, both boys were already there. Leander was grinning, his eyes wide and very green. Senrid, too, looked cheery, as he always did. Kitty scowled.

"Kitty—good morning! You're the first to hear—Senrid wants to stay with us."

Kitty gasped. "But Leander, I have something to—"

"Your approval is required," Leander began.

"What? No!" With a desperate idea of whispering her warning in his ear, Kitty approached her brother, but she had to pass by Senrid's chair.

She did not notice his foot out. She tripped, and when he tried to catch her, somehow his elbow thrust straight into her stomach.

"Oooog," Kitty gasped, fighting against nausea. "Uuuungh!"

"Oh no, I'm so sorry," Senrid exclaimed. "Accident!"

Kitty bent both her arms over her middle and ran out.

She made it upstairs and collapsed on her bed. Slowly the cramp loosened and she began muttering to herself—until she heard her door open quietly.

"Who's a rot-faced lumberhead?"

It was Senrid.

He sat on the edge of her bed. "I'm sorry," he said, with his disarming grin. "Please come downstairs. Leander wants to explain everything."

Kitty sat up. "He does?"

"Sure. Come along." He held out a hand.

Kitty avoided it, pressing her forearm against her middle, which was still tender. Senrid took her free arm and guided her out, his manner so apologetic her bad feelings died away.

To her surprise he headed not down the hall to the library, or down the stairway to the dining room, but for the back stair leading to the courtyard.

"Is he outside?" Kitty asked, trying once to free herself from Senrid's grip. He didn't squeeze her arm, but his grip was impossible to break.

"Yes," Senrid said.

They reached the courtyard, and Kitty saw no Leander. "He's not here," she accused, the bad feelings rushing back.

"Right outside the gates."

Outside the *gates?* Kitty stopped—that is, she tried to. "I don't believe you." And she sucked in her breath to yell for her brother.

Senrid's hold shifted, and she felt something sharp prick her neck under her ear. She glanced down, and gasped in surprise. "That knife—it's from the camp!"

"Yep. It's a good blade. Much too good to be consigned to cutting vegetables. Just a few steps farther, till we clear the perimeter of the castle, and your brother's wards—"

"You'll stay where you are."

"Leander!" Kitty squeaked in relief.

From the very edge of her vision Kitty saw Leander standing at the big doors. From behind him came Arel, and Alaxandar, and Pertar, all armed. Alaxandar had an arrow nocked and aimed.

Senrid looked around. He sighed.

Alaxandar raised the bow a trifle.

"Let Kitty go," Leander said.

Senrid lifted his hands, keeping Kitty between him and that arrow, she being too surprised to move for the crucial moments it took for him to back up hastily, muttering under his breath. He made it through the gateway a moment before the arrow flew, whistling, right where he'd been standing.

Senrid had vanished—by magic.

Kitty wailed in relief.

"Thank you, Alaxandar," Leander said. "You were fast."

"Not fast enough," Alaxandar growled. "That shot would've winged him, nice and tight."

"Well, then what? I wouldn't know what to do with him. At least he couldn't do any magic to damage us, which is what mattered." He turned to Kitty, his frown changing to worry. "Are you all right? I'm sorry I didn't talk to you before, but I had to get the others, without him knowing. He was with me almost all the time, and I didn't know if I was fooling him or not."

"I'm fine." Kitty sighed. "I was desperate to talk to you! I wasn't really *sure*. What made you suspicious about him?"

"A lot of little things."

"Conrad hated him—"

"Yes, Conrad's behavior was a puzzle, but that could have been explained by your sudden dislike. The real problem was that Senrid tried too hard, too fast. And he lied to me about breaking into my library—"

"He made me promise not to tell you!"

"What happened? He fall asleep?"

"Yes!"

"Hah." Leander grinned, feeling almost giddy with relief. "I had a ward in there against black magic. What did he do, make a zaplight?"

"Yes! I thought it was yours."

"That's all it would take," Leander said. "I've been afraid that he was some sort of Marloven spy."

"Ugh," said Kitty, rubbing her stomach. "He's worse than that."

Thinking she was just being insulting, Leander went on. "I didn't know what to do next when I realized magic was involved, except try to play along and fool him. Get him to be friendly, to talk, to reveal what his purpose was. He dissolved one of my castle wards—I didn't know for certain until last night. This was after a weird day at the old hideout, ending with him palming one of our supply knives without asking. I didn't think he'd use it against you, or I never would have let that get by. But I didn't know what he was after! I renewed the wards— spent half the night doing it—and he must had been able to tell, because he was trying to drag you beyond the walls, which are the ward perimeter. I didn't expect that at all! Why would he take you as a hostage—what could he possibly want from us?"

Kitty said, "I couldn't really believe it was *him*."

Leander stopped walking and looked down at her. "What do you mean? That he's some kind of mage-apprentice, as I said, sent to spy—"

"Then you *don't* know," Kitty gloated forebodingly. "I guess you haven't had time to go through the records. Me, I did—one at a time, since you wouldn't help me—and last night I found some stuff about Marloven Hess. Mother didn't destroy everything."

"I know that, but all she left were outdated list-books on old taxes, land transactions, trade and treaties. The Guild houses have all that stuff copied, but I left them anyway. What did you find out and where?"

"In this trade and treaty book, like you said. Here and there, back ten years ago, fifteen, twenty, were some deals with *them*. Marlovens."

Leander whistled. "Of course the Guilds wouldn't copy any of that. Go on."

"Buried in the list about ten years ago was a note that their last king—not the grandfather, who was long dead, but his son—had died, and a child was now king. The king's brother, his name is Tdanerend, became regent, because the treaties were signed by him, in the child's name, and not by King Indevan. Then I fell asleep. This morning I counted up the years."

Leander whistled. "And this child's name?"

Kitty nodded. "You guessed it. I didn't believe it either. Kept thinking the same name showing up was an accident. But after what just happened, and the years adding up, well, I believe it now."

"Believe what?"

Kitty said grimly, "That Senrid is the king of Marloven Hess."

Leander's laughter echoed up the castle walls.

PART TWO

An Excerpt
from the Records
of
Cherene Jennet Sherwood
of Mearsies Heili

ONE

Winter hit us like a splat in the phizz from a week-old fish.

When that first storm finally left us alone Mearsies Heili lay frozen, all blue, silver, and white, under a deep-winter frost. The air was heartlessly clear and cold, and though the sun shone it gave no warmth.

At the west end of the city on the cloud top, the white palace gleamed like a castle of ice. It felt a bit like a castle of ice to those of us inside, for despite the warmth of very old magic, occasional cold drafts drifted through and we, the occupants, shivered.

In one of the upper bedrooms lay a figure under a pile of warm, fluffy quilts—

Wait.

Since I began letting others read my records, I can no longer assume that they'll only be read by Mearsieans further down the stream of time. That means any poor slob—ah, person trudging through my records in the future might not know anything about us.

So here are some quick details.

I am Cherene Jennet Sherwood, right-hand splat to Clair Sherwood, Mearsies Heili's queen. Being a princess doesn't mean fancy clothes (who'd see them?) or fancy rituals (who'd attend 'em?), but being in charge when Clair's not at hand. We have no court, and no aristos, in small, mostly-farm-and-wood Mearsies Heili. We're kids. We can stay kids here on Sartorias-deles, I hope you're aware; I didn't know any Old Sartoran history when this adventure occurred, so in case you're still learning old history, I'll just tell you that people in the ancient days used to control a lot of things—including their aging process. The white magic non-aging spell is a kind of faint echo of that, added to the fact that time and space on this world are not as, well, *predictable* as they are on Earth.

Anyhow, Clair didn't have any siblings, just one friend, a little girl from the city. When the Yxubarecs killed her Clair was lonely. She spent most of her time learning magic, but she missed having a friend. She wanted someone who liked *her*, not her rank, so in her free time she zapped her way around on our continent, finding girls who were lonely or in rotten situations, and offered them a new start—and then she discovered the World Gate. It was on Earth that she found me, and later Gwen. And back in history centuries before my time four of our kid regional governors originated, in their first lives.

So there were nine of us—not counting Clair's cousin, meanly named Puddlenose by the Chwahir who kidnapped him when small (that's again another story) and his traveling buddy Christoph, who was a friend of one of those governors, from Earth long ago. They were itchfeet, and regarded Mearsies Heili as home base, rather than home.

That's us. Now, back to late autumn—or early winter—a few months after Faline's adventure.

As always, Clair's curtains were drawn back and low sunlight slanted in, sparking highlights in her white hair. The only signs that she was alive were her breathing and the sneezes that erupted now and then, punctuated by rattling coughs. The sudden cold weather had caught her; already overtired from too much study on top of her regular queen chores, she'd gotten chilled, kept working anyway, until she was too sick to move.

Down in the vast, silent throne room, the old crown nicknamed Six-Stix sat atop a black-haired head, the crown gleaming in the winter light with its own majesty. The black hair was mine, and there was *definitely* no majesty about me.

This was the dull part of being a princess, having to do Clair's open court while she was sick. Not that 'court' meant much in Mearsies Heili, because there aren't any courtiers. 'Interviews' would be more accurate, but the old words were used out of habit.

However, we weren't exactly piling up people for interviews. The weather kept even petitioners from wanting to travel, for below us the roads were shiny and dangerous with ice from this early storm. But duty required me to sit there, in case anyone did come.

There was nothing to do but eat and read. My favorite things to do alone are reading, drawing, writing, and eating. The order of those changes around a lot, but right now it was too cold for writing, and that stupid throne—handsome carvings, old and impressive, but completely uncomfortable, especially if you are short—was impossible for writing or drawing.

So. I had a copy of an old record, an empty mug that used to be filled with hot chocolate, and on my lap half a big slab of chocolate pie, but from time to time I stared moodily at the light from the high windows inching its way along the glistening walls.

Far too much time to go.

ഇരുഅ

While I sat in wintry stillness high on the cloud city above Mount Marcus, those who walked in the forest below found it equally quiet. The air was so cold a person couldn't even smell the trees. Sniffing hurt the nose.

Most of the girls were snug in our underground hideout. The outside was even too cold—and too dry—for Diana and Dhana respectively. No one wanted to be in the frigid air, but we felt the need to patrol, for we knew that the Chwahir might think this a perfect opportunity to try something nasty. *We're kids, so we're targets for anyone who wants my land and thinks kids are too weak and stupid to defend it*, Clair had said not long after I came to this world—and wow, had her words proved true!

So, patrol duty. And, after a whole summer of being stuck indoors unless everyone left together, Faline had convinced Clair that she could take her turn. Kwenz and Jilo's nasty trick—pinching Faline—earlier in the summer had scared us all, but nothing had come of it since Faline's surprising reappearance, and Clair had told Faline a couple weeks before the storm hit that she could do her patrols again.

Poor Faline! It figured that when she was finally back in the rotation, it was in time for rotten weather.

So today was her turn, and she tried to make it as quick as possible; all the routes that lead in and out of Kwenz's Shadowland underneath the cloud city to the east of Mount Marcus had to be snooped for signs of Kwenz's scouts and spies.

Cold bothered her much less than being alone did. It was hard to have fun alone, and Faline was a firm believer in turning all chores into fun. Time whirled by faster that way, which meant a person was likely to take longer, and thus do a better job. (Or so her reasoning went.)

But no one had wanted to come out with her, not in that weather. Underneath the piles of white snow lay ice from the first night's storm and freeze.

She trudged along as quickly as she could, which wasn't all that fast. The ice was too treacherous for racing. Her Yxubarec background (living on high clouds in cold air) kept her from minding the weather too much, but nobody likes slipping and falling on ice.

So she was delighted to spot someone else in the forest, ahead on the pathway she'd chosen. She hid, an automatic reaction, and peeked. The someone was not a Chwahir, and he was a kid—two things in his favor—shorter than Christoph, blond hair, and ordinary clothes. A Mearsiean? Lost, perchance? Well, that was part of patrol duty, helping lost travelers.

"Hi," she called, stepping out where she could be seen.

The boy turned quickly. He grinned at her. She liked that grin at once. It was the kind that seemed on the verge of a laugh. "Hi yourself," he said—in Mearsiean, but with an accent.

"Lost? Need directions? Looking for someone?" she asked, then realized that he hadn't seemed surprised to see her.

He shrugged. "Wandering."

"Garbacious weather t'wander in," Faline said cheerily, hoping that Clair's world-traveling cousin Puddlenose and his pal Christoph—wherever they were—hadn't got stuck in this kind of weather, or had managed to find shelter (preferably not in a jail for being slackers, practical jokers, and prone to snappy answers at the wrong people, like pompous border officials) if they had.

"It is," the boy said. "But company keeps me from noticing so much."

"Same here," Faline exclaimed. "I'm stuck on patrol. Lookin' for Kwenz's slobs, which you aren't one, I can tell—"

"Never," the kid said, with his almost-laugh grin.

"—so if you got nowhere else to go, why not come along with me? I know the whole forest, and when you wanna leave I can point you in the right direction."

The boy opened a hand. "What's your name? I'm Senrid."

"Faline Sherwood."

"Glad to meet you." Again the quick grin, almost a laugh.

Faline grinned back. "Well, then, this way."

Senrid seemed to be perfectly content to follow along where she led. As they walked they talked, Senrid mostly asking questions and Faline answering happily. Strangers were rare enough in the forest—strange kids, anyway, and when they did come along, it mostly fell to others to do the explaining. Faline thoroughly enjoyed being Senrid's guide. Remembering her experience with poor lonely Kyale, who seemed to want to talk about herself, Faline made an effort to talk about the kinds of things she thought another kid would like to hear.

She was especially pleased when she made him laugh. Her description of Prince Jonnicake of Elchnudaeb caused the first snicker. He really seemed to appreciate her artistry in insults when describing villains; and at his encouragement she talked more about the Chwahir, and why they had a centuries-long grudge against Mearsieans.

"So what you say," he commented finally, "is that tangling with the Chwahir has gotten you involved in world affairs?"

By that time they were at the Lake, dangling their bare feet in the water, which was pleasantly warm, and sent up clouds of iridescent steam. None of the Lake beings had shown up, and the water looked placid and empty.

Faline wrinkled her nose. "I don't know why we got mixed up in world events, as you call 'em. I call 'em nasty messes." She looked up, expecting a laugh.

Senrid gave her an appreciative smile.

Faline continued. "CJ thinks it's bad luck—'luck' is something from another world, you see. Puddlenose thinks it's happenstance—that's Clair's cousin. He's an itchfoot. Never stays in one place long. Clair says there aren't any happenstances, not when it comes to people wanting power. That is, the only accidents are to the people who get caught in the way—and if they resist, they get swept along, like sticks at the edge of the river."

Senrid drew in a long breath. "She said that, did she?"

Faline shrugged, looking down at the placid waters of the Lake. Weird, that the beings stayed away—maybe they felt cold after all? Except the water was warm! Faline mentally shrugged it off, as she did any question she couldn't answer, and said, "Hey, you want to meet the girls in person? Much more fun than hearing about them!"

Senrid hesitated. "Well, if your queen is sick—"

"Oh, she's safely upstairs in the white castle. You won't disturb her." Faline pointed to the mountain visible through the trees. They stood in silence, Senrid gazing up at the white palace, iridescent in the winter sun above the vaporous magic-bound cloud that crowned the mountain.

"What is that made of?" he asked, shading his eyes with his hand. "It's not any stone that I've ever seen."

"We don't know. Only that it's really, really old. Older than records, by far. And rare, so we've been told. Seshe thinks it goes all the way back to the days of Old Sartor, but some people think we're being show offs for saying that, so we usually don't." She grinned. "Except when I do. Like I just did."

Senrid uttered a soft, low whistle, still gazing upward. "And...is that a city? On a cloud?"

"Yep. Something some old mages did. On account of those stinkacious Chwahir I mentioned, who are stuck below, living under the shadow. Not that it stopped them from playing, as Clair's cousin Puddlenose says, the most popular of all

Chwahir games: *What's yours is mine.* Their ancestors, I mean. As well as the ones now."

"That must have taken some mighty spell-casting," he said. "And more to keep it there."

Faline shrugged. "I dunno. You can ask Clair. She's the one with the magic—her and CJ. And poor ol' CJ is stuck up there throne-warmin' so you won't get to meet her either, unless you want to go upstairs."

"No, that's all right," he said. "Why don't we meet your other friends, and then you can come and meet my family."

She was vaguely surprised. His family? She'd thought he was an itchfoot. But she was too excited about showing off the Junky and the gang to think about it further. "Okay," she said.

"Okay," he repeated, pronouncing the word with a slight hesitation. Experimentally.

"It's another of CJ's words," she said. "She brought over some good ones! Good foods, too. Like tacos."

As she spoke, Faline led the way to the Junky. Why not? True, not many people outside of us girls had seen our underground hideout, but some had. Faline thought. CJ and Clair brought visitors, the most recent being Devon, the Earth kid who now lived in Imar. As long as the visitor wasn't a Chwahir, or a grownup, who could object?

And admiration was obvious on his round face. Faline grinned, pleased to show off something she knew was really great.

"... and so we call it the Junky—from Junkyard. That was CJ's idea," she explained as they walked down the tunnel—after he appreciated the cleverness with which the entrance was hidden inside the ancient lightning-blasted tree. "Grown up nosers who might hear us say 'Let's go to the underground hideout' would probably want to search for it, but who cares what a 'junkyard' is?"

So saying, she led him into the main room. Senrid sniffed appreciatively at the air, which always smelled good to us girls, like loam and pine and the lingering scents of good food. It was the smell of home.

Faline gestured proudly at the tunnel to the rooms below, at the bookcases, and the Mural, explaining how everyone had worked together, lovingly recording each ghastly, repulsive detail of the loathsome, arrogant Queen Glotulae and her obnoxious son Jonnicake. As she explained how the disgusting duo were making the surrounding people faint from the stunning garishness of their outfits (those two were the only people I've ever met who wore *every* fashion—all in the same outfit), she saw Senrid looking puzzled, and for a time she pointed at the various details, laughing so hard by the end she could scarcely talk. "S-s-s-eee, it never fails to cheer us on the gloomiest day," she exclaimed finally. "Never! Clair s-s-s-says the world can never s-s-seem so b-b-bad when it has such silly people in it!"

She turned to her guest, who smiled politely, and Faline gave up. "Maybe you have to know them."

Senrid opened his hand, a gesture she couldn't interpret, but it didn't seem unfriendly. He looked around slowly and appreciatively, his eyes lingering longest on the root-veined ceiling. "What sort of magical ward protects this dwelling?"

"I dunno. Clair sees to all that." Faline twiddled her fingers. "And CJ helps."

Seshe wandered in from the kitchen, a cup of fresh cocoa in one hand and a book in the other. "I thought I heard some snickering," she said, looking with question at the newcomer.

Faline introduced the two. Seshe nodded, her smile shy, then she vanished down the lower tunnel in the direction of her room, her long hair swinging against her skirts.

Noises came from below; Sherry, Gwen, Dhana, and Irene were playing some kind of game. Faline took Senrid down a level, explaining how a lot of the rooms had two entrances and exits, one rope and one tunnel. The four girls looked up from their game, gave Senrid a polite look or greeting, then their attention snapped right back to their play. Diana sat on a hassock watching, dark braids flung back as she polished her knife collection.

Senrid's gaze lingered on Diana's treasures from past adventures. Diana noticed, and she looked him over with faint interest, though there was no expression in her dark eyes.

After the tour Faline remembered that he had wanted to go someplace. "Well, that's it."

"Thank you for showing me," Senrid said politely as he led the way back up the tunnel. And after he gave the place one last look-round, he walked out, and paused, his face expectant.

She was hungry, and would have been glad to let him go his way so she could stay and eat, but he seemed to be waiting. She recalled that he'd said something about his family, and she was trying to be a conscientious representative for her country, so she grabbed her sturdiest coat, belted it on, and followed, hoping they didn't live far.

The air outside was even colder. Blue light from the westering sun gave no warmth at all as it filtered through the trees. The two kids began walking, Senrid once more asking all kinds of questions. Did Mearsies Heili have an army? No? What kind of protections?

"That's Clair's stuff," Faline said. "Hafta ask her. Or CJ. That reminds me. Wanna hear about ol' Six-Stix bein' lost, thanks to a slime-arooni named Tzydes? That time, see, he was at the head of these baglio sapheads from Norsunder who tentacled in, and Clair and Puddlenose ended up going clear up north, almost to the top of the world, where they have this old, *old* magic city..."

By the time she'd finished that story, they had nearly reached the No Man's Land between the forest and the Shadowland and Wesset North at the far point of the triangle. Dark was almost on them.

Surprised, Faline said, "Hey! Where we goin'? There isn't anyone lives here, not in a straight line all the way to the ocean."

"Really? I wish you hadn't asked me that," Senrid said. "This day has been fun."

"So?" Faline was now completely confused.

In the darkness, Senrid's smile hadn't diminished. "In fact I wish you hadn't ruined my plans, Faline."

"Your plans?"

"Reuniting Vasande Leror and Marloven Hess. You have to die for interfering—"

"What?"

"A custom in our country with the force of law," Senrid explained.

"Fine for you," Faline squawked, "but it's not any custom here, and we're in my country!" She stamped. "MH!"

"Out of MH and into MH," Senrid said, as though offering her a joke. By now he knew how much Faline loved jokes.

"Huh?"

He explained the coincidence of initials.

She didn't laugh. Instead, she whirled around, head down, and started to run. Senrid caught up in two steps, reached for her wrist, and performed the one spell he'd allowed himself in a white magic country—the transfer spell.

TWO

They appeared in a room of stone walls and floor, and Faline recovered first from the transfer-effects. She looked around quickly for a way to escape. The room was small, lit by glowglobes, containing a few pieces of darkwood furniture. The windows were narrow, through which she glimpsed torch-lit towers and high, sentry-patrolled stone walls. It was a Destination room, closely guarded to prevent unwanted arrivals or departures.

And it was deep inside an enormous castle.

Senrid still had hold of her wrist. His face was pale, his eyes glazed the way that CJ's or Clair's often were after a very long transfer, especially a double one.

She yanked her hand away, startling Senrid. With grim thoroughness she wiped her wrist off, shook her fingers toward the floor, then stomped vigorously on the touch-cooties.

Senrid watched all this in silence, then gave her a sarcastic look. "You whites are all the same. Friends until you lose. Now you're the Righteous and Noble Hero, just like that." He snapped his fingers. "Hypocritical."

"But you weren't being friendly, you were just lying to set me up for a nasty trap. Who's the hypocrite?"

Senrid grinned. "I didn't lie—"

"Senrid!"

The sudden, loud voice made Faline jump. Senrid's head turned sharply.

"Uncle! You interrupted me—"

"I meant to. Once you've secured your prisoner, no need to fraternize further. Remember that. It shows a tendency toward weakness, and you'll never be able to rule if you are weak."

"Yes, Uncle."

"Otherwise, very commendable." The harsh voice was patronizing now.

Faline stared, already hating the speaker. The man was tall, or seemed tall, with brown hair and eyes. His expression was a combination of arrogance and sneer that reminded Faline of Shnit Sonscarna, King of the Chwahir—which intensified her dislike.

Senrid said in an obedient voice, "Very well, Uncle." And once again he grabbed Faline's wrist and transferred.

This time the transfer magic lasted scarce moments.

They appeared in a very dark, close-smelling environment. She recognized that smell immediately: stone-enclosed air seldom open to the outside, usually found in dungeons.

Senrid dropped Faline's hand. "You have to stay here."

"You are a lying, rotten, garbanzo gnerg of a bonehead and a disgusting pigfat, you know," Faline stated, crossing her arms.

"A pigfat? I don't think I am, though I'm not sure what it is." Senrid snapped a tiny zaplight into being. "Another of CJ's words?" It was clear from face and voice that he was enjoying her conversation. He offered apologetically, "A clean death won't be that bad—"

"I suppose you've died and know all about it," Faline asked, loading on the sarcasm.

"I know as much about that as you do about pigfats," Senrid retorted, once again giving her that grin-on-the-verge-of-a-laugh.

"You got me there." Faline couldn't help but grin back. "I s'pose you mean that's better than being tortured. I guess I'll agree that far. But, well, I'll be getting out soon enough. White magic always wins out over black."

"Why?" Senrid asked.

The question startled her. She was used to threats, explosions of anger followed by sinister speeches, or at least derision. Though that expression narrowed Senrid's gray-blue eyes, he seemed to want a real answer.

She blinked. "Because it's in harmony with the world," she said, waving her hands to encompass the entire universe.

Now came the derisive snort, though even that didn't match the magnitude of most villains' hitherto. "Explain the Fall of Old Sartor, then," he said. "See you at the execution tomorrow—or possibly tomorrow, depending on whether Ndand gets here tonight."

"What's a Ndand?"

"It's who, and she's my cousin," Senrid said. "I did say you'd meet my family."

"And who was that pickle-faced man with the nasty voice?"

"You mean my uncle? I see he made a good impression." Another quick grin. "He's regent until he feels I'll be a good king. And he's the rest of my family."

"You'll never be good at the rate you're going," Faline said firmly.

"Why?"

She expected it this time. "Cuzz a good king is one who works to help and protect the people, not bullies 'em."

"But I do work to protect my people," Senrid said. "We work constantly to make sure no one can attack us. You're wrong on that one, Faline." He seemed reluctant to leave. "Well, see you tomorrow."

"Oh, goodie," Faline yodeled.

Senrid raised his hand and disappeared.

The zaplight dwindled, leaving her alone in the empty, dark cell.

৵ඏଔ෴ଈ

While poor Faline sits there, I have to return to the Junky.

Just as Faline and Senrid left the lower room, Diana put away the knife she'd been polishing.

Diana thought about that kid, and as the sound of his and Faline's voices vanished up the tunnel, her curiosity altered into suspicion. Now, she liked having people admire her weapon collection—but that boy hadn't been admiring, he'd been assessing. Like someone who knew the difference between a Colendi dueling dagger, a Chwahir assassin blade, and an old-fashioned sailor's utility knife.

She hadn't said anything. Diana seldom says much, even when the others pester her to. She reflected on how sensitive Faline was on the subject of Kwenz having snaffled her for that stupid plan overseas somewhere. Until Clair had relaxed the rule about Faline staying hidden, Diana knew Faline's feelings had been bruised—as if she couldn't be trusted to pull off a patrol any more.

So she wasn't about to speak up. But because she felt suspicious, she grabbed her coat and ghosted up the lower tunnel. She was by far the best of us girls at wood work, so she decided to satisfy her suspicions on her own. If nothing happened, Faline would never know.

She stopped just outside the entrance to the main room and watched the kid looking around. He and Faline began to leave, and once more he glanced back, a glance of obvious longing. That was normal—kids always loved the underground hideout—so normal that Diana almost retreated back inside.

Except there was something funny going on because Faline clearly wanted to stay, but the boy expected her to go.

So she pulled on her coat and shadowed them outside and along the trails.

When she wants to be, she's completely invisible in a forest—even Seshe isn't as fog-footed. And no magic involved. The kid only looked back once or twice, but never saw her. Meanwhile, he started in with questions about Clair's army and magic protections, his voice clear and carrying in the frosty air.

Army?

But then Faline made a joke about PJ and they both laughed. Muttering to herself—was there something wrong about this boy, or wasn't there?—Diana shadowed them all the way to No Man's Land. As the trees thinned she had to drop farther and farther back, which made their conversation hard to hear.

But when they reached the fields, darkness mostly hid her. Diana ran forward to close some of the distance—in time to see the boy grab Faline by the wrist.

They vanished by magic transfer before she could get to them.

So Diana turned around and began the long run back.

She was tired and hot when she reached the Junky. On watery legs she trotted down the tunnel and dropped onto the rug.

"Diana?" Seshe exclaimed, startled. "What's wrong? Chwahir attacking?"

"CJ...get CJ," Diana gasped, her gaze roaming the ceiling as she fought for breath.

Seshe moved to the magic slate and wrote a message.

౸ᲪᎩᏚᏓᏉᏛ

Up above, the twin to the magic slate showed the message at once, and because it was within my field of vision, I saw the words appear. I hopped up, glad for any kind of break in the monotony, and did the summons spell.

Diana appeared a moment later. She wiped her damp hair back from her brow, then shrugged out of her worn old coat. Meanwhile, she fought to get enough breath in order to talk.

"Faline...taken. Kid...magic-transfer..."

"Chwahir?"

"Don't think so...not Kwenz's. Normal eyes...didn't seem like...he could be from Shnit. Nah. Accent's wrong," Diana added, frowning. "He called her Flinuh, not FAL-in-uh, like the Chwahir do—or Fa-linn-eh, like us. And when he said your name, it was Shrenuh, not CHAR-en-uh, like ol' Kwenz gorbles it."

CHAR-en-uh. I shuddered, remembering that terrible Kessler Sonscarna—and his Chwahir accent. I'd almost come to hate my name, and had had to whisper it over and over after I got home, *Cher-en-eh, Cher-en-eh*, in order to get it right in my head again.

Before I could speak (and I would have begun with a few dozen insults against Kessler before we got down to work trying to figure out what could have happened to Faline) a flash of transfer-dazzle and a brief spurt of displaced air made us both whirl around. Someone had transferred in, and from the flash and the way he blinked as if dazed, it was a very long distance transfer.

Diana and I stared in amazement at an unfamiliar boy, about Puddlenose's height, more or less the same age—around fifteen. He had curly dark hair and eyes as green as summer grass.

Neither of us spoke (me forgetting that I was supposed to be the hostess) until the boy said hopefully, "Mearsies Heili?"

"Yes," I said, and to Diana, "Is this the lunkhead who bagged Faline?"

"No," Diana said. "Other's blond. Short. Younger—I think. Called himself a funny, foreign-sounding name. San... Sonrad..."

"Senrid!" It was more of an exclamation than a question from the newcomer—catching a familiar word that he hadn't wanted to hear.

"That was it, by cracky," Diana said, looking pleased.

The boy didn't look pleased at all. "Are you the queen?" He spoke in his own language.

I responded in his language—though I don't know how it works. I only know it does. "No, are you?" I retorted absently, and then I remembered the situation and gabbled, "Oh! Uh, heh-heh, I was thinking about Faline, and—no, I'm not the queen, I am thankful to say. I'm throne warming for Clair, who's sick. Now, who are you? And do you know where Faline is? Why are you here anyway, and what's up?"

"All is down." the boy said grimly, "if you'll excuse a not-quite-joke. Stupid but true. I'm here because I believe your Faline might be in Marloven Hess—"

"Where?" I squawked.

"What?" Diana hooted.

"—and that means they'll kill her unless we can do something fast."

Kill? *Faline*? My brain refused to comprehend it. Meanwhile here was this stranger before me. "And you are?" I hinted subtly.

He grinned. "Leander Tlennen-Hess of Vasande Leror."

"Of course!" I exclaimed. "I have you down in the records. Faline's adventure, when she was stuck with that magician Latvian. And Hibern—though Faline says her nickname is Fern—and Stefan, who sets fire to things. But you and your sister are from that other country. I'm Cherene Jennet. Call me CJ. Now, what's this about Faline, and a cornpone named Senrid?"

"Half a year ago, all I really knew about our current neighbors to the west," Leander said grimly, "was that they were a big kingdom with a very bad past full of wars, and that their rulers relied on black magic. After something that happened I pledged money we don't have to order some more recent histories, and the more I've been reading about them, the more I feel that if they stayed on their side of the border and left me to mine we'd both be happy."

"Just like we feel about the Chwahir," I said.

"Faline told us a little about Kwenz," Leander said, holding his nose for a second. "I guess he's an old friend of Latvian."

"Is he still shopping around for victims for his experiments?" I asked.

"No, he seems to be angry with the Regent. Collet— she's a white magic student in Marloven Hess—"

"I remember," I said, nodding. "Faline told us about her. Fern's cousin, right? And you know her?"

"I didn't, until after these events I just mentioned. Hibern heard about them, wrote to me, and offered her cousin as a contact. Now Collet gathers information for us. Her father is part of the regional government, and Collet hears everything that's going on. Through her I've been finding other contacts, and I recently got a couple placed in the royal castle in Choreid Dhelerei itself, though in lowly positions. Not that I like spying much, but if those Marlovens want to invade us, I've got to know about it."

"That's why we have a spy, a kid named Ben," I said. "Only against the Chwahir."

"Anyway, Collet reports from Hibern that Latvian has given up with messing in politics. Now he only wants to cure Stefan." He grimaced. "The Regent isn't interested in sanity, he wants control of the kingdom."

"Ugh!   So glad Faline escaped from all that." I remembered Faline's story about how Stefan had nearly burned down Latvian's house because her hair was red.   The kid apparently has this craziness about fire. "So, back to how we fit in?"

"Last summer Faline found out about the Marloven king's plan for annexing Vasande Leror, and when she escaped she came to us and told us the plan so we could squash it."

"Right," I said. "We know that part."

"Well, none of us knew at the time that that king is Senrid.   He's king in name, but not in power.   His uncle is the regent, and he doesn't want to give up the throne any time soon, from everything we've learned."

"So where does Faline come in?   And executions?"

"Don't you see?   She messed up Senrid's plan, so he's got to make good—make bad?—well anyway, he's got to correct the 'mistakes' by killing everyone who thwarted him, according to Marloven custom."

"That's a custom?"

Leander said grimly, "To the Marlovens.   More of a law: You don't cross their kings and live."

"So can't you send your spies in to rescue them?"

Leander shook his head.   "They're spies.   They have no power at all—I can't even contact them, except through a complicated route that will take days.   I don't think we have that long.   We have to act fast.   By the time I could reach them, the execution might well be over."

I turned to Diana.   "Not that it compares in disaster points, but this kid saw *our* hideout?"

Diana nodded solemnly, then grinned.   "He saw it, but if he ever finds it again, it'd be more'n I know."

"True," I said, and rapidly tried to get my mind around the bigger problem. With no success, as usual. "No way can I solve this one on my own. I hope ol' Granny got a good rest, because it's ending now."

We'd long ago settled on an emergency signal and summons spell if we needed one another quickly. I did the signal spell, then the summons transfer, and Clair appeared before us, looking like a ghost in her white nightgown and long white hair. A ghost with a red nose.

She looked at us blearily, sneezed, then said, "CJ? What's this, a joke? If it is, I'll—what? Who's that?" She pointed at Leander, who looked slightly embarrassed. Maybe in his country, no one appeared in the throne room in their nightgown, even though Clair's was as long and plain as one of her gowns.

I'd taken a bite of my pie in order to fortify myself. "No joke, and I'm sorry to roust you out of bed," I said around the pie. "It's Leander. You know, the algae-eyed one Faline told us about." Leander looked a little sardonic at the 'algae' comment. "Hey, don't bust a gut. Clair's got 'em too, as we never fail to remind her." I pointed at her hazel eyes, which she was trying to blink into alertness. "Anyhoo, Whitey-granny, Faline's going to be executed unless we think of something fast. He's here to help—I guess."

Clair's breath whooshed out. "Clothes. Cleaning frame." She did the transfer magic and vanished.

When she returned, she was in a nice, warm woolen gown, and her hair was neat and orderly. "All right, you tar-topped, slobbinizing chocolate-pie guzzler, off my throne!" She grinned.

I took off Six-Stix, which I'd forgotten about all this time, and tossed it to her. She made it disappear to its proper place: Court was officially over.

"Gladly," I said, hopping up.

Clair settled down, sneezed, frowned, then got up again. "Why are we in here? It's freezing, and this stupid throne is about as comfortable as a cactus. Let's go up to the library."

I led the way upstairs. Leander looked around in appreciation, stopping at the first window. We all stopped as he took in the westward view over the snow-blanketed forestland, all cool and blue in the fading light, far, far below.

Clair sneezed a few times more, then coughed, leaning against the wall. She closed her eyes and began muttering a complicated spell. I recognized some of it. She was summoning all the stuff for that weird pinkish drink.

Sure enough, it appeared in her hand—contained in one of the kitchen cups—and Clare stared at the thick rose-colored liquid with a grim expression.

Leander pulled himself round, as though remembering the emergency at hand, and we continued on until we reached Clair's magic chamber, full of several generations worth of magic books, as well as books about magic history, and different magic workers' writings.

Leander watched with even more appreciation, but he didn't say anything as I parked myself on the study table, leaving the two comfortable chairs to Clair and our guest. Diana joined me.

I said, "So what can you tell us about Senrid?"

Clair held her nose and drank down the liquid.

Leander said, "I didn't know anything about Senrid before he came to us during the summer, and tried to fool us into accepting him as a friend while he nosed out everything he could about our recent history, and our strengths and weaknesses. But he was in too much of a hurry and made little slipups that gave him away."

"Little ones can be lethal." Clair's voice was hoarse.

Leander nodded once. "Exactly. So I figured my only defense is to learn as much as I can about the Marlovens, and plan for every eventuality, as best I could. Meanwhile Hibern wrote me a letter, as I said, and offered help. She and her friends feel responsible for the government's bad actions, I guess. Anyway, they agreed to help me out by being my eyes and ears. That's been going on since the end of summer."

Clair looked impressed, but she didn't say anything.

"Now that I've learned more about his situation, I believe that his visit to us was the first time his uncle had ever let Senrid do anything on his own, and he was on a time limit."

Clair nodded, setting down her empty cup. Her eyes were much clearer. Later she'd need to sleep for a whole day, but for now she'd be fine. "So there's a definite danger as well as the time question," Clair said. "This kid himself."

"Right," Leander agreed.

"He certainly learned something between visiting your place and visiting ours," I said, "if he could pinch Faline so easily. If it hadn't been for Diana, and if you hadn't come, he would have gotten away with it, too. We never would have known where she was."

Diana spoke for the first time. "Eyed my hardware collection. Made me suspicious."

Leander gave us a very wry smile. "I haven't told you the rest."

"Oh, great," I snarled. "There's worse?"

Clair bit her lip.

"He tried again to grab my sister Kyale, and this time he got her. She was three rooms from me, same floor, in my castle, with all my people around. *And* Kyale's cats—who didn't like Senrid's sunny smile and winning personality the time he was there before."

"How'd you know it was him, then?"

"Two things. One, Llhei, Kyale's governess, heard her yell Senrid's name—and two." Leander looked sardonic. "I happen to have Senrid's cousin. Who was with him for her very first mission."

"You don't have wards up against black magic?"

"Oh, I had plenty—I thought," Leander said. "And he ripped right through most of 'em, got around the rest. Nabbed Kitty, and afterward I guess he came straight here. Quite a day's work!"

Clair frowned. "A lot of transfers..." She started in with technical talk.

I interrupted. "If you two are going to gabble spells and wards, I'll leave. I hate that stuff because I don't know it all yet, and I'm hungry."

"We need to plan," Clair said.

"Then you can do it without me," I said firmly, "since every single plan I've ever made has gone floob. Diana? Want to stay or come?"

Clair laughed. "If we have to be fast, best without your temper."

"Temper? Whom? I?" I exclaimed.

Nobody looked convinced—not even Leander.

Diana said, "I'm going with you," and we zapped downstairs—leaving behind the sound of their laughter.

Seshe was waiting anxiously.

Trading off explanations and pocalubes (whenever Senrid's name was mentioned) Diana and I told her.

"This sounds bad," she said, sighing. "And he seemed so friendly a sort."

By then the other girls had heard our voices—and the various insults—and had wandered in. At the end, after Seshe's comment, we looked at one another in silence. Gwen grumbled under her breath; Sherry's blue eyes were round with worry. The moody two, Irene and Dhana, both exclaimed and insulted and stamped, looking ready to go to Marloven Hess and try some kid-grabbing on their own.

Despite what I said about planning, crazy ideas started sprouting in my head like a bunch of demented weeds. Before I could pick one and call for volunteers, I found myself on the receiving end of the signal-and-summons magic.

"Uh oh—" I started. Then I blinked, staggered, and found myself back in the library, facing Clair and Leander.

"CJ. " Clair gave me a funny smile. "We have a plan. And only one person is able to pull it off. By going into Marloven Hess in disguise."

"I sure pity that poor slob," I said feelingly.

Clair's grin widened into a silent laugh. "Then get a mirror and start pitying."

"What? *Me?* You nauseating..."

She let me go for maybe two minutes; I was just warming up for some real insults to vent my pent-up feelings, when she said (past her snickers), "CJ—remember Faline. If you pocalube us until tomorrow, it might be too late."

"Me? Why me?" I whined.

Clair continued as if I'd answered with cheery enthusiasm, "You know some magic, and it's our only chance to act fast, since both Mearsies Heili and Vasande Leror happen to lack armies—"

"And even if we had 'em," Leander put in, his face serious again. (During my pocalube he'd been so wooden-faced I suspected he was suspiciously close to snickers, but he didn't know us well enough to give in.) "Marloven Hess is bigger than both our countries put together—at least twice over. And it is *all* army."

"And apparently it's not an army of badly-trained, half-enchanted bumblers, like the Chwahir," Clair added. "If Leander's sources are true, they're good at it."

I snorted. "That guard who blabbed their plans to Faline to kill time sounded like a bumbler, nice as he was."

"True," Clair said, turning her attention to Leander.

Leander shrugged. "A Marloven would be quick to point out that he was only a foot warrior, and the best all go into their cavalry, but still. There's idiocy and corruption aplenty over there. But all of those warriors, rotten or not, train all the time. They *like* fighting. They don't do anything else, Collet said— their holidays are mainly wargaming in the middle plains, and they take it seriously. And Senrid and Tdanerend have got plans for the entire Halian subcontinent, which they once ruled and so think they should again, so they'll have lots and lots of war to look forward to, and it'll make 'em even better at it."

"Yeccch," I said. "And you think *I* can go up against *that? Alone?* Remember how successful I was last time I was spackled into an army!" I thought back to that crack-brained snabloon Kessler Sonscarna, and shuddered.

"But this time you'll have your magic, because there's no ward against you. And you won't be sneaking in because you'll be expected, you'll have a place. Disguised as Ndand—"

"Who's that?"

"Senrid's shortsighted, enchanted cousin," Leander said. "She's a year or so younger than you, but you're about the same size, so you'll pass. She's got magic wards on her, so no one will detect the slight illusion magic to alter your features a bit—

no full transformation necessary, which might cause tracer-alarms to warn them."

Clair said, "Anyway, we've got to get started. Lots to do because Senrid will expect her to escape at midnight from Leander's. Midnight their time, which isn't long from now."

"Midnight?" I repeated.

Leander said, "She was part of the plot to grab Kyale— this was her very first time away from home—but she fumbled, and I believe Senrid must have expected she might fumble, but he wouldn't be able to come right back and get her because I'd be raising the alarm. Which is exactly what happened."

"What's this about midnight?" I asked. "It sounds suspicious."

"Not if you know Senrid, and meet Ndand. His alternate plan required her to sneak along and hide in my library until we'd finished searching and running around and so forth. Midnight. By then he'd also be done with his end of the tasks his uncle had set for him."

I nodded, still uneasy.

"When you meet her," Leander said, "you'll understand. I found her lurking around in the hall outside Kitty's room, looking terrified. Mad as we were, we soon saw it would be a waste of time to blame her for anything. So I remembered what Faline had told us last summer, and got the idea of coming here, figuring that the midnight spell might actually work in our favor. It gave me a little time."

Clair nodded, sneezed thrice, and wiped her eyes. She waved a hand at Leander. "Bring her?" she asked hoarsely, then coughed.

Leander did the transfer magic and vanished.

I sighed. "For Faline. *Only* for Faline."

"Of course only for Faline," Clair said with a wry smile. Her eyes looked tired, and her lips were cracked. "If I weren't sick I'd be going, because I know more magic than you, but I don't think I'd last out the day."

"No," I said quickly. "Better send me. I'll manage."

Clair looked around, and because Leander wasn't there— we were alone—she said, "Don't give me the 'You stay here because you're queen' argument, because I don't believe in it.

Mearsies Heili would survive if I never came back, but Faline won't if we don't act. If I weren't sick I'd be the best for this plan, because it needs a short girl who knows lots of magic. But I am sick. You're next best, because you don't know as much as I do, yet, but you know some. Don't you see?"

"I *see*," I groaned. "I'm *scared*."

"Me too." She sighed, and sat up straight. "Leander says that Senrid seems to like his cousin. So if you're quick—and you're the quickest of us all—and careful, no one gets hurt on either side."

"I'm not the carefullest of us all," I moaned.

"But you know how to be," Clair said. She was smiling but her eyes were serious, and a little worried. Seeing that, I knew it was time for me to quit jellying and buckle down to business.

"Right," I chirped, faking confidence. "I'm hoping that if I whine a lot now, then all the bad luck will go away and I'll not mess up."

Clair grinned. She loved exotic Earth superstitions like 'bad luck'.

Before either of us could speak, transfer-dazzle warned us of arrival, and air puffed our faces as two people appeared. Leander stood before us with a girl. She was short, though not as scrawny as I am, and her eyes were blue and long-lashed behind spectacles. Honest-to-Earth spectacles! White magic has long been able to heal eye problems, but I guessed black magicians were too tough for that. Her face was shaped differently from mine, and her long hair was a thicker texture and colored dark reddish-brown, but Clair and Leander were right. Since I have blue eyes and long black hair, it would only require a minor illusion spell to make me resemble her.

"Hi, Ndand," I said awkwardly, wondering how she was feeling about being a prisoner of kids. Not that we'd stick her in any dungeon (even if we had one) or give her rotten food. Just the opposite. But we were supposed to be her enemies.

Ndand blinked, looking numb and very unhappy.

"Please sit down, Ndand," Clair said as kindly as she could in her croaky voice.

Ndand plumped onto a chair, with no change in expression. Her instant obedience made me edgy.

"Okay, CJ, on a chair next to her."

I splatted down, but not without a grimace and a roll of the eyes.

Clair had a very old book at hand. She studied us both, then performed the spell—an illusion spell meant to last through a full day. I felt my vision blur slightly when I looked down, then it snapped into clarity. My hair now looked wavy and thick-stranded and reddish-brown, but when I touched it, I felt the familiar ruler-straight fine black locks. A very well-made illusion.

A quick trade of clothes, a trip through a cleaning frame, and Ndand wore one of Clair's best gowns. I now wore Ndand's: a heavy brushed linen gown with a fitted waist and long flared skirt. The dress was plain, which I liked, its only ornament being a sash, which pulled the loose waist snug. At least, I thought in resignation as I smoothed my skirts across my knees, this wasn't Colend, where the court people wear ribbons and lace and gems on everything. Of course in Colend—though its king was about the strangest person I'd ever met for someone supposedly on the white side—there weren't executions.

"All right," Clair said, recalling my attention. "Time to study. Ndand, what can you tell us about your father?"

Ndand said in a high, flat voice, "His name is Tdanerend Montredaun-An, and he was younger brother to the former king, and is regent to the present one, my cousin Senrid..."

And so began what seemed a long, horrible stretch, but was probably no more than an hour. Pure misery for me as I tried desperately to master a lot of facts utterly new to me, exasperation for Clair and Leander as they questioned Ndand and repeated things for me. Only Ndand sat patiently throughout the whole, answering every question put to her, and never making any comment or even showing any curiosity.

She never reacted to the idea of Kyale or Faline being abducted for execution—or to our plans to save them.

She seemed so apathetic it was like she'd been turned into some kind of mechanical doll, except as time wore on one emotion became increasingly clear: she was terrified of her father. She didn't have any friends at all. That (like everything else that seemed a part of normal life) was "white weakness". But she didn't seem to care. Senrid was her only companion, and about him she gave no reaction—no liking or disliking either. He seemed part of the furniture of her life. Her only comment, when asked what he talked about when they were alone was, "He talks too fast. I don't always understand him."

"Does he get angry with you?" I asked.

"No." She shook her head. "He just talks and talks."

Surprisingly, (at least she believed) he didn't get her into trouble with her father, but protected her.

It seemed a horrible life—her only "help" being a rotten black magic creep of a kid—and *I* was going to be living it.

THREE

Faline flopped down on the stone floor, groaning. How to get out of this one?

A voice echoed hollowly: "Faline?"

Faline looked up, wondering if it was, as CJ called 'em, the harp brigade (or pitchfork platoon) lining up for recruitment.

The voice came again, stronger. "Faline! Put your ear to the wall! It's '3!"

Faline popped to her feet and pressed her ear to the stone wall.

"'3?" she called. She remembered her guard from Latvian's—713!

"Ah, there you are. Best we don't yell. This way we can talk. Heard everything the king told you. I guess we're in for it together tomorrow."

Faline grimaced. "Yah. Fun. Can hardly wait," she said with 100% lack of enthusiasm. "So what happened to you?"

"What do you mean?"

"I mean, you tell me what happened to you and I'll tell you what happened to me. We can pass the time that way. It's nice to hear your voice again, though not like this."

"In spite of everything," the warrior agreed.

Faline said, "I hope you're not too mad at me. For escaping and telling Leander what you'd told me, in order to save them in Vasande Leror."

"No."

"It was my duty, y'see. And I didn't lie, not really, because—"

"I know," he said. "Everyone's doing their duty as they see it. Everyone except me. I shouldn't'a been blabbing."

"I was glad you did," Faline said. "I met the leaders over in Vasande Leror, and I liked 'em a lot."

"They have dungeons?"

"Huh?"

Faline looked around. This dungeon she was in could have been a Chwahir one, either in the Shadow or the Land. Stone, damp, dark, except for the faint glow of torchlight from the hallway outlining the little barred window in the door, shining on stone of a warm peachy color, not the gray granite of Chwahirsland. But the horrible sense of weight, of tons and tons of heavy stone, all squared off and silent to imprison people away from light and air and greenery and normal life, *that* was just the same.

"I don't think so," she said. "Least, when I first got there'n tried to get in through a window, they didn't threaten me with any dungeons or death squads or any of that nastarooni."

"Do you have dungeons in your country?"

"Now, that I can answer! No. Not a one."

"Prisons?"

"Yup. But they're above ground, and people stay in 'em while they do restitution. They sleep there at night and work during the day."

"So if someone betrays a state secret?"

"Well, we don't have any state secrets. At least, if Clair has 'em, she only tells CJ, 'cause it's her job. But say CJ did up and blab one, by mistake, well, Clair would change the plans. Not that she'd ever plan to take over another country. I mean, in all the time I've lived in Mearsies Heili, we've never had an execution. If people break the law they make restitution, and Clair tries to figure out why it happened in the first place, if it's a big enough problem. But the grownup governors help with that—like ol' Kanos, who's lived a long time, and he knows a lot about people."

"I wondered about that," 713 said.

Faline didn't claim to be any kind of mind reader, but it seemed to her that ol' '3 had been going through some serious change of heart.

She said, "So after I got away from Latvian's, what happened?"

"Fellow on tower duty was demoted temporarily, until Latvian figured you'd used some kind of magic to escape. Fellows at the gate, same thing. That was it, until the king's plan was thwarted so neatly. I knew you'd managed that, and I spent the summer waiting for them to come for me, and I did some thinkin'. You didn't know anyone in Vasande Leror—you hadn't even known where it was."

"I found out real quick." Faline chortled. "So someone blabbed on you, I take it?"

"Don't know. The king himself found out. Took great pains, I was told. I knew I'd get stood up against the wall, but I didn't think you would."

"So you confessed?"

"Soon's the king asked. Why lie? I'd done wrong. Knew it. He knew it."

Faline thought about Senrid, who'd seemed so friendly. "Was he mad at you?"

"Not at all. I think..."

"What?" Faline prompted, when 713 fell silent, and all she could hear for an unmeasured time was a slow drip somewhere.

"I think that's why the two days of recreation, with the Regent watching. Regent said it was to make an example of me for any warrior in future who fraternized with prisoners, but it was actually a kind o' threat to the king, I think."

"'Recreation'? Oh. You don't mean, like, yecch, torture and junk?"

"That's what I mean," 713 said with a kind of wheezy laugh.

"So Senrid got to watch, is that it?"

"Had to. Not the whole two days. Regent came often. Enjoyed it. King didn't, I don't think. No expression."

Now Faline knew why 713 was rambling so much, he was probably feverish. She was glad she couldn't see him—but she knew what she ought to do.

"What the heck and would you believe," she groaned, hating the whole situation more than ever.

"What?"

"I'm disgusted!" Faline said, thinking: *I'm squeamish!*

"With who?" 713 asked.

"All these uniformed clod-hopping pickle-spleens—ooh, reminds me of a very fine joke!"

"I miss your jokes," 713 said wistfully.

Now Faline *knew* he was sick! But she said in a rallying tone, "Well then we simply have to live, so's you can tell the rest o' my gang. They'll NEVER believe ANYONE could miss my jokes! You got water in there?"

"No. Nothing."

"Are you by any chance tied up and all that junk?"

"No chance." 713's laugh was sad. "Truth."

"Argh! I'll come over and help you out. Only neighborly."

"You won't want to see what I look like."

"You'll look better when I'm done," Faline promised, hoping it was true. Then she scanned around the bare cell, now that her eyes had grown accustomed to the darkness. In the faint light from the grill in the cell door she saw notches all along the top of the stone wall she'd been leaning against. She discovered that she hadn't been hearing through the wall—which seemed impossible—she'd been hearing through shared air holes.

And who'd put her in this cell?

Faline shook her head. It did seem weird, all right, but she wasn't going to complain. Instead, she said, "This place is pretty old, isn't it?"

"Yes."

"Well, then. Lock'll be a cinch. Diana's the only one who can do new locks, but she taught us all how to pick these old ones, and we all carry something—me, it's on my belt buckle thingie—that works on locks. In case, you know, we meet up with your villain who likes slinging people into dungeons without letting you go home and pack first. Anyhoo," she said as she pulled her belt free, "Diana *understands* locks."

Some frustrated feeling about, fumbling, and pressure— and the ancient mechanism sprung, the door swung open, and she eased out.

A quick look—no guards in sight. Only the flaring torches as the stale air stirred slowly. So she hopped quickly up to the next cell and picked the lock—an easier job from the front.

"Hey!" she said softly, easing inside the door. She was afraid to open it wide. She knew that these old dungeon doors could graunch and groan.

"You little fox," 713 exclaimed in admiration. "How'd—"

"Toldya I could floob the lock," Faline said, grinning at the surprise in 713's wheezy laugh. "Now, where are you? My cell is like daylight compared to this'ee. Ah." She sat down beside 713 to wait until her eyes had adjusted a bit more; his cell was farther from that hallway wall torch, and barely caught any light at all.

"Nice to see you again," she said. "That is, if I could see you."

"Glad you can't see me," he said ruefully.

"Oh, don't gloom. We won't croak. Now, I'll get some water, and—"

"Why?"

"Why what?"

"You said we won't die. Why?"

"Cuzz we're allies of white magic," Faline stated. "Well, I think you are, you didn't know it."

"I don't know anything," 713 said. She could hear the shrug in his tone. "I never thought. Ever. When I was little I wanted to go for a warrior, like all my friends. Never even thought I'd be good enough for cavalry, foot warrior was all right. I could be with my friends, have the good life."

"War is a good life?"

"Drill's fun," he said. "Wargames fun too. Talk, regular meals. I liked it fine. Guard duty is boring—you know what happened because of that." He laughed again, that rueful laugh.

Faline stirred. "I guess I can't see it as fun. Fun is what we girls do. Losing your home, your name, your—your place in the world is fun?"

"I don't come from any family with a rep. I gave up my name without a second thought when the Regent started the number system. All we wanted was rank, see, and you get rank through war, and since no one attacks us, we were all rarin' to try out our skills elsewheres. But, like the king said, when I was tryin' to explain, attack in the abstract... Still not sure what he meant. But sounds right." His voice faded.

Faline struggled to follow the slow, fever-wheezy dialog. "D'you mean you didn't think your enemy had a face?" She remembered that being something Clair had said once, after reading an old record.

"That's it," 713 said.

Faline sighed, deciding she'd think about what all that meant some time later. Like when they weren't in a dungeon, awaiting execution.

"Well," she said. "CJ says the only white-magic people who die young are great and noble heroes, or martyrs, and so far it's been true, because we girls are not noble, or heroes, we like pie-fights and pocalubes too much. And we're all still alive! My jokes are *much* too rotten for me to make a great martyr, and you're not sure whose side you're on, so you can't be one either. Therefore we will escape, we just don't know how yet."

"I like your way o' thinking," 713 said, and wheezed another laugh. He was sounding awfully tired.

"I think I'll get the water now," Faline whispered, and let herself out again.

She locked herself back in the cell, shed her jacket and kicked it into a corner. "Hey! You guards! You ugly, pop-eyed globules, cummere!" She kicked and banged on the door.

A few seconds later a key clanked in the lock and two huge guards stood there glowering, one holding a torch.

She blinked against the sudden light. "Don't we get any grub?" she asked forlornly.

"No."

"How about clean water? And while you're at it, a nice big roomy warm shirt or somethin'? I'm real cold—and if I get cold I get sick, and if I get real sick I might croak before tomorry, and then where'll you be? Eh? Short one execution victim, that's what!"

The two guards turned away without speaking and locked the door.

Faline looked back up at the air holes as if to reassure herself. If she'd gauged Senrid right, she oughta get some kind of answer soon...

She'd sung to herself a dozen verses of one of her favorite anti-villain insult songs (making up two new verses, one for Senrid and one for his uncle) when the door clattered and clanked open again, and two objects were set on the stone ground: a good-sized bowl of water, and a thick folded square of cotton-wool cloth.

"You are requested by the king not to mention this to the Regent," one guard said in a flat voice.

Faline grinned, saying (in Mearsiean) "I bet you were 'requested' too!" In their language, she said, "Tell 'im thanks."

The cell door slammed shut.

So—she'd been right. Senrid did feel sorry for her. Not enough to stop the execution. But to make things bearable beforehand.

Faline picked up the cloth thing, to discover a fray-cuffed, bag-elbowed tunic much like the black-and-tan ones the warriors wore. It was a bit too small for 713, but it'd do. And the water would take care of whatever wounds he had, after the Regent's two days of 'recreation.'

Pocalubing the Regent, Senrid, dungeons, and her own squeamishness, Faline quietly unlocked the door again. She slipped out, carrying her booty, and let herself in next door to do what she could for poor old 713.

Possible escape could be thought about later—right now the poor slob had to be able to move.

&)CR&)cs

Clair, Leander, Ndand and I had to be done by mid-evening, because that would be midnight in Vasande Leror and Marloven Hess. By the end of that time (seemed like a year) my head felt like someone had stuffed it full of rocks. A week's practice might have made this kind of masquerade thing easier. A very tense session from early to mid-evening made me feel like I was living in a nightmare.

Two nightmares, mine and poor Ndand's.

"All right, that's it," Clair whispered finally. Her voice was completely gone. "We're out of time. CJ, you and Diana deserve medals—or better, chocolate pie and ice cream."

"Just have it ready," I said, trying to subdue my boiling guts. Truth was, I don't think I could have eaten anything, even chocolate pie, if I'd tried. I turned to Leander. "I wish you could go with me."

"I do too," Leander said. "But if something goes wrong, it won't be much good for both of us to be stuck in Senrid's capital."

His part was going to be tough in a different way. Because of complicated border wards, Leander had to sneak into Marloven Hess inside the border somewhere as a transfer designation for me to focus on, since my transfer was going to be difficult enough without picturing a destination I didn't know, and planning for wards no one was sure of.

To send Faline and Kitty to a person would be much easier. But Leander would have to sit and wait until either I got the others to him, then transferred myself—or the Marlovens did, if I flubbed up. If I did manage, and we all made it, then we could both concentrate on avoiding whatever border tracers they had, and get ourselves out a short distance. Short distances always being far easier for magic transfer, especially when you are 'carrying' others. And if I flubbed, he'd have to figure out what to do, probably with one second's notice.

We went over the plan one more time, though we all knew our parts. It was kind of reassuring to say, "Yes, and then I do the transfer to you..." and to hear the corresponding, "And after that you get Kitty and Faline to me, and if I haven't broken his ward spell by then and can't get us out, we'll cross the border on foot..."

When that was done, Leander stepped beside me. My insides really churned now.

Clair sneezed, said, "Fare well. I'm gonna sleep. Tomorrow I'll get a start on removing the enchantments from Ndand."

I looked over at Ndand. She sat there staring into space. I shivered inside, then turned to Leander, who nodded, took hold of my shoulder, and said the transfer spell.

FOUR

We splatooned into the courtyard of a castle. I caught a glimpse of wide glass windows and lots of green ivy rendering light gray stone somewhat less grim. When the transfer daze had unfogged a bit, I said, "This your place?"

"Yes," Leander said, leading the way inside and straight up some stone stairs. "And I hope to give you a full tour when we celebrate the success of our plan. Okay?" He added the last as if tasting the word.

I grinned, thinking of how much slang from Earth I'd spread over this world so far, and jammed a pair of spectacles over my nose as I followed him down a long hall to a wooden door. The glasses were twin to Ndand's. They were just glass, but with an illusion spell laid over them to resemble the grind of Ndand's lenses, or else there'd be no distortion of my eyes to others. This meant I had to see the world distorted. I looked through them, and a vice seemed to squeeze my skull as the world blurred around me. "I hate these things—I can't see."

"I know," Leander said, and opened the door to his library. "Peer over the tops, take 'em off and polish them on your skirt or chew the ends when you have to see clearly. But she wears them—"

"So I haveta wear them. Ugh."

The single toll of a midnight bell rang then, sounding to me like a funeral. Mine.

"See you later," he said with a sympathetic laugh. Leander was such a comfortable person, it was like we'd always known him.

I gave him the nod, and sucked in my breath. I carefully said the transfer word that Senrid had set up to shift Ndand home, and magic seized me in a much harder, faster wrench than I was used to. I splorched to the ground outside of Choreid Dhelerei, the capital of Marloven Hess.

Why not inside the palace? As I got shakily to my feet and waited for the dizziness to pass, I wondered if the Regent was so worried about traitors and invasion that no one could transfer in except him, and then I remembered that this transfer was Senrid's backup spell—apparently made just to protect Ndand. If you could believe him protecting anyone. I couldn't.

The time was midnight, the air chilly. I was glad of the thick fabric of my gown. According to Ndand the castle was drafty and cold because the Regent didn't like fires in any rooms until there was actually snow on the ground. He considered it weakness.

I walked slowly onto a well-tended road, while looking around over the top of the spectacles in order to get my bearings. Mentally I reviewed my story. Ndand had fumbled when Senrid got ahold of Kitty, who'd struggled mightily. She'd backed away from Kitty's flailing legs—right out of the range of Senrid's initial transfer. Then she panicked, just standing there uncertain what to do until Leander found her. But that part I wasn't going to tell Senrid. My new story was going to be that Leander and his people had run outside first, looking for enemies in the courtyard, and leaving me time to get to the library and hide until midnight, at which time I could say the activation word Senrid had set up for transfer.

Chilly as the air was, my palms were sweaty. I had to keep my own scrawny hide intact, as well as rescue Faline and Kitty—and I had to do it well enough so that poor clod Ndand would be able to slip back into her life.

If she wanted to, that is, when Clair was done removing all the spells her father had put on her to turn her into a clod. Clair would never force her to go back against her will. If she had any left. After Ndand told us about her father's experimental spells, Clair did a quiet scan, and while Ndand was eating some dinner, she told Leander and me privately that there was enough nasty magic laid over that girl to distort not just her eyes but her mind. Nobody in Marlovan Hess was going to question any magic 'feel' coming off my illusions, not with poor Ndand radiating bad magic.

As long as no one touched me—then looked into my face.

The sound of horsehooves called my attention to the present. My heart thumped like crazy.

Very shortly a neat formation of horsemen appeared over the top of a round hill and clattered to a stop when they saw me. "There she is," one of them said, and half-heard words of surprise riffed through the patrol.

"Are you all right?" one asked me in a cautious voice.

"I guess," I said in a flat voice, hoping I sounded convincing.

No one reacted. Instead, they reformed their lines, and I realized that a ride would be ahead. Could Ndand ride? We hadn't asked that, had we? Was I already starting to forget things?

Then I saw a saddled horse with no rider, its reins held by someone. All right. I was expected to ride—and this patrol must have been sent by Senrid.

One man dismounted and cupped his hands. Well, Ndand obviously was bad at mounting on her own. I moved slowly, hesitantly, looking at the starlit black-and-tan-clad warriors for clues to what they expected. Most of them were barely grown up, and all but one light-haired.

Placing my foot in the cupped hands, I found myself expertly pitched up onto the horse's back. Reins were tossed to me. I took them, and then—no warning—the two leaders started out at the gallop. So I let the horse follow at their pace.

Presently we crested a hill. Beyond, stark against the brilliant night sky, was the torch-lit outline of the fortified city, built along the top of three low hills. The royal castle on the central one. It was gigantic! Gigantic, and threatening. It was also supposed to be home, so I tried to look expectant, and not afraid.

Before we started up the road to the city gates, we were met by another patrol, but as they slowed a yell halted us all.

"Ndand!" A kid's voice. "I thought you might have gotten lost in the dark," the kid added. Added with meaning.

I was about to meet Senrid.

Again my heart started trying to escape past my ribs, except this time good old anger kept me steady.

Starlight glowed faintly on a white shirt. I peeked over the glasses, glimpsed a running figure.

"Senrid!" came a man's voice, loud in reprimand.

The white-shirted figure slowed to a sedate walk.

Remembering what Ndand had said of their relations with Tdanerend, the Regent (and her father), I leaned forward, and when Senrid reached us, I said in an undervoice, repeating something Ndand had observed over and over again, "He hasn't lifted that rule *yet*?"

The leader of the outer-perimeter patrol had stopped a little distance away. It was he who'd yelled at Senrid. Tdanerend had given various people in his own personal guard authority to correct Senrid for his own good. Running eagerly to greet his cousin was apparently not good for kings.

It also served to check any authority Senrid might be trying to gain, Clair had pointed out.

Senrid turned his palm up. Even in the dark I could see irony in that sharp, tight movement. I slid off my horse; the nearest rider held out his hand, and I tossed my reins to him. It was the right move.

So I began walking beside Senrid, since he clearly expected it. I could barely make out his features in the dark. The starlight glowed off his shirt, and in his yellow hair. He was maybe a hand taller than me. At least, I thought, he can't see me any clearer right now than I can see him.

Senrid set off toward the castle. The two patrols rode away, one to continue patrol and the other back to the city, leaving us alone.

As soon as they were out of hearing, Senrid said, "Good girl. You remembered everything."

"Everything," I repeated, my heart doing a chicken dance behind my ribs.

Senrid galloped right on. *Talk, talk, talk*, she'd said. "And I've done everything *he* ordered. Found 713 of the 44th

Foot. Grabbed Faline Sherwood from Mearsies Heili. Grabbed Kyale—*we* grabbed Kyale, though I think that particular plan is a waste of time. What happened? I told him you'd stayed behind for a while to spy on Leander. He liked that—that you'd choose to spy."

"Spy," I said carefully. Ndand had frequently repeated the last word anyone had said, when she was agreeing.

"And that you would report after you took a walk to get rid of the mental residue of being around whites. He actually believed it! To the patrol I said you'd gotten lost again, because you can't see. Everything as planned, and if your story matches mine, you won't get into trouble. So what did happen to you?" he asked.

"You didn't see her kick me?" I talked in my flattest voice, telling the story we'd concocted.

At the end Senrid snorted a laugh. "So Leander didn't figure out I'd broken his wards, did he? I didn't think he'd be that stupid." His voice was a regular kid-voice, his manner of speaking quick, with lots of humor. Humor in a black magic wielding creep. Ugh. Unsettling. "Just as well, since now you're safely home, and Uncle won't gripe." He sighed. "Says I'm not ready yet. I'm too weak. Somehow it's my fault about 713, though I see him as another example of corruption in the training system. Very lax training. Someone pays lip service to someone else, and they scant their duty with the recruits."

"Oh," I said, wondering if dealing with Senrid was always going to mean these headlong speeches. Following him—staying in Ndand's persona—felt like I was trying to swim down a rushing river.

"Don't-tell," he said, an automatic-sounding phrase, one I instantly recognized from Ndand's flat narration: whenever the two had real talk with each other they began it with *don't-tell*, meaning not to tell Tdanerend.

Not that she'd used it much. Those experimental spells her father had been trying on her made thinking slower and harder than ever, she'd told us. And if the Regent thought they worked properly, Senrid was going to get them next.

"Don't-tell," Senrid said, "but I think I'd as soon they live. Faline is funny! And she has no political ambition.

Absurd to pretend she had even the remotest idea of the consequences of her actions. 713 either—he was trying to impress her with our greatness! And now he's going to pay the price of his bad training. He should be a horse tender for some cavalry riding. A few moments of conversation and I could see that's where his talents really lie. But he's big, so they put weapons in his hands and gave him the most basic lessons in what to do with them."

We reached the city gates then. Magic-burning torches, glary-red and fitful, highlighted Senrid as he lifted his hand to the watchful sentry-silhouettes on the gate. I smelled fire, and iron, and steel, and dust, and horses. I sensed danger. These Marlovens watching us didn't have the glass-eyed stare of the Chwahir. They hadn't had initiative beaten or enchanted out of them, which meant they'd be harder to fool.

When we were past the sentries, Senrid added, "Kyale's okay, I guess, but not now. Like that word, okay? Got it from Kyale and Faline. Means yes, well, good, agreement. Okay. Short. I like it!"

"What about Kyale?" I asked, glad I hadn't accidentally said 'okay.'

Senrid said sarcastically, "Remember when Uncle found out—through my grrreat and precise report—that she gets shut-in mad?"

"Mmm?" I wasn't going to repeat *that*.

"Think, Ndand, back to summer. Remember when he sent me, was sure Mara Jiniea's daughter would be on our side? He really thought Leander Tlennen-Hess had enchanted her to be a white. I still can't believe that."

"Believe," I said, realizing I was hearing some of the stuff we'd been trying to guess at. So I tried a careful question. "Still?"

Senrid flexed his hands, throwing them outward. "No, of course not. The idea is to enchant her and send her back against her brother. Do our work for us from the inside. So he shut her up in one of the smaller cells with no peephole until she consents. Idea was for a full watch. Been there since I got back—the whole time I was gone getting Faline. Been at least a watch, more like three. He's probably forgotten about her," he added.

We passed through a torch-lit intersection. The streets were broad, well paved, and clean. Apparently the Marlovens also had wanders, the people who patrolled about zapping away animal droppings, like in white magic countries. The houses were big and surprisingly they weren't all ugly; most were built of a light peachy-gold stone, like the huge royal castle, others were built out of light gray granite. But they were all thick-walled, designed to withstand attack.

Light flickered over Senrid as we walked. I peeked over the glasses, saw a roundish face, and eyes that looked dark blue. Waving blond hair squared off short at collar length in back—the Marloven military cut, I would realize later. Elsewhere in the world, the toffs had long hair, but not here, where being an aristocrat meant first and foremost you were trained to hold rank in the military.

Was he sorry about Kyale? He almost sounded sorry. No, he was just annoyed with his uncle.

"Why don't you put a loyalty spell on her and have done?" I asked, and then I wondered if Ndand could even ask such a question.

Senrid's voice softened, patient and slow, as automatic as *don't tell*. "Remember, it needs consent to make his loyalty spells easy. That means you resign your will: either you obey, or go blank. But no consent is different, especially the kind of loyalty spell uncle wants. There isn't any good non-consenting loyalty spell—at least that I know of—that destroys will but leaves you able to think well. And sending Kyale against Leander as a walking doll won't net us anything, he'd know in a heartbeat something was wrong." He stopped and faced me. A sharp pang zinged through my innards. Was he suspicious before we even reached the palace? "Has he been experimenting on you again?"

"Again," I repeated, not sure what else to say.

"Don't consent, Ndand," Senrid said. "I told you. He'll rant and rave, but if he was going to really kill you, he would have by now."

"By now," I mumbled.

"And remember what I told you about those spells. I don't think he's really perfecting any loyalty spell for us, no matter what he says to you. We're both loyal. He wants an obedience spell. For me. Something that takes away my will, but manages to spare my skills with magic, since he's such a rotten mage." Senrid grinned. I did not like that grin, and the uneven torchlight didn't make it any more pleasant. "More I think on it, more I'm sure that's what he was harassing Latvian to cook up, and on a foreigner, so I wouldn't find out. But Faline got away, and I did find out!"

He was walking even faster by now, and his speech had gone back to a tumble of quick words. Like he was thinking out loud. I was sure by now that that was the way most of his 'conversations' with Ndand went.

I had to struggle to keep up, but keep up I did. It was, strictly speaking, mid-evening in my own home, but this had been a long day, without any supper—Ndand was the only one who'd gotten any.

Well, it was really midnight for Senrid, and I knew from Ndand that no one in that castle slept in. That was 'white-magic weakness.' I hoped Senrid would conk out soon, so I'd have some time to look around, and think over what I'd seen and learned.

But first: "Kyale," I said, hoping to get him back to my rescuees.

"We can look in on her. Excuse will be to see if she's given in. If you want to."

"Want to," I echoed.

"She'll probably rant at us. She's funny when she rants! So very self-righteous. When she's not mad she's all right. But keep that to yourself," he added sharply. Not a *don't-tell* at the beginning. It wasn't a confidence, it was an order.

Annoyance prompted me to snap, "You think I would?"

"My, how we forget," he retorted. "The last time you yapped out one of my prize opinions it was two weeks before I could set my shoulder-blades to a chair-back."

Yeccch. My hunger vanished, quick as that.

He snorted a sort of humorless laugh, and looked up. We'd reached the second set of gates. These were before the royal castle, which was gigantic. The gates were as high, and well-guarded, as the ones surrounding the city.

Again Senrid raised his hand. A couple of the sentries raised spears or swords in salute. No words were spoken.

I wanted to get him back on the subject of Kyale, so I tried a tease. "You're such a softie." An impulse—and a bad one.

He shot me a fast look of annoyance as he said, "I don't know that I am at that."

I wondered if it had rankled because he was afraid it might be true.

But it wasn't much like Ndand to point it out. So I said, "I don't care. I'm tired. Hungry, too." I sure needed to keep up my strength, if I was going to make this mess work. "Aren't you?"

"Hungry, no. Tired, definitely—and an execution tomorrow. Could chew up the entire day if 713 lasts. And he will, if just to spite Uncle. Not that I blame him, but then it'll take that much longer to get chores done."

"713?" I asked. "Not Faline?"

"Just gets shot. For him we have to run through the entire list of tortures ordinary and extraordinary."

"Why all that?"

"Price of treason." Senrid frowned at me. "Use your head, or at least your memory. He's ranted on about it enough."

I snorted my disgust.

Senrid laughed softly. "Don't-tell, but sometimes I'm inclined to agree."

We reached the immense courtyard, and hiked across it toward the massive iron-reinforced doors. One of the waiting guards opened one. I noticed how heavy those doors were—and wondered uneasily if I could get one open on my own.

We walked down three very long halls. The stone walls had been partly masked by tapestries, mostly by frescoes, and here, at least, the dreary torches had been replaced by fine sconces. Furnishings carved out of dark wood could be glimpsed here and there.

I followed Senrid's quick steps, sneaking peeks in all directions but trying to appear to the silent guards posted at nearly every intersection as if I knew where I was.

We came to a plain door—guarded, natch.

The warrior before it (alert and clear-eyed, and very heavily armed) gave us a short nod, and unbolted the door.

Down we bucketed, into the familiar dank, musty smell of centuries-old dungeon. Does any villain ever have them cleaned? I mean, on Earth this would be a health threat, because there they don't have the Waste Spell, and dungeons were invented long before indoor plumbing. Here on this world the smells are mainly mold and old sweat, and in some horrible places old blood—but then I guess nobody cares what the prisoners think about their lack of fresh air.

The stairs downward were narrow and steep and railless. The intermittent torches made the steps seem to move. I blinked; I was more tired than I had thought. My eyes burned.

"The Mearsiean and 713 are in next to each other. I convinced Uncle to think it was his idea. He thinks they'll spend all their time in mutual accusations, once they discover that you can talk through the air shafts." His voice echoed weirdly.

We walked downward again, deeper underground, and the smell *didn't* get worse. Nothing rotting, like in Shnit's land. Just the damp mustiness, which, in itself, isn't so bad, if you don't equate it with dungeons.

Several sets of guards had to be passed. None of them were drunk, or even playing cards. We could hear them talking in low voices; they fell silent when we drew near, but didn't act particularly guilty.

"Here's where he put Kyale," Senrid said at last, indicating a storage door at the end of a long row. "Give me a hand and we'll go in by magic. Simpler than demanding the key and having to explain why. Crouch down," he warned.

That meant he didn't have to tell anyone.

Making a mental note to scrub later, I hunched down next to him and stuck out my hand, bending my head forward so he wouldn't see my face, and trusting to the darkness to shroud my hair. Senrid's fingers closed on it, his palm callused, like

Puddlenose's; he muttered the transfer spell without looking at me.

We zapped inside an utterly dark space, close and cold. Senrid dropped my hand and snapped a light into being. The closet was stone, no windows, nothing.

Squeezed into the corner lay was a bundle of blue cloth with silvery hair lying in tangled skeins over it.

"Kyale, get up," Senrid said.

But the girl didn't move.

FIVE

"Stupid, can't you see she's out?" I whispered fiercely, completely forgetting that I was supposed to be Ndand.

I frog-waddled forward a few inches and pulled the girl up. Her face was white except around the eyes, which were red and puffy even closed. "Obviously she's not going to do much consenting like this," I said, struggling to sound uncaring, but in reality I was so very close to transferring out with her—if I could have located Faline I would have, despite wards, no transfer destination, or preparation.

"I knew it was a stupid idea," Senrid said—unknowingly avoiding a signed and sealed CJ tantrum. "I guess we'd better take her out." So saying he grabbed my shoulder, and since I was still holding the limp Kyale, we all transferred.

The room we appeared in was large, with very fine furnishings, lit by glowglobes high on the wall. It was painfully tidy, except for a shirt lying half-off a dresser where it'd evidently been thrown in haste; there were no pictures or tapestries, the only decoration being an enormous map of Marloven Hess on the wall opposite the bed.

Senrid closed his eyes as the transfer-dazzle faded away, and I backed out of his grip. Finding a handsome, carved chair behind us, I dropped Kyale into it. Her head sagged against the back.

"You waken her," Senrid said. "It'll only make her madder if I do it."

I tried flapping a corner of my dress near her face, like a fan. Then I shook her gently. Nothing.

"Wake-herbs?" I looked up at Senrid over the tops of the spectacles.

He frowned, then grunted, as if mentally locating where they would be stored. Then he murmured another transfer spell, and a small crystal vial appeared with a pop onto his extended palm.

I unstoppered the vial, wondering why these militant people would have such a handsome item—the Chwahir wouldn't. I waved it under Kyale's nose. The smell of distilled aromatic herbs made my eyes water, and she moaned and coughed, and tried clumsily to push it away. I kept at it, and was rewarded when her eyelids fluttered up. Her eyes were a pretty silver color, a couple shades darker than her silvery blond hair.

She raised a hand to her eyes and I faded back.

All this time I'd let the spectacles perch on the very end of my nose so I could peer over them. It'd felt safe enough in the dark, but in this well-lit room I didn't dare not look through them, at least in Senrid's direction.

So I shoved the blasted things up and looked through them at the two blurry kids before me.

Kyale spoke. Her voice was high, and clear, with a hoarse edge. "All right...you horrible rat. Do me in if you're going to. Hurry up! I won't help you... I won't join you... and you and your disgusting creep uncle can go rot for all I care!" Her voice wobbled. After a moment, she sniffed, then asked tearfully, "Who's she?"

Fear zapped me hard. Kitty didn't know me—had she met Ndand, and was she seeing through the disguise?

"My cousin Ndand," Senrid said. "Ndand, Kyale Marlonen. You don't remember Ndand, Kyale? Right before we transferred here?"

"All I remember is trying my hardest to scratch your ugly face off," Kitty said fiercely.

I liked this girl at once!

"Hi, Kyale," I said, stepping forward, and turning my back to Senrid. I grabbed the spectacles off my face and polished them, staring hard at her. "Remember Faline? She's down in the dungeon." I pronounced Faline's name *Fa-linn-eh*—

with a Mearsiean accent—and Kyale's eyes flickered from Senrid back to me, her brows puckering.

Senrid spoke. "Well, Kyale? My uncle will want to know if we have your consent to his spell."

"I won't even bother to lie like you do," Kyale said, struggling upright in the chair, and flinging her damp, snarled hair back. "You don't have my consent to anything except sending me home—unless you'd like to turn yourself into a snail. And your uncle along with. *That* I'll consent to, promptly and cheerfully!"

Senrid raised his eyebrows. A moment later I had the spectacles on again, and his face blurred, but his voice was wryly humorous as he said, "I guess you've got courage. I like to see that. But my uncle doesn't because he'll have you back in that cell quick as—" He snapped his fingers. "When he finds out. Uh oh ... there goes the courage..."

For a second fear squinched Kyale's features, but at Senrid's last words she made a sour face. "Ha ha," she snarled. "Shutting me up won't work. I'll start choking again. Eurgh! Spider webs in my hair!" Her voice rose to a wail. "Don't you have any cleaning frames here?"

"Baths," Senrid said.

I got an idea, and turned to Senrid—and saw a blur. "Let her clean up," I said, trying to sound flat. Unconcerned. I peeked. Senrid seemed uncertain—not surprising, as it was a weird idea, but I was desperate to get her alone and explain things. "If she looks neat and tidy, Father might change his mind about sticking her back in the closet."

I couldn't believe he was even wavering. He wasn't stupid. But I would soon learn he was amazingly fastidious, which I never expected any villain to be.

"She can fix up in my room," I offered, as flat as possible, not believing he couldn't see the obvious.

"Okay. One turn." He reached for the small sandglass. So the Marlovens used the same thing that most people on this world have for short measures of time—what I think of as about fifteen minutes. I still found it interesting that everyone relies on bells, colored candles, and here and there some honest-to-Earth clocks, but I'd never seen any with a second hand, or even minutes: they chime on the hour. Time is regarded differently here than on Earth, and I was still getting used to it.

"Thanks," Kyale mumbled—to me.

I led the way out, peeking over my spectacles at intervals. The stone of the walls had been covered with plaster in subtle gradations, curving and straight lines that gave the illusion of depth. On the plaster were magnificent paintings in shades of gray. Magnificent in design, but spare in detail, and in subject: they were pretty much confined to running horses, or soaring and stooping hunting raptors. I was to see a lot of those throughout the residence part of that castle.

I shifted my attention from those to the carved-wood doors, hoping I hadn't gone past Ndand's without seeing it. Two down from Senrid's, but what a long way—I looked back—counted—opened the second door—and sighed with relief. I recognized the furnishings from her description.

Her bedroom was as large as Senrid's, with pretty blue and gold hangings and cushions and rugs, the furnishings the same fine carved walnut we'd seen in Senrid's. Didn't these war-mad Marlovens regard nice furniture as 'white-magic weakness'? They sure are weird, I thought, as I led Kitty inside.

The bedroom was cold (no fire—*those* are for the weak) and I held my chilled fingers over the lamp that a servant had obligingly left burning. Only Senrid had glowglobes, which he'd made himself, so he could read at night.

I snatched the spectacles off and turned to Kitty, who was just opening her mouth to bombard me.

"No time for questions. I see a brush on the dressing table. Listen as you work," I said in Leander's home language.

"Oh! I *thought* there was something funny going on." Kitty paused in the act of smacking grit and mildew from her gown. "But why is he letting us talk alone?"

"Probably because he'd never think Ndand would have anything to say that he couldn't hear. Look, I'm a Mearsiean, in disguise, to rescue Faline, who they intend to kill tomorrow. Leander is in on this plan. The only thing we could think of to get you out too is for you to do what you can to get yourself included in the execution, so I can get us all out at once. I'll only be able to do a single transfer, I'm afraid, but I practiced and practiced. Because I'll only have the one chance. As soon as I do that spell, they'll be laying on wards right and left."

Kyale nodded, looking pale and sick.

"And when you see Leander, tell him *first thing* that if there's a warrior with us, it's 713, so he's not to attack him or anything. If the guy is on our side, fine, if he's not, Leander can zap him somewhere else. But I can't let them execute him. Faline likes him, and I know without seeing her that she'd feel it her fault forever if he was killed. Especially the way they plan to do it. Now, let's talk about something else before Senrid snouts in."

"Thanks...whoever you are." Kitty looked ready to cry.

"The thanks go to Leander and Clair. Now, brush your hair! Groanboils! There's no time for a bath, but there's a pitcher of water, and that room has to be the bathroom, so at least you can wash your face and hands."

I bounded to the door of the wardrobe and pulled it open, deciding I'd better change into a warmer gown, if I could find one.

All Ndand's things were much fancier than I'd choose, though not nearly as fancy as Kitty's dress, with its silken lacings down the front and the embroidery and flounces. Still, Ndand's clothing was very well made—a wardrobe fit for a princess. As I looked over the many gowns, I wondered if Tdanerend really loved his daughter after all, or if that fancy wardrobe was a kind of proof of his ambition.

So far, everything pointed to the second choice.

I picked a sturdy woolen gown that had close sleeves and ought to keep me warm even in a drafty, unwarmed castle on the verge of winter. Moving fast, I unlaced the old linen one, stepped out, and got into the other. Just as Senrid's knock came, I finished tying the sash.

After ramming the spectacles onto my nose, I sprang to the door and opened it. Senrid was a blur. I hate not seeing danger.

"Did she try to run away?"

"No. Too busy," I said shortly.

A quick peek at Kitty showed her clothes brushed, her face clean, and her hair damp but orderly down her back. She

looked tired and limp, and not in the least like someone about to
make a mad dash through a castle that seemed to be guarded by
as many people as our entire population on the cloud-top city at
home. If not the entire population of Mearsies Heili!

"Come on, Kyale," Senrid said from the doorway.

Peek. He had also changed, into one of those black-and-
tan uniforms, a high-collared, close-fitted black tunic with a line
of gold stitchwork edging the stiff collar and narrow long
trousers, black except for a narrow gold stripe down the outer
seam, high blackweave riding boots, plain black sash round the
fitted middle. His uniform was completely bare of any kind of
rank markers or insignia. Ndand had said in her bland,
emotionless voice that Tdanerend insisted on protocol whenever
any of them were in the throne room or overseeing military
exercises, but Senrid had not earned any rank in their military
academy—he wasn't even allowed to go, yet—therefore he had
no army rank.

Not until we had gorbanzoed down what seemed another
500 miles of rich-but-somberly-furnished castle and entered a
truly spectacular throne room did I begin to see what this meant.

Ancient banners alternated with newer ones high on the
vaulted walls, many of them tattered and spattered nastily with
old brown bloodstains. Below each was mounted a sword,
sometimes a sword and a crown, the polished metal glimmering
with baleful red highlights like a beating heart in the inescapable
torchlight. The dimensions of the vast room, the heavy black
stone and steel and gold all were meant to intimidate, and it
worked.

The throne was a great thing, mostly highly polished
blackwood gilt with finely worked gold, with some dark blue
gems set into the carving along the top in a pattern of galloping
horses. The black and gold were the same colors as the great
screaming eagle banner, gold on black, hung high behind the
throne: the flag of Marloven Hess, emblem of ages of bloody
war.

Next to the throne was a smaller chair, and on it
Tdanerend sat, alone, waiting for us, I guess. Or maybe he liked
to lurk around in there and brood. Anyway, when we entered,

except for the guards at the far doors, we appeared to be alone. The hour was very late by then, and I kept fighting yawns.

"Senrid. You have wasted too much time," the man on the lesser throne said, as soon as we were within hearing distance. His harsh voice echoed. "Were you fraternizing again?"

"No," Senrid said. His voice sounded light and kid-like by contrast. "Not at all, Uncle Tdanerend. We—Ndand and I— got lost in a long discussion of how well you are managing the kingdom for my sake, and how much I must learn before I am to be deemed worthy of the title to which I was born."

Wow! I wouldn't have believed *that* gas even if I'd been totally unconscious—but Tdanerend seemed to swallow it right down like fresh chocolate pie.

He nodded slightly, his frown-lined face creasing in obvious self-satisfaction. He was, I could see, a man of medium height, with neat, short dark brown hair that shone with reddish tinges in the torchlight. His uniform—glittering with awards and rank markers—made him seem imposing.

"We forgot about Kyale until now, but I remembered my responsibility," Senrid continued. "Isn't it so, Ndand?" He turned to me.

Ndand did not mind lying to her father, so long as Senrid gave her the words. "Forgot Kyale." I didn't mind lying, either. This creep wasn't anyone I felt obliged to be truthful with.

Tdanerend's gaze shifted to me, and my heart slammed again. "What did you accomplish in Vasande Leror, Ndand?" There was no emotion—no fondness or familiarity in his tone.

"What I was assigned, father," I said. "I helped Senrid find Kyale, and then I stayed to spy, and I saw many rooms, but all were empty, then I had to hide when I heard voices." I kept my voice flat.

"I see." He visibly lost interest in me, and turned to Kyale. "You. Have you decided to consent to our plans?"

Senrid had passed us by; he leaped up the steps before the thrones, and sat on the great one. He looked small, almost lost, except for the light on his blond hair.

"No," Kitty said, her voice high and angry. "I will NOT consent. And so you may's well kill me because *nothing* you do will work. I got a good rest in that silly closet of yours!" At the end her voice shrilled.

Tdanerend's thin mouth curved in a malicious smile. "Very well. I'll grant your wish, since you are worth nothing to us otherwise. You may witness two deaths tomorrow, after which I'll ask you once more. If you remain obdurate, yours will be the most entertaining of the three."

Poor Kitty looked like a sun-bleached sheet.

Pocalubes piled up behind my lips, but I kept myself quiet and unmoving.

Tdanerend motioned casually at what I'd taken to be inky shadows between the great stone supports of the vaulted ceiling, and two henchminions approached. A point of the Royal Avuncular Finger and these flanked Kitty.

"Since her fear of closed-in spaces appears to be selective," Tdanerend said sarcastically, with a glance at Senrid in the great throne, "she will be housed on Execution Row."

Senrid said nothing, but I saw one hand lift, holding three fingers together. Briefly, a slight gesture.

The henchies showed no reaction to anything.

Poor Kyale was hauled away. The sound of their diminishing steps had barely receded when Tdanerend said to Senrid, with a patronizing expression, "You have completed this task and acquitted yourself appropriately. You may sit in judgment at Convocation." He indicated the throne under Senrid's royal butt.

Senrid gave him a fast look that would have made *me* suspicious, but if Tdanerend even saw it, he thoroughly ignored it.

"Now, go off to bed, both of you. It is well past midnight. You have plenty to do tomorrow, Senrid, if you are to be finished with your work by third watch, which is when I have scheduled the executions."

He looked expectantly at Senrid. I'd been peering over my spectacles; by the time he turned to me, I had lifted my head and saw him as a blur through the lenses. Easier on my stomach, but not *safe*.

"Yes, Father," I said meekly, since he seemed to expect a response.

"I will check on you shortly. If you are not asleep, I'll make you sleep."

I repressed a shudder, but Senrid grinned as he slid off the throne and hopped down the steps. "Don't worry, we'll both be asleep. We're tired!"

We left together. Neither of us spoke during the thousand-mile hike back to the residence area of the castle. Senrid was deep in thought, the way his eyes moved sightlessly past all the guards, fine furnishings, and zillions of magic-torches.

I don't know what he was thinking about. I didn't want to know. I was thinking about Tdanerend and the throne and Senrid, and some of the things that pitiable Ndand had said. Now, I didn't care at all who sat on the throne of Marloven Hess. In fact, as far as I was concerned, they could all get themselves turned into tree stumps. But I was also thinking about that execution, and so, tired and unsettled and angry, I gave in to impulse and said when we reached his room, "Does it matter if he enchants us? Aren't we already acting enchanted when we practice unreasoning cruelty?"

Senrid looked sharply at me, and when our eyes met, his narrowed.

I lifted my head. His grayish-blue eyes blurred.

He opened his door and motioned me in, then shut it. "You've never asked that kind of question before," he said slowly. "What exactly happened at Leander's?"

My heartbeat seemed to thump behind my aching eyeballs, and I wished I'd kept my mouth closed.

Except it had felt so *good* to say it.

"Lots of time to think," I said in my dullest voice. "Sitting alone in the library."

He took quick steps across his room, turned, paced back. "I have to prove myself. Uncle is right about that, though I sometimes think he's preventing me from learning more than he's teaching me. I don't know! I thought my father was strong—stronger than anyone—but he wasn't if he could get himself killed. Maybe Uncle is right about his going weak by marrying a white, and I'm weak because of their influence. It's as if our mothers put spells on us through their white influence, and Uncle has to find ways to counteract it."

"Oh. Thank you for telling me, Senrid," I said in sickly-sweet gratitude. "Though if our mothers died so early, when we were too small to remember them, how great can their influence have been?" I opened his door and walked out, shutting it behind me.

Once I'd settled into Ndand's bed, my tired brain sent thoughts and images skittering about, like sightless mice. But when Tdanerend tromped in, as he'd threatened, I faked sleep, and he tromped out again after a short scan.

I heard his boots thump down the hall to Senrid's room.

Bed checks? He *couldn't* be afraid that Ndand would be up and plotting anything. But he was afraid of what Senrid might be doing—like learning.

⅋◖੨ⅎ◗⅘

While we were mountaineering back up to the bedrooms, poor Kyale found herself marched back down into the everlasting darkness of the dungeon by two hulks who didn't bother to shorten their mile-long strides. Once she tripped over a torn flounce and fell headlong, skinning her elbow through the flimsy fabric of her gown, but they just hauled her up, set her more or less on her feet again, and gave her a shove to get her moving.

Down down down some more, until what seemed ages later they pushed her into a cell, slammed the door, and marched away.

She paced the perimeter until her eyes adjusted, rejoicing over every indication of space. She couldn't reach any ceiling, and the grating in the door let in a distant flicker of torchlight. Above—she could just make them out—tiny air holes.

She wouldn't feel closed in here. No, she *wouldn't*. There was plenty of space. Not like—

No, don't think about it. But she wouldn't give in, even so, no, she wouldn't.

She stood on tiptoe and peered through the little grating in the door. Space. And—she heard voices, a high voice. Yes! One sounded like a kid!

Familiar? She heard a laugh, and memory bloomed. Faline! Knowing Faline was there too made everything less frightening. It had to mean the girl with Senrid was telling the truth, and there really was a rescue plan.

Kyale curled up on the floor, using part of her skirt as a pillow, and soon fell asleep.

SIX

We had yet to learn that people who get drawn into others' power struggles seldom stay isolated; the results of their actions eddy out in ever widening circles, intersecting more and more lives.

World events intersected our lives on a personal level, because while we have no interest whatsoever in politics or war, we do get caught up in the causes of people worth helping.

Well, an old adventure was about to intersect with my life once again, causing change for us all. Today was the first ripple, made by two very tired kids who stumbled over the border of Marloven Hess as a bleak dawn began to lighten the landscape.

One was feeling sick, and she could hardly walk. She didn't look for reason or relief. These things had become as meaningless as the passage of time.

They spied a cave in the hills through which they'd been wandering aimlessly—or what seemed to be aimlessly. They did not know they were drawn by a well of hidden magic pooled over centuries.

"Over here, Laurel," said the girl's twin brother. "A little farther, then you can lie down and rest."

"Is this a Place?" she asked listlessly.

"I don't know. You too sick to sense anything?"

"Yes," she sighed.

They picked their way up a short, rock-strewn trail, and reached the cave. To them the world was shades of gray, black, and white, all wearying, the other senses diminished to small irritants that served only to push them ever onward in their wanderings.

Now they fumbled with brief, weak gratitude into the cave, which was large, and would be easily spotted by anyone with a mind to search, but they didn't consider that. It felt like a Place. They didn't know, or care, that their Places were always spots—usually long forgotten—where ancient magic concentrated.

The girl paused inside, kicked rocks away from a spot, then she sank down, groaning crossly.

"Quiet," the boy said.

"Oh, you be quiet, Lael," she retorted with no energy. "I wish you were sick instead, so you could feel what it's like."

"I'm sick of your complaining. Tired of it, too. Tired." The boy sat disconsolately on a rock, kicking at it with his feet.

The girl endured the rhythmic tapping for a short space, then cried, "Stop it!"

For a century of outside time they had wandered, though they had no sense of day or night. They didn't need to eat or drink, nor had they aged; decades had slid by without anyone seeing any more of them than their shadows. It was a nightmare sort of existence, and they had become nightmare versions of themselves during the long years of their roaming.

"Make me," he responded, with the empty threat of unthinking habit. But he blinked at her in slightly bewildered annoyance. She really did sound sick.

"I hate it," she fretted, then stopped, too worn to continue. And likewise the boy was too dispirited to ask what 'it' was—even if he had cared.

Their thoughts drifted like fog vapors as they sat in the cold, dark cave. Memories, or scraps of memories, flickered in minds that had dwindled into distortions.

Presently the boy reached into a pocket and pulled out a stale crust that had petrified long ago. He looked at it without hunger. "Want some, Laurel? There's enough for a bite or two."

"No! Where'd you get that disgusting stale..." The listless whine died away.

Even though he felt no hunger, it was something to do. He bit off a piece and munched it methodically in a dry mouth, and when he'd swallowed it down, he moved across the cave from Laurel, where the sharp reach of the wind lessened.

"Lael?" Laurel's voice sounded odd. "I was trying to count up the time we've been away. Winters. *Years*. Winters, winters, winters!"

Lael felt the impact of those hundred winters, as if someone had opened a well in his head and he was about to drop down. "Quiet," he said, without any force. "It's making me sick, too." He sounded small, and young.

Silence shrouded them, and eventually they slept.

∞⟨ЯᴣᎧ⟩ʊ

Well before dawn in the royal castle in Choreid Dhelerei, I awoke as though being forced up through heavy waters. Unwillingly I moved stone-weighted limbs, burying my face firmly in the pillow.

"Uh...don't," I groaned.

But the something persisted in disturbing me. The something resolved into a hand on my shoulder, shaking.

"Ndand," a soft, nervous voice whispered. "Ndand! Wake up! You overslept!"

Ndand? Who was—?

Alarm zapped through me, fletching the arrow of memory. I had to wake up before the unknown person touched my hair and noted that it didn't feel at all like it looked.

I flung off her hand and sat up in bed, staring at a young serving woman dressed in gray. She bore a lamp in one hand, and its light shone on her frightened face.

"The king sent me. It's late, almost dawn. The Regent will be down to breakfast very soon."

"I'm awake," I croaked. "I'll be quick. Thanks."

The woman touched her hand to her heart, her expression relieved, and she hurried away.

The room was already lamp-lit, and I saw light glowing from the dressing room next door. I got up and ran in, and found a steaming bath waiting. Steaming! For a moment I stared down at this evidence of more Marloven arrogance; cleaning frames use far less magic than transferring, heating, and then filtering lots of water. Usually baths are made for everyone, like for a village, or everyone in a castle, and then are almost always diverted from streams, so the only magic is heating and what we on Earth would call filtering. That we all had private baths high up in the castle was so wasteful of magic I was disgusted, but not disgusted enough to refuse to thoroughly enjoy warming up in that clean water. Though I dared not stay long.

Then I thrashed into a sturdily made cotton-wool gown. The room was bitterly cold. Ran a brush through my hair, shoved my feet into Ndand's shoes, which were wider than my feet, so they more or less fit, grabbed the spectacles, and ran.

The hallway outside was empty. I paused at Senrid's room, then remembered what the maid had said. Senrid had sent her, which meant he was already awake. What had we gotten, then, maybe six hours of sleep? It felt like six minutes' worth.

I rubbed my gritty eyes and looked around. Without Senrid, I'd have to make my way to the dining room on my own.

What had Ndand said? I pictured her description of the castle in my mind, and bucketed down the hall to a very grand stairway. An instant of temptation to slide down the long, polished banister was easily squashed. Ndand would never do such a thing.

Instead I plodded down, polishing those horrible spectacles on my skirt so I wouldn't risk tripping on the stairs, until I reached the first floor.

Past high carved doors that opened into somber but beautifully furnished rooms. The occasional guard or servant kept me from nosing into each. Ndand wouldn't do that, either.

As it turned out, my sniffer clued me in. I smelled coffee and hot bread and some kind of baked fruit. Shoving the spectacles into place, I walked into the room from which the food smells emanated.

A long table hove into view, with two blotches at the far end, the big one pulling out a chair.

Peek.

Senrid at the head of the table, a half-eaten breakfast before him. He was dressed in his usual clothes—a plain button-shirt with long sleeves, and plain trousers and shoes. Tdanerend was in a uniform, though he didn't have all the medals and junk on. He was sitting down, his face lined with ill-humor. He looked at Senrid, who returned his gaze with a bland smile.

"Good morning, children," Tdanerend said. It sounded like ritual.

"Good morning Father," I said.

There was no reaction, so I'd done that much right.

A moment later Senrid said, "Good morning, Uncle," in a bland voice that matched his expression.

Senrid then turned to me.

I ducked my eyes behind the lenses, saw only a blob.

"Good morning, Ndand," Senrid said politely. "Sleep well?"

"Mmm," I replied, for I couldn't lie without sarcasm.

Quiet, efficient gray-clad servants set plates down before Tdanerend and me.

Peek.

Relief. Ndand's breakfast foods, toasted oatcakes and eggs-and-cheese, were nothing I couldn't stomach.

Tdanerend started talking about the day's plans. The way he described all he had to do sounded suspicious to me. Not like he was complaining, more like someone who talks in a foreign language in front of people—while making it clear he's talking about them.

I snuck quick peeks at them both, but I have a feeling I could have thrown the spectacles across the room and stood on my head for all the attention Tdanerend paid to me. His focus was completely on Senrid, who sat with his hands in his lap, his round face blank of any expression but innocent inquiry.

I would not have trusted a kid with an expression like that for one second, but Tdanerend's sharp looks slowly turned into complacency.

After Tdanerend had made it clear how helpless and ignorant Senrid was of the crown matters pressing for the Regent's attention, and how much incomprehensible work said Regent was doing on Senrid's behalf, he rose with a dismissive gesture, promising Senrid that he could preside over the executions. If he finished his own work by then.

Tdanerend had scarcely eaten half a piece of bread—but I'll bet he had a big, tasty meal waiting somewhere else. Not that he was fat, but he wasn't nearly as thin for a man as Senrid was for a kid.

He left.

Senrid gobbled down a few more bites of food. I noticed that his knuckles were splotchy pink.

I was already done, since I hadn't had to talk—or to hide my hands.

Senrid jumped up. "Let's go."

I didn't ask where. Did Ndand already know? Probably. And in any case she wouldn't ask.

With quick steps Senrid led the way down more halls, and finally through a door. He didn't speak until we were outside, out of hearing of all the guards. Then he laughed. "Don't-tell, but I got *real* practice today, a training session with Keriam, not just the usual, but also with swords. Now I know for certain my dear uncle doesn't want him doing it. Nothing he says, it's what he doesn't say. 'Kings don't lower themselves to using their hands. They have warriors to do that.' Hah! Keriam told me my father fought three duels, one of them when he was not much older than I am now, and won all three. Three duels, yet *I'm* not 'ready' for serious training with steel. The masters're all afraid of Uncle. But Keriam isn't."

All this gabble rambled right past me. In the bleak early morning light Senrid looked really tired, his eyes marked almost like a grownup's. 'Practice'?

I found out it meant training himself in stuff he could practice on his own, like rope-climbing, and knife-throwing, and archery. This Keriam (whoever he was, and I didn't want to meet him) had seen to it Senrid also learned contact fighting, though he was reluctant to directly cross Tdanerend and teach Senrid sword fighting. When he couldn't have Keriam, Senrid drilled himself on the ones he could do alone, every day, on his own.

What it meant at the time was that Senrid had been up a lot earlier than I had.

"You look awful," I said. "Dead."

Senrid grinned. "You look worse."

"Don't."

"Do."

"Don't." I said it flatly.

"Do." He seemed to enjoy being contradicted.

"D-O-N-O-T," I said, forgetting Ndand for a moment. Panic!

But Senrid said only, "We'll ask someone."

We reached the stables, which were enormous, and already a hive of activity. Beautifully bred horses were being led out and in, and everywhere in sight were black-and-tan-clad warriors, some with these sabers at their sides with a subtle and wicked-looking curve at the very end, and their helms, instead of having a steel point, like the guards', had long horse-tails.

Senrid walked up to one of the stationary guards. "Who looks worse, her or me?" he demanded.

The guard looked expressionlessly from one of us to the other, then—of course—he pointed at me. "You," he said.

Senrid gave me a triumphant grin. "See?"

"Bias," I said—realizing that that was what had caused the grin. Senrid had been testing his status.

∞CRISO∞

When Kyale woke up in that dark cell, the first thing on her mind was Faline. The second thing was an aching elbow. With wincing care she felt the scab, then she turned to the wall.

"Faline?"

"Kitty!" The voice was faint but cheerful-sounding. "Get up close to the wall!"

Kitty pressed herself up against it.

"Can you hear me?" Faline's voice was now much louder.

"Yes!"

"Then I can talk normal. You must be in the last cell, then, on the other side of me. Thought I heard 'em stick someone in, but I didn't know who. How are ya?"

"Oh, Faline, I'm so sorry I got you and that warrior fellow into this mess."

"Kitty!" Faline laughed. "Yer a dumb cluck—though not as dumb *or* as clucky as these-here Marloven gaboons—if you think you have to apologize!"

"But I'm the one who told Senrid how his plan was wrecked."

"Oh, he woulda found out anyway," Faline returned comfortingly. Or, at least, she tried—and Kitty appreciated the attempt. "So. How'd you end up in this stinkpot?"

"That Senrid," Kitty exclaimed with as much disgust as she could muster. "I was standing in my room, and all of a sudden he was right there in front of me! I hardly got a chance to yell before he grabbed me—and the next thing I know I'm in that horrible throne room, and that disgusting slob Tdanerend spouted a lot of gunk at me about how my mother was black magic so I ought to rejoin the 'right side' and help join the kingdoms again—which means betraying Leander! And would I consent to a spell to 'help' me see the right way again!" She sighed. "I pretended to go to sleep and he got mad, and stuck me in a closet..." She stopped, remembering what had happened afterward, and wondering if the guards listened.

"Oh, Kitty, you don't have to say any more. We all know Tdanerend is a footling clackbrain."

"That's for sure," Kitty said, trying to figure out what was safe to say—and what wasn't. "So what happened to you?"

Faline told her story, with lots of colorful insult added, so much that Kitty found herself laughing in spite of fear, and aches, and hunger.

Then there was a pause; apparently the warrior in the far cell wanted to know with whom Faline was talking. Faline ran back and forth between walls, and so the three whiled away time having a sort of lopsided conversation with Faline in the middle.

◦○⋆○◦

While they were talking, I was riding in the wind.

The low hills around Choreid Dhelerei were beautiful, dotted with smooth, pale-barked winter-bare trees. Plains stretched away to the west so vast they met the sky without a bump, covered in the tall golden grass of impending winter. In the distance, to the north, was a line of slightly higher hills, like baby dragon teeth.

The horses we rode were fast and strong and mettlesome, the saddles mere pads, the reins attached to halters and not bits. I was glad that I'd had plenty of practice at bareback riding, because Senrid liked going at breakneck pace. We raced, one horse pulling ahead and then the other. Senrid was by far the better rider, but I'd learned how to hold on through leaps and turns by riding Hreealdar, who has a tendency to turn into lightning and zap across the countryside—the horse form being an occasional diversion, not a natural form.

The cold, clean-smelling wind revived me despite my lack of sleep, and got my brain racing again. We dared each other, doing stupid tricks. At first I was wary, not certain if Ndand ever did anything reckless, but Senrid never seemed to question, and I wasn't about to let any *boy* out-dare *me*, especially a black magic clod.

Not that he acted like a bully or a creep toward me. That was the weird thing. I enjoyed that ride, and so did he—I could see it—and he didn't seem to mind when my horse pulled ahead. His company was almost agreeable as long as I didn't think about how this cheery kid had cheerily nabbed one of my friends in order to have her put to death. I was glad I'd soon be gone. I didn't ever want to see Senrid again. I felt guilty for enjoying his company—and I didn't want to know what kind of horrible creep his skunk-stench of an uncle would twist him into being.

His mood changed when, at last, it was time to go back to the castle. Senrid grinned occasionally, but it was a toothy, arrogant, challenging grin.

At the time I didn't know why his mood had changed, but I know now. He hated being kept out of the real work of ruling, but didn't know how to learn what he knew was an enormous job. Tdanerend's 'teaching', especially of late, was mostly sessions with magic books while Senrid, who showed a natural aptitude for magic, was assigned to come up with complicated wards, or spells to break wards.

What I did figure out, from his running stream of words, was that magic protections spells of various types were his 'chores'—and he'd already completed them while I'd been asleep. Before all that exercise with Keriam, whoever he was. Just so he could have time for this ride. It indicated a ferocious amount of self-discipline—much more than I had. It was all very unsettling, and I wanted to get away and forget them all.

So at last the ride came to an end, and we trotted through the great city gates. I marked the way carefully, peering over the tops of those accursed spectacles. Senrid had actually stopped talking for once. He brooded in silence until we rode through the castle gates, and reached the stables.

When we climbed down from our mounts, I felt exhaustion press on me again. Senrid tossed his reins to the stablehands who ran up.

I could not prevent a gigantic yawn. Senrid laughed, and I shrugged. "I'd like a nap." Surely Ndand would say that.

"Yep," Senrid said, squinting up at the blank windows of the castle. His eyes were marked underneath.

"But Father—" I started to amend.

Senrid cut in, saying in a low voice, ""Don't-tell, but I can hardly wait until I really am king. No more of his humiliating rules disguised as teaching. How I hate wearing the crown and knowing...and knowing that everyone else knows... that I have no power. That they think I strut around wearing the crown and don't know the difference."

None of this had been in Ndand's information about Senrid. She'd told us—and it was plain that she'd believed it— that Senrid loved wearing his father's crown.

"Almost as much as I hate standing there in an academy scrub's rankless uniform. I don't believe he's ever going to let me train with the others. Just excuses and more excuses until..." He opened his hands. "Either I win, or die."

I didn't say anything.

Senrid said, not with his usual careless cheer, but in a low, hard voice, and without the don't-tell preface, "I'd send him up against the wall today instead of those others if I could."

Cold fear gripped me; we were in the main courtyard now, and what if someone overheard? Maybe Senrid had enough self-discipline for five kids, but he wasn't any better than I am at regulating his moods when he was overtired.

I said carefully, "So you don't want to wear the crown today, is that it?"

Senrid lowered his voice to a whisper, shaped by the angry snap of his consonants. "I'll try to pull rank today, see what happens. And if it doesn't work, back to the cheery little boy act. He doesn't see through it yet—which is probably why I'm still alive."

"Hah," I snorted.

He gave me an odd look. "Why did you say that?"

"Father's gullibility." I bit my lip hard.

Senrid, luckily, didn't think it worth worrying about. He shrugged, glaring up at the castle towers. The tiredness marks made his eyes look more gray than blue. "Second watch. We've got a bell or two to kill, since his scutwork got done long ago, so what'll we do to look busy?"

"You're the boss," I said.

"Cut the sarcasm," Senrid retorted. He turned to face me, his eyes narrowed with question. "Not that I mind, but..."

I knew from his tone that 'Ndand' was acting out of character.

Glad that Leander had thought to ask Ndand for any private lingo, I retorted back, "Don't tread on me."

Senrid laughed. "Wow, last time I heard that was, what? You couldn't have been much more than six, and I thought I was so old and tough, copying the academy boys' slang—"

"But you're still just a little boy," I said in a sappy voice.

He laughed again, the subject successfully changed. "As long as Uncle keeps seeing me as a little boy I stay alive," he said, still laughing. "What d'you want to wager if I'd sprouted up like Leander—" He drew his finger across his neck.

I laughed too, because Ndand would, but it wasn't really funny—it gave me the stomach-wheems.

∞CRSOcs

Meanwhile, in the cave on the border, both kids had sunk into fitful slumber. Little rays of sun fingered into the cave as the morning progressed, and eventually one touched the boy's left foot.

SEVEN

The remaining hours before we had to get ready for the execution were not exactly relaxing.

We ate lunch—or gobbled it—and then came Senrid's idea of fun. I had to stand on guard at the door while he sorted through papers in Tdanerend's study, and all the time the Regent was down the hall in the throne room, acting like the Big Cheese in front of a gaggle of his klunks. I could hear his voice echoing and booming away as he speechified. I dared a peek into the study once, wondering what Senrid thought he could possibly learn while pawing so quickly through the piles of papers, but it wasn't my problem.

When he came out, muttering about corruption, and how Keriam was outflanked by incompetent bootlickers, I ignored this babble and paid attention to where we were walking. The castle was gigantic and confusing enough without Senrid always taking different shortcuts.

Finally he declared it was time to get ready. By then I was really tense. The prospect of managing the execution rescue was scary, but I tried to console myself with the thought that if I succeeded my reward would be to leave this terrible place forever.

If. A mighty frightening 'if'; this was not like pulling off a caper against an old bumbler like Kwenz.

Senrid led the way, and we slogged upstairs for the usual forty-year trudge. At least this time I recognized a lot of the turns and stairways before we got to them.

When we reached his room, I said, "Hurry up. I'll wait out here."

Senrid looked critically at me, and I glanced down and saw horse-hair on my skirts, and my muddy hem. "There's time for a bath, I made certain of that," he said.

The idea of having to be spruce for an execution annoyed me so much that I zapped him with 100-proof CJ-patented sarcasm. "Yeah, thanks, very thoughtful," I snarled. "Gotta look nice to watch people die hideously."

As soon as it was out I regretted it. Too tired to think of a recovery, I blundered away and slammed into Ndand's room, where I jellyfished onto the nearest chair and stared in horror at the floor. Had I ruined everything?

"Nice work," I snarled in Mearsiean. My home tongue was not comforting. "CJ the bigmouth. Arrrgh! Talk about squidbrains!"

Deciding that I needed to soak my head, if not my self, I flung off my gown and got into the ever-ready steaming bath. Someone had laid out an especially fine gown of black with gold trim—their colors. Groaning, I got out, dried off fast, for the bath chamber was cold. I was busy lacing up the dress when Senrid called from the other room:

"Ndand? Done? Come out."

Remembering the illusion, I flipped my hair back, and opened the door. All right, time to face the music.

Senrid stood before me, his hair damp, wearing that black-and-tan uniform and the polished blackweave riding boots.

"I know you're tired," he said. "I am too. So why try to pick a fight? And then run off like that?"

"Don't want to watch an execution."

"You never cared before."

In a panic, I hazarded a guess, "But not kids."

He flicked his right hand palm up. "True."

Sheer nerves got me across the room. I shoved my feet into Ndand's shoes, picked up the brush and gave my hair a couple swipes, and he said, "You look fine. We're going to be late."

Late—for an execution. Oh dear.

I sucked in a deep breath, trying to get my emotions under control. I could not give in to temper; lives depended upon my doing exactly what Leander and Clair had planned.

Even so, as we galumphed downstairs again I snuck a glance Senrid's way, and thought about how he could have been a friend. He was smart, and funny, and interesting—when he wasn't boring on about local politics and power—but the fact that he could actually not want to be late to see kids be killed, and not seem to care, made it so much worse. I was angry at liking him, angry at him, angry at myself. The sooner I was out, the better.

As bells tolled Senrid grabbed my hand and did the transfer. I loathe black magic transfers. They might be faster, but it's a jolt that hurts your bones and your head and makes you much dizzier than the displacement miasma of white magic transfers.

We appeared in a courtyard—what they call a parade ground—in the garrison area, and I yanked my hand free while he was still recovering.

Shaking off my own transfer reaction, I pulled off the spectacles and polished them on my skirt. After a few blinks I scanned the territory. Well, even with the spectacles on I would have been able to see that danger lay 100% of everywhere—and a second glance made it even worse.

What seemed to me a gigantic army was lined up on three sides of this courtyard, but actually it was only the castle's guards, plus the top-ranking splatniks from the cavalry academy adjacent to the palace, which was where they trained their future officers. This wasn't even an important execution—no high ranking victim, no political significance. There were no factions to whom Tdanerend had to underscore his power—not in killing off a bigmouthed foot warrior and a couple of kids.

Tdanerend was aiming this particular reminder of who held the power at one person: Senrid.

I didn't know it at the time. All I saw was, there were way too many of them to kick, scratch, and bite my way past if my plan squelched (as my plans usually do). I had to make it work.

But.

Directly opposite a bare wall—no less a sinister sight than all those uniformed and armed klunks—was a stand with seven chairs on it. Chairs! Like this was a theater! Warriors stood directly behind and beside this stand, within arm's reach of the end chairs.

There'd be no way to slip between the lines of warriors in order to take hold of the victims, which was what I'd planned. I had to be able to perform the multiple transfer without contact, because I was going to be stuck on a chair within reach of no one but enemies.

If the transfer wasn't warded, and *if* the three ended up close enough for me to bind them, and *if* I successfully transferred them—I would still have to get myself out, because I wouldn't be close enough to include myself in the binding.

Two spells. Not one.

Two spells, and Tdanerend and Senrid right beside me.

"Are you all right?"

The whisper was close to my ear. I jumped, my nerves firing as if struck by lightning. I looked up into Senrid's face. He stood close by, closer than he ever had; as I glared witlessly into his face his expression changed, and he rubbed his eyes.

The illusion! Did he see it? Sense it?

"I'm fine." I backed away.

He rubbed his eyes again, and I was grateful that he'd had far less sleep than I'd had.

Before he could speak a bugle pealed out several running chords.

Tdanerend appeared in the archway opposite, dressed with all those medals and the rest of that flapdoodle. Everyone snapped to attention. He looked the happiest, no, the most satisfied, that I'd seen him yet as he strutted across the courtyard with everyone watching him, and chose the chair next to the middle one.

Senrid and I splorched up the steps to join Tdanerend. I had the spectacles on, of course, but peeked over the tops in time to see Tdanerend frown at Senrid's head, which was bare, his blond hair dry now and lifting in the cold wind, like so many of the heads all around us.

We were joined by three men, two Tdanerend's age and one older, and all of them wearing plenty of rank markers—but not as many as ol' Uncle Modesty. They closed in on either side.

Senrid sat down next to Tdanerend, and I on his other side. Senrid's face was utterly bland.

Tdanerend lifted a hand, and this time through the archway, between double columns of marching knucklebrains, walked Faline, Kitty, and a tall, big-boned, messed-up looking young man who had to be 713. His face was all bruised, and he wasn't smiling, so one couldn't see the gap between his two front teeth that Faline had thought so funny, but who else could it be? His uniform was a wreck—the tunic-coat didn't fit him at all, but the rest of it looked worse.

All three had their hands bound behind them, which seemed sort of stupid—where would they go? How would they get any weapons, when surrounded by an army of armed hulks?

Faline looked around, blinking a little in the sun, her freckled face determinedly cheery. She and Kitty, whose silvery hair glinted in the wintry-gray sunlight, looked very small in the midst of all those tall and muscled clods.

The girls looked small—and so did Senrid.

I turned my attention back, making a long, fake yawn—so long that it caused a real yawn, so big a yawn my eyes watered. Senrid was right, I thought as Tdanerend gave me a sour look. He did look silly and little-boyish next to Tdanerend. No, that wasn't right. He looked powerless. He knew it, too.

Yawning again, then muttering "Excuse me," I forced my attention back to the stone wall with all those ugly brown stains, and the victims at either side. They still weren't close enough together yet.

Faline smiled, but her eyes were a little forlorn as she searched me out—Kitty had managed to tell her the plan. Faline would know how dangerous it was.

Tdanerend gave me another nasty glare, but I didn't care any more. Either I'd be gone or discovered; meantime, I yawned once more, yearning for the clods to shift the prisoners closer together.

Tdanerend turned his attention away from us and to the prisoners, at whom he had not yet bothered to glance, and he gave a hiss of displeasure. At what? The tunic on 713!

The warrior was supposed to be in total disgrace, and Tdanerend wanted everyone to see whatever they'd done to him, and the coat hid most of it.

Tdanerend looked mad. "Where'd he get that tunic?"

Faline glared up at us.

Tdanerend began a spell, but Senrid raised his hand. "No."

The creep uncle looked at him, surprised. "What's this?"

"I said Faline could have it. I take responsibility—but we'll deal with it later. Let the execution go on. No more delays," Senrid said grimly. He spoke without looking at any of us, only at the scene straight ahead.

Tdanerend's frown increased, and I could feel him assessing the others all around, who stood there stone-faced, but had to be listening. He then sat back, apparently not wanting to be seen arguing with Senrid in public. He waved his hand, and once again whoever was in control below us started getting people into position.

I settled my head against the back of my wooden chair. The spectacles blurred my vision and made my eyes hurt, my insides were a pit of boiling snakes, but I laid my hands in my lap. It was not only important to look like I was falling asleep, I was about to attempt an extremely difficult spell to do to on even one person, a transfer without physical contact. Yet I had to make it work with three. I would need every bit of energy I had in me. And then some.

They marched Faline to the wall first. Then, just as Tdanerend had threatened, the other two were ranged alongside, with an uninterrupted view—

And in range of one another.

My heart clumped against my ribs. I let some of my hair fall across the lower part of my face, hiding my mouth and nose, which were tucked against my shoulder.

Peek.

The death squad marched out next, a neat, orderly row, each with a blackwood longbow and arrows.

I noted the position of each prisoner, and started my spell. I had to hold in my mind their position, binding each to the next, yet keeping all three spells open so I could finish with the transfer.

Someone shouted a command. The death squad raised their bows. It was all slow and deliberate and orderly—as cruel as possible for the victims. It threw me back in memory to another, similar situation, and I lost my thread on the second spell. I forced the memory away—and the accompanying terror—and concentrated again on my spells, this time whispering faster.

And felt one hold.

Two.

"Nock arrows!"

Peek. Faline now looked scared, 713 stone-faced, and Kitty gazed at me, her face blanched, as I bound each name into the transfer spell, whispering into my shoulder, and I felt the energy holding—my own fear gave me more control than I usually had. I closed my eyes so I could see Leander in my mind.

"Aim!"

I could hear the creak of the bows, the wind on the stone ramparts, and somewhere the placketing of a flag as I forced myself to pronounce the triple-weighted transfer words—

"Shoot!"

Snap! I *felt* the spell hold, peeked through my lashes— and saw them vanish, with three soft pops of displaced air.

And a heartbeat later, the clatter of the arrows against the empty wall.

I closed my eyes and sank back, as waves of magic-reaction sogged my mind and clawed at my empty innards.

Tdanerend gasped, then said something very nasty that I won't even write.

The commander next to me started firing questions at the one next to him, who was gabbling his own questions. Behind us, a quick susurrus of whispered comment riffled through all those neat rows, quickly silenced.

I heard Senrid's breathing; he'd turned my way. I held my pose, my head buzzing severely from the magic reaction, but tried to gather what was left of my energy for a second transfer spell—

Hard fingers dug into my arm.

I didn't have to fake a violent start. "Huh? Who—"

"Ndand! They transferred!"

I looked at him—or the blur of him—in horror. "Oh, no!"

"Yes," he said grimly, then blinked, and I saw a blurry hand rub at his blurry face. Then, in a soft undertone, "And I've a feeling there'll be a long night ahead."

"Oh, no," I said again. He was still holding onto me—I couldn't transfer! This time there was no need to fake horror, because I felt it, right down to the bottoms of my feet.

I peered over the glasses. Senrid's eyes were shut as he muttered. The air charged with that intense inward hum of extremely powerful magic.

Wards snapped into place around us, preventing anyone from transferring either out or into the castle.

❧ CЯ℘ ❧ ℘

Meanwhile, poor Faline had shut her eyes at the last moment, scrunching up to make herself as small a target as possible, awaiting instant interior ventilation.

Then her head felt that weird almost-dizzy sense that she associated with transfers. She opened her eyes, breathed experimentally—and found no arrows in her middle.

"Am I dead?" she muttered, then looked around. "Nope. In a shack." She was perfectly happy to be in a shack. The shack was more welcome than the finest palace, because there were no Marlovens in sight—and more welcome than eternity, because it meant she could go home, crack jokes, and see Clair and the girls.

She became vaguely aware of voices around her, including a familiar one. "Faline, please get up so I can untie you."

"By Klutz, it's Cracky! I mean Leander! Hi!" she exclaimed happily, cackling in joy.

She turned around and soon her hands were free. She saw 713 and Kitty then, both looking puzzled and relieved; Kitty had, true to her promise, explained 713's presence, though Leander had guessed the moment he laid eyes on the poor slob.

Now Leander closed his eyes, began a spell—and abandoned it.

"Wards," he said. "Up as fast as I expected. So much for the easy way out. Okay, you three," Leander added briskly, trying to hide his alarm. "We must get moving, before they can try a tracer on CJ's spell, or get the searchers out. I've got everything all ready—" He looked at 713 and frowned. "The shirts I brought aren't going to work out."

Leander had brought a bundle of raggedy clothes from Vasande Leror, thinking to disguise himself and three girls. He was surprised—and pleased—to see 713 rescued, but it meant a scramble with the disguises.

"Don't worry about me," Faline said quickly. "Give me that old blanket to hide my jacket, that's all I need." Faline loathed using her Yxubarec shape-changing powers, but to save a life, she'd do it and not complain.

Leander nodded. "Right. 713, you be the shepherd, and I'll stay a boy, since they don't know me. Kitty, you're about to become my brother. Go up in the loft and change. This hole I dug here is for our old clothes. Put yours in, and we'll smooth it over before we leave."

Faline ran outside. Clouds gathered on the horizon. Cold wind whipped at them, and she wrapped the moth-eaten blanket tightly around her shoulders and head as a shawl and cape. The patched brown riding pants Leander had brought she pulled on over her own.

Within a short time the others emerged, 713 with his bruised face now dirty, and a knit cap pulled low over his head. The shepherd's smock Leander had selected for himself had been far too big, which worked to their advantage now. It fit 713 fine.

"Here's the walking stick," Leander said. "And the bag of coins for the wool we sold. You'd better hold it, since you're now the oldest brother."

All three had dirtied their faces with the soil that Leander had dug up. Leander's wavy dark hair hung in his eyes, and he'd pulled over his own clothes the tunic he'd brought for CJ— luckily too large again. On him it was too short. Kitty looked completely unlike herself, except for her silvery eyes. She was dirty, with her hair stuffed up in a ratty old cap, wearing a ragged tunic and baggy trousers and cloth shoes laced up over her house-slippers.

Behind the shack was an old plow horse that Leander had bought that morning. Faline and Kitty climbed up on the horse— Kitty holding tightly to Faline—and the other two walked beside—after 713 had checked it over, including its shoes, the horse whuffing into his neck.

Leander knew Senrid had magic and was smart. He'd assumed (rightly, as he'd just found out) that some kind of nasty border ward could be initiated within moments.

So they were going to have to get across the border without magic.

They started toward the northwest, heading back toward the capital—Leander explaining that as soon as the inevitable searches were over they'd turn right around and cut east over the mountains. But until then they couldn't be seen heading east, it would be instantly suspicious.

No one talked much after that. The rescuees were too tired and apprehensive from their close call. 713 might not have been scared, but he was in such rotten physical shape it was all he could do to make himself march, the stick carried like he'd carry a quarterstaff.

Within a frighteningly short time they heard the steady hoof-beats of a search party.

Faline looked over, and gasped. "'3! Stop walking like a warrior!"

713 shuffled his feet on the dusty road, leaning on the stick and hunching over.

A few seconds later they heard the galloping horses slow as they came into view, and a loud voice commanded them to halt.

"Who are you?" the leader rapped out to 713.

'3 blinked. "Claid's my name."

"No," the leader said impatiently. "All of you—who are you, where are you going, and what is your business?"

"Shepherd," 713 said. "Selling wool."

Another warrior edged his horse near Leander, then reached down and roughly grabbed his hair to yank his head back.

"That the one?"

"No. Too young, hair too dark." The warrior frowned. "Familiar... Who are you?"

Had this creep been on the expedition to conquer Vasande Leror? It was possible, for they were relatively near the border.

Then Faline said in a high, crotchety voice, "He's m'middle grandson."

Everyone looked up, including the fugitives, to see a very old woman riding the horse.

"We've sold our wool at market, an' we're goin' home, y'see," she cackled. "I'm tired, and if I have to sit here one more heartbeat, I might up and die right here."

"Have you seen two girls and a warrior on this road? They are traitors, wanted by the Regent himself, in the name of the King. Turn them in, and you will be rewarded."

"Oooh, from the king, are you?" Faline crotchetted respectfully. "Gold?" she asked with even more interest. "How much?"

"Plenty," the leader said, edging his restless horse away. "Thank you. Go your way." He saluted them, fingers flicking briefly to his heart, and the posse thundered off, mail jingling, weapons clattering, the horses raising dust to choke the four.

Leander—knowing that Faline hated her powers—said only, "That was fast thinking. Now we can leave this road and cut directly north, cross-country."

Faline glanced at the endless plains to the west, the broad sky with birds arrowing northwards, then scrutinized the border mountains not so very far to the east.

"This looks kind of familiar," she exclaimed. "We wouldn't be anywhere near Hibern, would we? She'd know what to do, if we could get to her."

Leander's face changed. He wasn't considering the map he'd spent the morning studying, he was remembering the summertime when he'd received, without any warning, a strange message from Hibern of Marloven Hess, promising a contact within the country *If your intentions are to protect your own kingdom, but not to harm mine.*

Then he nodded. "We're straight west of Crestel, my city, a day's ride inside the border, well away from their patrols. And she does live relatively close by! I know where Latvian's castle is on the map, more or less. But, judging distances in a land I don't know—"

"I don't care," Kyale said, her voice high and strained. "Faline's right! Let's go to Hibern. Faline says she knows magic."

"All right. Sounds like a better idea than attempting the border on our own." Leander sent a doubtful look at 713, whose face was tight with pain. "Though it means walking more west than I'd like."

They floundered into a field of late-growing seed-flax. The silvery-topped stalks were so tall that the two girls were mostly hidden. When they finally reached another road, they cleared the late autumn brambles and prickles off their clothing and started trudging along this path.

Presently Kitty said fretfully, "How much farther? I hate walking so much, and we didn't get anything to eat at all today."

"We should be in the right province, but like I said, I can't judge distances."

"I'll recognize Latvian's lair," Faline assured Kitty. "Not much longer. I keep recognizing things, like that funny shaped space, like a bite missing, between those two mountains over that way. Saw 'em through the window every morning when I woke up." She pointed east. She used her normal voice, though she wore the form of the old granny. A change would deplete her energy even more, and the disguise might still be needed.

ఴ෬෫෪ఴ

As for me, my head buzzed from all the magic, and I drew in a deep breath to fight off the nastiness. Tdanerend's voice rose over the hubbub around us, vicious cursing and threats punctuating his orders. Senrid had let go of my arm and sat with his hand over his eyes, his lips moving.

Leander, I hope you made it, I thought, as Senrid looked up. He gasped, cleared his throat, then spoke. "Uncle. Uncle! The border wards are up. No one can transfer out of the kingdom, or in, without a tracer alerting us."

Tdanerend flicked his hand upward, then continued firing orders at those guys with the medals and junk for search parties, inside the castle, the city, as well as along the borders.

Senrid poked me. "You'd better cut along. Stay out of the way for now, or you'll catch it for sure." He tipped his chin toward his uncle.

I bit back a groan, wishing he'd told me that earlier, instead of holding onto my arm while he deployed the castle wards. I could have cut out, all right—all the way home.

Tdanerend rose, still snarling curses as well as orders, and aides dashed this way and that. I was alone in the crowd, and glad to follow Senrid's advice.

I slipped off the stand and followed some of the aides inside. I was going to have to get out the hard way.

Now wasn't the time, though, not with all these search parties being sent out to grill every living thing they found. And I was tired—beyond tired. The magic had drained me far worse than the hunger and lack of sleep combined.

I bumbled my way along, with everyone too busy to notice me, until I finally found a section of the palace that seemed familiar, then I retreated up to Ndand's room.

What to do? What do to?

It was thinking about Faline—worrying that she was safe—that finally gave me the obvious solution. I would have to find Hibern.

Only how? I hesitated, standing there in the hall, my head pounding. I remembered the big map on the wall of Senrid's room, and hesitated about half a second. Sooner in, sooner out.

It was my only hope—otherwise I'd ride around this horrible kingdom forever, because I had no idea where the capital was located in it, much less anything else.

Senrid's room was cold, scrupulously neat. So neat I felt the urge to stomp on the bed, knot the sheets, and throw all his clothes out the window, but I did not touch anything, just moved to that map, and forced my tired eyes to focus.

It really was an enormous map, neatly lettered. In fact, a work of art of its own. I touched it, and the neat Marloven lettering flickered into an alphabet I could read, thanks to Clair's language spell. I wondered if every single stream and village and glade was lovingly listed there.

I located Choreid Dhelerei, the capital, which I stood in the middle of. I felt my first spurt of hope when I discovered it was closer to the eastern border than to any of the others. Latvian, I remembered, had also lived fairly close to the same border. His job was mage-protector of the east.

I started searching between the capital and the neatly drawn Aurum Hills for a couple of the little towns that Faline had named on her run the summer before, and which I had obligingly put in the record of her adventure.

There they were! Up north a little ways, and east. Feeling more apprehensive by the minute I memorized the roads, noted landmarks, then oozed out, looking both ways. No one in the hall.

I sat down at Ndand's desk, and put my head on my crossed arms, not daring to really relax or even to remove the spectacles, lest I fall so deeply asleep I'd betray myself on waking up. I tried to mentally review the map, but dropped almost immediately into the uncomfortable slumber of total exhaustion.

EIGHT

Faline and the other fugitives walked until sunset.

Two more search parties rode by. They gave the same story to the first. The second they were able to hide from because they heard it coming as they neared a huge stand of thick old willow. After the danger had passed, 713 suggested to Leander that they should let the horse go—it was tired, head drooping, and would do much better on its own. And they would have difficulty hiding a horse a second time.

So they freed the animal, and resumed their trudge. By then the girls, at least, had recovered enough to ask questions, so Leander whiled away some of the walking by explaining the plan that he and Clair had come up with.

He talked in detail, partly to pass the time, and partly to draw the girls' attention away from 713, who was forcing himself to move at the same speed as the others, but his face, his entire body, were expressive of someone nearing the end of his endurance, as he leaned more and more on the stick that Leander had bought to be part of his own disguise.

713 was the oldest, and he was a Marloven, but it was clear that even if he'd wanted to take over command of their party, he was not capable of it. Leander paused, feeling a wave of pity. Here was a young man who could never go home again, for no Marloven survived a treason judgment, however unfair, that much he'd learned. Had the poor fellow even thought about what might happen if he actually lived? From the look of him he hadn't.

"Leander?" Kitty said, the familiar shrill note in her voice breaking his reverie. "Is there danger? Why did you stop talking?"

"Sorry. Just looking around. So anyway, we transferred CJ up to tell her the plan—"

"Wait!" Faline interrupted, wheezing so hard she could barely speak. Kitty looked at her in round-eyed surprise. "Wait! CJ didn't know she was going to be sent to Marloven Hess? Right smack in the middle of a nest o' villains?"

"Nope." Leander shook his head.

Faline gave a loud, quivering sigh. "Oh, please, do you remember what she said? Now think! There have to have been some good ones!"

"Well, let me see," Leander said with a judicious air. "There was a lot about bagfaced cornpone-noses—what is a cornpone, anyway?—that was to us generally. For me, there were a couple that did stand out in my mind. Ah! Something about frogbelly-faced stenchiferous wights—I believe that would be addressed to the color of my eyes—and your friend Clair came in for some commentary on the color of her hair, apparently likening her as a close cousin to Shnit of the Chwahir—"

Faline clasped her hands. "Any other good words? Snilch? Grelb? Gnarg? And spackle!"

"I believe she used all those at some point or other, yes."

713 grinned wearily as Faline sailed off into gales of laughter. "Oh, to have heard that!"

Leander bowed. "I shall always consider myself privileged to have been on the receiving end of such artistic and inspired insults. And I'll remember them," he added, "in case I meet up with an equally deserving recipient."

Kitty whispered, "I hate it when he talks like that to me."

Faline snickered. "I think it's funny. Hey! That's it," she said, pointing to a many-spired silhouette projecting above a grove of trees with pumpkin-colored leaves. Latvian's castle was singular, built of dark stone and full of turrets and towers. "There can't be another like it."

The others looked up, 713 in obvious relief. "She's right," he said low-voiced, having confined his attention for the past few miles to the ground before each foot.

"And that's Fern's tower," Faline added, pointing to the highest one.

"How'll we get up?" Kitty asked.

"How'll we get in past the guards?" Leander amended.

"No more guards," 713 whispered. "Except his own. Two fellows. Front gate. Go round back."

"And that's where Hibern's tower is," Faline said. "I think I know the way to get her attention."

They walked around the long way, using the clusters of trees as cover, so as not to be spotted by the guards, one on the front wall, one at the gate.

"Faline, what if she isn't there?" Kitty asked, that shrill note in her voice again.

"Oh, she will be," Faline whispered reassuringly. "She's fake-lame as well as fake-nutso. She's locked up there—her dad doesn't know she travels by magic when she leaves at all."

"But she might have gone by magic," Kitty whined, wringing her hands.

"Sh," three voices responded, low-voiced but urgent.

Kitty fumed in tight-lipped silence.

They emerged from the cover of a thicket of fir and stood right below Hibern's tower, which was at the extreme end of the castle, with walls extending away from it at either end.

Faline peered up at the wide window, then selected some small rocks, and tossed them up. They did not reach anywhere near. Leander had a try next, and the stones clattered against the glass.

Moments later a casement opened, and a long, thin girl-face framed by dark hair peered down, then the dark eyes, sidelit by lamps within the tower, widened.

"Fern? Fern!" Faline called.

"Faline? It *is* you!" The familiar cool voice was low and quick. "Quiet. I must transfer you all up. Take hands, and do not move."

A sudden wrench, and when the transfer wore off they found themselves in a round stone room, facing a tall, thin black-haired girl Leander's age. She frowned at 713, and quickly bade him sit down on a chair.

He collapsed gratefully.

She faced Leander, and he discovered she was as tall as he. "You are Leander Tlennen-Hess?"

He nodded once.

"I wondered, soon as I heard the news. Well done."

Leander's face heated up. "Wasn't I. Entirely. There's a Mearsiean girl in the capital who took the biggest risks. CJ Sherwood, who managed the transfer."

"Ah." Hibern glanced at Faline, and it was clear she recognized the name. Then she said in a low voice, "We'll have to talk softly, as Father is housing the headquarters for the local search. Stefan is locked up, Faline, so don't worry." Fern's grin was somewhat wry.

Leander said, "How did you find out what happened? Magic of some kind?"

Hibern opened a hand. "Yes. Messages went out by magic to all the regional commanders, and from our local one to my father, who will be expected to maintain the border wards that the king set up. Such terrible ones will be a taxing job that must be renewed daily. I felt them go up."

Leander grimaced. Those black magic wards would destroy a tremendous amount of magical energy. But he said nothing.

"At first I hoped you'd think of me, but I fear I cannot send you over the border, for the wards are far too strong. I tested, and it's not surprising that they've got an intercept spell woven in. I'm trying to break it right now—that's what I was just doing." She nodded toward books lying on a table.

Kitty moaned in disappointment.

Hibern said, "What I can do is send you *to* the border. I'm afraid that's going to be dangerous for you because Regent Tdanerend and the king have riders all along it. The strongest concentration is directly east of the capital, but we have our share up here. But if I send you farther north, you'll have a better chance. There is a place I have in mind, an ancient ruin I discovered by accident a year or so ago. Magic pools there, I don't know why, it was ancient before the Iascans settled here, never mind the Marlovens."

Leander was impressed. Collet, the spy Hibern had arranged as his contact, had said in her first letter that Hibern was a powerful magician despite her youth, and here was the evidence.

Kitty looked horrified. Faline tried to hide her own disappointment, and she saw the same struggle in poor 713.

"How about food?" Kitty demanded.

"Bandages for ol' '3, here?" Faline asked.

Hibern's brow furrowed. "I wish I could do more for you—with the house full of warriors I don't dare transfer up quantities of food, or even bandages." She looked doubtfully at 713, who lifted a hand and shook his head. Hibern pointed to a side table, on which she'd set a tray of food still steaming. "I was just about to sit down to dinner. Help yourself, and here's some water." She indicated a pitcher.

Kitty sprang at the water, drinking down a glass. Faline poured some out for 713, who took it with wordless thanks—she saw it in his face. He drank down two cups, and then she had some, and Leander got his last, while Kitty wrapped all the food into a napkin.

Leander said to Hibern, "I thank you, and hope we can meet some day when there is more time for talk."

Hibern laid her hand flat to her heart. "I wish for the same. But I'd better send you now."

"Double good to see you," Faline said fervently. "Thanks for helping us!"

Hibern wove a long spell and the four transferred.

They appeared right in the middle of a blinding, drenching rainstorm.

"Yow!" Faline yelled as hail struck her face.

"We'll wait it out," Leander shouted, worried about both 713 and Kitty's endurance giving out long before they could make the ascent through the rocky hills to the border.

"A cave in the middle of that ruin," Faline called. "Right up there—openeth yer eyeballs, kiddies!"

"Let us progress to yon cave, rightest amst I-eth?" Leander joked, an anxious eye on his sister, who even in the fading light looked tired and cross as well as cold and wet. Behind her, 713 was clearly miserable.

"Yesseth thou ye! Forwardest and forthwith haulest us-eth ourst carcassethes yonder to," Faline yodeled, windmilling her arms.

And so, joking back and forth in super-fake Old Sartoran in an attempt to jolly the other two along, they picked their way up the rocky little animal path that led to the cave that had once been a storage chamber to a mage outpost silent milennia ago.

When they reached the mouth at last, Faline was panting and shivering. She knew the others had to be at least as tired.

The last of the daylight showed in a faint glow under the clouds in the west, casting peculiar light up the scrub-choked gully; rainbow shimmers glistened at the edges of their vision as water ran and splashed down below them, a sudden stream.

They all sank down onto the nearest rock or wind-worn stone and worked on trying to catch their clouding breath. Kitty shivered hard, muttering complaints to herself as she opened the napkin and divided out portions of a small loaf of fresh bread, some steamed cabbage, and a small chicken pie. A skinny fifteen-year-old girl's dinner was not going to stretch very far four ways. Kitty was scrupulous about making the portions equal, laying each on a cabbage leaf.

A gust of rain-laden wind made Faline shiver more violently. "Maybe we can go f-farther in," she managed past chattering teeth, as she reached for her share of the food.

"Let's try," Leander agreed, then wolfed his down. Regretfully it seemed to be about two bites.

Faline worriedly watched 713 moving like a very old man as he tried to stand, then sank back down. She took his food to him, then ducked around and began to explore further inside the cave.

Where she jolted to a stop. "Hey! There's someone here!"

"Who'd want to b-be in this h-h-horrible p-place?" Kitty's teeth chattered, and she shivered harder.

"Someone hiding," Leander said. "If they're still alive."

"Well, go see," Kitty ordered anxiously.

One of the shapes shifted and let out a groan.

"This one's alive, anyway," she called back in relief, and encouraged by this sign of life, she felt for the other shape. Reaching down, she touched a face that was clammy and hot with fever.

"This one's alive too, but sick. Shall I try to wake 'em up?"

"No." 713 spoke for the first time. "If they're asleep, leave 'em in peace." His voice was barely above a whisper.

"Okay." Faline picked her way back to the others. "Wowee. After being back there, it's almost bright up this way."

"Storm's passing," Leander commented. "Starlight appearing."

"So what now?" Kitty asked.

"We wait for CJ—or sunlight," Leander said. "Here, let's sit together. Warmer that way."

They got into a group, sitting back to back, except for poor 713, who didn't want anyone touching his flesh.

Silence fell. Presently Kitty, pressed between Faline and Leander, fell asleep with her chin on her knees.

713 sat near the mouth of the cave—hands gripping the walking stick, his profile to the stars—keeping guard.

NINE

When the door to Ndand's room slammed open I woke up instantly.

Some soft-footed servants had brought in a lamp while I was asleep. Its light hurt my eyes through those blasted spectacles. I looked up, blinking, my mouth dry and my head achy from the frames having pressed against the side of my nose, but I knew right where I was—and who I was supposed to be.

Senrid entered at his usual quick pace, but his hands flexed and gestured with nervous energy. His hair hung down in yellow fangs in his eyes, as if he'd been running his hands through it without being aware.

"Well, that's that," he said. "For a while. You awake? C'mon, let's go get some air."

How strong was the urge to kick him out! But Ndand would never do that. Besides, I'd better hear what he had on his mind, in case he said something I needed to know.

So I got up. "Okay."

A few minutes later we sat together on a couple of battlements high on one of the castle towers. Senrid perched there in his black uniform, kicking the heels of his riding boots against the stone. The wind was chilly and rainy-smelling, the stars overhead glittering with all the warmth of ice chips, except in the north, where the blue glow faintly revealed a long, low band of clouds. I hoped the others were all right—wherever they were.

Though I shivered the wind revived me a little, so I could think.

"So what did you get done?" I asked in Ndand's flat voice.

"Not as much as I'd like. As much as I could have if I'd been alone. He kept cursing, messing up the spells." Senrid shook his head. "Hadn't realized how very bad he is at magic when there's an emergency. His temper gets in the way of accomplishing anything. You can't threaten magic with death for not cooperating the way you can with people," he finished with cheery sarcasm.

Great ruler, I thought.

"I have an idea for a tracer," he continued. "Didn't get a chance to try it because he kept insisting it wouldn't work. When am I going to remember he only likes me successful with *his* ideas, not mine? I should have taken the time to lead him to discovering the idea, but I thought speed was necessary. I was a fool."

"Hmmm," I said, not daring to repeat 'fool'—I would not have been able to keep my tone flat. He was beyond don't-tell.

He drew in a deep breath. I heard it hiss between his teeth. Then he said, "I don't really care if they get away, though I know I have to search. Weak of me or not, I like Faline. Kyale is harmless. And 713 is walking, talking evidence of what Keriam's been insisting all along, how poor our foot warrior training really is, how lax the overall maintenance of regs. What was the use of my father overhauling the regs if they aren't universally enforced? Promotion isn't really on merit, it's on threat and favoritism, and it's at its very worst right here." He jerked his chin back toward the rest of the castle.

I didn't care about Senrid's army problems. What's more, I knew Ndand wouldn't either. Senrid's acceptance of my lack of reaction had made it really clear that she mostly sat in uncomprehending silence while he talked. But she hated her father too, so she was a safe confidant.

Well, my part was now done, and his careless *I know I have to search* killed any vestige of sympathy I might have felt for him. Our plan to save lives was to him just a puzzle to be solved as quickly and neatly as possible. *You don't cross their kings and live.*

"Go to sleep," I said. "You can plan better in the morning how to make him try your spell, with your usual winning ways."

Had my tone been too flat?

His head turned quickly, and though it was too dark to see his features clearly, his manner was alert. "Heh," he said. "If you weren't my cousin and on my side I'd say that last comment was loaded. Deadly, even. Well. You're right." He slammed his hands on his knees, then got up.

I did too. We walked sedately past the ever-vigilant sentries, Senrid flipping up a hand in greeting. No one questioned us, I was glad to see, so there wasn't a curfew except when Tdanerend set it and enforced it himself.

After Senrid left me outside Ndand's room I stood inside the doorway listening. His door clicked shut. I counted slowly to one hundred, and then backwards.

At least, I made it to 39, then tiredness made me fumble. Since I had an all night ride ahead, I decided I'd better get started.

I opened the door and slipped out. No one in sight. Light glowed under Senrid's door; I wondered if he'd ever sleep. Then I thought, who cares? Let him sit up all night figuring out his stupid tracer, as long as I never hear his voice again.

I moiled grimly down a few thousand long, torchlit hallways, and down to the stable. Ironic that I'd finally learned my way around in time to leave.

There's a symbol in that somewhere, my tired mind yammered. Or maybe a joke. Faline would know. But I'm not laughing until I'm out of this nightmare.

My heart clomped faster as I walked up to the stable. The huge exercise yard was mostly deserted, but not completely, and the sentries were alert.

"I'm going for a ride," I said to the guard at the stable door. "Have my horse readied."

He marched inside to roust up a stablehand, and very soon there was Ndand's favorite mount before me, fresh and energetic—and fast.

Feeling a spurt of energy at the prospect of getting away, I mounted up and rode out, keeping the horse at a slow pace while we exited the castle and then the city. My shoulder-blades crawled; any second I expected Senrid or Tdanerend to come tentacling out to zap me.

No hurry, I thought. Don't get anyone's suspicions up, because these crazy people think midnight rides relaxing. Well, who wouldn't, in such a home? Sheesh!

Out the gates. Wave at sentries.

One lifted a hand in salute.

Ride at an easy pace over the hill, around the next.

Slow, slow. Look back...

And the *moment* the towers were out of sight I urged the horse into a gallop, and we pounded to the northeast, me watching the stars to keep my bearings.

ಎಂCR಄ನ಄ೞ

What a long, miserable ride! I don't need to describe it—I don't want to describe it. A long cold night of riding through pre-winter Marloven Hess was bad enough without adding in the danger. Mindful of searches (not to mention the fact that the illusion over me ought to be fading any time now) I stayed near shrubbery and trees as much as I could. I did encounter a couple of patrols, but I heard them well before they heard me, and both times I was able to get behind cover; I think both were returning from long fruitless searches, and they were tired and expecting no one from my direction, or I might not have had that much luck.

It was dawn, my horse stumbling with weariness, when I reached Latvian's region, and I had to ask at a farmer's cottage where Latvian the Sorcerer lived. The people were rising to begin their day, but gave me directions readily enough.

Just before I reached it I topped a hill in time to see a foot patrol on another hill.

They called out to me to stop, but I wheeled my tired horse and set her moving quickly across someone's unharvested winter barley, which was tall and waving in the wind. In the middle of it I slipped off the horse and hid; in a frighteningly short time a mounted posse came flashing by, following the path of trampled barley-stalks as the horse cantered away back toward home.

I trekked on as fast as I could, and soon spotted the turreted castle silhouetted against the gray eastern sky, the way Faline had described it.

My eyes were so tired and gritty I was afraid I was dreaming it, but I put my head down and ran.

Moving silhouettes on the castle gate indicated a pair of guards. I figured I would have to circle around to the back, where I could see the tallest tower, which Faline had said was Hibern's. Finding a smooth, flat stone, I tossed it up; the stone tapped squarely in the middle of her window.

A minute or so later the casement opened and I saw long dark hair framing a pale face. "Someone out there?" called a soft voice.

"I'm Faline's friend—CJ."

A few seconds later I stood in a warm room goldenlit by a welcome fire in the fireplace. When the transfer woozies faded I saw before me a tall, dark-haired girl who looked at me in some perplexity.

"Illusion," I croaked. "Illusion—to look like Ndand Montredaun-An. Will they trace that spell you just did?"

"No," Hibern said. "I already have protective wards here, laid down by my mage-tutor's direction. I can transfer in and out of this castle, and transfer people in and out." She smiled. "As for my reaction, it's that black-and-gold gown, and those spectacles perched on the end of your nose."

"Spectacles!" I'd forgotten about the horrible things. I pulled them off and threw them savagely to the floor. "The gown I can't help, but these I'm done with! Rotten torture devices. Can you get me to Faline and the others?"

She bit her lip. "I can, but I've been unsuccessful at keeping transfer-tracers dissolved. The Regent has my father helping, and his abilities are considerable."

"You mean they might find me?"

"I don't know. I did dissolve the previous tracer, and I don't sense the negating of my spell, but that doesn't preclude another way around it. I feel I ought to tell you these things," she added in a quiet voice, her expression apologetic, and I nodded, repressing a groan of annoyance.

My head swam, and I was hungry, thirsty, and tired. I wanted—badly—to go home. But she was doing her best—she, too, had been up all night.

"My friends're close to the border, right?" I asked finally.

She nodded. "I believe so. I don't think they've moved, for the weather there has been terrible all night. We even caught a brief edge of it here, lightning, thunder, and hail." She pointed out her window.

"Then send me, please," I asked. "I'll take the risk. Use Faline as your transfer-focus."

She opened a hand, and performed the spell unerringly. I waved my thanks just before the magic wrenched me out of the physical world and then shoved me back in again. I wavered, stumbling in a shocking cold, wet place. The bleak, blue early-dawn's light outlined the entrance to a cave in the middle of a mossy, wind-worn tumbled ruin. The ground smelled of wet rock and weeds; all the trees were bare, and thick shrubs dotted the western cliff-faces.

I trudged to the cave entrance. Short as the distance was—you don't transfer people right to someone else, which is dangerous, but fifty paces away—the nasty crunchy-topped mud made me glad of Ndand's shoes.

Since I couldn't see anything I called out softly, "Are you in there?"

"Is that you, CJ?" Leander's voice was a whisper, easily heard in the utter stillness. He sounded as tired as I was.

"CJ!" Faline appeared, sounding joyful. "You nearly scared my freckles off!"

I snarkled, and heard a laugh from Kitty.

"Listen, CJ," Faline said, waving me inside. "There are some others here, but they're sick in some weird way. Uh oh—hear that?"

A tall shape slowly stood; 713. He was right by the cave entrance, looking groggy and half-conscious.

All of us fell silent. We heard footsteps. Soft ones, hesitant, crunching gravel and swishing by the leaves of a shrub.

My heart clomped again—but not from danger. A breath of flower scent tickled my nose, a familiar one, and I wondered if I was finally going nutso—uh, more than usual—but then the silhouette of a girl moved toward us from the top of the hill. She brought a sense of healing magic.

"Who is it?" I asked.

"CJ?" A familiar voice! "Is that really you?"

"Autumn!" I exclaimed in total amazement. "What are you doing *here*? Bermund is a million miles away—*everything is a million miles away*—"

She was too preoccupied to hear my blabbing. "They're here." She looked around, her face that I'd remembered as calm and merry now tense and anxious. "I feel I am being watched," she whispered as she looked around at the silent hills. Then she sucked in a breath almost like a sob. "They're *here*." And she pushed past me.

I remembered the story that she'd told me so long ago, and despite the danger I snapped a zaplight. The shadows jumped back, revealing Leander, and Kitty beyond 713, all three tired and grubby-looking.

Autumn didn't spare them a glance.

She dashed inside, her distracted gaze on someone beyond. I followed, and saw to my amazement two thin, wraith-like kids curled up uncomfortably on the stone ground. They were impossibly pale and drained-looking, like shades, with color just barely visible in their hands and faces.

Autumn was, as always, barefoot, wearing only a light shift, but she glimmered with her own inner light. The cave seemed to answer with its own light as she walked farther in. Now we could see them all clearly in the soft glow as she reached down toward each kid. The air filled with sparkles of gold and white and blue as she touched each dirty brow.

Nothing happened for a long breath, though the air in the cave had filled with a scent like fresh summer-grown herbs, and it was no longer cold. I snorted that lovely aroma, feeling my headache diminish slightly, and the others with me sighed. Even 713 straightened up a bit, drawing in a long, deep breath.

Meanwhile, color flushed through the strange kids' faces. They opened their eyes and sat up, looked around uncomprehendingly, then the boy saw Autumn and his face changed from fret to wonder.

"Lael, Laurel," Autumn said kindly. "Wake up— Autumn's here, and you are safe at last. The spell is broken, and I found you as I promised I would."

To our amazement both kids' faces, so wretched and pale before, now glowed with health. Their bodies took on normal contours, as they rubbed their eyes and stood up. They looked as if they'd woken from a good night's sleep.

"Autumn!" Laurel exclaimed happily.

"Where are we?" Lael asked. "May we go home now?"

Laurel blinked around, shoving back light brown hair. Lael, tall, thin, with slightly darker hair, looked perplexed. "The Old One lost, then?"

"He lost," Autumn said. "It took a hundred years to beat him, and the world has changed, but I think you will like the changes, for there are places for kids like us now. You are the ones who broke the first enchantment, so it's right that you break the last."

"Oh, let's go home," Laurel exclaimed fervently.

"You may go any time you like," Autumn said, opening her arms. "Nothing will happen to you now."

The two threw themselves into her arms and they all hugged, and for a time talked swiftly in their own language, but then Laurel tugged at her brother, and said, "Let's go! Let's go! I can hardly wait!"

And so they took off, scampering up the trail to the hill, and over it, faintly glowing, protected by very, very old magic indeed.

"I'm free," Autumn said, sitting down on a rock. She looked around as if she'd never seen rocks before, or the ground, or her own bare toes.

I killed my light, small magic that it was. "You aren't bound to your search any more?"

"No more. I am free to follow the wind," she said, sighing happily. "But—it's strange, I feel I ought to stay put, and not go home with them." She looked around in awe. "This is a place of magic."

"I wish it was a place of beds, " I said feelingly. "Magic's great—and I'm so glad I bumbled in at the end of your quest—but we just finished a real nasty adventure, and we need to—"

Leander heard it first.

713 looked up sharply.

Outside the cave torchlight flickered, red and glary, banishing the weak blue light of dawn. Leander stood there, arms crossed, gazing out into the night. Against the glare of the torches his profile was tight with anger.

Now we all could hear the unwelcome sounds of clanking weaponry and bootheels crunching stones. The unmistakable sound of a patrol rekindled all my anger, and then came a familiar voice—one I detested.

"Leander," Senrid said, coming up the last of the trail at the head of a number of heavily armed hulks, all in those Marloven uniforms. "I didn't expect to see you," Senrid continued, his tone bright and cheery as always, though his voice was somewhat hoarse. "So much the better, for I decided tonight that the time has come for me to run my own affairs. Kyale—713—"

He saw me, and stopped, his hands going wide in surprise. "Ndand! So you did ride north. Why? Did they abduct you?"

Sheer, hot, boiling, sizzling, *steaming* RAGE fazoomed through me with all the fury of a volcano.

"Don't you *ever* sleep, you boneheaded, oatmeal-faced, blob-eyed, splat-brained gabboon? I am NOT Ndand, and never will be!"

"Who are you, then? I sometimes thought—never mind, another time. Who's this?"

"Autumn," Autumn said politely. "Of Bermund."

"Are you with these others?" Senrid eyed her curiously, for she looked as she always had—barefooted, dressed in a light, shapeless travel-tunic, her reddish-brown hair crowned with a garland of summer blooms. Autumn's flowers never faded or withered. When she was done with them she replanted them, and they always flourished wherever she put them.

"I'm with CJ, yes," she said, standing next to me. Her gaze was steady, as it always was, her smile friendly—but Senrid must have seen something in her face that I never had because for the very first time I saw him drop his own gaze, and look away.

Toward me, as it happened.

"CJ?" Senrid repeated, frowning slightly. He looked as grubby and tired as I felt, for he was still in that unmarked uniform, his uncombed hair hanging down in his eyes, and I loathed the sight of him so much I was hopping from foot to foot.

"Faline." Senrid addressed her in a normal voice, as if he hadn't tried to have her killed half a day ago. "Didn't you mention someone by the name 'CJ'? I didn't know she looks like Ndand."

"I don't," I snarled. "You stupid, rat-brained fatwit of a lying stench!"

"Come along," Senrid said to me, his smile grim at the corners.

I started a transport spell, and the others pressed close, Leander grabbing 713's thick wrist, and he too began the transport spell.

Senrid started a counter, but I knew that spell and I was faster.

So he reached forward, now weaving another spell—a powerful spell, one he'd worked on all night—his fingers grasping 713's unresisting other arm as tangled, super-powered magic blasted us away.

TEN

I woke up when a foot nudged my side, causing me to roll over. Feeling like a disassembled wooden toy, I groaned. Bright sunlight shone on my eyelids.

I cracked them open (which took about as much effort as it would take to lift the average horse and set it onto the average roof) to find myself looking up into a round-headed silhouette that was very familiar.

I groaned again, lifted a hand to block the sun, and Senrid's curious gray-blue gaze met my own.

"That transfer seems to have blasted our magic—including your illusion spell. I wanted to see what you really look like," he explained, before I could croak out the insults already piling up in my head.

My tongue felt sprained, and all I could do was grunt and wheeze and cough.

And before I could recover, Senrid gave me a smile that looked to my bleary vision like a smirk, and moved away.

While I lay there trying to recover from the smashing reaction of that monster magic-transfer, Senrid wandered about on the sandy beach. The air was balmy, and smelled heavily of brine; Senrid and 713 and Kitty and Autumn had never been near the ocean before, but the rest of us who had were reminded of shores at home.

Blue-green waves crashed nearby, each foamy run of water coming in a little farther than the last, covering very white, very soft sand. Scattered about on the beach sat or lay the others, who regarded Senrid with wariness or downright hatred.

Except 713, who looked tired and sick, and Autumn, who was just curious.

Inland appeared to be a dense jungle, with no inviting pathway.

Before long we were all awake, exchanging exclamations about where we could be (no one knew) and how we felt (nasty) and what was to come next (again, no one knew). All, that is, except Senrid.

I ignored him as I yanked off Ndand's heavy winter shoes and threw them as far from me as I could. Shoes! I never wore them at home, except on winter patrols through the woods.

Autumn gave Senrid troubled glances from time to time. Kitty kept her back to him, and everyone else was too busy with our conversation, which circled round and round, punctuated by Faline's jokes, and went exactly nowhere.

Finally 713 observed, from the rock on which he'd been sitting, "Tide's coming in."

"Nosy, ain't it?" Faline commented, adding, "That's a joke, '3, so you have to laugh."

The warrior gave her an absent grin, which was good enough for Faline. She liked the fellow, and didn't like seeing him look so worn out. For Faline, a grin meant a person was next thing to feeling great. Nothing too bad could happen as long as people could laugh.

Kitty put her hands on her hips and said loudly, "Maybe we'd better explore before that stinkard plans how to kill us next." She sent a sour glare in Senrid's direction.

He sat there on a fallen log with weird scaly bark, his uniform sandy and grubby. Absolutely nothing could be read from his bland kid-face, except that sarcastic shadow at either side of his mouth.

Just the sight of him brought back the worries and fears of the past couple of days, and since I no longer had to hold in my thoughts, I marched right up to him.

"So what now, great and mighty king? Executions before lunch, or after?"

He said, "Do you have access to your magic?"

Truth to tell, I hadn't tried—my head was still ringing weirdly. I shut my eyes, reached for knowledge of the transfer spell, and felt the words skitter away like frightened mice. Words I'd worked and sweated to master.

I opened my eyes and began forming an insult, because I was not about to admit any weakness to Senrid. But he'd been watching. He said, "I don't either. I can frame a spell but not perform it."

"Good!" I *know* I was smirking.

"We've been warded," he said. "That means we're all at someone else's mercy."

"Oh, I've gotten pretty used to being at the mercy of rock-brained spackelodeons in the past couple of days," I snarled. "This will be a refreshing change—whatever happens. It can't possibly be worse, or more stupid, than you and your uncle."

"Want a bet?" Senrid fired back.

I opened my mouth, but he was already looking past me.

I turned, envisioning hordes of sword-waving villains, but all I saw was that the tide had come in farther. As you'd expect. Except that after a time wasn't the water supposed to recede before it came in again?

When I turned back, Senrid was walking away.

So I rejoined the others.

713 had shifted higher up the beach, studying the vast expanse of gray-green ocean with a very troubled look on his bruised, messed-up face.

Leander, who hadn't spoken much, announced that he was going to try to explore inland, and that functioned as a cue for everyone else to pick a direction in which to nose about.

So we did. Senrid moved farther down the beach. It became apparent even to my jumbled mind that he'd already explored—having been the first to recover—and hadn't found anything of help. But he said nothing, and one by one the rest of us reported the increasingly worrying news that we seemed to be stuck. Leander came back, sweaty and scratched, to say that the jungle was impenetrable except maybe by insects.

And the tide kept coming in, a little at a time.

After the futile search Faline and Kitty started making a sand-city, as if having fun might make this weird situation turn normal. Leander watched, and I could tell from his grin that he was waiting for a good chance to splat one of the castles and start a sand-fight. Faline's snorts and snickers made it clear she hoped it would be one of hers.

I helped for a time, until hunger and tiredness and left-over transfer malaise made it easier to sit on the sand, let the fading sunlight warm my skin, and watch. We didn't seem to be in any great danger, and I was too tired and hungry and worn to plan.

Kitty and Faline chattered happily, busy with roads and walls and tunnels between their houses. Beyond them 713 sat motionless until Senrid approached him, his back to us, and began talking.

713 was a mess, but he was big. Would he take out Tdanerend's nastiness on Senrid? He didn't look angry, I thought, as I watched Senrid kneel down by 713, his hands gesturing as he talked. The ex-warrior didn't look angry, or happy, or really much of anything—except maybe tired. But then he said something brief, and after a moment he made a gesture with one of his bruised hands, touching his fist to his heart. I hoped it was some kind of insult. Senrid's back was still to us and I couldn't see his face. He got to his feet, and walked up the beach toward the jungle.

That was strange, I thought, closing my eyes. Did 713 get mad at him—or not? Marlovens! Who can figure them?

And a voice spoke next to me: "What happened to my cousin?"

Senrid! He'd circled around while I was thinking, and snuck up behind me. I jerked away, though Senrid hadn't threatened me. But I was not about to trust him.

"Wouldn't you like to know," I said rudely, savoring the exquisite thrill of being able to say what I liked to a creep and a villain.

"Yes," he said. "That's why I asked."

"She's safe from you," I sneered. "That's all you need to know."

"So you've got her locked up as a prisoner?" he retorted.

The idea of Clair making anyone a prisoner boiled my blood. "Hah! She's free to go anywhere she wants! Or will be, when Cl—when the spells are gotten off her."

"Cl—?" he prompted.

"Clear off, nosy," I snapped back.

"Clair? She knows enough magic to undo my uncle's tangle of spells?"

I said, "If you think for *one stinking second* that you are going to add Clair to your little list of future pincushions, you can forget it, you rat-faced, lying gnackle! She's going to *help* your cousin—something you will never be smart enough to understand the meaning of—and then she'll send her anywhere she wants."

"Even home?"

"Yes. Though I doubt Ndand would be that stupid."

"But she liked home—when my uncle wasn't scaring her," Senrid said. "And as soon as I get back, it's time for my uncle to retire."

"So you can run your own executions?" I shot back snidely.

Senrid gave me a look of disgust and turned away.

"Hah!" I yelled at his back.

"Good one," Kitty said, coming up next to me. "I heard every word, and didn't he deserve it!"

I shrugged, feeling somewhat odd. I mean, it's one thing to exercise my grudge, and another to have someone cheering me on. So I tried to think of a subject change—but Kitty beat me to it. With a furtive glance Leander's way (he was at the other end of the beach) she said, "Faline said you came from Earth."

"Yes?" I hated remembering Earth.

"Were you of royal blood there?"

I laughed. Couldn't help it, even though Kitty looked a little offended. "Nope. Not even. In fact, where I come from, there aren't any nobles, or kings, or emperors. And even if there were, I wouldn't have been one."

I braced for more questions, but Kitty had obviously lost interest as soon as I said there weren't any nobles.

Autumn appeared from the other side of a thick-leafed plant right then, and gave us each a slight grimace. Her arms were laden with gourd-shaped fruits. "I found these up the shore a little," she said. "They taste pretty good, and I waited, and nothing nasty has happened inside me."

"But you're not really human," I said doubtfully.

"I am as much as Faline is," she replied.

That made sense—sort of. It means, when others have human form, they more or less work according to human rules. There are a few exceptions, but eating doesn't seem to be one. Anyway, I waved and yelled, "Food!"

The others came running, all except Senrid. Autumn handed out a fruit to each person. I'd hoped she hadn't gotten him one, but she had. After a quick glance at him (his back was turned as he watched the sea) she laid his share on a rock, and moved away.

I never would have been that generous. And though I promptly reassured myself that such a thought was perfectly justified, I couldn't really hold onto it. So I turned away, and bit into my fruit. The skin was thick, a little like Earth banana-skins, except it tasted good. Inside, the fruit was a little like citrus and a little like pomegranates. It had a faint sweetness, lots of juice, and felt refreshing going down.

I finished mine and buried the core in the white sand, straightening up in time to see Kitty take Senrid's share off the rock and throw it, with all her strength, into the sea, where it bobbed about on the tide.

Leander said something to her in a low voice, to which she yelled, "I don't care!"

I winced, not wanting to hear an argument, because I sympathized with both of them. So I wandered away, and found myself near Autumn. Her changeable eyes reflected the sinking sun, looking all greeny and browny and blue, as she smiled at me. Her skin was dotted with new freckles, which on her were pretty, just like Faline's are funny.

"I feel magic," Autumn said to me. "I think—I think I have to look about for it." She rubbed her hands up her arms, then opened them, palms turned upward. "I feel that I can do anything."

She seemed just an ordinary girl, standing there in her worn old dress, her ruddy brown hair hanging tousled down her back, but the way the sinking sunlight lit her so brightly, it seemed as if she glowed. Very hard to explain. She was both familiar—and different.

"Well, if you find it, I hope it can get us home," I said.

Autumn grinned. "So you feel it too? This isn't our world. I don't know how I know, and nothing looks or feels or smells that different, but I know it."

"Me too," I said. "Though that jungly-stuff sure looks different. I've never seen plants like any of those behind us. They look like plastic." At her puzzled look, I amended hastily, "This disgusting stuff that everything is made of on Earth."

Autumn turned around to gaze into the shadowy depths of the jungle. Broad, waxy leaves waved a little in the cool breeze that now fingered through our hair. She shrugged.

The others came toward us. The sun was sinking fast. Our long shadows were going dim, melding into one big shadow.

Leander said, "I guess we ought to settle down and sleep right here on the sand."

I nodded. "Sounds good to me. A nice change," I added in a louder voice, glancing Senrid's way out of the corners of my eyes, "from the total lack of sleep that seems to be Rule Three in the Villains' Handbook."

"Rule Three?" Kitty repeated.

"What's Rule One?" Faline asked, snickering. "You have to have a white beard, like Kwenz and Shnit, and mean faces?"

"Oh, you have to be a liar, a coward, and a cheat," I replied as loudly as I could.

"Ha! Ha! Ha!" Kitty fake-laughed in a loud, hard voice.

I added, glaring now at Senrid, "And Rule Two is, Kill Everyone Who Disagrees. A real popularity plus, and you're sure to always hear the truth!"

No answer.

Leander shook his head a couple times, then stretched out onto a mounded sand dune. 713 was already asleep. He'd lain down not long after eating his share of the fruit.

Before long we'd all settled down to sleep, and once I was comfortable, I dropped off fast.

My dreams, bland enough at first, slowly altered into vaguely uncomfortable ones that featured wet, cold toes, but I didn't actually waken until a sudden splash of cold water drenched me thoroughly.

I sat up, gasping, to find that the tide had come all the way up the beach to where I lay. I had settled on what I'd thought was the highest point of the beach, not far from the jungle, but now I looked out at an unbroken expanse of water, fear scrunching my innards.

The others, some of them wet, stood ranged along the edges of the jungle—which began abruptly, with thick, tough pale green plants growing out of the sandy soil. The blue-white light of dawn revealed somber, worried faces. 713 kept rubbing slowly at one arm, and he twitched his shoulders and winced as though his back hurt.

At the far end of our row, I saw Senrid making motions with his fingers, his hands expressive of anger. Magic spell! Magic spells that were not working.

Leander crossed to his side, and addressed a few words to him. Senrid looked up sharply, then out to sea, and then snapped his hands out as he said something back. Then Leander shrugged

To my surprise, he came back toward us.

"Why did you talk to that disgusting stinkard?" Kitty asked, folding her arms across her front.

"Truce," Leander said. "No more execution list."

"Sure," I said. "While we're here. But what if he gets access to his magic first?"

Leander said, "He told me—for what it's worth—that he really hadn't wanted to see you three dead, but couldn't figure out a way around it."

I opened my mouth to scoff, but a certain vivid memory blasted my brain from inside—another near-miss execution not so long ago. Somewhere very different, with different people. I hadn't wanted to see it happen, but I'd been unable to stop it—and it wouldn't have stopped, despite my most agonized wishes, until someone else's ambition did the trick.

I hadn't gone and collected the people for it, but someone could make a case for the whole thing having been my fault for picking a fight with a very, very nasty and vindictive villain.

So I sighed, and was about to say, "Truce," but first Kitty yelled, "Hah! Why even waste the time talking to a liar?"

"I think," Leander said, "we should not waste any more time talking at all, but get up into some of these trees—"

Just as he spoke a big wave came rolling at us, sounding like a great ripping of sailcloth, and we dashed and floundered in the stiff, waxy shrubs, which tore at hair and clothing. Seawater foamed and splashed at our feet.

The trees were rough and scaly but fairly easy to climb.

The tide seemed to be coming in almost as fast as we climbed; within moments the water now swirled and hissed round the lower levels of the trees, covering the shrubs entirely.

Kitty wailed in fright, crying, "I can't swim! I can't swim!"

"Climb higher," Leander called, holding down his hands to her when it became obvious that she also didn't know how to climb trees.

Poor Kitty clung to her branch as water splashed against their tree right up to their chins, fanning her silvery hair out around her. Senrid had gone up another tree; he'd taken off his tunic earlier, and now it was gone, leaving him shivering in shirt and trousers and boots.

Ndand's black-and-gold dress dragged at me, soggy and heavy. I was highest, so I saw the others one by one forced away from their trees. Kitty wailed, too frightened to hear 713 and Leander trying to reassure her. Farther away, Autumn scanned in one great, slow circle, and then, with a calm, deliberate movement, dove cleanly into the water.

She did not come up again.

Faline bobbed near me. I held out my hand to rescue her—and then a big, cold, gray wave washed over me. I clung hard, but the water sucking at my heavy, sodden skirts pulled me relentlessly away from the tree. The waves tumbled me into the water, the cumbersome gown now dragging me down.

Kicking hard, I broke the surface.   Sucked in a shuddering lungful of air, then sputtered and spat the nasty salty water out.

Fighting to tread water, I wondered how long I'd last when something brushed my foot, and I kicked back at it in frightened reaction. Nothing. The touch again—tentative, and then a quick little tug on my skirt.

I held my breath and peered down into the water, ignoring the sting. I made out a blurry shape: Autumn. Who gestured downward.

Dive?

She was already far below, tiny bubbles like pearls rising from her face. I became aware of the sense of magic tingling through my fast-numbing body. Autumn swam up to me, and showed herself drawing air in.

I ducked my head again, and though my heart kaboomed in fear, I let a little water trickle into my nose—and it didn't hurt!

Almost at once Autumn became clear to my eyes, and beyond her the others. Nearly invisible bubbles glowed around their heads: magic.

"Who?" I asked—I had a bubble as well.

To my surprise, she seemed to hear—and I realized our bubbles were touching. She pointed downward. I peered past my billowing skirt, and spied an old man, human, his hair waving in the water. He gestured sharply for us to follow—fast. Below him were some dark shapes that I couldn't make out; as I peered, they seemed to flicker and speed away into the depths.

Puzzled, I looked around, to find Senrid on my other side. His bubble touched mine with a soft sound like a hand-pat, and he said, "I'm not sure, but I think we're being chased."

And he pointed off in one direction, where a cloud of dark shapes was boiling rapidly toward us.

We tried to swim away, but they were much too fast.

Within moments we were surrounded by long, sinuous beings of a dark bluish color, who took hold of us with long, sticky fingers. Senrid fought the hardest—713 not at all—but none of us won free, and we were forced down and down and down until the light was only intermittent weak shafts, and then nothing, until weird blue glows lanced out from the beings—from their foreheads.

Rough rock scraped at my arm. We were being forced down into some kind of fantastically large rocky grotto.

Still farther down, until they stopped. My hair floated round my face like live black snakes, and my body felt squeezed, as if I were wrapped in a tight cloth. The water was cool, but at least we could breathe in our bubbles.

Then a nasty voice spoke directly into our heads: *Leave here the way you came, or die.*

"What?" I bellowed, shock making it impossible to think. Shock—and anger. "Do you think we *want* to be here? And I've had enough death threats to last a lifetime—"

It felt a little as if I was shouting into an empty room, except I heard Senrid's snicker on one side. Then his sharp intake of breath.

I turned my head to discover Autumn drawing her fingers apart in a peculiar pattern. I could see her face clearly, though her bubble was smaller; her eyes were half-shut, and again she drew her fingers out as if she wove invisible threads, and this time tiny bubbles streamed between them.

Again, and more bubbles came, and then she gestured a huge circle through the water, and bubbles whooshed out around us, millions of them, like glowing blue crystals. A hard hand gripped my arm and tugged. I yanked back, trying to free myself, but the grip was too hard to break, and Senrid snapped a command: "Get Faline!"

We were making a human chain. I groped about for where I'd seen Faline last, found her small, freckled hand, and gripped it.

We swam—pushed along by a hissing, tickling froth of bubbles.

It seemed a long time—longer even than hiking to breakfast through Senrid's kingdom-sized castle—then the bubbles abruptly cleared, and light glowed from above.

Above?

I swam upward toward the wavering blue light. My bubble had shrunk and now barely enclosed my head. But then I broke a surface, and breathed in dank air that smelled like wet rocks. The water had felt merely cool when the bubble was round my head, but now I was chilly, and my dress dragged horribly at me as I pulled myself up some barnacle-encrusted rocky steps.

All around the cavern paintings glowed on the walls, surrounded by a flourishing script that I couldn't read. I looked down, blinking salt from my eyes, to see a short, thin old man with greenish skin and short, thin greenish-white hair waiting patiently as, behind me, Faline emerged, and then Kitty, Leander, and last 713.

The old man spoke—and we couldn't understand a word of it.

We stared at one another, drips from our clothes echoing in the cavern, until Autumn held up her hands. "Wait," she said to the man, her palms toward him. "Wait!"

The old man made a sign with his hands, then retreated to a stone bench, where he sat down, water dripping from his hair and robe, his head bowed.

Autumn dove back into the water and vanished.

ELEVEN

Well, in these records I do try to tell the truth as I saw it, so I have to say that what happened next was mostly confusing.

First we had to wait.

713 sat, looking tired but patient. At the time I figured that was because he was feeling rotten, but I think now he was also waiting for someone to give him an order so he'd know what to do.

Leander wandered along the walls, strudying the glowing paintings and the mysterious script, completely entranced—except when Kitty (who was complaining non-stop about the cold, and Senrid, and her wet gown, and Senrid, and being hungry, and oh yes, Senrid) tugged at him or got louder when he didn't answer.

Senrid sat on a rock, looking down at the water, his brow furrowed as he pulled off his boots and stockings and set them aside to dry.

Faline plopped beside me. We caught up on each other's stories after Senrid had zapped her to his snackle-grundge of a capital. I was fascinated by the cave, but I kept sidling peeks at Senrid as if—oh, I don't know. I really can't say what I expected. Did I want him to do something villainous? With him away from Marloven Hess I found it harder and harder to keep up a good, brisk hate, until I looked at Faline and remembered what he'd tried to do to her.

In short, I didn't stay mad at him—until he spoke to me. Then it all came rushing back.

The old man, meanwhile, sat on a worn stone bench, his long fingers laced together, his eyes closed. After a time there was a rustling sound from the back of the cave, and two women emerged from a narrow opening. One woman was old, one young, both green, with browny-green short hair.

They all wore long PJs of a kind of shiny, lightweight material. Waterproof? It sure looked easier to swim in than my woolen gown.

Water splashed and ringed outward as Autumn reappeared, and with her a squid-like critter that gave me the shudders. She kept her hand on its head, though, and its great stalked eyes wove in a gentle pattern as it observed us all.

Autumn said, "They talk mind to mind."

"Eugh," Kitty said softly. "They're disgusting-looking."

Leander murmured something in a voice too low to hear, and Kitty turned away and folded her arms.

"So what can they tell us about those creeps down under water?" Faline asked.

Autumn looked up our way, as the man and the two women came down the steps to the edge of the dark waters. They extended hands, tentacles reached up to wind round their arms, and for a moment everything was quiet.

Then Autumn said to us, "The weird thing is, I don't think there are any villains—not like how we mean. At least, no villains from *this* world."

Kitty pointed at Senrid. "So they know about him, too?"

Autumn shook her head. "Strangers."

I said, "What? Those blue creatures threatening to kill us sure seemed to be a clue."

Autumn shook her head, and droplets flew from her wet hair. "They thought *we* were the villains. Something's gone wrong here—those creatures talk in mind-pictures, not in words. Kept showing me over and over this kind of mind-picture." She waved her hands side-to-side, and rocked. "Off-balance? Something is out of balance? I dunno—I hope they can tell us."

Senrid said, "How did you find that thing to communicate with?"

"It found me," Autumn said. "When I made the bubbles. This water—this world, is full of..." She shrugged.

"Magic," Senrid said. "It's full of magic potential. Feels like the power-build before a big spell."

"Ah!" Leander let out an exclamation. "It is! I thought it was some kind of residue of the transfer. But it really is."

A flash of blue light crackled between the squid-thing and the three humans.

Then, with a surge of water, the squid dove below and vanished.

The three faced us.

The youngest woman said to 713, "Please accompany. We go to find you sustenance, and bands. We then discourse." I heard the words as Mearsiean, but they sounded strange even so.

We followed the people up the stone steps into what turned out to be a city inside rock. A city! That easy word doesn't begin to explain the great, carved lacework of railings and stairs and rooms and balconies arching and swooping and curling with a soaring, airy beauty that you would never expect of rock. There we found more of the green people, of all sizes and ages, including kids running about and playing. A few tentatively approached us, but were waved away by cautious grownups, who brought us food that was completely strange, but not bad tasting. The only thing I recognized was a kind of flat bread made of rice, onto which they put vegetables that seemed to be stewed with spices.

After that a woman came and said, "We will give you access to the water. But there is much to be learned, you from us and us from you, until danger is averted."

₧(R₧)₧

Just as I wouldn't expect any visitor to Sartorias-deles to suddenly know all our main kingdoms, leaders, villains, and the rest of the mess, I can't really say that I completely understood that world or what was going on, even after what I believe was a couple of weeks.

So I'm sticking to what was important for us.

First were the bands. The squid-beings were the ones with magic, and they provided gold arm-bands like the local humans wore, so that we could breathe underwater, and not feel cold.

Then Leander and Autumn disappeared on an exploratory **dive**. Eventually the rules relaxed when we caused no one any **harm**, and Faline and I made friends with the local kids, trying **hard** to learn all their games, which had to do with swimming. **Wow**, were they fast! But when we came out of the water into **those** caverns, then we taught them some of our word games, and **they** seemed to like them.

Senrid stayed silent and listened.

713 slept a lot in the little cave they gave us, with alcoves carved round the walls, and nests made of soft woven material that felt odd, almost like smooth plastic but very soft, a little like that fake grass they put in Easter baskets on Earth. I found I much preferred sleeping under water than on stone—especially when there was too much talking going around me.

Kitty glared at Senrid, got bored with games she couldn't win, and complained when we were out of the water. She was worried about Leander, I guess, but I dove a lot to get away from her temper: I liked her when she stood up to villains, but she could get tiring when she whined about how a princess ought to be treated.

Finally, after a week or so (it was hard to judge the passage of time under water), Leander and Autumn returned. The rest of us were asleep (and sleeping underwater is probably more comfortable than anything else in the universe, as long as magic keeps you from being cold), but a hand on my arm woke me instantly.

I blinked awake to see Leander drifting nearby, his dark hair floating crazily about his head. I'd already made a braid of my long hair so I wouldn't get choked or blinded by it; I could see why all the people we'd seen in this world wore theirs short.

In silence I followed Leander up to the cavern, which was always lit. There, Senrid already waited, and the four of us each picked a stone and sat down.

"We're the ones who have magic," Leander said, pointing to Senrid and me and himself. "Autumn hasn't learned it—not the way we know it—but she's got a talent for finding it."

She IS magic, I thought.   But since she didn't say anything, neither did I.   Autumn had spent a century not learning, but running, in order to break a creepy enchantment that had involved the generation before.   Her learning was about to begin.

Leander went on, indicating the four of us, "It's we who have to figure out what to do, so we can go home."

"We can't use our magic," I said.   "I've tried.   Something stronger makes my spells flub up."

Leander nodded, his green eyes reflecting bits of light from the water.   "Same here.   Senrid?" He lifted his head.

"Yes.   Same."

"Yet someone wants us here.   It's not a mistake that we landed here—someone wants *us*.   There's something that four kids can do, and we're going to have to do it."

Someone with a whole lot of power.   I could see that thought strike them all, and they reacted in different ways: Leander frowned, Autumn looked pensive, and Senrid very, very angry.

Remembering that last hour in the cave on Marloven Hess's border, I turned to Autumn.   "You said, just before you found Laurel and Lael, that you thought someone was watching. Was that—" I jerked my thumb toward Senrid.

Autumn shook her head as Senrid said, "Wasn't me.   I was at home until the tracer I'd put back over the border three times alerted me that someone had transferred.   Then I had to find the nearest patrol."   And to Autumn, "So what did you learn?"

He'd been perching on a rock, but at my words about being watched he got up and walked back and forth along the water-splashed stone, his bare feet making a slapping noise, his hands gripped behind his back.   I could see his knuckles turning white.

"That the islands are supposed to sink," Autumn said. "Twice a year.   The old man we first met is always the last to go, and he was worried that we'd be sucked down with it.   The squids gave us the breathing bubbles."

Leander continued, "And the tould-hayin—that's the blue creatures—get to harvest something that grows on the islands, but needs both water and air in order to grow. The humans who live on the islands all swim down here to the caverns during that time, and carve some more of the city as their numbers grow on the islands. Our island is a small one. The people on it live at the other end."

"How does that fit with our being at the wrong end of the island when it sank and then getting death threats from the blue guys?" I asked.

"The humans leave a week or so before the islands sink," Leander explained. "Our being there was misunderstood."

"How?" Senrid asked.

"That's what we can't find out," Autumn said. "Leander and I think maybe the tould-hayin thought we were going to steal their whatever-it-is they were gathering to harvest. They won't tell us. They don't trust us enough yet, and the—the squid-people—their name is an image, not a word—well, they don't have a name for the harvest either. Anyway it's all part of how life goes here, and our appearance interrupted it. But I think something else might have been here before, because why else would they be so scared of visitors? But again, I can't get any images. I mean, ones I can understand."

"So the islands and the harvest and all the rest is a false trail, is that it?" Senrid asked, still walking back and forth.

Leander shrugged. "You tell me."

Senrid cast a look over his shoulder, and I realized he was looking for Kitty—like he didn't want her to hear what he was going to say next. "Back to how we got here." He stopped and faced me. "You and Leander both performed the multiple transfer spell. Mine was a counter, a disintegration meant to take you, though we were all included—by rights it should have destroyed us all." He made a kind of sour, sarcastic face; he'd been a lot angrier back in Marloven Hess than I'd known.

Including at himself, I know now.

But at the time I thought: well, him and me both. But *I* had a *right* to be.

Senrid swung around and glared at Autumn. "You did something, didn't you? You're some kind of mage. Why are you hiding it from me? I can't do anything to you."

"But I'm not hiding anything," Autumn said. "And I'm not a mage. Magic comes to me, it has all my life—to my three sisters and to me. But I've never done anything with it. Not in the sense I think you mean." Her smile was crooked. "My own life until days ago has been a long search over the continent, *between* time is the only way I can describe it. I don't know enough about where our people originally came from, or how our magic works. That's what I will be doing when I go home again. Learning those things."

"But you know we were being watched," Senrid countered, his eyes narrowed. "That is, you were, at that border cave. The air just happened to be filled with magic."

Autumn spread her hands. "I know it sounds strange, but it is the truth."

I was about to stick my oar in with a nasty *SHE always tells the truth, unlike Some People*—except he'd never lied to me. To Kitty and Faline and Leander, yes, but not to his supposed cousin. Again I felt uneasy and unsettled.

"So how did we get here?" Senrid turned to each of us.

Leander sighed, rubbing his eyes. A mistake; a moment later he winced. We were all covered with salt when we dried off. I'd already learned not to rub my eyes. The people here didn't have cleaning frames, though they did have the Waste Spell. I guess they didn't mind the salt. But then their skin was different from ours: shiny, sort of, like the leaves of their plants, and their clothes. Maybe the salt didn't crust on them like it did to us.

Autumn said, "I tried something by instinct when I felt your magic spells clash." She nodded at me, and then at Senrid. "I don't know, I guess I'd say I mentally reached for the big knot of fire that the magic was making, and threw it before it could burn us up. But I did not direct it in any way. Someone else did that."

Senrid shook his head. "How do you know?"

Autumn pressed her lips together, then said, "I—I felt it. Someone took that magic-knot, and shaped its direction after I threw it."

Senrid's eyes narrowed. "We have to figure out who stuck their unwanted snout in, and why, before we can get out of here." He was walking again. "I hate being shoved about on someone else's game board."

"So," I snarled, unable to stay quiet any longer, "do Faline and I."

Senrid gave me a fast, nasty glance over his shoulder. "Then why did she open her big mouth in the first place?"

"Because some rock-brained fleeb—naming no names— was about to invade another country that was no threat and had done absolutely nothing to warrant it," I shot back. "*She* felt she had a moral obligation. Is that your claim?"

"Of course it is," he said derisively. "'Moral' just translates out to 'I'm right and you're wrong,' therefore I had a *moral* obligation to reclaim our old lands until your friend elbowed in—"

I was so mad I had to get out of there. It was either that or strangle that creep. So I flung myself into the water and whooshed out my breath in a big storm of bubbles. I couldn't hear voices—couldn't see anything but the blue-lit spheres rising like perfect round crystals to the surface.

I didn't go anywhere. Where would I go? So I lay there underwater, enjoying the magic, and trying to get rid of my rage, justified as it was. Anger was useless, and my temper had gotten me into too many messes for me to give in to it now.

So I decided I had to go back. I wouldn't apologize—that would be fake, since I regretted nothing I'd said—but I'd go on as if that exchange hadn't happened, and if Senrid did the same, then, well, at least we could work together long enough to get away from this world, and never see one another again.

So I let myself float up to the surface, but when my head broke, I heard Senrid say, "...another bigmouthed, cowardly hypocrite as bad as Kyale. Worse, because she's managed to learn a few spells." He had to be talking about me. My anger *whazoomed* back!

Autumn said, "I don't know Kyale, but I do know that CJ is no hypocrite—what she says is what she thinks—and she's no coward. No one who stands up to Shnit of the Chwahir, on behalf of not just friends but people she doesn't know, is a coward."

"Shnit of the Chwahir, eh?" Senrid said, and he laughed. But it wasn't a mean laugh—not a *haw haw!*, but more of a *hoo, really?*

Severely embarrassed, I ducked below the surface again. Leander had also gone into the water. He was way below me, almost out of sight.

Stretching my arms before me into a point and kicking hard, I dove downward, the water streaming around me, and followed him.

We swam like that for a long time, Leander diving ever deeper, and looking around; he saw me because you can't hide in the water, but then I wasn't trying to hide. Finally he slowed, waiting for me to catch up, and stretched out a hand—we could 'talk' by thinking at one another, if we touched. I grabbed his wrist.

I didn't think it would be easy, but it shouldn't be nearly so hard if all four of us look. Let's go back and get the others.

I thought back: *What are we looking for?*

What Senrid said: evidence of an outside agent of some sort.

Not someone lurking around, spying? I made a face—as if someone really were watching me.

No. If someone sent us, then what we're looking for has to be outside of the norm, and it has to be reasonably close by, or why weren't we dropped anywhere else on the world? Leander thought at me.

In silence we swam all the way back, and when we broke surface, Leander explained his idea to Senrid.

Lights shining from the city indicated that others were waking up. Senrid said, "Let's go now."

We all knew he didn't want Kyale insisting on accompanying us, which she would if she saw Leander leaving. Leander said nothing; I looked at his face as he treaded water near me. His dark hair was plastered down over his forehead, and his face was completely blank. I was not the only one who wanted to get this mess over with and get home.

Autumn gave me a rather rueful grin, then she dove. I followed.

This time Senrid led the way, and we swam down and down, looking for I-didn't-know-what. The others seemed to know; at least they kept scanning back and forth.

Autumn shot ahead, swimming with a remarkable speed. We followed until we reached our island, now settled onto the bottom of the ocean. The trees waved gently in the water, which was dimly lit by shifting shafts from the morning sun far above.

We circled the island, striking into an even deeper area—and the next sudden move was from Senrid.

He flung out his arms, and I stopped, somersaulting. Leander swooped down and clamped a hand on Senrid's arm. Autumn next; I grabbed her, so I wouldn't have to touch Senrid, because the mean part of me wanted to pinch or scratch, to hurt him like his comment about Faline's big mouth had hurt me. Then I forgot my grudge when Senrid's thought came: *... sensed black magic—and hey! The binding is lifted. I have my magic back.*

Same here! Leander and I had the same thought at the same time.

Autumn's surprise and consternation flashed through us all. It was she who'd sensed the presence of magic that Leander had looked for, but couldn't find.

Senrid had found it because he knew that kind of magic.

Black magic, Leander thought. His feelings leaked through along with the words: he was worried about what we'd do now.

Senrid's thought came, sardonic as his voice, but with no other emotions. *Warded very neatly, too. It would have taken me longer to find it.*

What's 'it'? I asked.

Mirror ward, a vicious one. It's an enclosed area, so my guess is that someone is being kept prisoner inside.

Can you break it? Leander asked. *I sure can't.*

Don't even try, Senrid said. *This kind of mirror ward is especially designed for white magic. It'll send your magic right back onto you instead of disintegrating it.*

Can you break it? Leander asked again.

Yes. Easily. I had to practice setting them up for my uncle, and I always memorized the antidotes to his spells.

Question is, are we ready for whatever happens when we break the ward? Especially since we just got proof someone put us here, and has been running us like yearlings on a longe line? Now some of his feelings leaked through—he was ready for a fight.

Leander's perplexity matched mine so closely that for a moment or two I got almost dizzy; Senrid might be ready for a battle, but what if we faced an army of mages? Even with our magic mysteriously restored, we weren't ready for that. Or even an army without magic could do us in just as easily, I thought in disgust. May's well be sweating it out in Marloven Hess all over again!

But then came Autumn's thought, sure and clear and kindly. *This is not our world. Black magic is new here. I think we have to let the squid-folk, and the humans, and the tould-hayin know—and let them decide what to do.*

ৡৎ CℜℰᎧ ও

𝒜nd so we did.

Why make this part any longer? It's not actually our story—we were only the "strange foreign visitors" who were the unwitting causes of events we didn't even see.

Autumn and Leander did all the talking. Senrid stayed by himself somewhere, and I slogged back and found Faline and Kitty, who were busy with the local kids.

"What's going on?" Kitty asked.

"Magic stuff," I said, too weary of it all to explain.

And they didn't want to hear it.

"Yeccch," Kitty and Faline said together. And laughed.

Two more days passed, and then Senrid broke the spells. He'd warned the squid-folk that he didn't know what kind of tracers were on the wards, and who they'd bring, but if they did bring some mages, we never saw them.

That was the weird thing. We never saw the prisoners *or* the villains—someone had found this world, I guess, discovered they had no black magic, and thought it might serve as a hideout for prisoners now, and maybe serve some other purpose later.

The squids shot from ignorance to a new, strong form of magic in those two days, with a speed that frightened us all—even Senrid.

But they were going to wait until we were gone, and then close their world-gate off.

And so we gave the bands back, and stood around in the stone city, and the humans all gathered to watch us go—

But before any of us could perform a spell someone else got in first. Someone very fast, very powerful.

Whazeem, suddenly *transfer!* Before anyone had a chance to say anything—which made me almost glad.

ಋಲ಼ಲ಼೧಼ఴ

Next thing I knew, I was sitting on the floor in the white castle, Faline next to me, our clothes making a pool of salt water on the glistening white floor.

Clair came in, grinned when she saw us both, and she dropped right down next to us. "What happened?"

"CJ got us outa bein' pincushions," Faline began. "But then we got splatted somewhere else, and nothing made any sense, except you shoulda seen their city!"

I told Clair everything, and she listened, as always, without interrupting.

"...so we never did find out who sent us—or why," I finished. "And we don't know who we rescued, where they come from, or who put them there. It's so ... so pointless!"

Clair bit her lip, making her thinking hard face. Then spoke. "Not pointless. Not that much magic. Somebody didn't want you kids killed, so he or she interfered. And sent you where magic was needed. Then brought you safely back when you'd done what you were sent to do."

"But who? Why? Why not just tell us?"

She shook her head slowly. "It could be that Autumn's magic at that cave place drew the eyes of someone very powerful. Or maybe Autumn herself is being watched." She smiled a little. "Or Senrid."

"I hope he figures it out, if it's he who's being watched. He's going to *hate* that," I gloated. "Eccch. Speaking of Senrid, how is Ndand? Where is she?"

Clair waved a hand toward the great doors opening into the cloud city. "She's probably still over listening to the musicians who play for the theater."

I sat up, my sodden gown squelching around me. "Huh? That little group with the flutes and the strings?"

"Yes. The day I broke the last spell she changed." Clair opened her eyes wide, drew in a breath, threw her arms wide. "Like this. She said she'd never seen color so bright, or heard sounds so clear and sweet—like birds. And wind through the trees. Her eyes were fine, by the way—or had been, until her father tried some sort of weird spell meant, I think, to make her able to see in the dark—"

"Spy in the dark, is more like it."

"Probably. Anyway, when it didn't work, he couldn't undo it. His ability with magic is about what yours was after your first year here."

"Because he keeps messing up spells by cussing! Wow. Is she, well, like Senrid?" I made a prune-face.

Clair grinned. "I don't know what he's like, except through your account, but she's very quiet. Very deliberate in her movements, when she finally makes one. That first day I took her on a tour of the cloud city, and she kept stopping. I think we spent half a bell before the stained-glass display on Glazier Corner. Then, when she heard the musicians practice, she wouldn't leave. She's gone back there every day since, and sits and listens. I guess her father never permitted any kind of music, so she'd never heard any in her life. She can't seem to get enough of it."

"She probably doesn't want to go back to that spackle-gnarg of a castle," Faline spoke up for the first time, hugging her knees close. She chuckled. "I sure wouldn't!"

"She's ambivalent. Afraid of her father. I told her there is no hurry in deciding. Come on! Let's tell the others you're home. You can get a bath—clear water—and get rid of that soggy-looking black dress, then how about that chocolate pie?

Janil's made one every few days, waiting for you to come home."

Faline jumped up. I got to my feet more slowly in that heavy, sodden dress. "Well, whoever the Prime Noser is who's watching and blasting us places right and left, I trust that he, or she, or it has decided that Mearsies Heili and Marloven Hess won't cross one another's history again for a hundred years."

As usual, my prediction was a hundred percent wrong.

So ends this segment of CJ Sherwood's records.

PART THREE

ONE

While Faline and CJ gratefully settled back into normal life, unknown to them, two more Mearsieans were about to meet Senrid.

Puddlenose Sherwood was very certain of two things.

One: he loathed and distrusted political power.

Two: he loathed and distrusted most adults, especially those who sought political power.

What shaped him this way?

His mother, oldest daughter of King Tesmer Sherwood of Mearsies Heili, had passed the throne to her next sister because she couldn't stand to stay in one place for long. She found and married another adventurer companion, and they had a child eventually, who it was easiest (they shortly discovered) to leave back at home with her sisters Mearsieanne and Murael.

Puddlenose's mother also had a brother, Doumei Sherwood, who had craved power right from the start. Since his two older sisters would not let him be king, he was early suborned by the Chwahir with promises of position and power if he turned against his own family and land, which he did.

His first order was to get the baby, again which he did.

Well, this isn't Puddlenose's story, so there is no purpose into going into the grim details of Puddlenose's life among the Chwahir. Take it as truth that it *was* grim, and life-threatening, and that by the time he got away for good, Puddlenose had developed some remarkable survival traits, all of which he hid under his natural desire to spend his life traveling, having fun, adventuring, and righting wrongs—the sort of wrongs he'd been helpless to right when he was small and held by Shnit.

By then Puddlenose was fifteen. His younger cousin Clair, now queen of Mearsies Heili, gave him the spell for not aging, and so he stayed fifteen—a tall boy who'd shot up to just under six feet, with thick brown hair, a square, friendly face, and brown skin from all that traveling. Clair had also found and performed on him the Universal Language Spell, so once he heard a tongue, it translated itself into his mind as Mearsiean.

On one of his visits home he met a boy named Christoph who was a friend of one of Clair's regional governors, originally from Earth, and together they adventured their way up and down the Toaran continent before they set out east over the sea.

They were on another continent now, between adventures, seeking a place to sleep.

And so a peaceful evening fell, that autumn of '735, not long after that day in the cave on the border of Marloven Hess. The sun moved west, leaving darkness over the rest of the continent—including Puddlenose and Christoph, asleep in a barn.

Everyone transferred straight from the water world to home, except for 713 (now Claid again)—whose wish for a future life had vaguely centered on a place with a lot of horses, and so he was shifted to another continent entirely, where he found himself sitting at a roadside, a scattering of six-sided Sartoran coins around him, gleaming in the moonlight.

Puzzled, he picked up the coins and trod off to begin a new life.

The other who did not transfer home was Senrid.

He was tired from the two sleepless days of magic preparation and the tense wait. He was dizzy from the long transfer. But he gathered the last of his energy and tried an assessment spell—and was not surprised that yet another ward against transferring home had been set against him. It would take access to his magic books to dissolve it. He was too weary to sustain more than a flash of anger, or even to explore his new surroundings. It was quiet, warm, dry, and smelled good, so he dropped flat into the fresh hay and slid instantly into slumber.

He was running in dreamscapes when Christoph woke first.

He woke because an outflung hand caught him squarely in the mazzard, which was an invitation to heave himself onto the snoring Puddlenose and try to choke him.

A wrestling match started, a frequent occurrence, and despite the energetic thumps and grunts and the flying hay, one completely without malice. The battle ended only when the two rolled onto a third person.

Puddlenose and Christoph scrambled back, and Senrid, rudely awakened, sat up, blinking.

The three stared at one another in the warm reddish morning light. Cracks of bright morning sunrays slanted in between old boards in the barn wall. The air was warm, and dust motes swirled around them, brilliant pinpoints of gold.

Christoph sneezed. He pointed at Senrid and said, in Mearsiean, "You smell like brine."

"I should think so," Senrid answered in the same language.

Puddlenose was silent. He noted the accent in the stranger's voice, and the watchful expression in the gray-blue eyes. Otherwise Senrid looked somewhat like Christoph—short, blond, round-faced. Only Christoph's usual expression was cheerful, his movements a kind of agreeable drift or slouch; this newcomer's expression was wary, his posture tense.

"Been in the ocean long enough," Senrid continued.

"In?" Christoph repeated. "Or on."

"In."

"How long?"

"Hard to say. Could have been a week or a month. Time being different on other worlds, and the passing of nights hard to count when you're far below the surface."

He spoke with precision, his tone bland.

Puddlenose said, "I'm Puddlenose. He's Christoph."

Wariness narrowed the other boy's eyes. "I'm Senrid."

Puddlenose shrugged, Christoph nodded. If it was recognition the newcomer was expecting, he didn't get it. They were used to strange adventures—and adventurers.

"Of Marloven Hess."

No one reacted.

Senrid ventured another question. "Your accent—are you Mearsieans?"

"Our home base," Puddlenose said, and he would have dropped the subject there, though his curiosity was now waking up and sniffing about. He'd learned to bide his time.

Senrid's face had gone tight, as if he were holding in rage as he glared at a pair of riding boots sitting neatly nearby. They had been transferred from the rock on the water world. Eventually it became clear that whoever had put Senrid here had done it without his permission or knowledge—and had left the boots as a not-so-subtle reminder that yes, he was being watched.

Meanwhile Christoph had considered the preposition; Senrid hadn't said 'from' as most people would, he'd said 'of' and in many lands that particular word often denoted dominion.

"Of," he asked, "as in it belongs to you?"

"What of it?" Senrid countered.

"Nothing," Christoph said, shrugging. "Curious, is all. I mean, you're here, and I don't recall you climbing up."

"I was put here," Senrid stated in a hard voice. "You wouldn't have happened to come here the same way?"

"No. We walked. Then climbed. My guess is, you're probably here as someone's idea of a joke, but I don't know who," Puddlenose said easily. "Now." He decided to do some indirect testing of his own. "If you like pulling rank—which we don't—ol' Christoph here had it a long time ago on another world, and if I get nabbed again, Shnit of the Chwahir thinks he can make me his heir."

He and Christoph said "Yeccch" together in what was clearly long-established ritual.

Puddlenose watched Senrid register the word 'Chwahir'. Senrid said, his disbelief clear, "A Chwahir wants a Mearsiean as heir?"

"Only if my brains are enchanted out. He thinks watching me betray my family would be the entertainment high point of his overlong life."

Puddlenose saw that impact Senrid. It wasn't an overt reaction—no more than a tightening of the corners of his mouth, a hint of a sympathetic revulsion—but it was enough to enable Puddlenose to decide that whatever else lay in Senrid's background, he was going to be no threat to Christoph or him.

So on with the adventure—whatever it was to be. "Let's seek out some eats," Puddlenose suggested.

Senrid turned his palm up.   Then, as they started climbing down, "Puddlenose? Is that a Chwahir name?"

Puddlenose laughed. "No, it's a Chwahir insult. Shnit's idea was to stick me with a traditional Chwahir name, but he couldn't decide if my poisonous Mearsiean self deserved one of their kings' names, or if he should give me a lowly one. To add to the insult to Mearsies Heili, you know."

Christoph, who'd heard (and told) this story many times over, added with enthusiasm, "So they mostly called him by insults. None of them being fond of babies. Puddlenose was the most frequent, but there are some other goodies—"

"Addlepate," Puddlenose said.

"Eckbittle—"

"What's that?" Senrid asked, looking askance. From the wariness of his expression, the tighness of his smile, Puddlenose guessed Senrid couldn't tell if he was the target of an elaborate joke or if these two crazies he'd been dumped with were serious.

"You don't want Eckbittle translated," Christoph said with a grim smile.

"But the girls think it sounds funny, so we keep it in the Royal Name," Puddlenose explained. "CJ amended some of the others, going by sound. Like Eluded-Glue. Oh, and Puddlenose in Chwahir sounds, according to CJ, like 'Prunebald' so that stays in. Then there's Louseface—"

"What's a louse?"

"A villain, according to CJ. Muttonmouth is another. And Dummkopf, but both Gwen and CJ insist they're real Earth words, or mutton is, anyway."

"Butterfingers, though, we can translate through," Christoph offered with a helpful air.

As the two traded off with the names they scouted around, stopping only when they found cribs of freshly harvested fruit. They helped themselves and slid out into the open air, Puddlenose ending with, "They never knew my real name at home, or at least the one aunt who did disappeared after Clair's mother died. And though I've considered many fine new ones—"

"My favorite is Erdelarintarsa," Christoph interjected. "Sounds good and pompous! But the girls favor some of the old stinkers in Mearsiean history." He snickered.

"Anyway," Puddlenose said, waving an apple, "anything I tried, I'd forget that they meant me when somebody used it. So I stuck with Puddlenose. Which does remind me every time I hear it that I escaped. Ha ha!"

"Ho ho!" Christoph said, and they eased out, silent as they looked furtively around.

The owners of the farm were all busy in the cornfield not too distant. The barn that the boys were in was auxiliary storage, at the edge of the property, so they reached the road unseen.

The sky was blue, the air warm. As the morning progressed the weather warmed, and it was with relief that Puddlenose spotted the line of trees bordering a meandering line across the fields that denoted a good-sized spring.

"Water," he said, pointing. "Shall we?"

Senrid's longing was unmistakable.

They found a dammed-off section that local kids probably used as a pool when they weren't busy with harvest chores. The three had it to themselves, so they stripped off their grimy clothes. Puddlenose stashed his sword in a convenient place, noting that Senrid had been sporting a wicked-looking dagger in a wrist sheath: he cleaned it first, examining it this way and that with an expert eye before resheathing it.

Interesting, Puddlenose thought. Bundling his clothes under one arm, he dove in.

Puddlenose and Christoph were content to wedge their duds against the rocks forming the dam, letting the water's own action do whatever cleaning it might, but Senrid took the time to scrub at his clothing with considerable vigor before he set it neatly on the rocks beside his wrist sheath and boots to dry.

Puddlenose, idly splashing, looked him over. Though Senrid was smaller and slighter in build than Christoph, he was solid muscle. He was also skinny in the way that people who don't eat enough are skinny, and his back across his shoulders showed the straight pink horizontal scars of caning harsh enough to draw blood. Puddlenose recognized those scars because he had some of his own, though not as many, and far older, from his days with the Chwahir. Lots of trouble, then, in Senrid's life, and chocolate pies smothered in cream few and far between, eh?

Puddlenose said nothing, though, except to propose a game of diving for rocks, to which Senrid readily assented. The three played about for a time, then climbed out and dried off in the sun, Puddlenose's and Christoph's clothes having also been spread on rocks by then.

When they decided to dress and move on, the clothes were not yet dry, but the cool, damp fabric felt good in the hot afternoon sun. Puddlenose noted that the dagger had vanished again into Senrid's heavy linen long-sleeved shirt. He also wore his trousers outside his riding boots, instead of tucked in. At first glance one wouldn't know he was wearing riding boots, unless one looked at the heels, which were made to catch against stirrups—usually for those in some kind of military calling, who might need that extra kind of balance.

Interesting.

After a short time walking along a road, Puddlenose said casually, "So you recognized our accent, huh? Not many know about Mearsies Heili, as it isn't one of your biggies in size or in rep."

Senrid turned his palm up. "I've met a couple Mearsieans."

"Like who?" Christoph added, walking backwards. "Here, let's cut across yon fallow-field. This road is boring. Any of the queen's friends? If you've ever sampled Faline's jokes, you wouldn't forget those in a hurry."

"I met Faline," Senrid said, following obligingly as the other two struck northward into a field. "You're right about the jokes."

"So you met the girls! Hear any of CJ's better pocalubes?" Christoph chortled.

"Pocalubes?" Senrid asked.

"Name the girls made up for their insults. They have rules, you know, for the proper insulting of villains."

"I heard a few," Senrid admitted.

"Ho! So the girls have had an adventure since we saw them last, eh? Tell us what happened, then when we go home, we can annoy them by already knowing."

"Oh, you'll get it better from them," Senrid said.

And the subject necessarily ended then because Puddlenose saw something in the grass at his feet, started back, then tripped over the end of his sword and fell full length in the grass. The smell of broken herbs made him sneeze, and he sat up dizzily, to find Christoph and Senrid staring at a girl apparently their own age whose friendly face was disconcertingly half-invisible.

TWO

At the same moment that Senrid landed in that barn in East Arland, Leander and Kyale were transferred directly to the courtyard of their castle in Crestel, where it was still light. When the transfer dizziness passed, they found themselves staring up at the familiar ivy-covered walls of home.

"Ah! My kits!" Kyale exclaimed, and ran inside.

Those of her feline friends in view were all hale and happy; only the smaller ones were around. Once she'd greeted each, and petted them, and crooned over them, she called to Llhei, her old governess, to prepare her a bath.

Leander paused, wondering who had transferred them, and only them, to their home in Crestel. Like Senrid, he felt the pressure of an invisible but powerful hand behind their strange adventure. No hints who, or more important, why.

Only one thing was clear: the unknown power was not inimical. So he dismissed conjecture with a mental shrug and ran down the main hallway to the anteroom that had become his unofficial interview room, and there he found Alaxandar, the tough, stocky liegeman who served as his steward.

Alaxandar's dark eyes widened in surprise, and then narrowed in rare, expressive relief.

"You're back. What happened?"

"Magic tangle with Senrid over the hill," Leander said, tipping his head westward. "We were thrown off-world for a time. News? Are our spies still in place? And all right?"

"So that was true, then, about the magic battle," Alaxandar said grimly. "Rumor had it that the Regent had killed the boy at last, and was taking over. Our spies are all right, but all they hear is rumor—that's all anyone hears. Tdanerend hasn't issued any statements that have reached Collet, whose latest letter reached Arel at the border two days ago. I opened it, as you instructed."

Leander heard the question in his voice, and grinned, relieved, oh, so very much to be home. "Right. As for 'the boy,' he was with us. I assume he was sent home as we were—though what that's going to mean is anyone's guess."

Alaxandar shook his head slowly. "Tdanerend is making a power play of some kind, and I'll wager anything you care to name that we've been selected as the hapless victims on whom he's going to exhibit his military prowess. He's prated too much over there about reunification."

"He wants the border mines," Leander said. "So what's he doing?"

"He's got riders all along the border, and there are military camps forming out beyond the pass. Here, I'll show you on the map."

Leander sighed. "I'll have to take a look, but a bath first. Not a frame-zap, but a real bath. I've been soaking in saltwater for weeks. What is the date, anyway?"

Alaxandar followed him upstairs, and while Leander had a fast bath, filled him in on the details.

When he emerged, and headed down toward the kitchens to wait for the hot meal the cook was preparing, Kyale joined him, eager for news.

Every statement Alaxandar made about Tdanerend or Senrid was punctuated by Kyale's heartfelt insults— interpolations which amused the other two at first, Kyale having memorized a lot of CJ's favorite expressions, but slowly got to be wearing as she kept it up with untiring energy.

Leander responded with patience. Alaxandar began looking sardonic, which made Kitty defensive. He'd been laughing before, so why wasn't he now? Because he was a sourpie, of course. And hated her.

And that in turn increased her belligerent tone.

"Since dinner isn't ready yet I think I'd better to look at the border," Leander said at last, when it was clear that the conversation was going to founder on Kyale's more frequent interruptions.

"I'm going, too," Kyale said promptly.

"No you're not," Leander said, and when she sucked in a breath to yell, he stuck out his tongue at her.

She choked on laughter; he did the transfer magic, and vanished.

"Huh," she said, and raced upstairs to the library where he kept his magic books.

Lessons in magic had been sporadic at best, because she loathed the dullness of elemental memorization that he insisted on. Her idea of learning magic was to get spells for wonderful things. His insistence on her learning the boring way, just because he had, seemed stupid.

She ran her finger along the books until she came to the one she'd mentally marked before, and pulled it down. She knew that in a transfer spell you were supposed to think on your destination. That was easy—she pictured Leander, but from the back, and slowly read the spell.

Nothing happened.

Huffing in annoyance, she wondered if he'd messed with it to spite her, and read faster—then gasped as magic sucked at her from inside.

She appeared behind Leander at a distance of about fifty paces, which placed her beyond a couple of tall ash trees. She felt sick to her stomach, and kept the book tightly clutched against her until the dizziness passed.

Scary, she thought, but when she saw Leander's dark head in front of her, triumph replaced the magic-reaction. He stood on the very edge of a rocky cliff, looking at something below. Since she couldn't see his face, she did not know what it was he was studying—or how he felt about it.

She looked beyond, to the plains of Marloven Hess, which stretched away into a purplish haze in the far distance. Forestland in the lower hills gave way to the squares of farms. Most of those squares were bare; only the grapevines were left, on the south-facing hills, and winter-hay, and some seed-flax.

It was a pretty land, she thought, if you didn't know who lived there.

She turned her gaze southward, toward the green hills that formed the borderland. On the Vasande side, she could see neat slopes of dark green—mulberry trees, a part of the silk trade that Leander was trying so hard to get going again.

Without warning Leander vanished again, and she felt a puff of cold breeze in her face. Alone, she felt apprehensive, and so she opened the book. Fear made her accurate; she pictured the library, and made it on the first try.

When the reaction dissipated, she shoved the book back into the shelf, and retreated—almost running smack into Leander, who was reaching for the door to the library.

"What were you doing in there?" he asked.

She eyed him, sorting his tone. He was annoyed, all right, but she could see the worry in the way his brows quirked.

"Standing on my head," she snarled, because she knew she'd been in the wrong. "What a stupid question."

"I thought you'd given up messing with my books."

"Well," she said, testing, "I could say I don't know what you're talking about."

He shook his head. "Won't work. You could have asked."

"I did, and you said no."

He opened the door. "Come in."

She gave him a narrow glance, then nodded regally. She'd already worked it out in her head that he was to blame.

Leander followed her inside, repressing a sigh. Kitty was twelve, but sometimes she seemed more like six. When he was twelve, he'd already had the responsibility of people depending on him, and because of it, he found it hard to understand a kid who'd been raised in luxury but was otherwise totally ignored by a cold, cruel, ambitious woman who killed anyone in her way with no apparent regrets. Kitty wasn't even a blood relation, but one forced upon him when Mara Jinea married his father, but she was here, she needed a family, or a semblance of a family, and so did he. So he had to find a way to make it work.

Though he didn't understand her thinking, he was beginning to predict her reactions. Getting mad would guarantee that Kitty saw herself as a victim, no matter how difficult she'd been.

So he wouldn't get mad.

"I'd love to teach you magic," he said. "It'd be great to have some help. But you've got to learn the basics. That transport spell—if you don't do it right, well, you saw what happened when CJ and Senrid's magic tangled."

She stared at him, her eyes huge. "I didn't think of that," she admitted.

"And the only reason why we're here—still alive—is that some stronger magic interfered," Leander added.

She was listening.

"It could be even worse," he said. "You could get caught between times."

"I thought it was only black magic that was dangerous. Not white," she retorted. "We got caught in Senrid's nasty spell, not CJ's. Or yours."

"Everything in black magic is dangerous, for it mostly is summoned for force, which spends magic with equally rapid force. But there are dangerous spells in white, and transport is one of them. Why do you think most people take months to get around the usual way—and some magicians even travel normally? If it was really easy, we'd all be using it all the time." He pointed. "Don't you feel tired right now?"

Her lips compressed, which was enough of an answer. Then she sighed. "All right. I won't. No more nagging."

"Then promise me," he said. "It's for your own safety, not mine. Promise you won't mess with magic any more, not until I can give you lessons." He blocked the door, risking a tantrum—and retaliation—but he counted on that residual fear he saw in her face.

And he was right.

Though she'd mentally blamed him for not teaching her, she was secretly relieved. Though she couldn't show it, for that would be giving in. "All right. I promise. Now, is the lecture over? I'm hungry."

"Lecture over," he said, relieved and not trying to hide it. "Let's go get something to eat, preferably something that has nothing whatsoever to do with the ocean."

Kitty laughed. "Sounds good to me."

They walked downstairs together.

THREE

The see-through girl greeted the three boys with tranquil politeness.

Christoph was too busy laughing at Puddlenose's clumsiness to pay much attention to her, and Puddlenose was distracted by Senrid's appalled reaction.

Christoph was the first to speak, after a protracted silence that might have been embarrassing to anyone else. But Senrid was too furious, and Puddlenose too curious about Senrid's fury, to notice.

Christoph said, head to one side, "Are you a ghost?"

"You can call me that, if you like," the girl replied with a smile. Her voice was clear, as clear as the golden afternoon sunlight on her face and form. She appeared to be an ordinary girl, wearing an old-fashioned gown of unbleached cotton. But they could see through her, and she cast no shadow. "What matters most is not who I am, but what I can do for you."

"Not delivering gloomy portents or the like?" Puddlenose asked suspiciously, remembering some of Christoph's more gruesome tales from his Earth history, and similar tales that had woven their way into Sartorias-deles legends from other Earth travelers.

She grinned. "No. You make your own future, you know that. But sometimes the way you are going is fraught with more peril than you are aware. And sometimes someone like me can see consequences of your actions that you cannot see."

Senrid said, "Speak your piece."

The flat, almost hostile tone of his voice, and his stance—arms crossed, head slightly back—startled both Puddlenose and Christoph.

The girl's blue eyes turned his way, and seemed to gather light and focus it, like gemstones in the noonday sun.

"When you want my help, Senrid Indevan Montredaun-An, ask for it. Once, only, you may call upon me and I will aid you."

Senrid's lip curled. "Really? What kind of help might that be?"

"You will decide what, and when."

"And if. Unless you'll waft me back home now and annihilate my uncle and all his adherents in one bloody strike."

The girl did not react, except the blue of her eyes seemed to intensify so that it almost hurt to look at them. "For that, you must go to Norsunder," she said. "As you know. And you know the cost. There would be no more freedom of choice, ever. Ever, before death, or after."

The mention of Norsunder silenced all three boys.

"You can call me Erdrael. I will be waiting." And she vanished in a flash of light that made the boys' eyes water.

"Well," Christoph said after another protracted pause, "that was sufficiently weird."

Senrid stared at the ground where the manifestation had stood. The grass was unbent, the flowers nodding gently in the afternoon breeze.

"It was a damned taunt," Senrid said. "And she was probably just an illusion."

Puddlenose whistled softly, sensing that he'd managed to trip over one of those moments that make vast and radical changes in history.

Those changes weren't going to be initiated by him.

"Illusions have to be cast, and little I know of magic, I don't think that kind is easy. Either way, someone has quite the interest in you," he said to Senrid.

Senrid cursed, with such venom both the others were taken aback. But as suddenly as he began he stopped, and shrugged, though they saw the effort it took.

"Someone," Senrid said, "has been messing with me for the past couple of weeks, and I wish whoever it was would step right up and we could discuss it my way."

Christoph glanced from Senrid's hands to his eyes, then said casually—it being clear to him as well as Puddlenose that whatever Erdrael really represented, it was definitely not the damnation of Norsunder's soul-eaters and timeless darkness— "Puddlenose, only you could manage to trip over a ghost."

"I didn't," Puddlenose said. "It was the sudden light. Made me dizzy. I tripped over my trusty blade." He slapped the sword at his side.

Christoph snickered. "No, protest all you want, but I am going to believe, no, more importantly, I am going to *inform everyone you know*, that you managed to trip over a ghost and take a header." He bent, gasping with laughter. Then he stopped, snorted, and exclaimed, "I smell the sea! And it ain't Senrid!"

"I smell it too," Puddlenose said slowly, as he felt that distinct inner 'pull'. "Hoo! You got it?"

Christoph nodded. "First felt it in my dream last night. My, what a day so far!"

"Got what?" Senrid asked, eying them askance.

"My cousin Clair put magic on us—and on Captain Heraford, who constitutes our navy—"

"Navy? I thought Mearsies Heili is landlocked," Senrid interrupted.

"Not on the east, though there's no real harbor. And then we also have the Tornacio Islands. Anyway, he's a one-ship navy. Two, now, if he has that Chwahir transport we took a while back. So if he passes us or we pass him, we know it. What's weirder is, he also seems to know it if we're in landing range and in trouble, and many times the *Tzasilia* appears on the skyline."

Senrid's brows quirked up. "I didn't know Clair Sherwood had access to that kind of magic."

"I didn't either," Puddlenose said, "but she does. Who knows, it may be not her magic, but the reason she's got white hair—we figure there's gotta be some morvende way back in our obscure ancestry—anyway, it works fine for us. C'mon, ready for a little sea voyage?"

Senrid turned his palm up.

They ran northeast, and soon found themselves on the palisade overlooking a small bay. A few ships were anchored off the shore; to the east lay a small town, but the boys did not head that way.

"There he is," Puddlenose said, pointing to a pair of three masters floating in the middle of the bay.

The closer one was elegant in line, masts raked for speed—evocative of pirate vessels, which are designed to be fast. The farther one was round-hulled and high at forecastle and stern, meant for transport and not speed. Both were rigged for square sail. "And he's got the *Lheit* out there as well!"

They butt-slid, whooping and tumbling, down to the beach; someone had spied them with a glass from the ship, and had sent a rowboat to fetch them.

The boys ran across the sand. Christoph kicked it up at Senrid, who laughed and kicked it back. Then they waded into the gentle breakers, swimming when the shoreline dropped off, and once again Senrid got his clothes briny.

The rowboat that met them had at the oars a skinny, mahogany-faced man. "Fradrici," Puddlenose called happily, climbing on board the rowboat with the ease of long practice. Then he asked, "Why are *you* doing boat duty?"

"Because I had to see your fascinating selves," the man replied, winking as he pulled Senrid up. "Because it's also my Name Day, and the ruses to get me off of *Lheit* and onto *Tzasilia* were mighty lame. Same when the Captain asked for volunteers just now, they almost threw me over the side, so I'm guessin' cook's got the last o' the eats fixin'."

"A party," Christoph breathed, splashing, and to Puddlenose, "Are we good, or what?"

Puddlenose laughed as he helped Fradrici pull Christoph over the side, and then the crewman squinted at Puddlenose. "What's that around yer neck?"

Puddlenose fingered the open neck of his shirt, and pulled out the chain. "Y'mean this?"

Fradrici squinted at the strange shell on the end. "Now, what kind o' adventure you gotten yourself into this time?"

"Listen," Puddlenose said, and raised the shell to his lips. He blew, and a low, strange note sounded across the water. The hairs on the back of his neck lifted, and he saw the others listen with the stillness that indicated a similar reaction.

Fradrici said, "Wheeee-euw! What's the story behind that one?"

"Disappointing. Some old peddler we met outside some town, I don't even remember its name. No warnings, sinister or otherwise, no mysterious offers, no news that we'd been picked as heirs to four empires. Just stopped us, gave it to us, and that was that. You know how it is with us," he said, not meaning anything, but he felt Senrid's attention on him. "Things happen, and we stumble into adventure. Or around it. Anyhow, I'm going to give the whistle to Clair. She likes this kind of thing."

Fradrici grunted, then nudged the second set of oars with his foot. "We gotta pull against the tide, so it's either two, or I take all night. So who's gonna match me?"

Puddlenose, being biggest, rubbed his hands dry on a cloth Fradrici had brought, then put some back into oarwork— the rhythm set by Christoph's cheerful insults about his weakness, interspersed with his own artistic groans and wheezes.

When they reached the side of the *Tzasilia*, Puddlenose watched Senrid watching as the rope-ladder was let down over the side, and Christoph started up. Senrid obviously knew nothing about ships. He climbed up behind Christoph, copying his every movement, and Puddlenose helped Fradrici help get the rowboat hooked to be boomed up to the waist.

Up on deck, Captain Heraford waited, looking much as he usually did—a tallish man with the weathered look of the sailor, and the sharp eye of the privateer who might have turned his hand to piracy at one time or another, though he did not do that any more.

"Welcome," he was saying to Senrid. "You've never been aboard a ship before?"

"No," Senrid said.

"You have to sign the ship's log," Christoph said. "We all do!"

And he led the way down to the captain's cabin. Puddlenose watched as Senrid wrote in block Mearsiean script his name, *Senrid*, and nothing else, but he did not comment. Neither did the captain.

"Get him settled in," Captain Heraford said to Puddlenose. "We're going to split off from *Lheit*—it's time Fradrici took his own command," he added, looking up toward the doorway, where the other man stood grinning. "But after the, ah, surprise party tonight!"

Puddlenose nodded. "C'mon. Ordinarily the first stop is the most important spot on the ship—the galley! But I think we're about to get plenty of eats. So we'll go below to storage. You'll want some swimming cutoffs while you're on board, and there's lots of extra duds." He indicated Senrid's heavy linen shirt, cotton-wool trousers, and riding boots.

Senrid flicked his hand up, and followed. Puddlenose suspected he was queasy, but Senrid clearly was not going to give in to it. In fact, after he found a hammock he liked, and changed into better clothes for summer weather on shipboard, he climbed up to the foretop to sit on a yard with Christoph.

When Puddlenose lounged over to the rail he was joined by Captain Heraford. "Your friend," he said. "Where'd you find him?"

"We woke up in a barn with him next to us." Puddlenose shrugged.

"Where's he from?"

"Said it's called Marloven Hess. No place I've ever heard of."

"Mmm," the captain said, but then he moved off to consult with the red-haired sailor at the wheel. She was someone new, Puddlenose noted, but as she was grown up, he lost interest. Sometimes Heraford hired on kids as crew, but so far they always seemed to be working their way from one land to another, and they didn't stay on crew long.

Instead, he spent some time asking old friends among the crew about the *Tzasilia*'s latest adventures, until he saw Christoph and Senrid come down. The latter's complexion had lost that greenish tinge.

He was still pale, though. Very pale—like he'd not been out in the sun much in his life.

A few days of sailing changed that. He turned pink from the balmy sunshine, and accepted the salve that the captain offered him, which caused the pink to go brown without the intervening pain caused by sunburn.

The journey was thoroughly enjoyable, starting off with Fradrici's Name Day party that first night. Ale flowed freely among the older crewmembers. Puddlenose had some—he liked the taste—but stopped when he couldn't remember the verses to songs; he noted that Senrid, like Christoph, didn't touch liquor.

The weather stayed balmy during the day, though the nights were cold, promising that winter would eventually find its way here, too. But Puddlenose did not worry about the future. He enjoyed the succession of warm days of steady wind, tacking eastward along a familiar route. Captain Heraford's few requirements of passengers allowed plenty of time for storytelling, music, and observation.

Puddlenose amused himself watching Senrid's fascination with the maze-work of ropes that controlled masts and sails, and the constant attention required to make the most of the subtle changes in wind. Senrid also watched the defense drills, when selected crew raced aloft with their bows, and the torch bearers waited below with cloth-wrapped arrows, fire, and oil, ready to light the arrows for shooting at enemy ships while the boarding parties practiced lowering their boats and clambering up the sides, weapons ready.

Senrid never said anything, though, or even asked questions. When asked to haul on a rope or even help reef or loosen one of the lower courses, he did what he was told without making any comment.

There was only one incident to mar the uneventful cruise.

The third morning or so, Puddlenose woke up before the others, a rarity. Usually Senrid was up before dawn, but he'd been poring over the captain's charts the night before when Puddlenose climbed down to his hammock, a study that apparently had kept him up most of the night.

Puddlenose and Christoph were used to waking each other with a pillow in the face, or an armlock, or some other form of clowning. Delighted at having caught Senrid asleep, he grabbed his arm to tip him out of his hammock.

Christoph laughed, expecting to see Senrid flail into wakefulness, but then he choked on his hot chocolate.

Puddlenose was only aware of a whirl and a thump that knocked his breath out; when the haze cleared he was flat on the deck, knees pinning down his arms, and thumbs pressing his windpipe as cold blue-gray eyes stared down at him.

Only for a moment. Puddlenose's breath whooshed back in as Senrid leaped up, hesitated, then extended a hand to Puddlenose. Puddlenose took it, and found himself pulled to his feet with no visible effort.

"Don't. Do that," Senrid said, his cheeks red, but his mouth white and thin.

Questions cartwheeled through Puddlenose's mind, but he banished them all, having learned one thing: Senrid did not like to be touched, or at least not taken by surprise. Whatever kind of background produced that kind of reaction raised nothing but sympathy in Puddlenose. "Right," he said cheerily. "So let's go see what's for breakfast, eh?"

∞⟨R℘⟩ᄨ

When they came in sight of land again, Puddlenose watched the uneven line for a day or two as they sailed northwards, feeling the restless pull of a new environment.

"Let's land," he said the next morning to Christoph, who was swinging in a hammock after having done a turn at deck-scrubbing.

Christoph shrugged.

Puddlenose looked over at Senrid, who sat on a barrel with the captain's telescope, surveying the shore. Senrid swung about, and smacked the scope closed.

"If you're inviting me along, I'm ready to land when you are," he said. "I'll put these through the cleaning frame and get my clothes." He indicated his borrowed shirt and cutoffs, then vanished down the hatch.

A little later Puddlenose found the captain standing behind him. "That's Everon," he said, nodding westward toward the coast.

Puddlenose shrugged.

"You haven't been up this way much, have you?" Captain Heraford commented.

"Something wrong with it, then?" Christoph asked.

"Something wrong indeed.   Everon's been under enchantment for years. Rumor has mentioned Detlev, from Norsunder."

Two sinister names seldom spoken out loud.

Senrid had reappeared; Puddlenose saw his eyes flicker to the captain's face and westward again.   His expression didn't change, but the names seemed to linger, rendering the sunlight dim, the air cold.

Puddlenose pursed his lips, feeling that draw again. "Years, huh?"

"*He* hasn't been seen for a long time," the captain said. "Just local bully-boys, half-enchanted.   The land lies under a drought, and it's reputed to be impossible to travel through."

"Well, we wouldn't have to travel through it.   But maybe we could have fun with those bullies," Puddlenose said, and scratched his head.   "I don't know why, but I've got the urge to get over there and mess about."

The Captain nodded, used to Puddlenose's trouble magnet, which he (privately) thought was akin to Clair Sherwood's abilities.   There was some kind of powerful magic buried back in that family's history—though the present generation did not know how it had gotten there.

But he knew how to keep his peace, and indeed it was some time before he discussed his feelings with Clair, who by then had learned some of what he'd surmised.

But that was much later.

Instead, Captain Heraford measured wind (coming out of the southwest, mild) against tide (flooding), and glanced up at the sails.   "If you want to go ashore, we'll stand in a little closer," he said only.

∞⟨ℜℰ⟩ℭ

"Must be the border," Christoph said shortly afterward, squinting around as the boys waded toward the beach. "Didn't he say something about drought?"

"Those shrubs and trees look all right to me," Puddlenose commented.

Senrid didn't say anything as he waded steadily, his boots and socks held up in the air so he wouldn't have soggy feet. Since neither Christoph nor Puddlenose had shoes, they didn't have that particular worry.

Puddlenose held his sword above the water, moving as quickly as he could. The breakers were greenish; he looked down, seeing plants waving back and forth, and tiny silver fish swimming about.

"Euk." Christoph was first ashore. He flapped his arms and kicked sand about, trying to dry off.

Senrid was out next. He ran his feet through the sand, and when they were dry, he sat down and reshod himself, then pulled his soggy black trousers down over the boots. Puddlenose noticed for the first time the tan piping down the outer seams of the trousers: some kind of uniform? His white shirt was plain but very well made of heavy linen, fastened by costly carved buttons instead of laces.

Christoph gave a squawk as the bushes up ahead thrashed like a herd of horses was coming.

He was nearest the edge of the shrubbery. Before Puddlenose could speak Senrid said sharply, "Cut along."

Christoph nodded, ducking toward the nearest bush.

A troop of armed men in rough country wear came boiling down a pathway in the shrubbery. Puddlenose groaned and whipped his sword free of its scabbard. A moment later he saw Senrid holding his knife, his stance a half-crouch. Senrid sent the knife spinning directly at the gut of a foe about to try closing with him. Only a quick twist kept the man from being killed outright, but the dagger caught him in the side.

Strange, that the kid would throw it (though it was an excellent throw) and not fight with it.

Then Puddlenose was too busy to do anything but try to keep himself away from the three who ringed him.

Inwardly he sighed, knowing that this was not going to be any fight he could win. *Why* did he have to come ashore here? The Captain had warned him. I'm a rockhead, he thought.

Puddlenose kicked up a fan of sand and the three backed away, one clawing at his eyes and bumbling into the second (there was a strong whiff of stale beer in the air, explaining a lot about the skills of their opponents); Puddlenose risked a glance. Christoph was nowhere in sight, Senrid rolling with a much larger antagonist—who let out a yelp of pain and flung himself backward in the sand, whooping for breath, arms folded across his midsection.

Three heavies dropped on Senrid then, two more hovering just outside the flailing feet, hands, and kicked-up sand.

Puddlenose realized a heartbeat later he'd watched for too long. He blocked a strike—late—his arm hurt, the remainder of the patrol rushed him, and the fight was over.

Senrid squirmed in the sand with his assailants, but moments later they stood up, Senrid gripped on either side. They were all covered with sand, right to the eyebrows.

Next came an ignominious march up the shore thick, prickly bushes and twisted alder to a sheltered grove of maple and hemlock. The air was noticeably cooler when they reached the shade, not that Puddlenose was comfortable. Their captors bound them tightly and left them under a tree, guarded by several of their number who stood behind them, armed and silent.

Senrid's eyes moved about ceaselessly, but he said nothing. Puddlenose didn't speak either. He waited for a sign from Christoph; as long as he was loose, the game was still to be played.

Sure enough, the two who'd left returned, motioned to the guards, and Puddlenose and Senrid were hauled to their feet and shoved along a narrow trail through thick, scrubby grasses. Puddlenose saw the dark, waxy leddas plants from which cobblers made shoes and boots, and he wondered again if they were on the border of Everon, or if the captain's information was old.

Abruptly they entered a clearing, and found themselves in a tent camp. To the biggest tent they were hustled, and in.

There, to their surprise, they found not only a commander of some sort—tall, out of shape, pompous face—but Christoph, who smiled innocently and looked at the boys without a trace of recognition.

"...and I was hoping for employment, since my brother's group was sent north," he was saying in whatever the local lingo was.

"Wait. Who's this?" the commander asked the guards, indicating the two prisoners.

"Three-master flying a flag we don't recognize dropped 'em offshore," one of the guards said.

"What for?" the commander asked, and then he said to Puddlenose and Senrid, "Who are you? Why did you land here?"

Standing behind the commander's elbow, Christoph shook his head once, and Puddlenose shrugged.

Senrid shrugged too.

"Can't you understand me?" the commander said loudly—as if volume would translate his words.

Puddlenose said in Mearsiean, "What's your game?"

"Oh, let's have some fun," Christoph replied in the same language.

The captain looked at him, startled, and Christoph said in a smarmy voice, "I learned their tongue when I was young. Shall I interpret?"

"Go ahead." The commander gestured. "Find out who they are."

"What'll I say?" Christoph asked. "Want to get in with these guys?"

"Why not? Maybe we can find out something interesting. At any rate, I don't want to do the prisoner role," Puddlenose said.

"Who are they?" the commander asked.

"They're Puddlenose and Senrid, and they escaped from a pirate ship. They're willing to work."

The commander looked them over, stroked his chin, and said, "Hmm. What can they do?"

"Tell 'em we'd make great spies," Puddlenose said, trying not to grin.

"Carry water, help with the horses. Spy, if you need it, because who'd suspect boys?" Christoph said with a helpful air.

The commander swallowed that without the slightest evidence of suspicion about Christoph's fortuitous appearance, and Puddlenose rejoiced inside. Whatever else might be out of date, Heraford's assessment of the local talent had been spot on. Maybe they'd have some fun after all.

The captain said, "We could use a couple boys for the scut-work. You'll need to translate."

"Well, I did come looking for a job," Christoph said unctuously.

The commander waved at the guards, who untied the two boys. They were promptly put to work doing various chores around the camp—all the dirty, tiring work no one else wanted. But while they worked, they listened as the guards talked.

And talk they did, the more freely because the boys supposedly didn't understand them. It was soon obvious that the fracas on the beach had been the most activity they'd seen for weeks. (And a couple of them endured some ribbing for the broken bones and the knife-wound that Senrid had dealt out, items of interest that Puddlenose noted but kept to himself.) One or two tended to look askance at Senrid, who did what he was told, his face bland and his smile cheery.

Puddlenose found Senrid's reactions interesting, and impossible to figure out. They didn't talk much; the border rovers got suspicious if they did, so for the most part the boys were silent.

Christoph oozed around flattering them all and asking nosy questions. From the resultant bragging and hot air a picture emerged, pretty much what Captain Heraford had indicated.

With one important difference: orders had recently gone out to pull the forces inland toward the capital. It seemed that someone in the high command thought that trouble was brewing, and wanted the cause winnowed out.

When Puddlenose was alone with Senrid, fetching pails of water from the nearby stream along which grew all the leddas, he said, "That's it—we gotta warn them."

"Who?" Senrid asked.

Puddlenose shrugged. "We'll find out."

FOUR

Kitty awoke abruptly when gravel clattered against her windows. She sat up in bed, and two or three catheads lifted as well. The sound of gravel tinkled down the row of windows.

She sprang out of bed and ran to her casement, flinging it wide.

The morning light was blue, the air frigid. "Who's there?" Kitty called.

"Arel. Important message." She saw the man's breath.

"Just a moment." Kyale sighed, running to get her robe, which she pulled tightly about her.

All the way downstairs she scolded to herself. Here they lived in this big castle, and Leander refused to hire any more servants. Said he didn't like people waiting on him, doing things he was perfectly capable of doing himself—and had for years.

Kitty told over the old arguments as she pattered barefoot down the cold marble hallway. "But a king oughtn't to be doing those things!" "Why not?" "Because that's the job of servants!" "Cleaning up after oneself should be everyone's job."

How many times had they had that argument? A few of his old gang still worked at the castle as servants—but since their return from the water world he'd sent most of them off to the west on various spy and messenger trips. Including the two who used to serve as footmen.

She sighed again. Leander did his best to treat her like a sister, and not hold her mother's actions against her, and she did like him. She *did*. She didn't stay with him because she wanted to be a princess, though she'd heard that hinted at once. It wasn't true! She had nowhere else to go, but even so, she did like him. He was smart and funny and liked games, but he didn't take time to play nearly often enough. He also studied way too much, and brooded over things that didn't matter—and ignored the things that did. Like living the way royalty ought to. So, she reasoned, her job was to help him learn how to be a proper king.

Appetizing smells drifting from the kitchen broke into her thoughts. So the cook and her crew were up. Kitty considered calling whoever was there to help, but then she shrugged. She was already awake, and here, and she could manage the door if Arel helped. The princess waiting on the fellow who should by rights be doing the carpentry work around the castle! At least she'd be the first to hear whatever news there was.

So she ran into the great hall, and struggled with the big iron bar across the front doors. As soon as she got it clear of the iron support Arel shouldered the door open.

"Come on in," she said. "Hurry." For, cold as it was in the hall, the outside air was much colder.

Arel came in, stamping his feet and rubbing his hands. His nose was red, his blond hair tousled.

"Go wait in the kitchen," Kyale said, wishing she had a proper anteroom—and a steward to do the running. "Warm up. I'll go wake up my fathead of a brother."

Arel looked at her blankly.

"Oh, don't mind me," she said with false cheer. "I'm always dressed thus formally at dawn."

The young man blinked as though he hadn't heard, and she wondered if he had gone deaf—either that or he had been riding all night and was half frozen. "Kitchen," she repeated, and ran out.

Leander was not in his bedroom. As usual.

She thumped down the hall, muttering about frozen toes, and ran into the library—and sure enough, there he was, asleep with his head on the desk amid a welter of books and papers.

She kicked him. Not hard, but hard enough that he snorted and sat up, hair in his eyes, his cheek creased from the edge of a book.

"Arel is back with a message," she said. "There are no servants around. I had to let him in myself. Nearly freezing my toes off—"

Leander did not seem to hear. He slammed the book closed and shot out the door before she could finish her lament.

Shivering, Kitty decided that whatever news Arel brought could wait on warmer clothes, and she continued down the hall to her room to change.

Leander took the stairs two at a time, skidding into the kitchen, where he found Arel.

The cook said, "We lit a fire in the morning room, if you'd like to talk in comfort there."

Leander grinned. "Meaning we're in the way here?"

The cook snorted a laugh. "Well, if you want these pies any time soon..." She waved at her daughter. "Nelyas. Breakfast rolls in the morning room. Butter."

"Some hot tea, and chocolate for Kyale, would be nice if you can manage," Leander added.

"Easy," Nelyas said, flapping her apron to shoo him out. "Be there soon."

"Come on, Arel. Are you frozen?"

"Not so bad," was the chattering answer.

"Horse all right?"

"Portan was in the stable, took her over. Came straight along. Door was locked, as the princess said." He frowned. "No one on guard?"

"They're all up in the hills on either side of the pass. That's where the Marlovens have to come over, if they do come. What's going on? Any news on Senrid along the border?"

"Not a word."

Leander sighed. "Nor from Collet inside the kingdom. What can that mean? I'm afraid it can only mean one thing: if he transferred home like we did, then Tdanerend was waiting. That day we got thrown off-world, he'd said something about taking over his own affairs. That has to have gotten back to the Regent."

Arel nodded slowly. "Rumor is the Regent killed him with his own hands, no witnesses. There's been no sight whatever, and Collet said that my cousin reported there's been lots of magic done in the capital—Latvian's been there helping Tdanerend."

"Traps," Leander said. "Has to be. Traps laying for Senrid. Anything else?"

"Yes. Tdanerend's not in the capital."

"Uh oh. Where?"

"No word."

Leander sighed. "Then all we can do is keep watching, and find out more information. If we can. I'll go up to the pass and put down more illusions, and if I can master this time spell—ah, never mind."

Arel smiled. He was a thin-faced young man whose preferred calling was woodwork. He'd been mixed in politics ever since his Uncle Alaxandar, the former queen's captain of guard, had switched sides in disgust. His sister was up in the hills as one of the watchers; Pertar, Portan's twin, was the other messenger. "We'll keep on the lookout—" He paused as the door opened.

Nelyas shouldered her way in, bearing a heavy tray.

The two helped themselves to hot tea and rolls, and Kyale appeared, smiling when she saw the chocolate pot. "What's the news?"

"Tdanerend is missing, and so is Senrid. I'm afraid Tdanerend's being out of the capital might be bad news for us."

"It's not *fair*," Kitty raged. "Why should he harass *us*? We never did anything to him! Why should he be *able* to harass us? What's the good of there being magicians in the world, if they don't protect us?"

"Because there's always someone stronger. That's what happens when people go after power," Leander said, rubbing his eyes.

"What does he really want with us anyway? Everybody in Vasande Leror could probably fit into his capital and there'd be room left over!"

"Everybody in Vasande Leror could be working in the old mines, or starting new ones, if he gains both sides of the Aurum Hills," Leander said. "A military country always needs steel—and people to dig it out and make it. Preferably not *his* people."

"I thought we had a truce about that," Kitty said, frowning. "I vaguely remember my mother talking about it. And I know I saw lots of boring stuff about mines, and the Aurums, in that book of treaties."

"Well, we did and do, but Tdanerend wants it all. Also, white magic makes mining easier—but it takes a lot of patient work and care to set up the spells. Black magic rends and spends. So he wants us doing the work so he can get the steel. Now, how do we keep him out? Help us think of a plan."

"Good riddance to both, is what I say," Kyale stated, looking up expectantly at Nelyas, but she was vanishing through the door. With a small sigh, Kyale reached to pour herself a cup of cocoa, into which she added a heavy dollop of fresh cream. "Kick them both from here to the moon when you do find them."

"That's better than any of my ideas," Leander said.

Arel folded a couple of rolls into a kerchief, drank off his tea, and rose.

"Don't you want to thaw out?" Leander asked.

Arel shook his head. "Tea did that. Rolls will help. I smell snow on the way, and I want to get back up to camp first. Portan said that Amber is fresh and rarin' to run. I'll leave Berry with you."

"Thanks," Leander said.

The man nodded, bowed in Kitty's direction, then left.

"I'll have to spend the day at the pass doing magic," Leander said. "I don't have that time-trap spell mastered. I wish I did! Tdanerend might be worthless as a magician but Latvian isn't. My illusions aren't going to hold against someone with his abilities."

"What else can we do?" Kitty asked.

Leander sighed. "What I've done. Warned the towns to be ready. Sent my best up to watch. We can't stand against any army, or even a portion of the Marloven army. I hope Arel makes it back all right. He and Alaxandar are the best we've got. They know something about military maneuvers, they'll know what they see, and I hope they'll know what to do. Our best chance is forewarning."

Kyale said, frowning, "Arel doesn't show proper respect, Leander. He should really call you 'your majesty.' After all, you're no longer stuck in the forest—"

"Say!" Leander leaned forward. "Is that your underwater band on your arm?" He pointed toward a faint line in her silken sleeve.

Kyale fussed with the ribbon binding her sleeve. The question had been a subject change, and perhaps a week ago—a month ago—she would have treated it as it deserved. Not now, though. Not after all those nights when his library was lit until dawn, or nearly, while he wrestled with magic books and worries about the kingdom. Kitty ran the ribbon through her fingers, repressing a sigh. He didn't want to listen even for his own good! What could she do?

She shoved her sleeve up to expose the golden band on her arm. "There it is! Handsome, isn't it? Since I'm not exactly drowning in jewels." She laughed—she didn't care a whit about jewels. Pretty gowns she liked, and she had plenty of those.

"Why didn't you give your band back?" Leander asked.

Kitty shrugged. "I wanted to keep it. As a keepsake. Autumn kept hers too," she added defensively, in case he was going to complain.

"Well, it might be of use some day," Leander said, smiling.

"That's what I thought!" Kitty grinned in relief. "Since I don't know how to swim, but this way I never have to be afraid of water."

"Sounds all right to me," Leander said, buttering another roll. "If they'd needed them all back, they would have asked. But if you change your mind and want it off, I'm afraid it's going to take a spell."

"I know," she said, shrugging. "Um, this is yummy." She reached for more chocolate. "So that creep of a Senrid is gone for good, huh?"

Leander looked out the window. The truth was, he felt ambivalent. He remembered those first days, before they found out who he was, how much fun they'd had. The lengthy periods of talk. What's more, he would wager anything Senrid regretted them as well—he was fairly certain he'd caught signs of it while they were on the water world.

But to say that out loud was to invite an angry response from Kitty, who had not only endured the close call with the execution, she crabbed with what Leander knew was jealousy whenever reminded of his short-lived friendship with Senrid.

"I don't know," he said.

FIVE

"Now."

Christoph was only a silhouette in the weak moonlight.

"The last one is snoring," he whispered.

"I'll take that," Senrid said, pointing to the commander's tent, from which loud snores emerged. "I want a crack at the maps."

"If you happen to see Lordsnordsword—" Puddlenose began.

"What?" Senrid's voice was breathy with laughter. "What's that?"

"My blade. I stole it from a pompous gasbag named Snord, and he was a lord, so what name could be better?"

"What indeed," Senrid echoed—and it was clear that in his country, though they had plenty of weapons they didn't name them. "I do remember seeing it in there."

Puddlenose shrugged. "Well, let's get busy."

While they'd worked, they'd learned everything there was to know about the camp, so it didn't take long to upend all the tent poles, let the horses all go, and get rid of the banner and attach to its pole one of the commander's undergarments that had been drying on a bush after having been laundered in the stream earlier—by the boys.

The guardians of the coast snored oblivious, all having partaken liberally of the ale one had brought in with the latest supply wagon, and into which Christoph had thoughtfully added a packet of powdered sleepweed, found in the cook tent.

As Puddlenose worked away at thrashing the camp, he kept looking over at the main tent, half-expecting to hear a roar for guards, but no sounds emerged until Senrid himself came out, his pale head gleaming in the weak light, with his arms full.

"Got 'em," Senrid said.

"Any trouble?" Puddlenose asked.

"I know how to be quiet," Senrid said. He lit a candle, spread a map out on the grass, and studied it intently.

Christoph came up then, lugging three woven waterbags. "I think that business about Everon being a desert has to be true," he said. "Look what I found in the horse tack, for the messengers. I filled 'em, one each."

"Good thinking," Puddlenose said. "Let's raid the cook tent, and get moving."

Not long after, they were on their way to the northwest, directed by Senrid.

ಬಂ⚮ಬಂ

𝐃espite the promising beginning, the remainder of the episode scarcely constituted an adventure. It was a journey, one that soon was hot, dry, and arduous.

Exactly as Captain Heraford predicted, Everon soon became a desert, only not of sand, like the Senyavin west of Mearsies Heili, but like farmland and forest denuded of growth—of life.

Travel was difficult, not because anyone interfered with them, but because of the unremitting heat. Blue sky curved from horizon to horizon like a bell, cloudless and bright by day, but curiously starless at night; a haze manifested between ground and sky each evening at sunset.

They did see a few other travelers, none of whom spoke to them. Once an old woman walked in the opposite direction, her face hooded. When they drew even, Puddlenose looked into her face, saw observant eyes, set amid the wrinkles of humor and of patient endurance, but she passed on by.

And once, horsemen. Thinking of their victims back in the camp, the three at first wanted to hide, but there was no hiding here. It soon became obvious that these were not the border riders, but something else indeed, for they rode white steeds that made Senrid stare in admiration, and they wore white livery edged with silver and purple.

None of the boys knew it at the time, but they were seeing the legendary Knights of Dei, sworn to execute the King or Queen's bidding. The King and Queen were enchanted, and so the Knights rode, silent for the duration of the enchantment, existing in an arid, dream-like half-world.

They did not stop or speak.

Puddlenose had the feeling they'd been seen, though— and assessed. When the three had galloped by, dust obscuring them, Christoph scratched his head and whistled a long, low note expressive of amazement. Senrid said nothing, but he seemed bemused for a long while after.

⤒

Most of their sporadic conversation (which dwindled over the successive days of hiking in that relentless sun) was between Christoph and Puddlenose, Senrid listening to their quick, easy, sometimes laughing exchanges. They had been friends for a long time, and shared humor as well as stories. They understood one another so well that they sometimes spoke in cryptic metonymy.

So that's what it was like to have a friend.

Senrid asked about some of their past adventures, which they were very ready to relate—especially the funny ones. Senrid also asked about the Chwahir, and it was Christoph who answered. Puddlenose's comments were largely restricted to pungent observations on Shnit Sonscarna's more disgusting traits.

Senrid enjoyed those as well, but some of his questions hinted at a background that, if it wasn't similar in all points, was similar enough to cause Puddlenose to speculate on who might have landed the kid with them—and why.

There was one important conversation on the evening they sighted the hills beyond the capital.

"Do you know who it is we are giving the news of this crackdown to?" Senrid asked.

"Nope," Puddlenose said. "I didn't catch any names, did you?" he asked Christoph.

Christoph shrugged. "Nary a one."

"Then...why are you doing it?" Senrid asked. "For the chance to score off the Norsundrians? A worthwhile goal," he added, not hiding his dislike.

"I guess," Puddlenose said, thinking, *Because it's the right thing to do.*

And Senrid said, in an edgy voice, "You're not about to inform me, most self-righteously, that it's the right thing to do?"

"If you already know it is, why ask?" Christoph bent to pick up a stone, which he skimmed ahead on the trail. He shaded his eyes as he watched it land, spinning, on the road ahead.

"Because I'm not convinced there's any such thing as the 'right' thing to do—outside of self interest," Senrid said.

"So opposing, say, Norsunder every chance one can get isn't right?" Puddlenose asked.

"Pure self-interest." Senrid looked sardonic. "From anyone on any 'side' if they have half a brain."

"True," Puddlenose said, shrugging.

He'd learned during his days as Shnit's prisoner, when the warped mage-king would force Kwenz's heir, Jilo, and Puddlenose into adversarial positions, that talking of right and wrong was worthless from the perspective of one raised to calculate human interactions in terms of degrees of power.

Puddlenose and Jilo had had to form a truce of sorts, to survive. They'd talked expedience, never ethics.

From what little Senrid would say of his own background, there were some startling similarities.

So Puddlenose added, "The chance for action. To snap our fingers, so to speak, under this Detlev's nose—even though I've never met him and hope never to have the pleasure. I don't know. It seemed the thing to do. If that's 'right' I can live with it. Why are you still here with us? Is staying right, or wrong?"

"Because I don't know if I'm still being watched," Senrid said, too hot and tired for anything but bluntness. "If I am, by whom. And why. Someone put me here with you for a reason, and I thought if I stayed I'd find out the reason."

Christoph said, "You must have an almighty sense of self if you think someone is watching us now." He looked around the empty landscape and above, which was even emptier. His grin, usually so friendly, was sardonic.

Senrid snorted a laugh.

Puddlenose said, "You can always test it. What did that spirit-thing call herself?" He tipped his head back. "Erdrael? Erdrael! Send us on a magic carpet? Not that I've ever heard of one existing, but CJ tells stories with 'em," he added. "What I can't figure is, why a carpet? Wouldn't you fall off? A magic raft sounds more sensible. Erdrael, hear that? One magic raft, please."

Nothing happened.

"Here, you try," Puddlenose invited.

Senrid said once, in a goading voice, "Erdrael, we'll take that magic raft now—and a feast on top of it."

Nothing.

They walked on.

Puddlenose said finally, "Everywhere I go, you learn that there are different kinds of awareness, some extending outside of time. Those people that Dhana—that's one of Clair's gang—comes from, they live in certain waters, and they all seem to know of each other, but if they know anything about land life I'd be surprised. And if you ask Dhana about her life in non-human form, she'll first say *What do you mean by 'know?'*"

Christoph said, "Some of those magic races apparently extend outside of time, or at least time passes differently for them than for us."

Senrid opened his hand, acknowledging the possibility.

Christoph kicked at a pebble, watching the puffs of dust it raised, light brown and fine as flour. "You must have done some kind of magic to catch the attention of some big blade, right?"

Senrid tipped his head back, wiped his sleeve over his forehead, then shrugged. "True. My magic and—someone else's clashed and we ended up thrown off the world."

"Off the *world*?" Puddlenose and Christoph said together.

"Yes. I told you that."

"I thought you were kidding," Puddlenose said. "Landed yourself in one of our oceans." He whistled. "Well, you definitely did come to someone's attention."

"Who plucked us away from that world when we finished, and then stuck me with you."

"Hoo. Well, I can't answer that one," Christoph said. He grinned. "And anyway it would suggest someone might be watching *us* too, from time to time, eh?" He looked upward and simpered. "Yoo hoo? How about some shade?"

Puddlenose thought, *So you know magic, huh? You didn't say what kind.*

He didn't speak, though; whatever kind of magic it was, Senrid didn't seem to have access to it at present.

Christoph bent and picked up another flat stone, shying it ahead and listening to the dry rattle and clatter.

Puddlenose felt Senrid's assessing gaze, but he watched Christoph's throw, then picked up a stone and tried skipping it. He sensed that the real subject was yet to be broached.

And sure enough, out it came.

"So," Senrid said. "Supposing you've a custom with which you might disagree, but if you don't perform it, at best you will be perceived as weak. At worst, someone else uses it as an excuse to get rid of you."

"Easy," Puddlenose said, chortling. "First, I'd have to find a reason to give this—" He showed the back of his hand. "—for what a bunch of rats think of me. And if I don't—and I am sure I wouldn't—I'm out so fast all they see are my heels."

"Suppose you have a stake in staying," Senrid persisted.

Christoph sighed. "I hate this kind of thing. What kind of custom are you talking about? Whether or not you button or lace your shirts? If you belch after drinking? And what happens if you don't behave according to custom—does someone paint your nose purple, or does someone come in the night and stab you?"

"The latter." Senrid's face was bland, but Puddlenose saw his hands flex once or twice.

"I'd skip out," Puddlenose said firmly. "Nothing is going to make me stay under those circs. I've had a bellyful of life-and-death game playing with the Chwahir, and none of it I chose. But if you were to ask my cousin Clair, she'd want to know first thing your stake in staying. Are you protecting someone, or are you merely playing life-and-death games for your own fun and profit?"

"Let's say that you see corruption and senseless misuse of power and know how to fix it, but you not only can't flout custom, you have to be perceived as strong or you won't be able to control those who will resist you."

Christoph whistled. "I'd say you have a big mess on your hands, and better get some allies who are awfully good— either that or start sleeping sitting up, with your eyes open and a sword in your hand."

Puddlenose shook his head. "I wouldn't do it. Clair would, though. If she believed it was for the greater good of those who can't protect themselves. Except then," he shied another stone, "you're not being logical. In the worldview where what matters is power and expedience, who cares about the weak?"

Flex. Senrid's hands betrayed a hit. He didn't speak.

A long silence ensued, the only sound their feet shuffling through the dry dirt. Senrid walked with his head down. Puddlenose watched, wondering if he was ever going to find out what had prompted the questions—and where they would lead.

Then Christoph tipped back his head, and let out an exclamation. "Are those our hills?" he asked, pointing.

On the western horizon, in the purplish haze of the ending day, they made out shapes like uneven knuckles.

"Hope so," Puddlenose said. "I don't know about you, but I only have enough water left maybe for tomorrow. Ditto the wen-cakes and fruit."

Senrid sloshed his waterbag, and Christoph groaned as he hefted his, which seemed as light as the others'.

"Why don't we camp now, and start as soon as we have light to walk?" Puddlenose suggested.

The others agreed, and so they did.

Morning was cold. They woke stiff and chilled, and ate the last of their food.

Another day's hike brought them much closer to the hills, which were now plain even in the shimmering heat waves of day. They discussed what to do when they got to the capital, but when they reached the first of the rocky hills, they encountered two standing stones, and Senrid halted them.

"There's magic here," he said.

Neither of the others asked how he knew.

"I've read about this kind of access. If you want to test them out, we walk between them from the north."

"Should we?" Puddlenose asked. "What kind of magic?"

"White."

"Which isn't always used for good purposes," Christoph put in comfortingly. "Now, for real evil it isn't much use. Obscure, though, does work."

Senrid looked over. "What does that mean?"

Puddlenose said, "It means though it's a white magic spell we still might be in trouble."

"I'm hungry—" Christoph began.

"Naturally," Puddlenose put in. "As always."

"—so I say, let's see what we find between the stones. We already know we've got desert and nothing else here. Whatever awaits in the hills might be swords and knives. Because our hosts on the coast made it clear their orders came from Ferdrian, the capital, lying there beyond the hills."

Puddlenose shrugged and circled around one of the stones. The other two followed.

Puddlenose felt the weird vertigo of transfer magic, but his feet kept moving forward on solid ground, and within an eyeblink he discovered he was in darkness. Darkness, but his next breath drew in the complex richness of young and old trees, of flowering shrubs, herbs, and loam, and underneath it all, the sweetness of flowing water. A second breath drove out the memory of the dusty, arid air they'd endured on their long walk.

His eyes adjusted rapidly.

He was surrounded by forestland.

"Whoo, this is weird," he said, gulping in the good air, as the other two emerged.

Christoph snorted in lungfuls. Senrid stayed quiet.

Puddlenose glanced behind them. The two stones were mere shadows, and the space between dark.

"Path." Senrid pointed.

"That's so," Christoph said, hands on hips. "Me, I'm glad to be out of that sun. It really was dead out there, wasn't it? Not just arid, but dead. No living things at all. I didn't notice until I stepped here—wherever 'here' might be—and smelled life again. Shall we see if this path leads to food?"

Puddlenose peered into the undergrowth, but the darkness defeated him. He nodded. "Path it is."

They trod cautiously; Puddlenose noticed at one point that Senrid had his dagger in his hand, but when they saw peacefully twinkling lights shining like lacework between the foliage of the trees, and heard cheery dance music rising on the soft evening air, the dagger vanished up the shirt cuff again.

The pool of golden light revealed a circle of travelers' wagons, brightly painted, some with wind chimes hanging in the rounded openings. In the midst of this camp burned a great fire, around which a dozen or so people of all ages danced, amid them a girl about Christoph's age and height, her golden hair swinging against her skirts. Her coloring, the way she moved, made it clear she was at least related to the forest-dwelling maulons.

Christoph minced forward, parodying dance. Puddlenose stuck out a foot and tripped him. Christoph fell down with a *foof!* that made the other two laugh.

The sound attracted attention; two men materialized out of the shadows between a couple of wagons. Both carried steel.

Senrid's hands were together, but he stood silently.

"Who are you?" one man called.

"Ourselves," Christoph called. "Wait! Check that!" He scrambled to his feet, dusted off his clothes. Then he bowed absurdly. "Christoph Uhlemann, heavenly fiend at your service—that's only a figure of speech, that service part. I'm too lazy to work."

"Clam up, you numbskull," Puddlenose said, noticing the stances of the men ease at Christoph's foolishness. "Do you want them to think we're insane?"

"But we are!" Christoph protested.

"Who are you?" the man asked again, in a considerably less belligerent tone.

Puddlenose decided it was time to at least pretend to be serious. "Travelers, come to warn you that your border riders have been ordered to move in for some kind of search. We didn't find out for what, but we figured it was worthwhile warning someone, since this land—that is, if we are still in Everon—is reputed to be under Norsunder's shadow."

One of the men drew his breath in audibly. The other said, "We're in Everon, yes. The right part. Out there is the wrong part. Come along. We'll talk inside camp, where we can see one another."

The first one slipped back between the wagons, and a moment later Puddlenose heard him call out: "Cassandra?"

"We have to check," the second man said somewhat apologetically.

The boys followed the man into the light of the campfire, where they surveyed one another. Puddlenose saw an ordinary middle-aged man, long hair, the bright clothing of the traveling player. Propped near the wheel of the wagon he'd stopped near was a woodwind.

A moment later the blond girl had joined them. She was about the age of Clair and the girls, barefoot, dressed in a plain gown much too big for her, bound close by a fringed sash. She pulled from the sash something that glinted with blue-silver light: a long pin, its head carved to look like either a leaf or a feather.

She held the pin out and Puddlenose wondered if he was supposed to take it; Senrid crossed his arms and Christoph scratched his head.

"They are not Norsundrians," the girl said, then tucked the pin back into her sash.

The man did not hide his relief. He gestured to Puddlenose, a friendly gesture. "Tell her your warning?"

Puddlenose repeated it, watching the girl's face. She listened soberly, and then sighed. "They must have found out that the enchantment is breaking over some of us. That's all I can figure."

Puddlenose felt a million questions piling up in the back of his head, but he squashed them down. He knew that they were on the very edge of impending action—something big, possibly just about to begin.

He looked over, met Christoph's eyes. Christoph shrugged faintly: he agreed.

Senrid hadn't reacted at all.

"Come! Join us for a meal?"

"Don't need to ask twice," Christoph said enthusiastically.

The players had plenty to eat, which was surprising to Puddlenose, but he didn't question that either. An atmosphere of tension tightened jaws, and caused quick looks, even though everyone appeared to be having a good time with their music and dance.

The girl Cassandra vanished after a while. Christoph wandered about looking at various musical instruments, but Puddlenose was content to sit with his eyes half-closed and watch the fire.

After a while he realized he was hearing a pair of voices.

"...you'll walk into a trap," an old woman said slowly. Was this the same woman they'd seen on the road? "You must believe that magic communication preceded you."

Senrid said, "Trap. South?"

Puddlenose saw images in the fire: them entering the southern forest again, by day, reaching the shore, being jumped by a patrol of Chwahir, sent by magic transfer...

The old woman's voice whispered on, low and slow, and Puddlenose couldn't make out the words. He almost dropped off to sleep when he discovered Senrid next to him.

"Come on," he said. "They've given us food and water. Said if we leave at night, we travel much faster through the outer land."

Puddlenose rubbed gritty eyes and scrambled to his feet. He found Christoph right behind him.

"We will?"

"And we apparently will run into transfer magic," Senrid said dryly.

"You don't sound pleased."

"I don't trust it," Senrid said. "I hate interference."

"So does everybody," Puddlenose retorted cheerfully "Let's go."

Silence stayed with them as they trod back up the path.

Through the stones, and into the hazed desert-land; a long night of travel brought them within hearing of the ocean, but before any of them could remark on it, magic seized them, and Puddlenose and Christoph found themselves in Mearsies Heili—without Senrid.

Clair was as used to their sudden reappearances as they, and was grateful it was midmorning, and not in the middle of the night, as had happened before.

"I just finished four interviews," she said. "No other appointments, so all I have to do is wait for noon, and then we can go."

"Go?" Christoph said; they were tired, but that could be ignored if something fun was planned.

"Yes. Diana and Seshe have laid out a treasure hunt. Team game, whoever loses has to do snow patrol against the Chwahir and all kitchen chores for the winners for two weeks."

Puddlenose rubbed his hands. "Are we good or what?" he gloated, as Christoph laughed.

Clair said, "So how did you get here—who sent you?"

"Dunno," both boys said, which was more typical than not. And, because it was not yet noon, they plopped down on the steps of the dais and told her everything, Puddlenose finishing with giving her the necklace.

Clair turned it absently in her hands, but there was a frown between her brows.

"I have to admit it bothers me, too, this feeling that somebody is watching him. It could happen to any of us."

Puddlenose shrugged. "And what can you do? My advice that no one asked for is this: pretend they don't exist."

Christoph sighed. "I have to admit I hope I never see Senrid again."

The cousins looked his way. "Why? Did you dislike him?" Clair asked.

Christoph grimaced. "No, I liked him. That's the problem."

Puddlenose cracked his knuckles. "Yup. He's sitting on the fence right now. Anything could push him either way. If he goes for the Norsunder side, I don't want to see him again either. He's too smart, too nervy—it's too likely you would end up seeing him grinning there at the head of an army. C'mon, let's roust us out some eats before the noon bells."

SIX

Kyale woke up to the sound of Conrad growling.

She opened her eyes, sat up, and flung off the bedclothes.

The growl wasn't just Conrad. Meta, the powerful black leopard who almost never came indoors unless there was a blizzard, also prowled about her room, back and forth, tail twitching, teeth gleaming, coat ruffled as she growled.

"Uh oh," Kitty breathed, and dashed into her wardrobe. She scrambled into a warm woolen dress, for the air was chilly. She hesitated at stockings and shoes, then decided against them. It would take too long to lace up her slippers.

So she ran barefoot into the hall—just as a young man in a black and tan uniform entered from the other end.

She whirled, ducked back inside, slammed her door, and bolted it.

She fled to the window, remembering Faline's climb up the ivy. If Faline could go up, Kitty could go down.

But a glance into the courtyard revealed a terrible sight— a group of fellows in those familiar black-and-tan uniforms, all of them with drawn steel. As she stared down, one glanced up. He was about Leander's age, his lean face framed by pale blond hair. He grinned. It was a challenging grin, not at all friendly, and Kitty whirled away, then drew her curtains.

Bang! Someone pounded on the door with something hard.

"Open up!"

Kitty looked around, shivering. "Under the bed, kits," she cried, dropping down onto the floor to follow her own order.

Her small cats were already there. The two large ones did not heed her.

The door smashed open, wood splintering. Two or three sets of iron-capped heels trod in, clumped around, then a voice said, in accented Leroran, "Come out, or these beasts are dead."

Kitty poked her head out from under the bed duster— along with three or four small cat heads.

Someone muffled a snicker at the sight, but the faces in view were stern, one in the back sneering. None of them friendly.

"Now."

Kitty scrambled out, and dashed for her desk. In one hand she grabbed up her letter-opener, and in the other a solid gold candleholder.

When the first Marloven took a step near her, she flung the opener, which spun through the air past the fellow's shoulder and clattered against her broken door.

"You went first," said the leader, a very young man with a determined face and serious light brown eyes. "Now it's my turn."

He drew a long dagger from the sheath at his side, flipped it expertly in his fingers so that he held it by the blade, and cocked his arm back as he sighted on Meta.

Conrad growled, crouching to spring; the others pulled their swords and knives with a hiss and ring of steel.

"All right," she said in a squeaky voice. "I won't throw this thing. Don't hurt the kits."

She put the candleholder down, and he sheathed his knife. Conrad stayed crouched, growling on every breath, ears flat back, but didn't move.

"Come along."

She came. All the Marlovens closed in around her. She heard the soft thud of cat pads on the marble flooring, and Meta and Conrad vanished down the hall the other way. A couple of the Marlovens watched, but they didn't react; one gave her a prod between the shoulder blades.

In lip-biting silence Kitty hustled to keep up with the others' quick strides. They thundered down the stairs to the old garrison courtyard, which was overgrown with weeds, and stopped when a pair of Marlovens crossed from the other direction.

"Here," said the leader from behind Kyale. He spoke in Marloven—which Kitty now understood, thanks to Leander's persistence, but she didn't let on. "Regent wants this brat stashed in the tower for now."

And, without warning, a gloved hand gave Kitty a shove.

She stumbled forward. One of the new ones crooked a finger at her, then pointed at the tower. She hesitated, heard them all breathing behind her, sensed their impatience. There was no way she was getting out of this mess, so she crossed her arms and stalked toward the old tower, which had been unused since her mother's day. Her toes bunched against the cold stones of the courtyard.

Up the steps, which were wet from the recent rain; the old-style arrow-slit windows were all open to the weather. To the top, and in. The door slammed, she heard the bar thrown, and bootheels receding back down the stone steps.

She looked around. The bleak gray light revealed moss on the stones, and a small pile of withered leaves against the far wall. Above her head a trap door—but it was well beyond her reach.

She sat down, pulled her skirts about her, put her head on her knees, and wept.

⊱⋅ᘒᘓ⋅⊰

Leander woke up with his skull aching and a nasty metallic taste in his mouth. Darkness surrounded him. He sniffed, recognized the dusty smells of stone, hemp, and the doggy smell of damp wool.

He was in the storerooms that in Mara Jinea's day had been a dungeon, under the unused garrison.

He lay without moving, breathing slowly, fighting the nausea that had wrung him in waves when he first moved his head. He was on his side; with cautious fingers he explored the swollen lump behind his right ear. Pain sent lightning bolts shooting behind his eyes, and he winced, then let his hand fall.

Memory came back, unwanted, humiliating: he had walked into the kitchen to order up some tea just as an assault team burst in through the door to the truck garden.

Nelyas had defended herself with a carving knife. Her mother had struggled with two assailants, trying desperately to brain one with a cooking pot. Leander had looked about him for something to use as a weapon, but he never got a chance. Behind him a sword rang as it was pulled from a sheath. He turned in time for someone to club him across the back of the head with a hilt.

And that was that. The great king Leander Tlennen-Hess, youngest of the family ever to come to the throne, taken down without having struck a single blow. His rule had lasted not quite a year—and his defense of his kingdom had lasted about three quick breaths.

Don't think like that.
Can't think at all.

ೞಛೞಖ

Up in the tower, the day wore slowly on, weak light changing in the two arrow slits then darkening. From time to time Kitty heard the echo of voices ricocheting up the stones, always in Marloven. Sometimes commands, other times punctuated by the ring of bootheels. A few times chatter, and even laughter. Not gloating laughter, aimed at her, but the snickers of fun.

Those Marlovens out there were having *fun.*

Kitty raged and fumed to herself, after trying to hear the talk below, but the echoes, the low murmuring voices, made it impossible. Some of the commands she did hear, but they didn't tell her anything other than one group was coming on duty and another going off. No sign of Leander, or anyone else she knew. Just Marlovens—some stationed on the walls, like in her mother's day. Their words were carried away by the wind the few times she heard their voices.

She stood on tiptoe and peered through the window slit that overlooked the courtyard. She didn't see much, just Marlovens walking about.

Once a pair clattered in through the gate, dressed like the others except their helms had long horse-tails, not steel spikes. These two didn't wear their helms, but carried them in their left arms. The Marlovens with the steel points on their helms all got out of the way; the two with the horse-tail helms crossed the courtyard, one of them talking in a low voice, the other laughing as they disappeared inside the old garrison.

Kitty's toes hurt, so she sat back down.

At sunset she heard someone tramp up the stairs. The bar was thrown back, the door creaked partially open, and a long arm set in first a jug, then a bowl with a wooden spoon sticking out. The door slammed, the bar clunked into place, and the steps receded.

Kitty crossed the cell, shivering. The dishes she recognized from the kitchen. The jug was cold, full of water, but the bowl was warm. She sniffed, smelled spiced cabbage and barley cooked in turkey broth in a thick soup. It seemed an insult—the prisoner slop you hear about in stories—but she ate it anyway, enjoying the warmth more than the taste.

A long drink of water, then she set the dishes down again, and crouched down directly opposite the arrow slit, where she didn't feel the breeze as much.

Dark fell.

After a time she roused from shivering half-slumber when the bar scraped up and the door opened, and someone pitched in a blanket. From the smell of dust and mildew it was one of the old ones from the unused garrison. She wrapped herself up in it and tried to sleep.

⁎CR⁎CG

Leander felt hunger and thirst supercede the pain in his head. He had no idea how long he lay there in the storeroom. Sleep came intermittently, with unpleasant dreams.

He was soggy with sleep when the door opened. Dream images flickered and died, chased by the flaring of orange torchlight. His head ached abominably, and he shivered.

Hands gripped his arms, pulled him to his feet.

"I'll walk," he said in Marloven, trying to shake off the hands.

One let go, but the other did not. Dizzy, he almost pitched forward, and the second hand grabbed hastily and this time did not let go.

An ignominious walk came next, with torchlight shifting the dimensions of his own storerooms and the servants' stairs upward, making the dizziness worse.

Into the castle, which had Marloven guards posted at all the main landings and doors. Some of them looked at him curiously. Leander noted that most of them were young men. He'd pictured them all being Alaxandar's age, only more grizzled. Bigger. These were his size, most of them fair-haired—like Senrid.

They were all armed. He was not.

His guides force-marched him down past the old reception rooms, empty this past year, toward Mara Jinea's throne room, which he had never used. He drew in a deep breath. They were armed, they'd taken his home—probably his land, or nearly. He strongly suspected he was about to meet Senrid's uncle, the Regent. He had nothing to help him but his knowledge of Tdanerend, garnered from Kitty, the Mearsieans, and the Regent's own daughter—that, and his wits.

Sure enough, the doors to the throne room stood open. The room was lit with glowglobes, but no attempt had been made to warm the icy, stale air. Leander had never bothered to get rid of Mara Jinea's obsidian-inlaid throne, or the black walnut chairs with their golden edging; Marloven colors, Leander realized belatedly. Just how far had her ambitions reached?

His dry lips twisted. She was gone. The threat now was Tdanerend, who seemed to like throne rooms.

The guards halted, bringing Leander face to face with Tdanerend. They were nearly the same height, but Tdanerend was far heavier in build. His hair was reddish brown, his eyes dark, his face lined with ill humor.

He wore a Marloven uniform, glittering with medals and rank insignia.

Leander imagined how he himself looked: filthy dark hair hanging in his bruised face, his weedy form clad in mildew-grubby shirt and old trousers and house slippers. He laughed.

Tdanerend's mouth pruned. "Your options are these," he said. "You will either consent to a loyalty spell, so that I may use you here in place of a governor, or I'll hold you against any uprisings—any trouble at all—and give your people the messiest show they've ever had as a demonstration."

Ice-trickle pooled inside Leander's innards. But those words—loyalty spell—sparked enough anger to make him determined: defeated he might be, but not without a fight.

He said as derisively as possible, "Am I supposed to be impressed? Or are they?" He jerked his head back toward the two flanking him. "It'll take more than a throne room, you sorry fart-wind."

Tdanerend's mouth thinned. "Out. Let Rathend teach him some manners. We'll try again in the morning."

Back through the door. Leander's heart slammed painfully in his chest, and his wrists felt watery, but exhilaration sang through him, sang until he was shoved into a cold, bad-smelling room with a cruel-faced man whose clothes were stained with blood obviously not his.

⅜CR℡ⅎ

The night was long and miserable for Kitty.

When she woke, it was to the sound of the door closing, and she sat up, her breath clouding, to find the bowl gone and in its place another bowl, this one with something steaming. She wriggled over, keeping the blanket about her, and discovered that it was oat slurry with boiled egg.

Only commoners ate dishes like that, and this slurry was watery, with only the faintest dash of honey in it, the egg overcooked. Disgusting! But the urge to throw it out the window only lasted about two breaths, then she drank it all down.

Her jug of water had a thin film of ice on top. She poked a hole through and drank a few sips, shuddering at the coldness, then she wriggled back to her spot. It was no longer warm. She lay down again.

Voices echoed up the court after a time, same as the day before. She wondered if she'd be there until she froze—either from the weather or from boredom.

The day dragged on, broken only when she crawled over to drink from the water jug, and at sunset she heard the expected footsteps.

But this time when the door opened the guards came inside, and one of them pulled her to her feet. The gut twist of fear made her wish for the boredom again. They couldn't have come for her for any good reason, not if Marlovens were fetching her.

Back into the castle, which was at least somewhat warmer. She was marched down the hall to the old grand reception rooms, unused since the bad old days with Kitty's mother. All the candles were lit, and once Kitty saw a familiar shadow in a doorway—Llhei! But she dared not turn her head to see for sure.

Straight to the old throne room, which held so many bad memories. Nothing had changed, that was what was strangest. It felt as if the year with Leander had been only a bright dream.

"Kyale Marlonen." That was Tdanerend.

Kitty gulped, and stopped when the guard holding her stopped.

"Where is my daughter?"

Kitty's thoughts careened wildly, and she remembered then how they'd found Ndand, and CJ had impersonated her—

"She ran away," Kitty stated triumphantly.

"And my nephew?"

Kitty gawked. "I thought you killed that stinkard!"

"Is that the rumor going around?" Tdanerend asked.

Kitty felt her sympathies veer Senrid's way. But she knew better than to let Tdanerend know. "Well, that was what we hoped," she stated. "But we certainly haven't seen that slime-crawler for ages—and good riddance."

"What exactly happened?" Tdanerend asked.

"You mean, when you came stenching into our home—"

Tdanerend waved a hand, and someone spun Kitty around and slapped her face. Stars danced redly across her vision. Pain lanced through her cheek, then it felt weirdly numb.

She put her hand up to it.

"Answer the question," Tdanerend said, smiling nastily. It was clear that he would really, really enjoy more chances for bullying.

Kitty had to swallow twice before she could trust her voice. Even so, it came out trembling. "A foreigner pulled us out by magic. Senrid found us. He tried to transfer us back to your disgusting castle, but the magic got all tangled, and we all got thrown off-world."

"And?" Tdanerend prompted. "You seem to have returned. What about Senrid?"

"I told you, I don't know! Leander and I got sent back here, and that's *all* I know. Or care."

"What was this other world?"

"A water place."

"Were there magicians present?"

"Yes."

"And did my nephew interact with them?"

"Interact? I don't know what you mean by that, but we had to get rid of some spell or other, and we met some interesting people, some green humans and some beings like squids. There were some fish people, too, but we didn't really see them but once."

"I see. And did my nephew stay?"

"How should I—" Kitty saw Tdanerend glance up behind her, and she flinched and said hastily, "No. None of us did. We were all together when somebody did this giant spell—I don't know who—and Leander and I landed here, and I didn't see any of the others. Including your rotten globule of a nephew. So there!"

"Who were these others? Faline Sherwood was one, I take it? And 713?"

"Yes, and a couple of their friends who got accidentally pulled in." Kitty had learned what Marlovens did to those who messed with their plans. She was not about to mention CJ's part if she could possibly help it. She'd never understood who

Autumn was or how she'd gotten mixed in, but one thing for sure: Autumn was nice, and Kitty wasn't even going to tell this monster her name.

Tdanerend drummed his fingers on the arm of the black throne, then he said, "You are utterly worthless to anyone as you are. I could kill you now and no one in the world would blink an eye. So we are where we were when we met last: I want your cooperation, so that I may find some use for you."

"I won't consent to a traitor spell," Kitty yelled, her voice shrill and desperate. "I won't."

"Well, we'll see. I've received word from the last of my detachments. Your country is now mine. All of it. Less than one day. A reprehensible record, even for you fools. You're about to witness a little ceremony."

"Oh no I won't."

"Oh yes you will—and it'll be the last thing you'll see for a while," Tdanerend said, and laughed.

His laugh was as nasty as his expression.

Kyale was jerked around and marched out, down the hall, and into the garrison court again. This time another group came out, and Kitty was stunned and sickened when she recognized the tattered, bruised figure being held upright in their midst: Leander.

One side of his face was too bruised and swollen to look at, but he tried to smile. Terror wrung down her in waves, but she did her best to hide it, for Leander was hiding it, he was trying to encourage her with his quirked brow—she knew it, even though his puffy jaw and purple eye distorted his expression.

"Hi," she squeaked.

"Hi yourself," he responded, his voice more like the croak of a frog.

Then they were pulled apart.

Kitty looked around—in time to see the sky blue banner of Vasande Leror pulled from the highest tower, and in its place the Marlovens put the one she'd seen in Senrid's castle: a screaming eagle of gold, edged with blue, against a black background.

She shut her eyes, and refused to look.

"Don't want to see it, eh, brat?"

Tdanerend's voice, shockingly near, made her jump.

"No!" she snarled.

"Kitty—" Leander's voice came, strained, warning, then a door slammed.

Kitty whirled around, scarcely aware of Tdanerend's droning voice, but she couldn't see the other side of the court. Where was Leander, and when had the darkness gotten so thick?

She couldn't see the court, or the Marlovens, or Tdanerend—or even her own feet.

Tdanerend chortled, endlessly entertained.

She couldn't help crying out, or staggering as the darkness closed in.

She was blind.

SEVEN

A sudden flurry of noise—footsteps, distant shouts, the ringing scrape of swords being drawn—sounded to Kitty's left. Instinctively she forced herself not to react, standing as still as she could, despite her trembling.

She picked out Tdanerend's voice—yelling orders, and cursing—from among the others. He was now at some distance, and rapidly moving away.

A hand touched her arm. She started, and covered her face with her hands, as though hiding her face would protect her.

"It's I," Llhei whispered. "Come along. Something's happened elsewhere, something he doesn't like, and maybe he'll forget about you for a time."

"I can't *see*, Llhei," Kitty whimpered. "Don't t-tell anyone—"

"Shhh, child. I'm taking you to your room. You'll soon be snug in your own bed."

And so it was.

Warm and clean at last, Kitty scarcely had the energy to eat the fresh bread-and-cheese that Llhei brought, but eat it she did. She drank down some warm steeped listerblossom, feeling the last of her headache fade, and then burrowed under her quilt and slept deeply.

When she woke, there was noise at the door. She sat up, looked around, saw only darkness and once again smacked her hands over her eyes.

Llhei said quickly, "It's I. With something to eat. And as much news as you can bear."

"Leander?"

Llhei sighed. "He might be visiting in a bit. We shall see."

Llhei had not answered the question directly. Kitty's stomached churned. But Llhei insisted she dress, and eat, before they talked.

When Kitty was full, and warm, Llhei said, "They think I am a cleaning servant, so I have a measure of freedom. I suspect Tdanerend was not happy to discover how few of us there are, and his warriors do not like being pressed into kitchen and cleaning duty." She chuckled. "So we are safe, because he needs us. Alaxandar, Arel, and some of the others managed to get away. They have been doing their best to make trouble."

"Some of the others?"

"Portan was killed," Llhei murmured. "As well as the others who were with him in the stables. They attempted to defend the front gates and would not surrender."

Kitty felt sick. She hadn't really liked any of those people, but she'd known them, and to think she'd never see Portan saddling horses again. . . She winced, and shook her head.

"The good news is that since yesterday someone has been making things very difficult for Tdanerend. A messenger was waylaid. Tdanerend's commands have been countermanded. Some strange magical interference as well, the latest one I overheard being that the wards Tdanerend has been putting round our borders are gone. He was furious!"

"I didn't know Alaxandar or Arel knew magic!"

"I didn't either, but maybe your brother managed to set something up. Anyway, Tdanerend intended to have you and Leander either enchanted or killed by tomorrow—we've been desperately trying to make plans for getting the two of you free—"

A quick tap at the door caused Llhei's breath to hiss in.

Kitty clenched her hands together. She heard the door open, and footsteps. "One turn," said a Marloven voice, in accented Leroran, and Kitty heard the click of the small glass being set on the mantel.

The door closed.

A sigh—Leander's sigh! A sigh of relief?

"Leander?" Kitty asked.

"He said he had a surprise. I thought—I thought it was worse than it was," he said.

The strain in his voice made Kitty's eyes burn.

"Oh, Leander, I didn't want to tell you, but I can't see."

"But it was done with magic," Leander said. He *did* sound relieved!

For a moment Kitty was angry—until she realized what he'd feared, and again her stomach squinched up at the vivid mental picture of the way that Tdanerend *could* have done it. She started talking then, describing every horrible moment from the time she'd woken to the sound of growling felines, ending up with what had just happened. "Why?" she wailed at the end. "Why?"

"He wants you whole and healthy," Leander said, ignoring a question he couldn't answer. The sand had nearly run out, so he talked fast. "In default of me. I don't think he's thought of using you against me—not until now. If he does," he whispered. "If he does, Kitty, will you forgive me if I give in?"

"Leander! It's not your fault!"

The door rattled.

Kitty said quickly, "Llhei says that Alaxandar and the others are causing Tdanerend awful trouble."

Leander sighed again. She was glad that she couldn't see him. She was afraid of what had happened to him to make him sound like that.

The door opened and a jumble of footsteps came in and left again. The door closed.

Llhei said, "Good girl. Tdanerend expected you to whine and cry and make things worse for Leander. That's the only reason why you were permitted the visit."

"What can I do?" Kitty whimpered, thoroughly terrified.

"Try to bear what you can. If Tdanerend does..." Her voice faded, and she sounded tired and old. "If you can, try not to beg Leander for help or aid, if the two of you are brought in together. You will be safer if Tdanerend thinks you don't really care for one another."

"Like him and Ndand?"

"Exactly."

"What's wrong with Leander?   What did they do to him?"

"You don't want to know, child.   But—as yet—it hasn't gotten worse because Tdanerend has hopes yet of using magic to make him a puppet.   I am so glad Leander put that language spell on us all!   That dreadful man doesn't know we can understand him, and Nelyas overheard some talk in the stairwell. He doesn't want to be here, he's anxious to get back home. I am afraid it will get worse before it gets better, unless we get some help. Do you want the window open, child? It's beginning to snow out there."

"First Snow," Kitty said in a small voice. "And I'm missing it." She bit her lip, thinking about how it had looked in the past. She told herself, use your imagination. Use your memory. Llhei's right. Don't whine. Don't make it all worse.

The touch of cold air on her cheek kept her from feeling closed in. The room did not stay really warm, but the trade was worth it.

"Open a crack. I need the air," Kitty said. "Or I feel like I'm in a box."

"Then bundle up and rest. When he gets back, I'm afraid you both are in for more nastiness."

℠(ℹℝ℠)ℂ

And so it was.

Kitty woke up abruptly with Llhei's hand on her shoulder. "They're here. Want you below," she whispered. "Remember what I told you."

Kitty had slept in her dress. She groped with her hands, caught at Llhei's fingers, and slipped out of bed.

At the door, unfamiliar smells swirled in—or rather, smells she was not used to smelling at home. Steel, horse, wet wool.   It smelled like the Marloven dungeon in Choreid Dhelerei, not like her own home. All that was missing was the odor of old stone and unchanged air.

Fingers grabbed at her arms. The pace was much too rapid, and she stumbled until the grip on her arms tightened. At least she didn't fall down.

The room they hustled her to was big, from the sound, and cold, and she was fairly sure it was again the throne room.

"Now we'll see some sport."

The hated voice made Kitty's insides tighten with anger and apprehension.

"We'll try a game that our academy boys often play. No blindfold needed! Let's see how well our mouthy little princess does."

The hands let go of Kitty. She stood for a moment, her feet cold on marble, listening to the scrapes of boots around her, the sounds of breathing. A lot of people were in the room. All Marlovens?

A sudden slap on her cheek caused her to gasp.

"Run," a voice said.

"If you get through the perimeter, you're free," Tdanerend called, his tone derisive. "You have to learn to listen. Something I don't think you were ever taught."

Kitty stumbled in one direction, heard the clunk of boots on the marble. They were close—and *Sting*! another slap.

She whirled about and ran, stumbling over her hem and falling, then getting up. She waved her hands before her, but they were smacked away. Again and again the footsteps, the cuffs, and all the while that single voice laughing, harshly, in the background. Tdanerend seemed to find every single slap, every fall, inordinately entertaining.

No one else laughed, none of the people around her. They were silent, except for the sounds of breathing.

"Harder," Tdanerend called, though Kitty felt that the slaps were painful enough.

Another smack caught her on the side of her face, so hard it took her breath with it, and her arms windmilled before she fell full length.

Tdanerend laughed so hard he wheezed. Then he said, "Aren't you enjoying it? Or would you like to take her place?"

Kitty's head was ringing now, but she could still hear.

Leander's voice came from the right, drawling with fake boredom, "I'd do it, but I can't seem to walk." It was fake boredom because Kitty could hear the tremble of rage underneath the drawl.

She remembered what Llhei had said, and yelled, "This is all your fault, Leander!"

And Leander snapped back, "You're the authority, of course, Kyale." It was so nasty a tone, so false, that she knew instantly that he was faking it as hard as she was.

Slap. Smash. She hit her elbow, felt splinters of pain shoot up her arm, and she decided she'd had enough. So she crouched down in a ball and wouldn't move. A few slaps—none of them very hard—and then silence.

Not silence. One set of new footsteps, quick ones. The rattle of paper. A messenger, then?

Tdanerend cursed in Marloven, then, again in his own tongue, "Get them out of here." And, his fast step and his voice diminishing, "Why haven't you fools caught those raiders? Every strike is getting bolder! These Lerorans are nothing but rabbits. Do I have to flog the back off of every commander until I see my orders carried out...."

Fingers gripped Kitty's arms again, and out she went.

Back in her room, Kitty held in her tears until Llhei had bathed her face, and then she buried her face in her pillow and yelled and screamed.

§

She was sitting up in bed, her fingers following the stitching on the quilting and the embroidery over it, when the vines outside her window rustled.

"Hoped you were here," came a whisper. "Ready for a rescue?"

"Who's there?" Kitty whispered back.

"There are no guards close by? Or servants?"

"Llhei's asleep, and those disgusting Marlovens only come in here when Tdanerend sends them. Who are you?"

She heard footsteps in her room.

"Um, it isn't safe to say." The whisper was completely voiceless. "But I'm against Tdanerend being here as much as you are."

"Oh! Then you must be a raider!"

"Raider? Oh. Yes. That's right." A breathy laugh. "So are you coming, or do you want to sit here and wait until Tdanerend comes up for a visit?"

"An escape?" Kitty flung back her covers and slid her feet, still in their bed-socks, into her mocs, which had been waiting at her bedside. Then she hesitated. The raider couldn't know she had been blinded, or maybe she'd be left behind.

So she crossed toward her windows, fairly certain that the dimensions of her own room were familiar enough not to trip her up.

Step, step, step, and—she reached. Yes! There was a windowsill. To the left, then, would be her wardrobe, and inside, on its hook, her cape. She risked the attempt, and her outstretched fingers groped once before closing on the familiar wool.

She pulled the cape on, thrust her arms through the slits—glad she'd not changed into a nightgown, but kept her sturdy walking dress on, in case those horrible Marlovens came for her again—and made it back to the window. If only she knew where Llhei kept her mittens!

The whisper came again. "Now the trick is, test the vine first. Grab the bigger ones, not the little, and make sure each vine is strong. I'll go first. See that your feet are placed right."

Sounds of slithering and rustling, and then the whisper came from outside, "Come on."

The journey down the wall was long and frightening. Her nose stung from the sharp smell of broken plants, and from the cold air, but she didn't dare sneeze. Her fingers ached from their tight grip on the plants. Halfway down she thought, what about the guards on the wall?

She didn't ask, in case her rescuer expected her to be able to see whatever was going on.

Instead, she concentrated on one foot, one hand, other foot, other hand, one at a time, until she made it down the wall.

At the bottom, a hand closed on her wrist. "Can you ride?"

Kitty shook her head.

But a moment later a triangular head butted against the backs of her knees, and she felt about, and found a muscular, sleek-furred feline body. "Meta?" she whispered.

A low raspy purr was her answer, and moments later she was seated astride the black leopard.

Meta paced slowly for a short time. Kitty heard the clopping of hooves, muffled by the snow, and then Meta's pace increased. Kitty leaned over, locking her arms around the thick, strong neck, as Meta raced feline-fashion next to a galloping horse.

The fast pace lasted a while, then the animals both slowed, and again Kitty kept expecting a halt, but it did not come.

Her fingers were numb and her arms and neck on fire from her bent posture when at last a voice said, "Here we are."

Kitty sat up, wincing, and swung her leg over. Her steps crunched in snow. Meta moved away, and Kitty said, "Thank you."

"Hmmph, very polite of you," said the voice, no longer whispering. It was a light, cheery kid voice.

Kitty's insides swooped nastily. "Senrid!"

EIGHT

"And you are blind as a post."

Kyale groaned, wishing Senrid was near enough to kick. "So what now, my own personal execution?"

"No," he said, sounding disgusted. "Think, Kyale, instead of drowning in self-pity. If I wanted you dead, wouldn't I just leave you there?"

Kitty sighed. "All right. What do you want?"

"Information."

"Oh, and I'm going to give it to you? Like *this*? Sounds like *you*'re the one who—"

"Let's get a fire going," he interrupted. "Now, I'll take that spell off your eyes if you promise me something."

"I don't believe you can do it."

Senrid snorted. "This way. No, this way. Sit there. Hah! From the look of things, someone was here recently—and maybe means to return. Huh. I'll be back in a moment. Have to start the fire and see to the horse. I note your cat friend is gone."

Kitty said nothing. Presently she smelled burning wood and felt faint warmth, and scooted toward it. As she held out her hands to warm up she heard noises: hooves, horse-breathing, then munchings; other horse noises that she couldn't identify, all punctuated by Senrid's quick steps crunching dirt against stone. Then at last she smelled the sharp fragrance of dry wood catching fire.

Senrid said, "Tdanerend knows something about eyes because his experimental spells caused Ndand's vision problems. He's too incompetent to completely correct his mistakes, but he knows plenty about damage. I found and memorized the antidotes—I always planned to fix Ndand as soon as my uncle let me take power."

Kitty did not care about Ndand. She interrupted sourly, "So what do I have to promise? If it's killing anybody—"

"You being so well trained."

Once again his sarcasm stopped her.

"Well, then, what?"

"It's easy. Nothing easier. You keep your mouth shut about my presence. That includes what I've done, and what I'm going to do."

"As if I'd tell that disgusting creep of an uncle anything, except how rotten and disgusting he is—"

"And Leander. Anybody. I don't want anybody to know. At all."

"Leander? But that makes no sense!"

"I don't care what makes sense to you and what doesn't. Promise, and you see. Don't, and I'll leave you here and get back to work."

"What are you doing anyway?"

"I'm having priceless fun," Senrid said. Kitty could imagine that toothy grin that she loathed so much. "I want Tdanerend back on home ground, where he and I can have it out, winner take Marloven Hess. But I don't want you involved, or your brother, or any other outsiders." He paused, then said in a harder voice, "No interference."

"So..." Kitty thought rapidly. "Alaxandar isn't doing magic after all. You're the one who took down the border wards, and other things like that?"

Senrid laughed. "'And other things like that.' All part of my plan. Well?"

"All right," Kitty said, sighing. "But you're a stupid, rotten, lying fool."

"Save the compliments for someone who cares a snap for your opinion. And sit still. This magic is complicated."

Kitty held her breath, listening to the low murmur of Senrid's voice. Beneath it, beneath the whisper of the wind through bare trees, she felt a hum, like a bee at the edge hearing, and her skin prickled. Then a sharp, sudden pang shot through her head, and sparkling lights flashed across her vision. Her tearing eyes slowly compassed a gray blur, which resolved into a dark cave at night.

A dark cave—Leander's old hideout!

Kitty blinked, looked about, and saw Senrid perched on an old log, face and hair golden in the ruddy firelight. At the familiar sight of those watchful gray-blue eyes, she frowned, loathing him all over again. "Oh, why didn't you get lost."

"Still the same perfect princess," Senrid retorted.

"Shut up," she snapped.

"The first plan is to spring Leander," Senrid continued.

"Why?"

"I told you. I want my uncle on home ground. If I get you two out, I can deal with him more easily. Right now with you gone he's going to be more careful with Leander, or he'll have lost you both. And if he loses you two, he loses this country, and he knows it."

"Why, because he has to put us in as puppets?"

Senrid flexed his hands. The firelight highlighted their contours, making them seem tense "Or else stay here and enforce every single order, and watch for uprisings. And use half his army to guard the mines. While home is left open for enterprising sorts, such as myself, to walk in and take the throne. He thinks having you might be a stopgap, but he really needs Leander ordering your people to do his will—and doing the magic to ease the mining."

Kitty sighed. "Leander sounded really bad. I hope he's—"

"Tell me what happened," Senrid cut in again, leaning forward. "Exactly."

Kitty shrugged, and outlined her experiences in detail. He said nothing, but his breath whooshed when she told him what Leander had said: *Will you forgive me if I give in?*

At the end, he said, "It's worse than I thought. If you want your brother back, we'll have to act fast."

"What? I don't get it. I mean, I know he said he'd consent if Tdanerend did anything creepy to me, but couldn't that spell be removed?"

Senrid's eyes were almost black, his pupils were so huge.
"Kyale. Don't you ever see anything past your own image in the
mirror? Leander's going to push them to kill him. He as much
told you that." He frowned as he stared into the fire. Twin
points of orange light reflecting in those black pupils did not
make his gaze any more pleasant, despite his round, fine-
featured kid face. "He thinks—I'll wager he sees it as the only
way to defeat Tdanerend for certain."

Kitty gave a cry of dismay. Then she frowned. "Why
should I believe a liar and a creep like you?" Anger and fear
made her feel shivery. She wanted, so badly, for Senrid to be
wrong.

"Believe what you want," Senrid said. "What I want
right now is the exact layout of those dungeons of yours. You
and Leander never took me through there on my visit." Now
Senrid looked and sounded as bland as ever.

Kitty glared at him across the bright flames, but he went
on. "I don't suppose you noticed where the guards are posted, or
when they change?"

She shook her head.

He shrugged. "I'll assume that watches and posts will be
will be what they would be at home, then. Never mind. Just
give me the layout." As he spoke, he knelt on the cave floor and
smoothed the dirt over.

Kitty closed her eyes, thinking. She'd been about to
deny the knowledge—and it was true she'd seldom been there.
But she remembered that the storage areas had been her best
hiding spots during hide and seek games.

All she had to do was think back, and she could picture
the first big room, then the hallways leading this way, then
bending, then that way...

She sketched with her finger. Senrid watched in silence,
his eyes narrowed.

When she was done Kitty sat back, eying him in dislike.
He was wearing the same shirt and trousers and boots he'd been
in during the adventure on the other world; in place of the tunic
he lost in the ocean he had a cloak now, way too long. A
grownup's cloak that dragged on the ground. The rest was the

same—except far grubbier. He had obviously not been home in order to change his clothes.

He scanned the finger-marks once more, smeared them out with a sudden movement, then sketched slowly. Kitty noted with sour disgust that he redrew it much faster than she'd done the first map.

When he was done, he looked up. "Is that it?"

"Yes."

He nodded. "Time to go."

"Why don't you use magic to go in and get him and get out again?"

"Tracer spells on the transfer," Senrid said. "And my uncle keeps putting wards on the palace. See, the smaller the perimeter, the easier the ward. Big ones are toughest."

Kitty nodded. "Oh. And you messed up the one over the country—"

Senrid grinned. "He'll have lost an entire day of very intensive labor. Longer, because he's such a terrible mage, and he won't have the guts to get Latvian over to do it for him again." He pointed back into the cave. "Extra blankets are back there."

"What? You're leaving me here?"

"You want to go back to my uncle?" He put his hands on his hips, smiling in derision.

"No no no no no."

"You're safe enough here. Tdanerend knows nothing about this place."

Kitty turned her back on him, and bustled about questing for blankets.

Senrid led his mount out, and hoof-beats rapidly faded away.

She was alone, except for the crackling fire, and the soft soughing of a cold breeze in the high pines on the hill. She wrapped up in three blankets, lay down by the fire, and drifted into dreams.

When she woke up, one side of her was warm, the other chilled. She had been dreaming of rumbling thunder—not horrific thunder, but a curiously comforting distant thunder.

When she opened her eyes to the blue-gray light of morning, she found Meta curled up next to her. Kitty sat up, reached for Meta's flat head. She scratched the great cat, who yawned, displaying her sharp white teeth, then stretched.

With a bound and a twitch of her long black tail, Meta vanished out the cave mouth. Kitty, peering after her, discovered that it was snowing outside.

Kitty stared at her fire, which had been reduced to a few dull red embers. Leander didn't keep Fire Sticks here—gave them all away. Leander—no, she couldn't think about him.

So she flung off her blankets and ran to the stack of firewood someone had cut from the dried-out old log. Picking up some small twigs, she returned and crouched down, poking the twigs at one of the last two embers.

The first burst apart and faded out.

She was more cautious with the last one, holding the twig above it. For a long time nothing happened, then it smoked, and at last she was rewarded with a tiny tongue of flame.

By working with care, adding wood slowly, she soon had a nice blaze going again—and she'd done it all herself.

She was hungry, but at least she was warm, and free.

The day passed slowly. She wandered about, and even spent some time standing on the pretty little arched bridge. She looked down into the cold blue water trickling past the ice forming in glass-like beads along twigs and rocks, and thought about what Senrid had said.

Leander was going to *die*?

She felt icy inside. What would happen to her if Leander did die? Even if they got rid of the Marlovens, nobody would want her as the ruler. She knew that. They'd put some grownup in, someone who wouldn't want Mara Jinea's daughter around, and Kitty would have no place to go.

And she would miss Leander. Horribly. He was the first person, besides Llhei, who was ever nice to her.

She sighed. Well, if that disgusting Senrid had a plan, then she would do whatever he asked.

When the sun began to sink beyond the frost-touched dark branches to the west she heard horse hooves, and scurried back into the cave to crouch behind some wooden boxes.

Shadows flickered, then a voice called out, "Kyale?" It was Senrid.

She ran out, relieved to see him, though she never would have admitted it. He slid off a horse—a different one than the day before—and leaned against it for a moment, blinking stupidly at the fire.

"You kept it going," he observed, then glanced at the woodpile. "I suppose you used half a winter's supply."

"I've never tended a fire before," Kitty said defensively. "It's a servant's job."

Senrid straightened up. "No more wood on it, we're not going to be here long. My plan requires darkness. I'm here to collect you and explain." He pulled a wrapped packet from the saddlebag and tossed it to her. "And you have to eat something."

He did some quick chores with the horse. She ignored that, wrinkling her nose at the smell of horse sweat. She didn't like horses. Tall, uncanny things! Cats were much preferable.

Senrid's packet turned out to be fresh bread—so fresh the middle was faintly warm—and cheese and a single tomato. Kitty retreated into the cave and found the plain clay plates that Leander kept stored. She pulled out a knife, cut up the cheese and tomato, then slit one side of the bread and poked the things into it.

It was the first time she'd ever done it, but she'd watched the cook often enough when she'd had to eat in the kitchen. When she was done she looked at it proudly, and took a bite. Wonderful!

She felt much better when the bread was all gone, and she'd had some more of the water that she'd earlier set near the fire in a pan so it wouldn't be so cold to drink.

About the time she finished, Senrid rejoined her; she was shocked at the marks of tiredness in his face.

"Yeuch," she exclaimed.

Senrid's upper lip curled, but all he said was, "Ready to be the great hero?"

She stared in surprise.

"I've set it all up. It's going to be all your doing." He pulled something from his pocket and tossed it into her lap. "That's the key to the row of cells he's in. Don't lose it!"

"How did you—"

"Never mind that," he said impatiently. "You need to listen. I've messed with the magic wards, another reason we have to be fast, but I don't think Uncle Tdanerend will find them all, and he sure can't replace them—not unless he admits he's incompetent and pulls Latvian in. And they've had a falling out." He grinned.

Mistrusting that grin, Kitty demanded, "You haven't done anything to Hibern, have you?"

"Never even seen her. It was all by messengers. Anyway, what's going to happen will be a lot of noise and fire and confusion on the opposite side of the castle, so don't get yourself in a panic. Tdanerend will go wild and summon the guards to defend him first, and as soon as they assemble, in you go."

"And what are you going to do?" she asked, still distrustful.

"Borrowing Leander's idea, I'll have a host of illusory light cavalry with me—another reason for darkness. And Tdanerend'll be my affair after that. You get Leander out and well away. If you can, take him to that old estate you were a child in—"

"Tannantaun?"

"That's it. Uncle'd never send patrols there, cuz it's too isolated."

"And?"

"And when you hear what the results are, the two of you decide what to do. If I lose, you won't be rid of my uncle but at least you'll have some freedom of movement. Understood?"

Kitty nodded once, then frowned. "I wish I knew why you were doing all this stuff. It seems to me you could fight Tdanerend just as well without rescuing us, though I'm glad to be free—"

"Because it'll make my uncle furious, of course. I want him so mad he can't think, and I can get around him easier."

"So why not let Leander know?"

"Are you ready to go?"

Kitty persevered. "If I could be sure that you don't have some nastier plan waiting for Leander. But then you're such a liar you wouldn't tell me the truth anyway—"

"Have I lied to you since yesterday?"

"You shouldn't have lied to us," Kitty pronounced loftily, sure now that she was completely in the right.

"I suppose you've never lied in your life." He checked the saddles.

Kitty said smugly, "Never to betray friendships or honor."

Senrid gave a long sigh, and looked up at the stars beyond the tops of the trees. "I just want to go home," he said finally. Then he gave her that derisive look again. "Speaking of liars, whatever did happen to my cousin? CJ wouldn't tell me."

"She's safe, according to a message from—from someone. And I'm sure she's now quite happy. And you won't find out where."

"Just so that my tender-hearted uncle never finds her, I'm content."

"Then let's get busy. Sooner we do it, sooner you're gone. And good riddance."

He laughed, and held down a hand to pull her up behind him.

Kitty backed off, frightened. "I don't like horses—"

A black shadow swarmed across the pale, gleaming snow, and Kitty cried in relief. "Meta!"

And so they departed as they had come, one on horseback, and one riding a leopard.

NINE

At first the plan progressed exactly as Senrid had outlined.

They left the animals some distance from the castle—outside the first perimeter, whatever that was. Kitty didn't want to know.

She hadn't talked on the long ride. Once they were on foot Senrid led, even though this was supposedly her territory, but she kept quiet, and was soon glad that she had because he used a way that she'd never seen before.

It meant following along a creek bed, with lots of stones, in the dark, but she did not complain, even when she almost fell twice, twisting her ankle with sudden, painful wrenches when she stepped on the sides of loose stones that shifted. He didn't have to warn her about the guards on the walls: she could see their silhouettes moving back and forth, making the red torchlight wink and stream.

When they were close to the castle, he said softly, "Behind me, and hold on."

She stepped behind him, and touched his arm. He muttered under his breath, and she felt that hum again, but briefer, weaker. The air around her seemed to glitter darkly. Illusion—she knew that much—the spell would cloak them both as long as they touched. The spell was on her, not him, which was why her vision had smeared.

She also knew the spell did not really make them invisible, though it was called 'invisibility illusion.' It mirrored their surroundings, but if anyone looked straight at them, closely, they would see a suspicious smear, especially if they were moving. So they must not make noise, or tracks, and cause anyone to look closely.

She felt exposed and defenseless as they laboriously made their way toward the castle; Senrid stepped in hoof prints, and Kitty in turn stepped where Senrid had, making certain she never lost her grip on him.

Their progress was slow, and Kitty jumped, her heart thumping, every time the men in the gleaming helms on the wall stopped in their constant pacing, or turned the nosepieces her way.

She and Senrid finally reached the old garrison supply entrance, which Kitty had never been through, though she knew where it was. And there they stopped.

After standing motionless for what seemed forever she leaned toward him to speak, but he raised a hand warningly, and she bit her numb lips, and huddled into her cloak except for her one icy hand, still gripping him. Senrid whispered another spell.

Not long after that she heard horsehooves, and then the gate opened. Riders galloped out, the horsetails on their helms tossing in the wind. They passed within a stone's throw of the two kids; some of the horses turned their heads Kitty's way, the huge dark eyes gleaming with starlight, but the riders clucked at them, and they moved on.

When the last one was past, Senrid nodded once and they ran inside, no longer having to bother about their prints as the horses had thoroughly churned up the snow into mud.

Once they were in, Senrid walked her to the archway leading down to the dungeon. They slipped past the two guards standing on either side of the archway, and Senrid motioned for Kitty to stay in place.

She nodded, knowing that she had to wait for the door to open before she could get inside.

Senrid slipped away. He was now visible, but he stepped hastily into the shadows and then moments later winkled out of sight: now he had an illusion spell on himself. Yes, she could see a vague, kid-sized distortion of the wall that he stood in front of, which rippled slightly when he moved, but she had to concentrate to make it out.

Kitty stood where she was, hands in her armpits, the stones cold through her mocs. She tried to keep her breathing soft, for the guards did not talk, nor were they inattentive. They swept their gazes back and forth every so often, and once she even saw one turn her way. A faint gleam from one of the torches reflected in his eyes, but then he faced outward again.

Her throat closed against a whimper of fear. She gritted her teeth until her jaw ached. How long would that stupid brat take?

Just then a huge, thunderous boom made her jump—her and the guards. The clatter of falling rubble followed, then an even louder boom, and a third: only in black magic could one deliberately transfer something into space already occupied. It took a tremendous amount of work, the spells were dangerously volatile, but three big boulders slammed into the wall from within, with spectacular results.

Two breaths later the garrison courtyard streamed with Marlovens, all of them putting on helms, pulling weapons free, and lining into neat defensive squares. Kitty pressed against the wall. As yet the dungeon door hadn't opened.

Then she heard Tdanerend. His harsh, angry voice echoed weirdly, punctuating orders with vile curses.

Someone dashed her way, his light brown hair stuck sweatily to his forehead. He banged on the dungeon door, which opened—and Kitty was almost on his heels. She knew she was supposed to wait until the guards came out, but what if they didn't?

She crept to the side, against the inner wall, as the young man's voice echoed down the stone corridor, "Assemble! Assemble!"

And then she had to flatten against the wall as Marlovens boiled out of the corridors. An elbow struck her cheek and she bit back a gasp. The man glanced back, and Kitty caught a brief, terrifying glimpse of a broad, puzzled faced framed by short lemon-pale hair, but someone shoved him and he straightened round again and kept going. She pressed herself flatter, not daring to breathe, until she knew they were past, and she was alone.

Her fingers closed over the key that Senrid had given her as she ran down the corridor he'd told her to use. Of course it was the last hall, the one that took longest to get to.

But she made it, her hands shaking so badly and her fingers so numb that she fumbled the key and dropped it not once but several times. She had to bite her lips hard to keep from whimpering in terrified frustration when at last she got the door open. Leander stood in the bare cell, lit by the torch behind her.

The sight of him made her stop still.

"Is that you, Kitty?"

"I—I can see," she mumbled, touching his wrist so he would be able to see her. "Oh, you look awful."

Leander smiled—as much as he could with a blackened eye and split lip—and said, "I'll heal. If I can get out of here. Is this a trick, or a rescue?"

Kitty gulped in air. "Rescue! Come on!"

"How—"

"Illusion," she said quickly, bracing herself against questions she couldn't answer. But Leander looked down at her fingers on his wrist, and his brow cleared, as though he'd managed to figure out why she'd grabbed him. "But I don't know how long it'll last," she added tentatively.

Leander nodded and started out.

She matched Leander's pace, which wasn't very fast. His breath hissed between his teeth at every other step.

But they made it to the door, and out. Kitty firmly gripped Leander's hand, according to instructions, and they ventured through the archway, though Marlovens dashed about in every direction.

Tdanerend began yelling from the wall above them.

Leander whirled around. So did Kitty, her arm wrenching badly. But she managed to keep her grip on Leander, and not to cry out. Leander looked up, and so did she. Tdanerend was waving his arms, pronouncing magic spells—

"Uh oh," Leander whispered.

Kitty realized that the dark glitter at the edges of her vision, which she'd gotten used to, was gone. Astonished faces turned their way.

Someone shouted, "The prisoners!"

"Run," Leander groaned.

"I am!"

They each managed about five steps in the direction of the gates before they were surrounded.

Someone shouted a warning up to Tdanerend, who looked down, and then back over the wall, and then down again. "Stash 'em! Until I deal with this traitor!" he snarled.

Kitty's eyes burned with tears of rage, but anger gave way to fear when she saw how Leander had fallen into the snow. Had someone knocked him down? He seemed unable to get up. Two Marlovens grabbed his arms and half-carried, half-dragged him toward the tower, which was closest.

Leander almost slipped from their grasp. He seemed unconscious. What had they done to him so quickly? The Marlovens hustled the two kids into the lower cell, and slammed the door. Bang! The bar thunked into place.

Leander grunted with pain. Kitty felt around for him in the complete darkness, wondering how she could revive him.

But then he whispered, "Hurry!" And she heard the muffled creak of a rusty hinge.

"What?"

"I hoped if I acted extra decrepit they'd dump us here rather than lug me all the way to the top, or back inside the old storage rooms. Here, Kitty. Trapdoor behind the rotting hay bales. They never even looked," Leander said. "Giving me hope for the other end. Come on, Kitty!"

She was feeling her way across the floor as he spoke, guided by his voice. She bumped into his knee. He caught her hand and guided her through a low crawlspace.

Spider webs brushed her face. She whimpered, shuddering, but forced herself to keep crawling, trying not to sneeze though thick dust tickled her nose. They crawled down the passage at the base of the castle wall, Leander's breath hissing.

Finally they reached the end. Leander fumbled about, then they squeezed through another opening, this time under an old, moss-ruined table; there was a faint, sharp smell of burned wood. "We're in the old stables," he whispered. "Tack room at the very back, the only space that didn't burn."

Mara Jinea had rebuilt the stables when she'd taken over, making more space for her new guards; she'd knocked down the adjacent wall and rebuilt it to include the new space, leaving the old stables outside the castle, where no one had to see them.

"That trapdoor and passage is where we used to get in and out during your mother's day. The passage used to be all enclosed inside the castle, but when she made the new wall, it opened to the outside. It was such a great way in we left weapons here even after she was gone." Leander sighed. "I don't think I ever believed she wouldn't come back."

After the darkness in the passage, the starlight and the faint reflected torchlight through the open roof seemed almost like day.

"Is this why you never fixed all this old burned stuff?" Kitty whispered.

Leander uttered a soft laugh. "Partly. I also didn't fix it because we can't afford that kind of reconstruction yet."

As he spoke he shoved empty boxes out of the way, lifted a blanket green with mildew, and pulled up something cloth-wrapped. In silence he unwrapped it, and Kitty gazed at a sword and dagger.

He offered her the dagger. Her fingers closed around the hilt. The world was fast becoming more and more unreal and dream-like; from the distance came a shout. It sounded like a kid's voice.

Leander stilled, listening, then shook his head. The sounds now were all men's shouts, and horse hooves, and clanks.

"Tdanerend wiped out the black magic illusion spell, which means those wards are gone—" He murmured, made signs, and winked out of sight.

Kitty gasped.

From the air next to her came a soft murmur, and again that magic-dazzle twinkled subtly at the edges of her vision. Leander took her hand, and he blinked back into view.

"Now we get away," he said.

And—slowly, carefully, steadily—they did.

ಚಿ(R೮)ಚ

Leander also felt that sense of unreality, as if he'd wandered forever into a nightmare and could not waken. The escape was too sudden to believe. He kept looking over his shoulder, bracing for Tdanerend to emerge, sneering, from every copse of willows, or from behind a cottage, torches flaring, his Marlovens waving swords.

But no one followed them, no one saw them, not even after the illusion magic wore off. Leander wondered tiredly if he ought to renew it. The spell would hold for an even shorter period this time; he had very little strength left.

His job now was to put one foot in front of the other, and hold onto that blade, which he used as a cane. Kitty walked in silence beside him. He was grateful for her lack of complaint, and lack of questions that he hadn't the strength to answer.

He had no strength—he also had no answers.

It was then that he realized that he had not brought about the escape. He'd not done anything. It was Kitty who had rescued *him*.

He drew a breath, which hurt—when had breathing not hurt? He couldn't remember—and decided that questions could wait.

By the time they reached Mara Jinea's old house outside of Tannantaun, Leander could barely walk. Dawn grayed the east as they plodded down the lane, their footsteps cracking the thin layer of icy snow. Anyone who came along the road would see those prints and know they were there, but he was past caring.

They saw the house, and reached it, and found it had been left unlocked. It was deserted. Leander managed a zaplight, and in its weak blue glow Kitty led the way to the kitchen, where she found a pair of candles and a sparker in a cupboard.

He leaned against a wall, swallowed a couple of times, and said, "How did you get your sight back?"

Kyale looked up, her pupils so large her eyes looked black.

Her lips parted, then she gave her head a little shake.

"And the illusions? And who made that noise I heard before you came? Was it Alaxandar and the others?"

Kitty's eyes flickered. "Yes—maybe—I don't know."

"I think you're lying," Leander said, calm as a dream. Nothing seemed quite real any more.

"Then don't ask questions," Kitty responded, sounding more like herself. "I want to go to sleep."

She lit the candles, handed one to Leander, and led the way upstairs. Leander wondered if he could make it up those stairs. Yes. One, two. Three. Four...

Kitty scuffed to her old bedroom, disgusted at the dust and spider webs. He continued down the hall—still counting his steps—until he found another room with a bed, and quilts folded away in a cedar chest. He pulled those out, tossed the candle into the cold fireplace, lay down, and snapped out of consciousness with the speed of his candle flame.

಼ಅ૨ℇᎧ૬ౚ

He woke up aware of someone else near him, and habit caused him to throw an arm up to ward a blow—a gesture that pulled painfully at his ribs, and thoroughly woke him.

He opened his eyes and looked up into Arel's somber face.

Arel stared back, his mouth compressed into a line. In the bleachy light coming through the window, Leander looked bruised, thin and ill.

"Pretty bad eh?" Leander felt the impulse to laugh, but easily squashed it.

Arel shook his head, looked away, then back. "Worse than I'd thought."

"It's all on the surface. Tdanerend wanted lots of pain. But no permanent damage. Like broken bones. Or worse. He wanted me still able to do magic. I think I might... have cracked a rib, though. Hurts to take a deep breath."

Leander hadn't talked so much in what seemed weeks, though he knew it had only been a few days. A brief time without end; he shook his head slightly, and tried again. "Amazing...isn't it...what you can endure if you know it won't last..."

Arel frowned. "I'll get you some food."

Leander sat up. His head felt light, but he knew that was mostly hunger. The aches had not eased any, but freedom made them bearable. "I'll come with you. I can't just lie here...I have to know what's happening."

He eased his way out of the bed. The dressing room adjacent had a cleaning frame. Feeling an intense pang of gratitude, he walked through it, and back again—just to feel the magic. It did nothing for his hurts, but the zap of cleanliness was good for the spirit.

Arel gave him a half-smile. "That shirt's got to go."

"Too bad frames don't mend rips and tears. Maybe something will turn up here."

"What is this place, anyway?" Arel asked.

"Didn't you know? How did *you* get here? This is Mara Jinea's old house."

"Faugh," Arel exclaimed, glancing about the silent house in disgust. Then he gave Leander a puzzled look. "I got a message to meet you here. Thought it was from you."

Leander waved tiredly. "Not me. What—? Why—? No. I can't think! As for the house, Mara Jinea was never in it, only Kitty, those last few years. Come on, let's scout out the kitchens. My guess is, no one has been here since she was defeated. The locals would be afraid of the place, lest it have magic traps, and legally it belongs to Kitty."

The kitchen larder produced some nasty-looking objects that had sat for the last year, but there was also a chest of carefully dried and preserved herbs and steeping leaves—including listerblossom, a wonderful healing brew. Another surprise appeared—a wax-sealed ceramic bottle labeled *Sartoran Leaf*, a rarity that might have sat there for at least a generation, if not longer, but if it was dry, it would be drinkable.

Arel had fetched water from the well outside the kitchen while Leander explored. Working together they got a fire going, and Leander measured out steeping leaf for brewing while Arel, with brisk efficiency, cleared out the ruined foods and then retreated to what he strongly suspected was a vegetable garden.

Leander, spent from so much effort, sat on a stool and leaned against the table to wait for the water to boil.

Arel returned presently, triumphantly carrying a load of vegetables. "Ground hasn't had time to freeze yet. Let's get a soup going."

Their years of foraging in Sindan made both adept at imaginative cookery with a minimum of equipment and supplies. Mara Jinea's unknown cook had taken most of the pots and pans.

Arel set Leander up with a small knife that had fallen between two storage chests, and he used his own dagger to chop vegetables. He said, "Alaxandar is at Erban Mine. We worked all through two days, and last night we collapsed it."

Leander laughed softly.

Arel grinned. "Thought you'd enjoy that. Was the only thing we could think of, for we were at an impasse: that soul-eater Marloven had ordered everyone from the region up to the mine by today, or else he'd send his murderers among 'em. So anyway, they're setting up traps against the Marlovens forcing people up there regardless."

Leander frowned. The roar of heating water changed to the quiet steam-cloud of boil. He stood slowly up, but Arel was quicker. He shoved Leander firmly down again, poured the steaming water into the pot Leander had found, and within moments the dusty air no longer smelled of chopped vegetables and fire, but like summer.

Leander breathed—and found he could take in a bit more air each time. The pain seemed easier from the mere steam. He sighed. "Then who did the magic last night? Why is a black magic wielder aiding us?"

Arel said, "It's not just magic. Unless you can shoot an arrow with magic?"

"Not that I ever heard of." Leander looked up, hoping for a clue to the mystery. "What shooting? When?"

"Second day or so. Tdanerend was in the town, with bully-boys at his back. Gathering in market-square. Told the people that he had you, and the princess, and that the countries were reunited, hoola-loola.   Mind you, I wasn't there, but Monale was, and you know she always tells the exact truth."

"So she does. Go on."

"Well, he had old Fanuther up there—as Mayor—and a noose. Hangman got the rope round his scrawny neck, all nice and tight, and was about to drop the trapdoor and hang the old geezer as an example of what would happen to guild leaders and then heads of families unless he had instant obedience.   And then a steel-tipped arrow split the rope.   Next one nailed the hangman's right arm in the act of reaching for the rope, third one hit one of Tdanerend's commanders in the knee."

"Split the rope!" Leander whistled.

"Yes. Fine piece of work. Even the Marlovens were impressed, Monale reported. Wish we knew who it was— Alaxandar's hoppin' to find him. Or her."

"No idea who it was?"

"Whoever it was shot from the rooftops, but by the time the Marlovens could get through the crowd to give chase—no one was exactly cooperating, mind you—he, or she, was long gone."

"Might be one of the deserters from Mara Jinea's day," Leander said slowly. "Since the effort was for us, not against, and nothing else untoward happened, I guess we can let that mystery go unsolved. But this magic, I can't."

He thought of Kitty, her eyes gray with fear—and effort. He remembered the illusion spell on her, and the returned vision, and the other evidences of magic. Of *dark* magic, which meant someone trained to spend magic in order to gain an end.

He would have to find out who it was and what they wanted.

He drank down his brew, ignoring the scald, then walked painfully back up to find Kitty.

When he entered her room, he stopped in blank-minded shock.

She stood in the middle of her room, dressed in one of her old black gowns. On her head was a thin, glittering black obsidian crown.

PART FOUR

ONE

Senrid Montredaun-An, deposed king of Marloven Hess, slung his bow over his back and sauntered out from the trees where he'd been waiting to see if anyone showed up at his offered rendezvous.

He'd left a message, with one of his arrows to pin it down, in the light cavalry riding-captain's tent, after a great deal of thought: the commander couldn't receive it as it would put him in a difficult position. But his captains were not under direct orders from Tdanerend.

In the note he'd said: *If you want to talk, meet me here.* And he described the rendezvous. Then signed his initials. He figured that, and the arrow, and the fact that he knew where their camp was but had done nothing about it, might bring them. Of course, it might bring them with orders to kill him on sight, but that was the risk he had to take.

Before him, the four cavalry captains had ranged themselves in a row, helms in left arms, right hands down—no one taking precedence, their aspect neutral. Helms on heads and hands on sword hilts would have meant trouble; at least they were willing to hear him out. Their freedom from the strict obedience of the foot warriors was a jealously guarded privilege, something he'd realized when he was small, so he made certain that he approached them straight on, favoring neither end.

As he closed the distance, his feet crunching the snow, he scanned the four faces. Three youngish, one old, all male. Tdanerend had permitted no females in the academy during the recent years—fool that he was.

Senrid would use that, too.

He saw respect in one face, blankness in two, and caution in the old one. He knew that the young ones would probably defer to the oldest, because he had a distinguished rep. Though it would be a mistake to talk to him only.

These are my people, Senrid thought. *If I don't know how they think, then I deserve what I'll get.*

It was his place to speak first.

He met each gaze, then: "I want your allegiance."

The old one—Tharend—spoke. "It was you who shot Darid Ndermand in the knee."

Senrid acknowledged with a hand-flick, palm up. "Warning," he said.

None of them mentioned the hangman, who had been one of Tdanerend's pet torturers; Senrid knew how the warriors despised that type. Torture debased the arts of war, the test of skills against the worthy opponent. There was no possibility of winning honor in torturing helpless people. They wouldn't care if he lived or died.

Tharend said, "Nice shot with the rope."

"That too was a warning," Senrid said, struggling to keep his voice flat and not give away his relief, or how hard his heart was galloping. "Tdanerend will know I could have potted him just as easily. But I want a duel on home ground. No interference from outsiders."

The one on the end spoke. "Why not aid us here first?"

"Because this is a stupid plan," Senrid said. "It's a fool ploy to hide his incompetence at home. We don't have the magicians to stay here and renew Tdanerend's wards, and wasting half the army to guard one or two mines is stupidity so great that we'll be laughed at in every kingdom on the subcontinent. He may as well assign warriors to dig, because otherwise they'll have to stand over every one of these locals with a sword to force them to do it."

Two of the captains stirred at the mention of warriors digging.

Tharend rubbed a callused thumb on the rim of his helmet. "Not if he had the boy besorcelled. He says you sprang him."

"I did." Senrid's heart-beat drummed in his ears. This was his weakest action—so he had to make it sound like his strongest. "Because the Regent's plan won't work. He doesn't know how these people over here view things. They got rid of their last ruler, and if we turn Leander Tlennen-Hess into a puppet spouting Tdanerend's orders, they'll get rid of him just as fast."

"But if he does the magic," Tharend said doubtfully.

"Another piece of stupidity. You don't have to use white magic to study what it can do and can't do. I've studied its strengths and its limitations—it's cautious and slow. Digging a new mine by magic will take years to set up. By then, if they're left alone, they'll have ready and willing workers who know what to do and how to do it. This is why," Senrid decided it was now time for the mantle of his ancestors to cloak his short, skinny body. "This is why my grandfather wrote, *The better part of wisdom is to wait until the Lerorans decide on their own they can make their fortune in mining and forging steel. When they make it possible, if they won't treat or trade then we take them back. Until then, no matter how loudly you threaten a frozen egg it will not grow into a chicken.*"

Two shifted position. Tharend smiled slightly, and said, "You had a look of the old king, there. I recall him well."

Senrid's heart still thumped. Had he won?

Tharend looked at his companions. One turned his palm out toward the others. The other two no longer kept their hands near their weapons; one scratched his head, the other had hooked his thumb into his sash.

Tharend said, "Will you accompany us to our camp? We can talk further."

And he struck palm to heart: the salute of captain to heir.

Relief flooded through Senrid, so strong it almost made him giddy. Almost washed away the headache that had been nagging for the past couple of days.

They began the long walk.

౫൦ℭ𝔏𝔖൦౬

Kitty stared at Leander. The expression on his face stunned her. He looked like he'd been hit.

She remembered what she'd put on when she'd wakened. "This is a joke," she said, pointing to the dress, which was black with silver trimmings, and then the crown. "I put on this old dress because it's warm, and I found this thing—" She pulled the crown off and looked at it, then put it back on. Leander hated metal on his head, and thought the whole concept of crowns was absurd. Kitty thought they were lovely—and a princess had a right to wear them! "I was having fun putting on all the old stuff and thinking how much things had changed. Because I was reading my old exercise books, see?"

She pointed to the bed, where several battered books lay. One was open, and on it Kitty's childish scrawl had been corrected by Llhei's neat hand.

Leander sighed, leaning against the door. He said, "I have to know who did that magic, Kyale."

Kyale. Not Kitty.

She resorted to annoyance. "Oh, so now you think I'm suddenly this mighty sorcerer?"

"No," he said gently. "But you could have made...some kind of bargain with one." He spread his hands. "Kitty, what am I supposed to believe, since you won't tell me?"

She winced, unable to meet his eyes. A bargain—like her mother—with Norsunder. That's what he thought. And what else could he think?

Kitty felt sick inside. She knew this tension was her own fault—that she should have thought it all through. Senrid had said, *You'll be the great hero* and she hadn't looked past that. The image of Alaxandar, and Arel, and all the rest of them admiring her instead of thinking her a useless princess had been so wonderful!

But now everything had fallen apart—and the worst thing of all was that Leander didn't trust her. But she'd promised, and she knew that Leander would think worse of her if she broke a promise even to a rotter like Senrid.

After a long, painful silence he said, "I'm going to have to find the rest of my group."

He hesitated. Her expression was usually a mirror to her thoughts, and he could see her unhappiness, uncertainty, the wince of regret at the corner of her eyes and turning her mouth down. Whatever had happened, whatever her reasoning, he knew she did not intend to betray him.

That's all that matters now, he thought. *If she cannot confide in me, well, that can wait.*

When she didn't speak—she couldn't think of anything to say—he left.

She listened to his footsteps recede, then groaned and flung herself on her bed. Maybe things had been rotten in the old days, but they'd been much easier!

She pulled one of her old workbooks over and leafed through it, looking with interest at her old drawings. Sour faces and monsters lined the edges of the pages, bringing back memories of bad moods.

She rolled over, the book slipping off the bed, and stared at the ceiling, watching the hypnotic shadows of winter-bare twigs on the ceiling, gently swaying in the wind, the same vision that had engrossed her each winter when she was small. Images, questions, emotions flowed through her tired mind, until she slipped back into slumber.

She woke at sunup—she'd slept through the latter part of a day and the night. Her mouth was dry, her dress clammy.

Her head felt strange when she got up. She walked through the cleaning frame, put on her old winter shoes, then she tripped downstairs. The house felt empty.

She reached the kitchen and found the warm remains of a fire, and some congealed soup. "Eugh!" she exclaimed, glaring at the mess in the pot. The house seemed less empty if she talked out loud. "Peasant food!"

Next to that pot someone had put a plate of vegetables. Hungry, she picked up a somewhat withered carrot, and ate it without any enthusiasm as she walked outside. No one there, either. Leander had left.

She realized what his last words about finding the group had meant: Leander had *left* her.

Indignation crackled through her. How could he *do* that?

She marched through the house, stomped outside, then stopped when she reached the stable. She heard a noise.

Tiptoeing with care, she peeked inside, to discover that someone had left a horse behind. It stood in the last stall, munching slowly on some hay.

There was no saddle on its back, but it was standing conveniently close to a wooden fence. Anger made her brave; she climbed the fence, pausing only when the horse swung its head over and looked at her.

She looked back into that great brown eye, fascinated, repelled, hopeful.

The horse swung its head down, and lipped more hay.

Kitty reached the top slat, touched the horse's back. The skin twitched, and she snatched her hand away. But the horse only shifted its weight from one leg to another, and so she eased herself over, until she sat astride its broad back.

It lifted its head again, swung it so that she caught sight of one of those eyes.

"Where's Leander?" she asked, wishing she knew how you commanded a horse. It wasn't like riding on Meta, who always understood her.

"Move?" she said, thumping her knees against its broad sides. Yuck, how nasty these beasts smelled!

The horse snorted, and began to walk. Kyale clutched desperately at the rough, stiff hair growing down its bony neck.

When it left the stable, it picked up its pace to a scary up-and-down sort of movement that made Kitty hang onto the mane with both hands.

The up-and-down increased, until it seemed to be flying.

Whimpering, her eyes closed, her head pressed against the horse where its neck joined its shoulder, she held on.

და ᲬᲔᲜ თ

Off and on that day Senrid talked, though his head ached and his gut growled. He sat on a rock near the cavalry commander's tent, for though he had a right to, he wouldn't go in unless invited—and the commander was still in Leander's castle, waiting on Tdanerend.

Senrid had thought it all out during the days he'd ridden about, sabotaging Tdanerend's efforts. He had to begin as he would go on. He would not make Tdanerend's mistakes. *As soon as you have to remind someone to salute, you have lost that warrior's respect for ever,* one of his ancestors had written.

Tdanerend had never bothered with history, except when he stumbled onto some custom, or story of an old battle, that justified either his plans or his insistence on the outward marks of prestige. He'd thought the study of history suitable for children or lackeys like scribes—and his motivation for assigning it to Senrid had been to keep him from learning anything about current affairs. Senrid knew that now. Despite the motivation, he was glad he had buried himself in his kingdom's past. He'd read everything written by the Montredaun-Ans—and those they'd deposed—because he'd figured out by the time he was ten that history was in fact a weapon, one his uncle would never recognize. So was map-making, again an activity Tdanerend thought belonged to lackeys.

Knowledge was a weapon.

And his uncle was too ignorant to realize it.

So he sat on a rock, ignoring the cold, and his own hunger, and watched covertly as the camp moved about its business—noting how the warriors covertly watched him. The camp aromas of horse and hay were familiar from early childhood, when his father had taken him to the academy. A vague memory of a strong hand holding him in place on a broad shoulder, and a voice saying, *You'll be here some day, my son* made him shake his head.

The days of the harmless little boy were over, but he knew his limits. He had to rely on brains, because he had no brawn, not against trained men. If he had to use a sword, he'd lose them forever—if they didn't laugh themselves to death first. In the other skills—the ones Tdanerend couldn't forbid—he could take his place unafraid. And they'd all seen the evidence.

When the guard changed, new arrivals came to him. Accompanying them were two of the captains who'd first met him. As time wore on and most of the others rode away, or were called to duty, these two stayed, and he learned their names. The dark-haired one's last name was Senelac, and the blond's Abreran.

"... saw the old king. I was about five," Senelac was saying reminiscently. He was silent during all the previous talk; Senrid was sure he had something on his mind, but had waited until almost everyone was gone. "He always used to judge the cavalry games. Never missed them, I'm told."

"True," Senrid said. "The academy was strong in his day."

"That's what the oldsters say," Senelac commented.

"That's probably what oldsters have said ever since the academy was first begun," Abreran put in, laughing.

Senelac shrugged. "Maybe." Senrid caught a flickering look from his black eyes. "But my grandmother, who won two firsts her senior year, maintains that standards are lower now."

"They are," Senrid said—knowing now what Senelac was after. In a casual voice he added, "Have to be, when half the talent in the kingdom can't compete because they happen to wear skirts when dressed as civs."

And the slight lift of the head, the narrowing of the black eyes, let Senrid know he had indeed got it: a sister, or a female cousin, well-qualified and kept out.

Abreran gave a soft snort. "A consistency evidenced every banner day."

Senrid drew in a slow breath of sheer delight. This was only two out of countless others, but so far again he'd been right: Tdanerend had insisted on wearing their ancestors' medals. Most everyone knew those medals, and who'd won them, for Tdanerend had won none during his brief stint in the academy. Indevan had won several, and now his younger brother wore those too.

Tdanerend also wore the medal one of their many-great grandmothers had won in a terrific battle against an earlier incarnation of the Brotherhood of Blood, the pirate confederacy whose leader at that time had had a hankering to carve out a kingdom and try his skills as a king. The princess Sharend Montredaun-An, serving then as a captain in the light cavalry, had led the expedition, a battle that every child in Marloven Hess had heard about through famous ballads.

I represent the crown, and therefore our ancestors' *majesty*, his uncle had said, but what Senrid had heard was: *I'm really king, and their glory is mine.* Except not in a kingdom where respect was supposed to come from skill and leadership, and not just tradition and force.

The talk veered almost at once to academy games of the past few years, and who had won under what circumstances. Senrid let it wash past him. He needed to concentrate his strength for when it would be required. Cooking odors wafted from the other side of the camp. He was desperately hungry, but wouldn't admit to it. He was afraid that would be taken as a sign of weakness. He knew nothing of woodcraft—and had only been able to eat when he could steal food in and around Crestel, once he'd gone through the meager store of supplies at Leander's old camp. At least he'd been able to find the camp! But though he knew nothing of woodcraft, he had a very good memory and a sense for geographic space...

"—don't you think?"

Someone had addressed him. Why was his mind wandering so badly? He looked up, ignored the pangs through his head, saw everyone's posture expecting agreement. He recovered a few words—academy—skills—games and opened his hand in agreement.

Smiles, flicks of hands. That was all right, then. Sit up straight. If only he could eat, surely he'd feel better.

The sun set, and the meal call finally rang out. Tharend himself returned to ask Senrid to join them. He got in line with the rest, claiming no precedence that wasn't offered. No one deferred, so he waited, and got his share when it was his turn. He felt himself being watched. They were judging him as he was judging them.

As he ate the talk became general—horses first, almost always, weapons next, and gossip about local events last. Senrid let it ride past him, and gauged his success so far. It seemed promising. But there were wary glances, and someone had to be on the way to report his presence to Uncle Tdanerend, if he hadn't already arrived there. It was inevitable that the Regent had long had his own spies planted among them.

But he'd worry about that later.

Right now, it was a relief to eat hot food, and drink down some strong coffee. It would help keep him awake, maybe through another night, if he drank more, and it might banish the soreness at the back of his throat, and the band of pain round his head.

When he was done he forced himself to his feet, dropped his dishes in the cleaning barrel, and poured more coffee. It was late; the early morning patrols had all retired. With the warm mug between his hands, Senrid sat down again, his back to a rock, his knees up, and put his forehead down on his knees to rest it, just for a moment—

—and woke up abruptly to the cold blue light of dawn, smelling fire.

His hand clapped to the dagger at his side, found it there. The fire was nearby, ringed with stones giving off warmth.

Someone had built a fire not two arm's length's away, and he hadn't even stirred. He stared at it stupidly, felt cold on one side of his face, realized he'd been drooling, and wiped his face on the grimy cloak he'd stolen from the garrison in Crestel.

He'd fallen asleep! He'd fallen asleep after admonishing himself not to show weakness. He nearly groaned out loud, but old habit held in the reaction, and instead he looked away from the fire to see two guards standing like sentinels at either side, their spears grounded. They were facing out, watching the camp, which was breaking; as yet no one knew he was awake.

So was this an honor guard—or was he a prisoner?

He touched the dagger—still there. He flexed his wrist. That one was also untouched. Same with the one in his boot. A quick look: his bow leaned against the rock, almost within reach.

If they'd decided to hold him as a prisoner for his uncle, he would have been stripped of his weapons. An honor guard, then?

Dangerous to act on guesses. Time to stir.

He stood up, slung his bow, and said, "Is there anywhere to wash? Or at least get something hot to drink?"

Both guards' heads jerked round, and he felt a tiny spurt of gratification that he wasn't the only one to be taken flat by surprise.

Both smacked their palms to their hearts in salute, and one said, "Commander wants to talk to you. In his tent."

Senrid flicked his fingers up, his heartbeat going from walk to gallop.

"Cook tent's right on the way," the other volunteered.

Senrid acknowledged with another gesture and started off with as much energy as he could muster. He loathed the feel of his grubby clothing and clammy body. He'd sweated hard during his sleep. His head ached. He smelled coffee, and wished that it was listerblossom leaf and not this hard stuff. His gut lurched but he controlled the reaction, accepted a cup, and continued on between his two sentinels to the big tent.

On their arrival everyone inside except the commander found business elsewhere. Senrid watched old Gherdred bend over a map. He'd mentally marked the commander down as one of Tdanerend's men—though he wasn't a toady. Gherdred had headed the cavalry academy under the old king, and Senrid's father had promoted him to commander of the light cavalry, the most coveted of all commands—except commander in chief. That position Tdanerend had kept for himself.

Gherdred straightened up.

Senrid waited in silence.

The old man's light blue eyes narrowed as he looked Senrid up and down. "The Regent will be wanting you in the castle," he said.

"Very well," Senrid responded.

That was to be expected. But it didn't mean he'd go.

"I'll tell you this, my boy," the man said. "I obey the Regent because he was strong enough to take the crown. I've listened to the meanings behind the heroic words in the songs. I know what happens to a kingdom if the ruler isn't strong, or if there is no ruler. My private convictions about a man's worth are nothing, if he's strong enough to command. On the other hand, if he leads us to war within our own borders, against our own people, then he has lost my allegiance."

Senrid wished his head didn't ache so much. "So," he said, aware that no one else was within hearing. "What you're telling me is, if I can take back my father's crown without causing civil war, then you won't oppose me."

Gherdred said, "What I am telling you is that I will heed no order to attack our own people. Defend, yes."

Senrid thought rapidly. "Have you told my uncle what you told me?"

"No."

Senrid touched fingers to heart. Nothing more needed to be spoken. The man had made it as plain as honor permitted that he disliked Tdanerend, and would be glad to see him defeated.

Senrid left the tent to find in the strengthened light that the camp was clear, and most were ready to ride. Hearing Gherdred's voice behind him—the sound, not the words—he stayed where he was. If Ghedred had wanted him to hear orders, he would have summoned the captains while Senrid was still in the tent.

"We will ride ahead," Senelac said, and stepped up on Senrid's right.

And Senrid felt the puzzle pieces fall into place. The light cavalry had been given orders from Tdanerend that none of them wanted to obey. Probably to converge on the city and start some local slaughter in order to bolster Tdanerend's crumbling prestige.

Gherdred had to obey that order and the 'capture on sight and send to me' that no doubt had been issued over Senrid's own name, but he could wait as long as possible.

Senrid had to get to Crestel first; the cavalry would be riding as slowly as possible. Between his own arrival and the cavalry's, Senrid had better prevail.

Or die.

TWO

Kitty could not tell one horse from another, so she did not recognize Portan's favorite gray. She did not know that Arel had brought two extra horses to Tannantaun once he'd found tucked under his horse's harness the mysterious note telling him where Leander was.

When he and Leander departed Mara Jinea's old home, the gray had been left behind as a fresh mount for a messenger sent to the house to carry news to Kitty, since poor Portan would no longer need it. It had never occurred to any of them that she would climb onto an unsaddled horse.

So while Leander and Arel rode, under cover of snowfall, round the outskirts of Crestel and into the town, Leander did not worry about Kitty. He figured she'd hide in her old home, and rest, and if she tired of the soup they'd provided for her, she could always walk to the town and find some old friends to feed her.

He had no idea when he woke that next morning after a long night of activity and far too brief a rest that the gray was now racing for home—with Kitty clinging precariously to its back.

Leander sank with relief into a stuffed chair. Alaxandar and the others who had collapsed the mine had drifted in ones and twos into the town just before the bleak dawn. They were now gathered at the home of Veria, a cobbler who lived on the eastern edge of Crestel. The house was small, so it took some doing to fit two dozen persons inside of the two rooms.

Exhaustion dragged at Leander's body, and his wounds ached.   He drank the steeped listerblossom that Veria's grandmother put into his hands. It helped—some. He'd been drinking it all the night before, and each time it helped less. What he needed was sleep, but he wasn't going to get any.

The last couple of people slunk in just after the midday bells.   They were greeted, squeezed in, then everyone faced Leander expectantly.

He said, "The border wards are gone, so I transferred down to Firel last night. The Besanan family is willing to cede all their hill land to Marloven Hess if he'll go away and leave us be."

"Those south facing slopes are all prime grape country," someone protested.

Leander shook his head.   "Tdanerend wants mines. Maybe he'll leave if we give him ore. If not..."

"But he wants everything." Alaxandar smacked his fist into his palm. "Not only the entire border, but workers to dig. Rather go down with a sword through my gut than sweat my life away shoveling ore under the sights of their crossbows."

"Yes."

"Yes!"

"Well said."

The murmurs made Leander sigh. Would his be the shortest rule on the entire world? Probably. What a claim to fame!

"Let us enjoy one last meal together, then march on the castle. I feel I have to try this one attempt at negotiation. He has found that we're not so easy to defeat as he'd thought, and maybe he'll listen. If he won't—then, I guess, it's our steel against theirs, until the last of us is gone."

Grim nods of agreement all around.

"How about magic?" Veria asked, and several others nodded or made murmurs of agreement.

Leander said, "Magic isn't much good for war. Especially that which I've been learning. But I will do my best to protect us as I can, if he employs his own magic to do something treacherous."

"When," Veria said, her face grim.

And so, while the people crowded there in the cobbler's home shared a meal of fishcakes and roasted potatoes-and-cabbage, Kitty's gray plodded through the snowdrifts northward toward Crestel.

Senrid reached it first.

Someone had gone on ahead, as he'd expected; Senrid tipped back his head, and even though the lowering winter sun had just begun to bend westward, casting the figures along the wall into silhouette, he easily recognized his uncle surrounded by taller guards. Moments later magic seized him right off his horse, and he transported to the wall next to Tdanerend.

He heard his uncle's voice, felt someone take his bow, and his dagger from the side-sheath. Senrid didn't try to fight it, or even react.

When the transfer reaction diminished, he looked up into an ill-tempered frown. His unceremonial arrival was due to the fact that he'd been riding free and unbound.

"You are a traitor," Tdanerend began.

Senrid glanced right and left. Surrounding them was the Regent's own personal guard—of course. One stood a spear's length behind, holding Senrid's bow and dagger.

He interrupted, knowing that he had to get his uncle mad, and keep him there. "Yes, we've all heard—a million times—how I'm a traitor, and a coward, hoola-loola. Why did you run our people into this stupidity? I'd rather be everything you call me than stupid. Your plan is ridiculous, Uncle, and you can be sure the Lerorans will be ridiculing us while you waste good warriors."

"Waste! You—"

"Forcing them to spend the rest of their lives doing guard duty on these worthless Lerorans is nothing more than waste."

"Yes, because of your interference," Tdanerend snarled, his face dark red with ready anger.

Below, someone had run out from the stable to collect the loose horse, Senrid was glad to see.

He shifted his attention to his uncle, bracing against the pang of headache. "No. That was to buy you time to think—that, and tweak you for deposing me. You could have waited! I got sent off-world, and when I finally got back, it was to find

you marching here, and everyone at home was talking about
your planned coronation at New Year's Convocation."

"That's because I thought you were dead. And you may
as well be dead. You are weak, Senrid," Tdanerend said. "I did
my best, but you'll never be strong enough to sit on the throne of
our great-fathers—"

"Uhn," Senrid groaned. "Not another long, dull speech!
I—uh oh."

He'd turned away, feigning nausea, as a sentinel on the
tower wall blew the signal for *Enemy approaching!*

Senrid, Tdanerend, and his guards all looked down at the
group of people who'd rounded a bend in the northeast road,
from the direction of the tiny market town they called their
capital city. At the front was a skinny kid with dark hair who
leaned on a stick.

Senrid sighed. He had to admit that Leander, puzzling as
he was, showed plenty of courage. Even from a distance he
looked bad, but there he walked, at the head what was left of his
gang, all of them bearing some sort of weapon, though they had
to know they were outnumbered many times over. No form, no
discipline—no training or skill—but they did look determined.

Senrid snickered loudly.

Tdanerend flushed even darker. "What are you laughing
at? Unless it's the sight of that fool down there—"

"I'm thinking of how he's going to make you look in
about ten heartbeats." Senrid lifted a shoulder. "My guess is
he's going to try a negotiation on you. And if you turn it down,
they'll fight, to the very last weakling. Look at 'em! They know
they cannot possibly win. But how many people are watching
from windows in this castle, maybe from behind those trees on
that hill yonder? If you make martyrs of 'em you might as well
get busy hanging the entire country, because you'll never settle
'em, as long as the last one lives."

During this speech Tdanerend cursed under his breath. At
the end he scowled, a vein beating in his neck, then motioned the
waiting messenger over—but before he could issue an order, the
bugle sounded again. And from the other direction came a lone
rider.

Leander's group stopped. Senrid stared down in surprise at the sight of a small girl clinging to the back of a very handsome, and tired, pure-bred Nelkereth gray.

The girl lifted her head and shrieked, "Leander!" From atop the castle wall her voice sounded like a bird's cry.

The gray, startled, sidled—and Kyale promptly tumbled off into the snow. She stood up, gowned in black and silver, with a gleaming black crown fitted round her brow.

She was in the midst of brushing snow off her gown when Tdanerend once more made summoning magic—and moments later Kyale appeared with them on the wall. She blinked, nausea contracting her features, then she saw whom she was with and her expression was such a peculiar combination of outrage and fear that Senrid laughed again.

Tdanerend said to his messenger in Marloven, "When Gherdred gets here, he can get rid of those fools." He pointed downward.

Senrid saw immediately that Kyale understood their home-language. How could Tdanerend miss it? He glared at Kyale and began a threat, but Senrid—thinking of Gherdred's orders—decided the time had come to take the initiative.

"Kyale," he said, "Go ask Leander if he wants to fight with steel or with magic. If magic, he'll have help."

Tdanerend jerked his head round, and while he assimilated Senrid's words—his face suffusing even more— Senrid braced himself against the wall and performed the transfer spell, sending Kyale down to Leander. It was important that magic seem to come easily to Senrid, if there was to be a battle ahead.

Poor Kitty felt all the effects of two black magic transfers. While she stood in the snow and fought against vertigo and nausea, Leander gazed at her in dismay.

What all these new clues seemed to add up to was that— at best—she had broken her promise and got into his magic books, figuring out various spells. And at worst, she'd made some kind of bargain with... With whom? The clothes suggested that Mara Jinea had come back. Kitty was loyal—fiercely loyal—but she had only begun to learn anything about ethics in the last year, despite Llhei's covert attempts to teach her during her early childhood.

He was afraid she had done something terrible in an effort to help—and to seem a hero in the process.

As he watched, Kitty swallowed convulsively, then she said, "Magic battle. Someone might help you. Or do you want to fight."

"White magic help, or black?" Leander asked, trying not to sound accusing, or threatening.

Kitty looked down at her shoes in the muddy snow.

Leander sighed. "I can't have black magic aid, Kitty. It'll turn on us. We'll have to fight, then."

She heard the intense regret in his voice, and winced, not knowing what to say. Avoiding his gaze, she turned her head up toward those on the wall. Tdanerend was visible, of course, but Senrid was out of sight. Drat! If Leander could just see him, surely he'd guess who it was doing all that magic!

On the wall, Tdanerend saw her face turn toward them, and again he did the summons spell.

Kitty appeared, and groaned, pressing her forearms against her roiling stomach. "I hate that!" She sucked in a deep breath. "Leander says, no black magic."

But Senrid had already seen it in their faces. By the time Tdanerend registered the news, and was ready to start on the offensive, Senrid had already begun on a series of spells.

And Kitty was in a panic.

On one side Tdanerend's voice, so loud and grating, poured out vile invective. On the other Senrid whispered steadily and a nasty, whining hum made all the hairs on Kyale's neck lift and her teeth ache. She felt as if the world had gone unsteady—and then *snap!* The hum was gone, but Senrid leaned against the wall, his face greenish.

Tdanerend glared at him, pointed a finger—but before he could finish a spell Senrid disappeared.

Tdanerend's expression was truly frightening. Kitty ducked her head and ran for the tower door, the skin over her shoulder blades crawling. She hunched over, listening for Tdanerend to order his guards to kill her, but he'd already forgotten about her, and the guards, lacking orders, ignored her.

They watched Tdanerend, weapons gripped—and to their surprise, he, too, transferred!

Kitty made it to the tower door, threw it open, got inside, and collapsed against it, her entire body trembling. She put her head in her hands. The black crown, loosened by her fall from the horse, dropped off and clattered to the stone floor, but she paid it no heed.

No one came—no one bothered her.

She ran downstairs, not to her room, but to the servants' quarters, and found Llhei, Nelyas, and a couple of the others gathered in one of their rooms. All looked up, startled, when she appeared in the doorway.

"Tdanerend—he—they—" She pointed, stopped, her head so light and dizzy she had to sit down abruptly.

Llhei sprang forward. "Never mind, child. You can tell us the news later. Right now, let's hide you here, and you can rest. Tdanerend has never once poked his nose in this wing."

и СЗ SO cs

While Kitty snuggled down in Nelyas' bed, a tray of biscuits and hot steeped leaf on her lap, Leander and his group were making their way back up the road into town as fast as they could. Since there was no one left to negotiate with, but a lot of shiny swords threatening anyone who came near the castle, Leander felt it was better part of wisdom to retreat. No one argued.

"He must be going to fetch reinforcements," Alaxandar said. "And when they show up, we're going to be in it hot."

"Why reinforcements?" Lisaeth asked, her arms held out wide. "They already outnumber us about two-hundred-fifty to one! Think they might need a few more, just in case?" And she flexed her skinny arm.

The others laughed, but Alaxandar shook his head. Loyal he was, and strong, but not exactly first choice in anyone's mind when it came to a sense of humor.

"Magical reinforcements," Alaxandar said. "Didn't you see that weird shimmer over the wall? Something's going on, magic-wise."

Leander frowned. "Something's missing. Something else is wrong. Who was that spell aimed at, since nothing happened to us? It was one *big* spell. *Something* happened. And right after it Tdanerend transfered so abruptly—to where? Could he have Latvian there, and they've fallen out?"

"Who cares?" Arel asked, flapping a dismissive hand in the direction of the royal castle. "At least they let us retreat."

"If we can use it..."

Veria sighed, her gaze skyward. "What we need right now is shelter. Look at that! If we don't have a blizzard coming at us, then I'm a hoptoad."

Leander looked up, saw the sky darkening to a flat, threatening gray. The atmosphere was tense. It could have been magic, or the weather, or both. One thing for certain: a storm was building with frightening speed.

At the crossroads, no one was in sight.

Leander said, "Let's disperse. Arel, will you and Lisaeth sneak back and scout the castle?"

Lisaeth threw back a braid and laughed. "Sure! Nice chance to be warm—"

"No it isn't," Arel said grimly. "Tdanerend doesn't like fires—except in his own personal living quarters."

"At least you'll be out of the weather," Alaxandar said. He turned to Leander. "Leave scouting his army to me. I want to know where they are camped and what they're doing before we make any more plans. We seem to have been granted a respite, and we have to use it well. All we know for certain is that we've got Tdanerend's foot busy with our mine, but those horse-boys should have been here long ago."

Leander nodded, grateful to surrender the military thinking to someone who knew how to do it.

Alaxandar added in a low growl, "And if you don't hole up and sleep somewhere, I'll brain you myself."

Leander groaned. "Ah, it hurts too much to laugh. Truth to tell, if a blizzard keeps them nailed down for a day, I'll be as happy to hole up. And sleep. And eat. And did I mention sleep?"

∞⦉⦊∞

The blizzard was not an overnight visitor.

It howled for five days, pounding the countryside with a white blanket that mired travelers, kept warriors huddling in tents, and had Lerorans grateful for homes to hide in while they dug up old weapons or tried to fashion farm or building tools into fighting tools for the coming battle.

There were a few brief encounters. The worst was near the mines, when a desperate group of farmers tried to flood out the warriors camped in the lee of a cliff by diverting a running stream onto them. They were spotted by vigilant sentries; they were caught—they fought—were shot.

A couple of other skirmishes near Crestel also occurred, to the detriment of Leander's people, who were untrained and ill-equipped.

Each time the news made its way back to Leander he felt sicker at heart, because each incident not only caused fresh grief for families and friends, but served as a harbinger of the inevitable.

How to avoid it, he had no idea.

At least Kyale was all right. Lisaeth and Arel both managed to get into the castle, as servants—desperately needed—and they reported that Llhei had her in charge. He would wait to see her until he had the strength to deal with her evasions, well-meant as they were.

∞⦉⦊∞

So where was Senrid?

On that fast ride from the camp to Crestel, he had not been idle. Fortified by enough coffee to make his hands tremble, he'd concentrated on magic spells. All those years of drill, and repetition when his uncle made mistakes, aided by a naturally clear memory, made it possible for him to recall and practice several sets of spells. All were dangerous, all could backfire and take him with them, but he was committed now.

To turn back was to die for certain.

As soon as he had seen in Leander's face the (not unexpected) rejection of his indirect offer of aid, he rattled through the first set of spells, which dissolved all his uncle's remaining wards.

He'd trusted to Tdanerend's temper, his inability to concentrate on any one thing when he was in a fury; that was his only protection, and it worked.

He had just enough energy left to transfer to his old guest room in the castle, the only close-by destination he could envision. He did not have the strength for a more distant transfer. Just as he'd trusted to Tdanerend's temper, he would have to trust to his arrogance; Tdanerend would never believe Senrid would have the temerity to hide right in his conquered stronghold, so he wouldn't send anyone to search. Or so Senrid hoped.

Senrid collapsed on the bed, but as soon as the transfer reaction eased, he braced himself for the next set of spells. With painstaking care he placed his own ward, with a tracer spell on transfer magic; he suspected Tdanerend was now busy poring over the magic books, desperate to reestablish his wards. Maybe try to set up some traps. Well, that would keep him busy for a time—but if he transferred home for help....

He needed to know where his uncle would go.

If the Regent thought of physically leaving the castle perimeter and transferring from somewhere outside the wards, then Senrid was lost. But he didn't think his uncle would put himself to that much trouble.

And so, for the last spell:

The weather.

He'd seen snow moving slowly in. Using strength from the land itself, he packed the storm with power, a spell so strong it left him lying dizzy and weak, unable to do anything for a long while.

But he'd managed what he'd intended: to pin down the various combatants so he could deal with them one at a time.

Then, shivering with reaction, he dropped into long-overdue sleep.

soαβεοcς

When Kitty woke up after a refreshing nap, she got up and made her way slowly to Llhei's room. That nightmare horse ride had left her legs feeling like barrel staves, only much sorer. The servants were all gathered there. The room was warm, and smelled of chocolate; the wind-driven snow drummed against the windows.

"Oh," she exclaimed. "Where's mine?"

"Right here," Llhei said comfortably. "I brought up an extra cup in case. Here, let us get you into a fresh gown."

The room was inordinately crowded. Arel leaned against the bedstead, wearing livery. Lisaeth, the one who Leander said was so good at spying, sat on the floor, dressed in a plain gown with an apron, and mending in her lap. What she was mending was a ripped Marloven tunic. Kitty blinked, feeling as if she hadn't really woken, but was lost in a dream.

She followed Llhei back into Nelyas's room, and gratefully took the cup. She sipped hot chocolate. It was warm, and tasted wonderful.

"Now," Llhei said, standing with her back to the door. "When I went up to your room to get something for you to wear, I heard a noise down the hall, and discovered that that boy is here—"

"You mean Senrid?" Kitty asked, making a face.

"Yes. He's asleep right now in the guest suite, snoring fit to tear the roof off. I'm not sure, but I think he may be ill. If I so much as mention it to Arel or Lisaeth, they'll rush right up and slit his throat. Is there any reason why I shouldn't?"

Kitty opened her mouth. Oh, she'd said—plenty of times!—how glad she'd be if Senrid croaked, but the fact remained that he had, for some reason, saved herself and Leander. She couldn't tell Llhei that, but she could tell her why.

"Don't," she said. "He's fighting against his uncle. He wants him to go home and he thinks the plot about the mines is stupid."

Llhei's eyes narrowed. "And you heard this how?"

"Warriors talking. While I was a prisoner," Kitty invented hastily, and she slurped up more chocolate in order to hide her face.

When she looked up again, Llhei shook her head. "I'll speak with him shortly. In fact, he might need sustenance as well."

"When you do, I'll go with you," Kitty said. "So I can report to Leander."

Llhei shrugged. "Very well. Now. Let's get you through your frame and changed into a warm gown before you end up as sick as that other one sounds."

∞CRƧꝃ∞

Senrid woke up abruptly as the wind shrieked round the stone tower above him on a rising note. His mouth was dry, and his head ached as if someone had been hammering on it. He was hot and cold at once.

Oh, just what he needed now. He was sick.

He sat up slowly. Had someone been in the room? The air current moved softly against his cheek, as if the door had recently closed, and though his nose was stuffy, he did catch a whiff of an herbal scent.

He lay back, but only for a few moments.

He could not stay. There was far too much to do. Gherdred had to be found—but he could use magic now to transfer to him—and then there were the foot...and last, there was Tdanerend.

He got up, and the room swam. He made it to the dressing room door, and through. The zap-tingle of a cleaning frame pulled the grittiness from his clothes and skin. It even seemed to unclog his nose slightly. Though he still felt clammy.

He drew in another deep breath, walked to the bed, and flopped down, cursing himself. He was still cursing when he slid right into sleep, waking when he heard the door open.

Darkness had fallen, and a candle flared. It was that old woman, the one with the Sartoran name.

He sat up, wincing against the headache. Llhei came in slowly, the candle set on a tray.

"Kitty wanted to come," the woman said, "but she's asleep too. I was going to say that you children should not be playing at war, for it is likely to kill you, but if your uncle is any example the adults are even worse."

Senrid said—discovering that his voice had gone hoarse—"I'm not sure I can parse that." He tried to laugh, but hadn't the strength.

"You don't need to parse it." Llhei bent to touch the candle flame to another candle, which she set into a holder beside the bed. Then she moved to the windows to draw the curtains, so that the light would not be visible through the fierce storm outside. "Just accept it as true. Now. Here is some healer's brew, and some food. Kitty says that you are endeavoring to get rid of your uncle, and leave us in peace."

"I want my kingdom back," Senrid said. "Get him on home ground first. Leave you people alone. There's nothing I want here."

Llhei nodded. "Very well, then. The Marlovens don't come up here any more—they think it's deserted. Tdanerend settled into the old royal bedroom on the other wing. The servants report he's ranting and raving in there over his books. I'll see to it you have food and drink, if you'll stick with what you told Kitty."

"All right," Senrid said. "What else did she tell you?"

"Just that." Llhei paused at the door, looking back. "Is there something else to be told?"

He was annoyed with himself. How could he slip like that? "I lifted Tdanerend's magic wards. As a challenge to him."

Llhei picked up her candle, smiled slightly, and left.

Senrid ate, drank, tried a spell, but the magic started to burn inside his head—he knew he couldn't hold it. He abandoned it, and slept instead.

⊱⊰

The next day, he made it to Gherdred, who was holed up in a bad position in the western portion of Sindan-An. Senrid did not tell him that magic had caused the storm—and that the magic was his. He did tell him where Leander's hideout was, so that Gherdred could relocate his wing there and hole up more securely.

When he got back he found food waiting, and lukewarm steeped leaf in a closed container, as Llhei had promised. He had enough strength left to eat, drink, and then collapse.

The third day, after some locals tried to unfreeze a stream above the foot warriors, who were weather-bound in the mountains, he made it to the trapped riding and ordered the commander to march back to Marloven Hess.

"On whose authority?" the commander asked.

"Mine," Senrid said. He stood before the man with his arms crossed. Opening one hand and murmuring a spell he'd rehearsed all the night before, he pointed at the wall of snow blocking the road upward to the west, and fire erupted, steam billowing up from the melted snow. "I am taking my throne back."

At least the cold made his voice sound deeper, but if he talked much more, he'd lose it entirely. He stopped there, hoping the threat was implicit. Otherwise, one more spell and he would pass out.

But it was enough.

The man said, "As soon as the weather clears." And his palm smacked against his heart.

Senrid made it back. Just.

On the fifth day, he woke up feeling the pull of magic.

Tdanerend had finally succeeded in breaking Senrid's wards, and was reweaving his own wards. Senrid would have to act now.

Murmuring the transport spell, he envisioned Tdanerend and zapped down to the confrontation he'd wished could be avoided until he was well.

ಬಂಜ೩ಬಂ೮ಆ

Even though her legs were *still* sore from that horrible ride, Kitty was bored.

She was so bored she decided to do some scouting on her own. Why did Arel and Lisaeth get to do it all? Didn't Kitty have ears too?

Via the servants' hallway she sneaked round to the other wing, where she knew Tdanerend had his lair in Mara Jinea's old rooms. Those were the nicest rooms in the castle—but as usual, Kitty thought aggrievedly, Leander much preferred living in the plain ones.

He *had* said that she could have them, but that didn't seem right. And anyway, she didn't like the idea of being all alone in a whole wing by herself, especially where her horrible mother had once lived.

The storm had kept the Marlovens from doing much. The castle ones mostly stayed in the garrison, except for a few guards on wall and hall, and those all tended to be posted at the entries rather than walking about in the wind.

Kitty prowled along the servants' corridor outside the morning room, and when she heard voices, she stopped and pressed her ear to a wall.

It was Tdanerend!

A hand touched her arm.

She gasped, whirled around. Llhei! She sighed in relief.

"You ought not to be here," Llhei whispered. "And you definitely ought not to be eavesdropping."

"But it's *him*. And I think Senrid, too!"

"Just remember what I said about eavesdropping." Having given her reminder about manners, Llhei pressed her ear to the wall—promptly joined by Kitty.

Who was frustrated because she couldn't hear the talk. It sounded like voices had on the water world, until they'd been given their magic bands.

Burble, burble, burble.   Then Tdanerend shouted something, and Senrid laughed.

More shouts—and Llhei gasped at the foulness of Tdanerend's language. Kitty felt her face go red, but she kept her ear in place, hoping to find out what was going on.

"Traitor!" That was Tdanerend. "[*Mutter mutter*] treason! [*Mutter mutter*] execution—"

"Huh," Kitty whispered to herself. "See how you like hearing that stuff, Senrid."

The argument escalated again, both voices talking at once, then silence.

Silence?

Slowly, increasingly, she felt that whiny hum again, and she gasped and pulled away. "Magic," she whispered. "We'd better get away. It feels *nasty*."

Llhei winced as well, and whirled back from the wall. "Something happened in there—" she began.

A loud smashing sound made them both jump. It sounded like doors crashing open.

"Stay." Llhei's voice was a command.

She bustled out into the royal hallway.

Kitty remained where she was, chewing the inside of her lip. She counted to ten. She counted to twenty.

She gave up, and ran back into the servant's hall, down the long dim-lit corridor, and out into the servants' wing, which looked out on the garrison court.

She saw movement outside the window, and paused.

The storm had stopped. Not a flake of snow in the air.

And floundering in the drifts as they lined up in neat rows, were all the Marlovens.

She stood there for a long time, afraid it was some kind of a trick, until they had all ridden or marched out.

Then she turned around, to find Llhei standing behind her.

"They're gone," Llhei said, and put her apron over her head, and wept.

THREE

At first no one believed it.

Nelyas and a couple of the others ventured cautiously through the castle, finding the rooms empty. The beautiful carved doors to the morning room were smashed, which caused cries of outrage—where Tdanerend's guards had broken in to arrest Senrid.

Both rival kings had vanished. No one knew who had given the order for the warriors to withdraw, but withdraw they did, as fast as they could, and what's more they had left the barracks wing reasonably clean—horse droppings all wanded underground, the barracks empty and swept, the only evidence of their stay a badly frayed rope here, a broken blackweave harness there, and a lingering aroma of wet wool and horse.

All Nelyas and the explorers found in Tdanerend's former quarters were the old Tlennen-Hess golden dinnerware (the warriors had brought their own) on a gold tray, a half-eaten meal still on the plates, and a fine woolen cloak, which Nelyas's cousin threw into the fire. The left-over food was burned and the dishes taken three times through the cleaning frame, an old ritual that persisted everywhere despite magicians trying to tell people that the second and third tries only spent the magic a bit more without doing any good. But three cleansings, one for physical, one for mental, and one for spiritual banishment of an enemy's touch made people feel that an item was truly clean.

Meanwhile Lisaeth had departed at once to toil her way through the mighty snowdrifts to Crestel, in order to apprise Leander.

By nightfall the castle was bustling again, people cleaning to remove any traces of the invaders, and cooking, and eating, and talking.

Leander walked through his castle, expecting anything but that emptiness.

He'll be back, he kept thinking. *It's not over. This is just a respite.*

He retreated up to his magic library, intending on getting started right away on more border wards. The room was largely untouched. Tdanerend had apparently disdained his small collection of white magic books—either that or he'd tried a small spell and was caught asleep, and when he was woken he did not know enough magic to break Leander's ward.

First, though, Leander had to activate the road-clearing spells for which he had so painstakingly laid down the basic magic, during early spring. For three weeks he'd traveled around, partly to get to know people, but mostly to set the spells against the next winter—spells his father had sought for a number of years, and had promised his people. It was one of the sad ironies of his life that he obtained the spells from far north right before he was killed by his own wife.

Leander picked up the book in which he'd carefully written out the activation spells, and moved to the window that overlooked a curve of the town road. Each road was named. He performed the castle-road spell first, then looked out. A sudden straight line of snow dashed into the air, sparkling in the sunlight—and there was the road, with snow mounded high on both sides.

He laughed in delight. What would it feel like, to be toiling on the road when the spell activated? A sudden white whirlwind all around one, and the unsteady sensation of magic... and suddenly a clean road?

Spell, recover, spell, recover. Down the list he ran, triumph infusing him with energy. After the days of defeat, of humiliation and helplessness, it felt good to accomplish this one thing.

The only roads he did not clear were those leading down from the mountains, whereon the Marlovens were probably marching westward toward home. He did not want them discovering neatly cleared roads and regarding them as an invitation to return.

When that was done, he was startled to see that the day was already gone, and he had mentally mapped out much more to do. So he clapped on the lights, shut and locked his doors so no one would disturb him for anything but emergencies, and settled down with his books.

Until late he worked, the five days of rest having done much to restore him. As he'd recovered physically, a different kind of fever had seized him, a fever of anxiousness, making him desperate to invent a way to protect his kingdom if he could.

Once, when he looked up, thinking about food, he remembered a summer campfire at the old hideout. His words to Senrid came back, an ironic echo. *Or maybe what I don't need is the foolishness of adulthood.* Had he really been that complacent?

Except was adulthood any guarantee of wisdom? Tdanerend, and Mara Jinea—and his father's foolish attraction for that evil woman's pretty face—were proof that it wasn't.

Back to work.

Of course he fell asleep over his books, just like the good old days.

In fact, it was almost a relief to wake up with the familiar stiff neck, dry mouth, and creased cheek. Maybe that meant life would return to normal, that the horrors with Tdanerend would diminish into a very bad memory—

He glanced at the window, which was day bright. He'd heard noise outside: horsehooves.

Fear drove him to the window, but when he looked out, instead of the expected formation of black-and-tan Marlovens, he saw Alaxandar at the head of half-a-dozen riders, and he remembered Alaxandar's vow to ride a perimeter check round the city as soon as the roads were cleared, and to venture farther at dawn.

They were returning so early? Something was wrong.

He ran to his rooms for a quick trip through the cleaning frame so he wouldn't have to bother changing his clothes, and leaped down the stairs, ducking through the door in time to meet a snowball on the ear.

"Huh?"

"Whose joke is that?" Kitty screamed. She swept up snow and flung it in the other direction. "Argh!"

Leander blinked away the snow that had dashed across his vision to see Kitty standing before Alaxandar's horse, her face mottled scarlet with fury.

"Thought it might be," Alaxandar said, making a sign to Arel.

What Leander had taken to be a saddle-bag across the horse's withers was, in fact, a person. As he registered this Arel grasped the scruff of its neck and slung it away from his horse.

Leander stared down in mind-flown surprise as Senrid Montredaun-An landed flat on his back in the deep snow, arms out, hands empty and loose. He was completely unconscious.

Kitty stamped around in a circle. "Why? That rotten rotten *rotten* Tdanerend—and *him* too!" She pointed down at Senrid.

"Where'd he come from?" Leander asked Alaxandar. "I thought he was dead!"

"Found him holed up in a burned-out barn to the west. Saw the princess's lion and a couple of the other felines running across a field, kept looking back at us. We followed, discovered prints leading to the barn, and there he was."

Leander turned to Kitty, questions chasing through his mind again, caroming off possible answers. "He's alive, then. And you knew it. Didn't you?"

Kitty waved at Senrid. "Ask him!" she yelled, then she whirled around and flounced back inside.

Leander sighed, looking down at the friend-turned-enemy. For a brief moment the sight of that pale face lying in the snow was overlaid with the memory of the same face staring down at him through the clear water of Sindan's river. Only this time Leander held the decision of life or death, and Senrid wasn't even aware.

Of course there was no choice. He waved a hand toward the inside, and Arel and his riding companion picked up the limp figure, one at each end.

"Where?" Arel asked, pausing to look back. His hands were under Senrid's armpits; Leander looked at Senrid's limp body, his pale face lifeless of any of the determination or wit that so characterized him, and turned away. Arel added, "And should we post a guard?"

Leander hesitated. *Was* Senrid his prisoner? What had he done to deserve it—and could Leander even keep him, if he wanted to get free? The answers there, at least, were clear: no, and no. "Don't bother," Leander said tiredly. "He has magic. More than I do. Just put him in a guest room. If he wants to leave, I can't stop him."

Kitty hovered in the hallway until Arel and the other trod past with their burden, then she pounded down the hall to the kitchen, which was blessedly warm and smelled like cinnamon.

"Llhei!" she called, and when everyone looked up, she beckoned fiercely.

Llhei smiled. "What is it, child?"

Kitty waited until Llhei had reached the doorway, and drew her out. "Senrid," she whispered. "They found him in the snow. They're taking him upstairs right now. Leander—he's mad at me, he gave me this *look*—"

"Go have a berry-bun, they're fresh," Llhei said. "I'll see to the boy. And Leander."

Kitty waited only until Llhei was down the hall, then she slunk after. She had to know what happened—what was said. That horrid promise—*just* when she'd thought herself finally safe!

Llhei chose the servants' way upstairs, which was shorter. It was also impossible to sneak there, Kitty had discovered. You saw everyone coming and going, as there was no furniture to hide behind.

So she ran to the grand stairway and skidded round the landing, racing upward. When she reached her own hall, Llhei disappeared inside the room Senrid had had before. Arel and his riding partner strode away down the hall in the other direction.

As soon as the clatter of their riding boots had diminished down the stairwell Kitty tiptoed up and pressed her ear to the door.

She heard a *wark! wark!* sound, kind of like a dog, and then a moan and a jumble of words.

Then Llhei's voice, "Yes, I know, I'm taking terrible liberties, but you simply can't sleep with wet clothing on, not to mention knives. We don't have enough bedding to risk your ruining this fine set of sheets with bloodstains."

Another jumble of words.

Llhei laughed. "No, but you've no authority here and cannot order me around, and you *are* in my charge. I already have charge of two children not the least related to me, so what is a temporary third? Now stop babbling and sleep. I hate the thought of how happy your wicked uncle would be if you conveniently died."

Kitty heard Llhei coming toward the door, and fled to hide in her room.

She'd get at Senrid later, and make him take back that promise, Or Else.

₧෬৪০෬

Leander was in his magic room when Llhei came through his study door with a tray.

"If you don't eat, you will end up like your guest," she said, setting the tray down on the table.

Leander gazed in bemusement at the tray, which was loaded with enough food for five or six people. All his favorite things, he noticed. The smells woke his insides up.

"I thank you, but if I don't work, we'll all end up like him. If not worse. I don't know when his uncle is coming back."

"If I can understand young Senrid's ravings aright, the Regent won't be, at least not yet. He'll have to settle things at home first."

"What happened? Why is Senrid here?"

"He appeared that one day, before the storm hit us—"

"That storm was magic," Leander cut in, frowning. "Black magic driven. It's going to pull more storms this way. We're in for a bad winter." He blinked. "I'm sorry I interrupted. Too many things in my mind at once, all of them equally important."

Llhei nodded, comfortable and imperturbable as ever. Leander had been grateful for her presence ever since he first met her.

"He was arguing with the Regent. He was sick then, but he told me he wanted only to get his uncle on home ground. He said he had no interest in us here."

"And you believed him?" Leander winced. "I believed him once too, and found out he's very good at lying—saying what you expect to hear."

"He did nothing untoward," Llhei said. "And Nelyas later overheard some of the guards gossiping about how angry the Regent was that he'd shown up. So perhaps that much, at least, is true, that Senrid is less interested in fighting us than with his uncle. You probably ought to interview him when he's rested a bit."

Leander sighed. "I don't really want to see him. What would be the use? You can't believe anything he says."

"He's raving right now. You won't get any sense out of him at all, lies or truth, not until the fever breaks."

Leander remembered their early talks, how much fun it had been to find someone else who liked history, who could think as fast as he could. Probably faster; Senrid had been outthinking Leander the whole time.

Regret was Leander's foremost emotion, not hatred or disgust. Those would come only if Senrid returned at the head of an army.

He looked up at Llhei, who was waiting, watching him with her usual mild expression. "Let me know if he asks to see me, okay?" he asked. "I really need to work on mastering these wards. If Tdanerend comes back, I intend to see that he won't easily use his black magic here again, if I possibly can. Since there's nothing we can do about that army."

Llhei nodded. "Yes, and in my turn, I admonish you not to let that food sit there like decorations. Eat."

"I promise."

She left, and Leander dutifully picked up a honey-and-nut loaded oatcake, munching it as he turned back to his book.

While Senrid faded from his mind as old magic once more engrossed his thoughts, Kitty hovered outside the doorway.

As soon as Leander's door was closed, she whispered, "What did he say? What did you tell him?"

Llhei laughed. "That Senrid is sick, and that Leander ought to eat. What am I not to tell him? Why are you so fretful, Kitty?"

Kitty scowled. "That Senrid—it's all his fault."

"What is his fault?"

"Oh, some stupid mess he caused. And I'll get blamed for it. You'll see." And, as they reached the door to Senrid's room, "Can I go in there yet?"

"Wait here, and let me check."

When she emerged, she shook her head. "He's asleep."

Kitty groaned. "He would be. He did it on purpose."

And she stalked back to her room.

For another day and a half she endured the long wait. No one talked to her, for the servants were all busy setting the castle to rights again, and Leander lived in his study. He never came out for meals.

Once she tiptoed in, but the first thing he said was, "How's Senrid?"

"A bad fever, Llhei says. She won't let me go in there—" She realized that Leander was not the one she ought to be complaining to, and stopped, and sighed.

"Is there anything you want to tell me?" he asked then.

He wasn't mad, but those green eyes were uncomfortably direct. She might moan about how he never really saw or heard her any more, but he sure was paying all his attention to her right now.

She remembered the mysterious disappearance of her blindness—and all those other spells. She remembered her promise to Leander about never messing with his magic books. Promises were important to Leander, so she'd tried to make them important to her too.

But now he looked at her as if, well, she'd lied.

And she *hadn't!* It was all Senrid's fault!

She groaned. "I want him out of here," she declared.

"Me too," Leander said, and turned back to his books.

Kitty didn't stop him.

A day and a half later, she was lurking in the hallway after Llhei's morning visit to the guest room, when Llhei came out, her eyes pitying, her mouth quirked in a strange little smile. "His sufferings have ended," she said.

FOUR

"You mean the fever's finally broken?" Kitty asked.

"And none too soon," Llhei said. "Now, do not fret him back into one. I managed to get this broth down his throat, and though he's got his wits back, his mood is a match for yours. I'd consider a wait if there's something you need his cooperation with."

Kitty sucked in her breath. "What do you mean?"

Llhei shrugged. "What do *you* mean?"

Kitty frowned. Llhei was getting awfully regal for a servant. But Kitty knew if she said something about that, Llhei would shrug, and smile, so she stalked past and into Senrid's room.

He was propped up on pillows, wearing a shirt of Leander's that was much too large for him. His eyes looked watery and his nose dull red. A besorcelled handkerchief was clutched in one hand, with which he kept wiping his nose.

"You look terrible." Kitty chortled in triumph. "Do you feel terrible? I hope so, because you deserve it!"

Senrid gave a brief, wheezy laugh. "I was counting the moments. Until you'd be by. To say something. Bright and cheery."

"When are you going to let me off that ridiculous promise?"

"Never. What would be the use. Of making it. In the first place?"

Talking, even that much, was an effort.

Kitty glared. "Leander has been asking about that magic. He thinks I did it."

"So?"

"I promised not to! And he—he *looks* at me. I can't stand it!"

"If he doesn't trust you...he should throw you out," Senrid said. "I would. But he's weak. Nothing will happen." He waved a hand, his voice going hoarse. "Few days, all will be. Same as before."

"You are talking about *my* home, and *my* comfort, all for some stupid mess of *yours*. It would serve you right if I told him everything."

"And you'd be foresworn," Senrid retorted. His voice had no force, but his eyes were exactly as derisive as ever. "And I'd know it. Forever."

"You've ruined my life!"

He winced. "Stop bellowing. I can hear you."

"If *yelling* will get what I *want* then I will *yell!* You don't *deserve* any better!"

"Since when—" He was taken by a fit of coughing.

It sounded nasty, and it lasted a long time. When it was done, both kids were equally embarrassed, she for causing it and he for not being able to control it.

Kitty eyed him, then flounced to the door. "You wait, Senrid whatever-your-name is—"

"Montredaun-An."

"—I'll get that promise back!"

"You won't."

She slammed the door.

Senrid lay in the bed, considering. He did not want to think about the dreams he'd had. Why? Though they had been difficult to endure at the time—harrowing—they were, in the light of day, meaningless. Just dreams, caused by the fever, and the residue of magic-poison. What he did need to think about was his place here, and his plan of action when he got home.

And how he'd get home, since he knew without even trying that Tdanerend would have destroyed all his magic wards, and would have tracer-wards on the border—on him, actually—for half-a-dozen spells, beginning with the transfer spell.

He reached for the steeped leaf that Llhei had brought. It was fresh, not too hot, and tasted good. It was gone in three gulps—even his throat felt better, though the swallowing hurt. Then there were the fresh oatcakes. Oats! At home, the oat crop belonged to the military first, for the use of the high-bred Nelkereth horses, or for warriors in the field. Only if there was a surplus did civilians get any.

He ate his oatcakes and thought about Llhei, who had tended him without fear of what anyone else might say. Including Senrid.

There was also the younger one, Nelyas. She'd brought the clean bedding in before Llhei came, and said, "So what happened to your uncle anyway?"

"Tried a summons-transfer against me, to send me home. Dungeon. I mirrored it. Sent *him*. Tried to go home, not enough strength for the long transfer. Got outside this castle, walked. Holed up in some burned barn. Don't remember anything else."

"So he'll be coming back at us?"

"Doubt it," Senrid said. It was all he had strength for.

She nodded and left.

No servant at home would ever question any of the family. They wouldn't think of it. Senrid wasn't sure if he disliked it or was just unused to it. He remembered that at home he had never liked the fearful glances, the closed faces that made it very clear thoughts did indeed go on behind those shuttered expressions, but he wasn't going to hear them.

Tdanerend arrogantly maintained that servants were stupid, and that's why they were servants. Senrid had never considered the truth of that, because servants did not present any threat, but he considered it now. Llhei wasn't stupid, and neither were these others—Nelyas, or that Arel, who'd carried him in to the bath at dawn.

If the same thing had happened at home, with his and Leander's places switched, there was no doubt that Leander would have been killed as soon as he'd been found. Unless someone wanted to make some kind of gesture and designed a more protracted end for him.

He couldn't remember what it was called, this attitude that you did not take a life except in defense. Maybe it came under the category of that mystery called morality. Tdanerend had taught him—and the writings of many of his ancestors backed it up—that there were no such thing as morals, only expedience. As soon as you acknowledged any kind of a moral standard, then you weakened yourself through the accompanying guilt. That was using your own power against yourself. Yet there were others among his ancestors who had felt differently, writing long thoughts about moral standards, passages that Senrid had read and reread, but the sense had eluded him, like a butterfly flitting beyond his grasp. His own father had written something about it, in the one record not destroyed by Tdanerend, probably because it had been appended to an older one, and missed. Yet Senrid had been taught that his father died because he was weak.

So who was smart, strong, yet moral?

The problem was, he did not know how to measure strength. Leander wasn't stupid. And their situations were remarkably parallel: both born princes, parents of both murdered by the usurper. Only where Senrid had kept his rank, Leander had lived as an outcast in the woods. They both had loyal friends. Senrid's were fewer in number if higher in rank, and they were trained in warfare, but he'd seen Leander's friends. Their loyalty—their mutual trust—was their strength.

He wished that Leander would come in. There were so many questions he had!

But the day wore on, and he slept again, and when he woke it was dark. He realized that Leander was not going to come. The only one he'd see would be Kyale, a loud, narrow-minded, utterly worthless kid who would not last a week in Choreid Dhelerei. Again, that loyalty. Though their actual connection was tenuous at best Leander accepted her as a sister, useless as she was, and that was that.

One of the dream images struck him again, this one from memory: Leander's face while Senrid held him underwater.

The fight had been initially a reaction of anger, and when he'd won and was drowning Leander he had thought in triumph, *I can take his little kingdom back right now, and nobody could stop me.*

He couldn't define the expression he'd observed in those green eyes looking up at him through the running water. Not betrayal, for Senrid had promised nothing. Nor was it surrender, precisely. Nor even anger. Regret?

Regret, and acceptance. An act of will, a profound sort of acceptance that had smoothed out his features. Leander had been ready to die.

That wasn't cowardice, though Tdanerend would deem it so. Likewise a coward would never have marched on the castle with an ill-trained rabble of a dozen servants in order to face, for all he knew, the entire east wing of Marloven Hess's light cavalry; if Tdanerend had had his way, Leander and his gang would have faced them. No, that was not cowardice, whatever else you might call it.

But civilians whose mages worked the weakness of white magic didn't have courage, that he'd always been taught.

All the old concepts seemed meaningless. No, it was their definitions that had warped until they no longer held any truth.

Was there any higher truth? Or was that all just a matter of whose perception could be enforced on others?

He was tired again.

He made a resolution: he would sleep, and by morning he would be gone.

He was not the only one making resolutions.

Senrid, Kitty, and Leander all thought about the other two as the evening wore on, but they all stayed in their rooms alone.

Kitty avoided Leander because she didn't want any more uncomfortable questions—or looks.

As for Senrid, she spent the day mapping out a verbal campaign. If she thought ahead to what she'd say, and what Senrid would say back, then she could have her answers ready, and not get mad—and maybe she could grind him down until he gave in. After all, it was only selfishness, pure and simple, that kept him from letting her tell Leander where that magic had come from. Her resolution was to have it out with Senrid and not give up until he took back that stupid promise.

Leander tried not to think about Senrid. What was the use? He felt stupid for having liked the kid at the very beginning. Of course a liar would know how to make himself likable to the fools he was trying to deceive. But he felt as the day progressed that he was going to have to visit Senrid, just once, even if only to say "How are you?" and listen to a one-word answer.

So he resolved on doing it as soon as he woke up.

When morning came, he dressed, walked down to eat, and then started back up to keep his resolution when he met Llhei in the hallway.

"He's gone," she said, and handed him a paper. Across it, printed in a neat hand, was *Kyale Marlonen*.

Regret and relief were Leander's strongest reactions. Leander said, "Thanks. I'll give this to Kitty."

Llhei nodded and passed by.

Leander continued down the hall to Kitty's room. Her door was open—she was coming out.

"Senrid's gone," Leander said. "Left this note for you—"

"Oh, no! He can't!"

"Kitty, please tell me—"

"Argh!" She reddened with rage as she ripped open the note, read it, then tore it into bits and stamped on it. Then she looked up, obviously determined. "I can tell you everything if you will send me after him."

"Did you two make some kind of deal?"

"Anything I say will make you mad and get me into trouble," Kitty snarled.

"How about if I say I'm mad already?"

"*You're* mad? Huh! You have *no* right to be mad when you haven't even—that is, you don't even—oh, what a mess. Send me?"

"No, because if he's gone, it's to Marloven Hess."

Kitty groaned, flounced into her room, and slammed the door so hard an echo came back, like the clapping of invisible hands.

Leander sighed. He just about had it figured out: Senrid and Kitty had formed some kind of unlikely partnership. What he couldn't figure out was why, and what they'd done, and why

Kitty couldn't tell him. That she was angry with her erstwhile partner was obvious—and unfeigned. *Kitty is no dissembler*, he thought. *What you see is what she feels.*

He stood outside her room looking at the bits of paper, then bent slowly and picked them up, and crushed them in his hand. Her motivation was easy to guess at: survival. Senrid's was impossible.

Leander retreated back to his room, and tossed the paper fragments into his fire, and watched it flare briefly. Whatever had happened, he had no part of it—both kids had made that pretty clear.

So the best he could do would be to get on with the enormous pile of work that did concern him, and leave the rest to sort itself out.

He shut the door, and sat down at his desk to begin.

ಎಂ⚭ೞ

Senrid walked along the western road, relieved at its dryness. Every time it snowed Leander was going to have to renew whatever magic he'd done, but Senrid had to admit that this was a fine piece of magery—something that he could use in Marloven Hess, especially if he wanted to move armies around fast. Though the hesitancy and over-caution of white magic probably made the spells roughly five times longer than they needed to be—even if the personal cost was less.

And so, for a time, he entertained himself trying to come up with something within his own magical knowledge.

But even with good roads a person who's been sick can only go so far, and before noon he was desperately tired, and all he could think about was rest.

He got a ride on a wagon by a cheerful man carrying bolts of silk, who bowled along behind his horses. The man kept exclaiming over the clear road—even his horses seemed happy. Senrid forced himself to respond to the frequent repetitions of how wonderful it was until they spotted a very small trade town crowning a hill at the edge of the border mountains. The town was built on either side of a river.

It, like Crestel, betrayed its origins in the way it was built, mostly of peachy stone, the light gray tile roof-gutters fashioned to take the load from the highest building, an interlocking geometric pattern shaping waterfalls downward toward the river; almost all doors facing east. This style of building was not Leroran, which was only a recent conceit in Senrid's eyes, they were like those over in Marloven Hess, evidence of their shared past, an ancient past, reaching clear back to the mysterious Venn far in the north of the world.

Just past the first hill the roads were no longer clear—at least by magic. The locals had done some dredging, but the horse, already tired, now slowed. The man leaned forward as if he could will more strength to his horses; all four were grateful when they reached the town at last. The man let Senrid down under the swinging sign of an inn.

Back in the Crestel castle he'd searched the drawers of the guest room, and had not been surprised to find money; he strongly suspected that Llhei had in fact put it there. Had Leander known?

Impossible to guess.

Soon he was sitting at a table, hot food before him, and the prospect of a bed waiting—though apparently he was going to have to share the room.

He'd scarcely taken a couple of bites of the eternal oatcakes and baked potato-cabbage-and-onion rolls that Lerorans seemed so fond of, when he felt uneasy. As though he was being watched. When he looked up, he made the unpleasant discovery that most of the patrons in the small common room were regarding him with a variety of expressions, most of them curious; some whispered.

"Is there a problem?" His voice came out sounding like the bark of a dog.

The oldest two in the room, a man and a woman, exchanged glances, then the woman said, "It's just that you came up Crestel-road on that wagon. D'you happen to have news out of there?"

Senrid opened his hand. "News like...?"

The old man said, "Are them pony-rumps from over west comin' back agin is what we want to know. There's a few of us wantin' to go home."

"So why don't you?" Senrid asked.

"And get shot for our pains? No one walks fast in the snow, you might have noticed," a young woman at the next table stated with congenial sarcasm, before holding up the squirming baby in her arms, sniffing expertly, then saying in an undervoice to a little girl of eight or so, "Frame your sister, will you?"

The little girl sighed and bore the stinky baby away

The boy who'd served him was about his own age. He said, "When they first came through, they shot two men outright. My father was one. Another the beekeeper. Crossbow-bolts— no warning. Someone else bawled orders at us, if we were seen on the road until we were allowed out by that soulripping Montredaun-An reeker, we'd be shot. Just like them. So everyone, even traders, been here since that day when they all rode through. Prisoned in our own town!"

"Ruined every herb-garden in town." The old woman added.

Senrid rubbed his tired eyes. "Everyone in Crestel thinks they're gone. Not coming back," he said.

"King?" the boy asked. "Is he alive?"

"Yes, and busy with magic protections," Senrid said, and then wondered why he would waste the breath defending Leander.

"Well, then." The old man smiled around the room as the others cheered, laughed, exclaimed. "Looks as if dawn'll find me on the road."

They all talked at once—celebrative talk and laughter, mixed with colorful invective against Marloven Hess. All of it was so heartfelt. Senrid ate quickly, drank down the hot cider he'd been offered, and climbed the stairs to sleep.

He woke up once, clammy and soggy-minded, to find it dark, and what had begun as another harrowing dream had resolved into noise: raucous singing, untuneful but enthusiastic, racketed from the common room, and outside in the market-square whoops and laughter and shouts. Intermittently, from closer, giggles and whispers; Senrid realized that a flirting couple were celebrating in their own way directly outside the ill-fitting casement above his bed. Disgusted, he turned over and pulled the quilt about his ears. Flirtation. Revolting weakness—an invitation for an enemy to gut you, that's what "romance" amounted to.

What was it Keriam had said? *Your father was never a coward. He was fast, and courageous, and everyone knew it. But after your mother's death, it was as if his spirit had died. I don't think he feared the knife in the back so much as invited it.*

That was weak. Senrid had vowed that he would never put himself in that position.

Remembering what Leander had said about that very subject, he wondered if he could find some white magic worker to put the no-aging spell on him as well. In this one thing he admitted that his own magic was less successful. But it was far, far better for defense, offense, and preservation of power.

He drifted back into sleep, briefly waking when his roommates tiptoed in. They did not speak as they settled in the other beds, and he soon slept again.

೪೦ଓଽଚ৩ଓଃ

Old habit had him up and through the cleaning frame before dawn. He was the first downstairs. A sleepy-eyed innkeeper served him a substantial breakfast, and lots of hot coffee. He paid for extra food to carry, and asked about walking distances between towns; he knew his map well, but dots on paper are very different, he had discovered, from real geography. He did not want anyone knowing that his destination was Marloven Hess, so he asked about various towns in either direction, mentally calculating distances and comparing them to the nearest Marloven market town.

Any way he looked at it, he had a long walk ahead. No help for it. Either he made it—or he didn't.

Bundling his bread-and-cheese under Leander's old tunic to keep the food warm, he pulled on his cloak and departed. He looked distrustfully at the bleak sky, and the snowflakes drifting lazily down.

As he plodded up the road to the west he thought again about the questions he'd answered, and the attitudes those people had revealed about Leander. Respect, that was clear. Concern. Scarcely a year on the throne, and defeated in less than a day by a detachment of warriors in training, yet they seemed to want him anyway.

He thought back, wishing Leander had confronted him. Even an argument would have offered a kind of exchange of ideas.

Well, he hadn't. That was in itself a message.

He tried to thrust Vasande Leror, and its kid rulers, from his mind. They were the past. What he had to face now was the fact that he would need to begin his own work all over again. Tdanerend had to be sitting in Choreid Dhelerei right now, preparing against Senrid's reappearance.

Senrid walked without really seeing where he was going, as he considered his encounters with his uncle since his return from his inadvertent side-trip to the water world and then with Puddlenose and Christoph.

Tdanerend had been appalled to discover that Senrid was alive. Of course. But what was behind the intensity of that reaction? His uncle had never been quite that ready to anger in the past, so easy to provoke into losing control. He seemed almost desperate, at times. The invasion of Vasande Leror was not just an act of desperation. It was an act of madness to claim the throne of Marloven Hess—and then leave. To try to smash Vasande Leror into producing steel for an even bigger army—

He pulled out his bread-and-cheese and munched slowly as he reviewed the past weeks. From the moment that mysterious transfer magic had whisked him away from Puddlenose and Christoph in Everon and slammed him down outside of Crestel he'd been on the run, his plans always just ahead of his own steps. Immediate actions and reactions had been all he'd been capable of, but now, with no one around (side-question: *was* he being watched?) and time to consider, he questioned things that he'd taken for granted scarce days before. The more he considered, the more it seemed that there was something missing. Tdanerend, on first seeing Senrid, had been so enraged because of what, fear?

Fear?

Fear of...what?

Longing to be home seized Senrid, but he forced himself to walk at a steady pace, to resist futile anger. To consider carefully everything he could remember.

He was reviewing the details of that last magic battle when a persistent bird cry broke into his thoughts.

It came from behind. He turned as the cry resolved into a voice.

When he recognized the short, silver-haired figure toiling up the road toward him, annoyance burned through him. It was Kyale—the person he wanted least to see right now, excepting only his uncle.

Arms swinging, she bustled the last distance. Her face was crimson. "There you are!" she cried, nearly out of breath. "I *thought* you'd be slower than a frozen snail. And I can see how welcome I am, which is wonderful, because I am going to stick to your side until you stop being a fathead and let me tell Leander everything."

"Shut up," he said.

Kitty had thought it all out, and she was determined not to relent. What she'd decided was that Senrid stuck to his promise out of a weird sense of... Well, in a normal person it would be honor, or maybe even embarrassment, but in a Marloven it had to be arrogance.

"Oh, I'm not going to shut up," she proclaimed, smirking with anticipation. No doubt about it, she was going to thoroughly enjoy every moment. How often, after all, did a person get to be nasty, loud, and insulting to a villain, and know she was every bit in the right? "I am going to be so obnoxious you won't be able to bear it, because you've made my life at home too miserable to stay."

"If you get yourself killed it won't be my fault," he honked.

Kyale laughed at the weird sound of his voice. "Not if I stick close to you. One thing for sure, you seem to know how to stay alive. I can't go home." She lifted her chin. "You've destroyed my honor."

He laughed—and coughed so hard he sat down inadvertently in the snow.

Kyale watched him with a weird mixture of hilarity and worry, and when at last he got control of the coughing, she said, "I don't think you're going to make it."

"I'll make it," he said, breathing fast. "But without you." He got up, disliking the way his head swam, and sniffed juicily, wishing he dared use his magic so he could get a besorcelled handkerchief. He wished he hadn't left Leander's behind, but he hadn't wanted to take anything from them, except that money obviously left for him. Stupidity!

He sneezed.

"Quite a concert of disgusting sounds." Kyale made a euch!-this-stinks face.

"You don't have to stay to hear it," he hinted.

Kitty eyed him, then started in with a few other gambits that she'd thought invented over the previous day.

Senrid scarcely heard her. His "Shut up," was automatic; what worried him was that the coughing fit seemed to have drained him.

He plodded one foot in front of the other, head down, arms folded tightly across his aching chest, letting the sound of Kitty's voice wash past as he considered how he might get around the tracers no doubt on him so he could transfer, and leave Kitty behind.

His thoughts vanished like dream images when he heard crunching steps in the snow behind him. And Kyale was right at his side, as she'd promised to be. She whirled around, looking up a moment before he did; he saw her expression of fear and distrust before he turned his attention behind them to the man walking not two paces behind.

FIVE

To Kitty, the sudden visitor seemed tall and dark with threat. Senrid, used to assessing adults, saw a man a little over medium height—no taller than Tdanerend—but there the resemblance ended. Tdanerend's face had become lined with ill-humor; this man, though appearing roughly the same age, had only the faint lines at the corners of his eyes that came of squinting against the sun. His brown hair was combed straight back, square-cut over the neck—the same military style Marloven Hess currently favored, and he was dressed in black and gray, the gray tunic unmarked. No weapons in sight, but his walk was that of someone who was well trained.

Another difference was that where Tdanerend almost never met anyone's eyes unless he was angry—and in control of everyone in view—this man's glance was direct, acute, and amused.

Senrid instantly distrusted him.

"Do I interrupt?" the man asked, the amusement pronounced. And to Senrid, "I am here to offer my aid."

"I don't want any help," Senrid said.

The man made a gesture, murmured a few words, and Senrid felt the sudden impact of intense magic. So did Kyale, who looked up in surprise and fear.

"My aid would advance your cause with relative ease," he said. "Go on, try your magic. The tracers are all gone."

The gesture might have been intended to be taken as altruism, but Senrid knew what he'd really seen: a demonstration of power. And a quick glance at that face made him realize the man was reading him without any trouble.

"I don't need your help," Senrid said, even more distinctly.

"Who are you?" Kyale demanded. "Go away!"

The man turned his gaze to Kyale, and it narrowed slightly. She stared up at gray eyes flecked with little bits of green, a steady gaze that she couldn't...seem...to...look...away... from...

Senrid *felt* Kyale's will start to dissolve. He drew in a sharp breath, knowing just where the man came from, and that the stories about ensorcelling—if not stealing—one's mind with a mere act of will were true.

He hooked his foot out, caught Kyale behind the ankle, and yanked. She collapsed in the snow with a "Whoop!"

The man smiled slightly, apparently waiting for a reaction.

"Who are you, Senrid's father?" Kyale demanded, her voice breathy with fright and false bravado.

Senrid rounded on her, but stopped himself in time. Idiot! To reveal anything to this soul-sucker, a *real* one—"Are you all right?" he asked her, hoping to cover.

"Yes," she snapped, getting up and brushing snow off her gown. "I know what that creep almost did, because I saw Mara Jinea try to do it, only with a lot of magic spells. Well, you won't get me!" She snarled at the man.

He looked down at her with the air of someone observing the antics of a puppy.

Senrid's heart hammered. Norsunder—the man was from Norsunder. The evil beyond time and the physical world that he'd heard about his entire life was real, and it was *here*.

And then he had it. Tdanerend had tangled himself with Norsunder, probably in a desperate bid to gain more power. He was sure of it with an instant but utter conviction.

The man turned his gaze to Senrid, and both kids felt a subtle but distinct focus of intent.

Kyale gulped in a breath, and said, her face stricken, "Hibern's tower!"

Hoping that its image was still in her head, Senrid did the transport spell, touched her hand, and they transferred, appearing in a warm round room with a tall black-haired girl staring at them in surprise.

The man appeared a heartbeat afterward.

Senrid stared, transfer-reaction and fear making red flare across his vision, but the man only said, "Impressive wards," to someone else, and then to Senrid, "We'll continue our discourse when I choose."

He vanished.

Senrid drew in a slow, shaky breath. The malaise dissolved, leaving him looking up at a tall, dark-eyed girl his own age.

"Kyale?" the girl exclaimed, having backed against the wall. "Who's this?"

Kitty grinned, relieved that the man was gone, and delighted to feel safe and warm again. "Who, him?" She pointed at Senrid, who leaned back against the opposite wall, pale and grim. "Your future P.I.L.!"

"P.I.L.?" Hibern repeated, her mouth smiling, but her eyes still wide with reaction.

"Partner In Life!"

"Oh. King Senrid, of course. Welcome."

For a moment they assessed one another. Senrid had heard about this girl, who studied white magic right in her father's home, and in Senrid's own kingdom. She was indeed tall, about as tall as Leander, a long thin, brown face framed by long dark hair. Her most dominant feature was a pair of intelligent black eyes under straight black brows.

"I am Hibern," she said, her mouth quirked. "Latvian's lame, insane daughter."

"Thanks for getting me out of a betrothal with your plea of insanity," Senrid said.

"You're welcome," Hibern retorted with good-natured irony. "But my motives were entirely selfish."

Senrid laughed—and endured another fit of coughing, which left black spots swimming before his eyes.

Kitty said, "Hibern, can you ward out Latvian and Uncle Nasty-face Tdanerend and them?"

"Already done," Hibern said. "This is the first time any stranger has ever transferred in like that. He must have put a tracer on you," she said to Senrid. "Who was he, anyway?"

"Don't know," Kitty said, and Senrid gave his head a single shake. "He appeared on the road, gabbled a lot of stuff about 'helping out', and when Senrid got us away by magic, he followed us here."

Hibern said, "My rooms have been warded against the Regent and my father for a couple of years. Obviously I need a more complex ward, a general one, though it will be hard work. I will get to that right away."

"Maybe second thing?" Kitty asked.

Hibern gave her a rueful smile. "Dare I ask?"

Exhausted as he was, Senrid could see that Hibern had been shaken by the man's appearance in her tower. She might have thought herself invisible to enemies before; the man's wry compliment about impressive wards was a more effective threat than any sinister speeches would have been.

Kitty flapped a hand Senrid's way, recalling his wandering wits. "Because if Boneribs here doesn't get more rest, he's gonna croak and make that disgusting uncle happy."

"Boneribs?" Hibern murmured, her brows raised in question.

"What CJ called him, on this other world we got thrown into."

"I see! You can tell me about it anon," Hibern said. "Senrid, you can tuck up in my bed. When the servants come up with food, don't talk. I'll put an illusion in the doorway and tell them I'm sick, and they'll put the trays down and run."

"What about us?" Kitty asked.

Hibern laughed. "Oh, we'll resort to a very fine bit of new magic one of my tutors helped me set up. There is a room directly above here, both warded and protected by illusion. That's where I keep my most important books! Watch, for it's only accessible by magic." She made a sign, and vanished. The other two copied it, and found themselves in what appeared to be a room exactly like the one below, only minus the bed. In its place was a fine desk, covered with neat stacks of books and papers at which Senrid glanced with weary curiosity. There was also a narrow couch, and rugs on the floor.

Despite her careless words, this kind of magic was difficult, exacting, and must have taken a full year to set up, transferring and binding each brick, stone, and board. And then shrouding them with illusion. Senrid was impressed.

"Records," Hibern said, pointing to the bookshelves all round the walls below the windows. "From all over the world, copies obtained by—" She glanced at Senrid and said, "—various mages. Senrid, why don't you go below and sleep?"

"I don't need—" he began to protest.

"Rot," Hibern interrupted unemotionally. "You do need. And you and I are going to converse after you do."

He met that dark, clever gaze, but had not the energy to challenge it.

"Use my nightgown," Hibern continued. "From the looks of you, size will not be a problem. The cleaning frame is in the door of the wardrobe."

Senrid flicked his palm up, made the sign, and vanished.

Kitty sighed with relief.

Hibern surveyed her, smiling. "It's good to meet you. Now, tell me everything. Beginning with how you managed to meet up with who, on further thought, I very much fear was Detlev of Norsunder."

Kitty jumped. "Norsunder? That man was from *Norsunder?*"

"If I am right, he's one of the commanders. Though not one of the Host of Lords who created it, so many thousand years ago." Hibern gave a rueful wince. "I'm so glad I didn't realize it at the time."

"Detlev?" Kitty repeated, wondering if she'd heard the name before.

"It's one of his names—or at least I believe that was he. The descriptions are very like. Has Senrid been courting Norsundrians?"

Kitty gasped. "I don't *think* so!" And, more rapidly than she had ever told a story, she outlined what had happened.

Hibern listened intently, leaning forward, her dark eyes every bit as acute as that mysterious man's—but without being threatening.

At the end, she said, "I do think it's Detlev. Now we're in trouble." She rubbed her hands up her arms, though the room was warm enough. "Detlev. *Here*. Just long enough to let me know he recognized the wards I have in place. What does it mean? Nothing that can even remotely do us any good whatever, that I can be sure of."

"Who? What?" Kitty asked. "Though maybe I don't want to know."

"Would you shut your eyes to danger?"

"Yes!" Kitty squirmed, loathing the question. "No. I guess not."

"I've learned a little about Detlev because I've been reading world history. How much do you know about Old Sartor?"

"Old Sartor?" Kitty repeated, surprised. "As in, before the Fall? Thousands of years ago?"

"That Old Sartor, yes."

"Nothing, really, except it was our ancestors, and they had glorious art and were all perfect and had all these incredible abilities."

Hibern grinned. "Well, they weren't all that perfect or we wouldn't be here talking about them as ancient history. They had their problems, though they did also have abilities we don't have, and their art was apparently something special. When they did have personal problems, they had these kind of mental healers who used objects made out of this, oh, silvery-white material with natural magic, not rock and not metal, that we also don't have any more, but it helped them focus their thoughts so the healers could fix whatever needed to be fixed." She paused.

Kitty nodded, comprehending so far.

"Well, this Detlev was supposedly one of these mental healers. The best of them, or so it's said. And Norsunder got him by some kind of really nasty trickery, and after a couple thousand years, he switched over to their side."

"A couple thousand... *years*?"

Hibern said a trifle impatiently, "Not like day-to-day. Norsunder exists outside of time—you have to know that."

"Well, sure. But I guess I never thought about what that means," Kitty admitted. "All right, so this Detlev turned from a good guy to a bad guy, and it maybe took a thousand years. Euw." She grimaced.

"For our purposes, he was gone from the physical world well over a thousand years, and then reappeared in the records, doing evil things. He also tried to locate and gather those dyr things—the objects I told you about—so they could be switched to evil purposes."

"But he didn't use anything like that on me," Kitty said. "His hands were bare."

"Right." Hibern flicked her palm upward in agreement. "That's because he only got a couple of the dyra and successfully managed to warp one of them to enhance black magic—so he could use one against an entire kingdom. With it, about a century ago, he did some really horrible experiments in powerful countries like Everon, and Sartor, and others, until he lost the dyra in some kind of big magical clash. Both have been hidden, though I guess he knows where the evil one is. Well, mages on both sides know, and the enchantment on it was broken recently. One thing for sure: Norsunder used to watch, but now they seem to be actively involving themselves again. And Detlev's one of the worst of them."

Kitty shuddered. "Yuk! So what has all that to do with *us*?"

"Well, that kind of depends on our friend asleep below, doesn't it?"

∞○››‹‹○∞

In the morning, Senrid woke when the door closed.

At first he thought he was still in Crestel, and his bleary vision tried to force his surroundings into the plastered-and-fabric-hung walls of his room in Leander's castle. But this room was not square, and the stone remained stone; memory came back, in emotion-charged shards, and with it the smells of herb steeped leaf and boiled oats—an expensive dish, here in Marloven Hess.

He sat up. Felt the soft folds of an old linen nightgown shift about him. He looked down at the fine pink embroidery and his sense of reality took a serious misstep.

A kind of perceptional vertigo sent his thoughts round in dizzying circles, and he groaned, and forced himself not to think at all. Instead, he got out of bed, noting with sour apprehension that merely lifting the tray and getting back in bed tired him out.

The tray also contained a small pot of cream, and some honey. He poured both on the oats, drank the steeped leaf, then ate. He finished it all, and felt incrementally better.

Experimentally, he made a small transfer spell. The tray and its contents vanished from the bed and appeared by the door.

Good.

Moments later, the flash and stirred air of transfer magic made him look up. Hibern said, "You did magic."

"Just transferred the tray from here to there." His voice was almost gone.

She nodded. "Don't do anything outside of this room, or my father will discover you are here. He has mirror wards up." She was taken by a sudden yawn. "Ugh! Read half the night, seeking the strongest possible wards. We both read."

"Kyale can read?" Senrid asked skeptically.

Hibern said, her dark gaze steady, "She doesn't like being ignorant, but no one bothered to put her in the way of a real education until recently. Leander's too busy to really direct her first steps, though I understand he does his best. She read some records that I have copies of..." She smiled. "You remember CJ Sherwood?"

"Do I," Senrid said, without enthusiasm.

Though he'd initially liked CJ, he'd endured far too many of her insults on the other world to maintain any kind of goodwill. And he couldn't just shrug her off as a hypocrite and fool, as he did Kyale, because she wasn't either, and he knew it. Once he'd recovered from his initial fury at the discovery of her masquerade, he'd respected the courage it had taken to go into the midst of his own stronghold, surrounded by enemies, protected only by a flimsy illusion-spell. And that transfer of the prisoners right under his own and his uncle's noses had been a superlative piece of work.

"The Mearsieans," Hibern said, "have stumbled into Norsunder's attention, and CJ has written about the experience. Kyale wanted to read up on it, considering your situation here."

"That man yesterday," Senrid said. "Did she tell you about him?"

"Yes, but before we go on, I have some questions for you," Hibern said, sitting down on her wingchair and folding her hands.

And Senrid remembered that they were enemies. Despite the situation, which seemed absurd—he in her bed, wearing her nightclothes, and she protecting him from his uncle—even here there was danger.

She said, "You tried to kill Kyale, and Faline, and you would have killed CJ—and Leander—if you'd gotten the chance, am I right?"

He opened his mouth, and hesitated. She was unlike anyone he'd met yet. She was a Marloven born and raised, but she studied white magic. That had to mean she'd accepted as guiding principles the moral standards that white mages professed. That made her a 'white', the pejorative his uncle had never uttered without scorn. White meant weak.

A 'weak white'—like his own mother.

Further, if what Kyale had let fall was true, she was part of a network of people with the same views, here in his very own country. People who had actively worked against his uncle—against *him*. A fact he'd kept secret from Tdanerend all this time, until he could assess it. Well, the time for assessment seemed to be now.

Third, she knew a lot more magic than he did.

He said, "Probably, yes."

"Probably?"

He didn't miss the tone of extreme skepticism. He said, "If CJ and Leander hadn't interfered, Kyale and Faline would be dead, along with 713, true. I don't know if it makes a difference, but I found it a disgusting prospect, and if I could have figured a way around it that would not have led to my uncle curtailing what few freedoms I had—on the grounds of weakness—I would have. As for CJ and Leander, my first idea was to hunt 'em down, bring them back to Choreid Dhelerei, and while my uncle was busy gloating over them and preparing one of his executions, to secure the kingdom. If I could."

"All right. Go back to the first execution, the one that almost happened. Never mind the warrior, I'm talking about two girls who never harmed you in any way. So you had some sympathy—while going right ahead with the plans. But you believed your sympathy was weakness, didn't you? So you could ignore the fact that what you were doing was not in any sense justice in the true meaning of the word? Do you know what justice is?"

These were questions he'd been avoiding all along. He couldn't answer any of them for himself, and wasn't about to get into the subject of justice with her.

She seemed to see it in his face, because she sat back and said, "Never mind. At least you didn't spin out some kind of lie. In truth, there are more people in our country than just you wrestling at midnight with the same questions—including, from what I understand, some of those archers who were pointing arrows at the midsection of a harmless red-haired little girl from another country who wasn't even remotely capable of military stratagems."

A network of spies that included servants—or guards— right in his own castle, then. Senrid felt a headache behind his eyes. How would he ever sort all these factions out? He wouldn't. He was going to die, probably in some stupid, pointless way, and figure in history as the boy-king who never actually ruled a day in his life.

A derisive laugh escaped him, which brought on one of those coughing fits that left his chest on fire and black spots floating across his vision. He flopped back onto the bed, breathing fast.

"I should let you sleep," Hibern said. "But I'm trying desperately to figure out if you really are in fact my enemy, and if my harboring you right now is a danger to those I am trying to protect."

"No," he whispered, his eyes closed. "If Tdanerend disappeared today, I would never shoot Kyale. Though I would send her. Back to her brother. As the biggest curse I could possibly give him. And the Mearsieans, I hope... Never to see again."

"So," the voice persisted, "if you had the throne today, for what would you be fighting? To clear out the corruption in Tdanerend's government, I know about that from other sources, but to what end? To better enable you to conquer the neighboring kingdoms?"

"I want..."

He searched back in memory, and saw his father's face, the cheering crowds, the whispers down through the years that had haunted Senrid's dreams: barely understood words, the most important one being *justice*...

"Justice," he repeated. And his eyes opened. "If I knew what it really was. But I know we don't have it now."

Hibern gave a short nod. "Fair enough. Go to sleep. I'm going to do so myself. I'm tired, after setting up what I hope are strong enough wards to keep Detlev from a return visit. But if we're going to be facing Norsunder outside of this tower, we're both in for some long nights of study."

Senrid closed his eyes, and was very soon asleep.

When he woke up again, the light had changed, and Hibern was back, now looking very worried.

"Kyale's not here," she said.

Senrid said voicelessly, "I'm grateful."

Hibern waved a hand. "You don't understand—she's disappeared."

SIX

When Kyale woke up, she saw Hibern asleep on a narrow sofa, an open book near her hand. The day was well advanced. She let her gaze travel about the study. All those records—exciting adventures happening to people. People she knew! CJ Sherwood, and Faline, doing really heroic things. It was obvious from her records that CJ didn't see herself as any kind of hero, but Kitty sure did.

No one would ever think of me as a hero, she thought morosely. *But then, I don't do anything heroic.*

She sat up on the pile of rugs Hibern had made into a bed for her. What could she do? Not fight, certainly. *Can I find out something everyone wants, some secret?*

Secret—spies. Who better to visit than a spy, particularly a friendly one? Hibern had mentioned her cousin Collet the night before, and Kitty remembered hearing about her during the summer, not long after Senrid's first visit. Hibern had put her and Leander together.

Hibern had spoken about the possibility of introducing Kitty to Collet, a smart and fun girl. She and her mother were part of a network of people seeking to change the government of Marloven Hess, something Kitty had scarcely listened to. Changing governments was boring. But girl spies were interesting.

Kitty not only wanted to meet her but talk to her. Maybe even be the first to find out some sort of interesting news no one else was aware of.

Yes, Kitty thought, exulting. *I can visit Collet, before anyone wakes up. Then, when Senrid snouts in again, I can tell him her news, if she has any, and that ought to shut him up about me being unable to do anything.*

She got up, pleased with her plan, and made the sign to go downstairs. Senrid was sound asleep in the bed, snoring away like people do when they can't breathe through their nose. Folded neatly on a chair were his clothes, and underneath the chair his boots, side by side. She glared, disgusted at his neatness. It seemed a silent reproach to her, who refused to put things away because that was the job of servants. Wouldn't it be fun to kick him and watch him scramble!

Instead, she moved silently to the wardrobe, a handsome piece of furniture with several gowns hung inside. She stepped in, stepped out, felt the delicious zing of being clean.

Then she looked at the door—hesitated—glanced out the window. Snow. Ugh.

She made the sign and transferred back up to the invisible room. Now, what was it Hibern had said? No magic outside the castle. But she'd said that Senrid could do some downstairs.

That had to mean that if Kyale did the transfer spell from inside the castle, she'd be perfectly safe! And though she'd promised Leander that she wouldn't mess with his books, she'd made no such promise to Hibern.

Moving with silent stealth, she removed a few of Hibern's older magic books, leafing slowly through them until she found the transfer spell. But how would she get back? She didn't mind taking Leander's books along—or hadn't—but she was afraid that Hibern might think she'd stolen it, if she woke up while Kitty was at Collet's.

Kitty looked around and spied a pencil and some scraps of paper. She carefully wrote the spell out, folded it, and tucked it into her sash.

Then she leaned over the book, firmly saying Collet's name as she did the spell. At first the familiar weirdness of the magic shifting one through space was all she felt, but then the magic changed, a blinding, wrenching change as if she had run into lightning, only a cold, numbing lightning as thick and terrible as a wall of ice.

When it released her, she gasped for breath and fell onto a cold floor of black marble. Footsteps approached; she let out a wail when she recognized Marloven uniforms.

Hands gripped her arms, yanked her to her feet. She was dizzy. She almost dropped, so they held her up in a harsh grip. Her head rocked on her shoulders as they bustled her down a long hall into a vast, cold room—the throne room.

She was in Choreid Dhelerei!

She saw the glint of torchlight on golden medals, then Tdanerend emerged out of the shadows, his expression of expectation altering to disappointment, which turned immediately to rage.

"That one! What are *you* doing here? How could *you*, of all the idiots I contend with, transfer into my tracers?" Quick suspicion pinched his features and he waved away the silent guards. As she wavered on her feet he grabbed her shoulder, painfully pulling her hair as he shook her. "Were you with Senrid? Where is he?"

"Dead, I hope," she yelled, pain-tears blurring her eyes. What could she say? What could she say? She couldn't mention Hibern! "I borrowed my brother's magic book."

"Where were you? You blocked the destination tracer—either you or someone else, but you did not ward the mirror transfer." His rapid words seemed more to himself than to her.

They certainly did not make any sense. Kitty struggled to free herself from those bruising fingers.

"Well?" He shook her again. "You were within my border, I know that much! Where? Why?"

Still dizzy, Kitty blurted, "I ran away from Senrid, who's at the head of a giant army, and they're marching this way!"

"You're lying."

Kitty winced, and shrugged, invention utterly giving out.

"Take her out and shoot her," Tdanerend said in disgust, flinging her away. She landed hard on the marble flooring. "And then we'll send her corpse to that soul-damned brother as a warning."

He stalked out.

Kitty trembled so badly she couldn't get up. The guards each took an arm, lifting her up and plopping her onto her feet. She began a violent struggle against their grip.

And kept struggling, dragging her heels and yelling as they bustled her out of the throne room, back down the corridor, and then through a door into a much plainer hall.

But here they were stopped by two more guards.

"His Majesty has superceded the orders," one of them said. "Wants to put her to the question, and we're to take her along. You're to resume your post in the transfer room against anyone else coming."

The silent ones let go of Kitty and she heard them walking away. The new ones grabbed her and bustled even faster into yet another corridor. Here the guards paused, and to Kitty's surprise, one of them let go of her arm and bent down.

"Princess," he whispered. "Don't you recognize me?"

Kitty gaped, as the ubiquitous uniform and square-cut yellow hair resolved into Arel's cousin, he who used to have long hair and favor forest clothing. He was Leander's spy in Choreid Dhelerei, she realized, almost sick with relief.

"Now, run," he said. "We're going to safety."

She needed no urging. The guards moved very fast; she had to skip and trot.

Hall after hall, stairs, an empty courtyard, neatly cleared of snow, and then she entered a door in the castle wall. In the distance she heard kids' voices, and she smelled food aromas.

Then into a plain, small room, with only a desk and a few chairs. The curtains were drawn shut, but she still heard kids' voices, and the occasional clang of steel.

The cousin (she'd never troubled to learn his name) and his friend let her go and stood silently at the door. Almost immediately the door opened again, and a fat man in an apron entered, followed by an older woman and then a uniformed Marloven with medals and a sword.

Kitty glared at him, wondering if danger had entered with this man, who was tall, old, with gray-flecked black curly hair.

This man came straight to her, and in an urgent voice said, "Where is Senrid? Is he still alive?"

Kitty turned to Arel's cousin, who motioned for her to talk.

"He's sick, but he's resting, and I don't think the fever is back," Kitty said.

The man gave a long sigh of relief, and turned away to face the drawn curtains. Kitty stared in amazement at that broad back. Why would he hide his face? Someone cared about Senrid? That was more than she would ever have guessed.

When the man turned around again, there was indeed moisture gleaming in his eyes, but his expression was grim. Before he spoke the door opened yet again, and more guards clattered in. This time there was no speech. The old one with the medals glanced up. One of the newcomers, who looked barely older than Leander, gave a nod, his expression bleak, and the older man shifted his glance from them to the door.

The newcomers left without having spoken. Kitty realized that some kind of nasty order had been carried out, and reported on, all in those exchanges of glances. She winced, remembering those two guards whom Tdanerend had told to see her shot.

Fear gripped her insides so tight she felt queasy.

The older man said, "You must give Senrid this message. It is desperately important. I am Keriam. Tell him Keriam awaits his command. Tell him that Gherdred is neutral. He will not follow an order to strike against our own people, but he will fight to defend. Tell him that the entire mounted is behind that, or most of them. The foot is under Tdanerend's direct control. Can you remember that?"

Kitty nodded, but looked accusingly at the cousin. "You almost let me get killed last month!"

The adults all exchanged quick looks, difficult to interpret.

"We couldn't act," the cousin said. "It was too quickly done, and we couldn't get near you, as the Regent had you three marked off in his own playground down below. Even the king couldn't interfere, other than seeing to it Rathend or any of the Regent's other pet torturers didn't go down there to play. Against you children, I mean. We couldn't do anything about the warrior."

Kitty realized what he meant, and her insides twisted again. She remembered Faline saying, during their long night of talk, *I can get us outa the cells, but we can't get past any of the guards at the doors—way too many.*

"We do have orders now. Just this morning, from the king, our king, himself: *To render Senrid whatever assistance he needs.*" He smiled. "We stretched that to include you."

Kitty sighed. "So these people are all our spies?"

Keriam said, "No. The rest of us are Marlovens. Only this pair—" He nodded at the cousin and the fat man. "Those are Lerorans, and I knew about them from the beginning, but since the castle guard is also under my control, all except for the Regent's personal guard, I permitted them to stay. The time has come, we believe, to join forces."

Kitty stared from one to the other, one of Leander's wry comments coming back to her: *I'm afraid it was too easy to get them in. I hope this isn't going to recoil back on us.*

The cousin said, "There are allies all over this kingdom. We have been slowly finding that out as they come to trust us. That young one whose father aids the regional governor, she didn't tell us until recently, but there's a much older webwork in this land."

"Collet?" Kitty whispered.

Keriam nodded, smiling faintly. "What we don't have are the civilian contacts in the central regions. I suspect that young girl knows them."

Kitty said, "But I don't know if I can—"

"You don't have to do anything," Keriam said quickly. "Just tell Senrid to find out who they are. He has to contact them all, one at a time. Show himself. The people are ready to rise and march on Choreid Dhelerei and demand the Regent revert to King Indevan's Law, and if Senrid has chosen to uphold those, the factions may all unite behind him. But he has to stand forth and say so, and then confront the Regent."

"Without touching off civil war," the cousin said. "No one wants Marlovens fighting Marlovens."

Kitty nodded, questions winging through her mind. But she banished them. The urgency she sensed in all the adults made her anxious to leave.

"Do you have all that?" Keriam asked.

"I think so."

Keriam looked up at the woman, who closed her eyes and muttered.

Kitty felt that weird hum of intense magic, and she hunched, bracing for some terrible spell. But when the woman was done, she sat silently, eyes closed, breathing slowly.

Keriam said, "She has temporarily broken Tdanerend's mirror ward, but it must be reformed again right away if he is not to find us out. Can you get yourself back to where you came from?"

Kitty fumbled with shaking fingers at her sash, removed the paper, pictured Hibern's room, and said the spell as fast as she could.

Transfer!

When she appeared in the familiar, warm room, she cried out in sheer relief, and grabbed hold of the edge of Hibern's wardrobe to steady herself.

When her vision cleared, she saw them both staring at her, Hibern relieved, Senrid sitting up in bed, still wearing that nightgown, unlaced in front, providing a disgusting view of skinny ribs. His mouth was pressed in a thin line and his eyes were dark, an expression she should have taken as warning, but as the magic-residue wore off and she remembered what had just happened, she remembered that her true goal had been met—she *did* know all the news!

"You tried transfer magic?" Hibern asked.

"Yes, and there was some kind of nasty spell waiting, even though I was careful to transfer from in here—"

"You can only do magic within this room, fool," Senrid cut in, his sarcasm in no wise impaired by his honking voice. "Tdanerend got you?"

"Yes! But I was rescued by—" She paused, and crossed her arms, and grinned. "I forgot. But I'll remember the rest if a certain promise—"

"What happened?" he demanded.

Hibern's lips parted as she looked from Senrid to Kitty.

Kitty shrugged one shoulder, grinning smugly. "That's for me to know, and—"

Senrid was out of the bed like a bolt from a crossbow. Kitty gasped, then squawked a laugh when he tripped on the dragging hem of the nightgown and fell headlong.

But hardly had her laugh gotten past her lips when he rolled, a flash of white linen and pink embroidery, and sprang up, his hands out.

He gave her a shove. Klonk! Her head bumped against the stone wall. She whooped in a breath to scream at him, but then his fingers closed round her throat. "Tell me. Now."

Though he wasn't much taller than she, his hands were longer than hers, and far stronger. She tugged ineffectually at his wrists, then, after he thumped her against the wall a couple of times, she dug her nails into the tops of his hands as hard as she could.

He didn't even flinch. "Who. Was. There?"

Hibern stepped up, taller than both, her presence somehow calming. "Kyale, your personal quarrel can wait. There are not only Marloven lives in danger, but Leroran as well."

Marloven.

She stared at them, Marlovens both, and for a moment she saw from their point of view how arrogant it was to hold a whole country against her own comfort. But as always, guilt was followed by anger and blame.

She ignored Senrid, and said to Hibern, "If. I. Could. Talk—"

Senrid hadn't squeezed, he'd just held her there, but now he let go, a sudden movement that made her head klonk back against the wall once more. "Ow, you stupid dolt," she snarled, rubbing her scalp, even though it actually hadn't hurt.

"Kyale?" Hibern prompted.

Senrid returned to the bed, Hibern's nightgown trailing behind him, but then he turned around, still very angry.

"Our two spies were with this man with medals, who said his name was Keriam."

Senrid's anger vanished. "Keriam," he repeated, and he let out a shaky sigh, which turned into another of those long, terrible coughing fits. Then he wheezed, "Go on."

"I will when you stop your musical concert," Kitty said snidely.

Senrid snorted a weak laugh, too spent to reply. He waved a hand—blood-smeared on top from where she'd dug her nails in.

Kitty looked quickly away, and satisfied that she'd gotten in the last word, she told it all, omitting nothing. Neither of the other two spoke until she was done; Hibern silently dipped a cloth in the water pitcher and handed it to Senrid, who looked at it absently, then wiped the blood off his hands.

When Kitty finished her story Senrid reached for his clothes.

Hibern put a hand out. "You can't do anything today," she said. "The snow is coming fast. And you need rest."

"I can't rest while—"

"You have to," Hibern cut in. "While you can. Now, here's what you have to remember. You're the enemy in the eyes of many. You could go to Collet's but she would never tell you anything. Tomorrow Kyale and I will go visit her, and tell her the news, and I will convey your words to me, if you still stand behind them."

"I do." He grimaced. "Though I hardly know— Indevan's Law. That much, though, I'm sure of. My father overhauled the regs to make them fair."

Hibern flicked her palms up, then said, "I shall find out what's to be done. Meanwhile, you rest, because I expect this is going to be the last rest you'll get."

"You're right." Senrid rubbed his hands across his eyes and up through his hair. "Keriam! Leander had spies in the castle?" He grinned. "I never would have thought it of him."

"Pure self defense," Kitty said, nose in the air.

Senrid snorted—and coughed again. When he was done, he said, "Well, we couldn't get any in your place, not when you only have half-a-dozen people, and most of 'em are related."

"Hah," Kitty said, for once pleased with Leander's refusal to hire more servants.

Hibern asked, frowning slightly, "Keriam didn't say anything about Norsundrians?"

Kitty shook her head.

"That was my next question as well." Senrid prowled around the bed once or twice, one hand bunching the nightgown inelegantly at his side so the hem wouldn't drag, the other pounding lightly on whatever surface was in reach. "The next thing I need to know." His voice squeaked and honked. "Is Tdanerend going to give in to them?"

"Do you think he's that shortsighted?" Hibern asked.

"I don't know. What can they offer him?"

"What can they offer you?"

Senrid looked up at Hibern. "Nothing," he said, his scorn plain. "They're stupid if they think they could offer me *anything* that would get my allegiance."

Kitty sneered, "If Uncle had told you to join them a year ago—half a year ago—you would have fast enough."

Senrid retorted promptly, "A year ago, if Mother Mara Jinea had told you to, you would have trotted right along."

"Would not," she shot back, but without much conviction.

"Oh, right, and you never lie."

"Well you're the king of liars, and anyway that was different."

"How?"

"If you have to ask, you're too stupid to know," she stated, nose in the air.

Senrid groaned. "Why do I waste the time?"

"Why indeed?" Hibern asked, laughing. "Come on, Kyale. You're overdue for breakfast—it's way past lunch—and Senrid is overdue for more beauty sleep."

"Overdue by a hundred years," Kitty cracked.

Hibern touched her arm and they transferred upstairs.

Kitty opened her mouth to complain about Senrid and his arrogance and stupidity, but Hibern spoke first. "Do you prefer to be called Kyale, or Kitty? I've heard both." She sat down at one end of the couch.

"Kitty."

"And I like Fern much better than Hibern."

"Fern! Faline called you Fern, now I remember!" Kitty exclaimed. "It's pretty. Though I like Hibern too."

"I don't," Fern said. "It's boring—means 'Right Road' in old Iascan, of all the dull things. Your name, Kyale, is much more interesting."

"It is?" Kyale was delighted. "I know 'Marlonen' means 'Death Conqueror,' because my mother told me that."

"Well, actually it doesn't. 'Marlo' is more 'outcast', and 'nan' was more 'dead' than 'death' but go on."

"She never told me what Kyale meant, only that it was a name for a princess."

"It is. For centuries, and the boy version is Kyle, without the 'ah' sound in the middle. Ky-lee. *Ky-ah-lee* means, sort of, 'royal girl-tree', from way back when some of our ancestors were forest-dwellers, before they came to these plains. Same with your brother's name, which was modernized from Anderle, which means 'Green Tree'."

"Green Tree! Wow! Will I have fun with that, when I get home." Kyale sighed. "If I get home."

Hibern laughed. "Now, let me tell you more about Collet, then we will have supper."

"Collet!" Kitty exclaimed. "I love the idea of a girl being in charge of spies!"

Fern said, "Collet's mother is the real link in the white network."

A grown lady? Kitty felt a stab of disappointment. "How did that happen?"

"Well, she's a distant cousin of the former queen, and her sister, who was Tdanerend's wife."

Kitty nodded, remembering that someone had said that Tdanerend had probably killed both those women, or had them killed. Kitty wondered if he'd drowned them, like Leander's mother was drowned by Mara Jinea—slipped over the side of a pleasure boat while asleep, after drinking wine laced with a heroic dose of sleepweed.

Hibern spoke again. "Collet's mother found out about my secret life through her connections with some of my mage teachers. She was the one who encouraged Collet and me to visit, with the excuse of family connection. It was made easier for us to get together because Collet's father, as assistant to the Jarl, and Latvian both felt it worthwhile to cultivate the other's good will, so our families socialized frequently, until Stefan got too unstable for Latvian to risk visitors."

Kitty grimaced. She hadn't seen Stefan—and did not want to.

"But by then Collet and I had established our secret method of keeping contact."

"Spies," Kitty said wistfully, thinking: *Everyone has an interesting life but me.* Then a yawn took her by surprise.

Hibern gave a soft laugh. "I'm sorry! I've talked you near to fainting. Here, let's get you supper and then you can sleep. We'll have enough to do come morning, I fear."

SEVEN

The castle looked formidable when seen from the road, its towers snow-topped, and one of the two guards that Tdanerend had assigned to Latvian—as mages weren't permitted to have personal guards—patrolled along the top of the battlements below all the turrets and towers.

Kyale didn't like the dazzle around her vision that indicated they were hidden by illusion, but she was grateful for it. They walked along the road, which was already rutted from wagons and horses, so their footsteps made no impression.

The magic wore off not long after they vanished through the trees that grew in a thick line near Hibern's tower. Now they walked quickly, their breath clouding. The air was stunningly cold, the sky overhead almost as white as the ground around them.

Kitty would not have enjoyed the walk anyway, for the shortcut meant stepping into snow that was calf-deep in some places, but the way Hibern kept frowning and looking upward made her particularly uneasy. Kitty glanced fearfully upward, but all she saw were low gray clouds coming out of the west, where before there'd been cool, weak sunshine. As they walked all the shadows vanished, leaving the world bleak and ice-blue.

They did not speak for a time; Fern had said that cold carries voices, something Kitty didn't want to test the truth of. She wanted to get to Collet, where there would be warmth.

After a long, silent walk, Fern said softly, "This is so strange. From my tower I usually can see weather coming, but I did not see this storm."

The clouds were now overhead. White drifted down, at first prettily stippling the evergreens around them, but swiftly thickening. Almost blinded, Kitty pressed close to Fern, her head bent, her cloak pulled up around her ears.

"Old shepherd's shack," Fern said, and veered. "We're not far."

Unquestioning, Kitty followed.

An eternity of slogging seemed to follow, during which Kitty kept her gaze on her feet. One, the other, one, the other. Would they go on forever like this? Then she stepped onto rough wooden planking, and the cold weight of snow abruptly lifted: they were inside a rough cabin. Warmth drew them instinctively toward a fireplace in which a leaping fire roared.

"This hut was abandoned years ago," Fern exclaimed. "Is there someone else—"

She stopped. Both girls had gone straight to the fire, their hands out, but when they turned, they saw the man seated on a rough-hewn bench in the shadows at the other side of the room.

Kitty felt a wail constrict her throat when a figure rose from the chair and advanced at a deliberate and leisurely pace, the firelight striking ruddy glints in the hazel eyes and brown hair of the man she and Senrid had encountered on the border road.

He stepped between the girls and the door.

Hibern untied her cloak and laid it down before the fire as if she and Kitty were alone in the room, but Kitty saw a vein beating in her temple.

Kitty was too scared to take her cloak off. She hunched closer to the fire, as if that would protect her, ignoring the sharp scent of singed wool that arose.

"I was hoping," the man said, as if continuing a conversation, "that you would emerge from your citadel, Hibern Deheldegarthe."

Fern's face flushed bright red. "I've never touched a sword in my life," she said—and then turned even redder.

"Guardian of the world, ready to take on everyone's battles but your own," the man continued.

Kitty had no idea what he was talking about, but she felt the sting in that smiling voice.

"Will you engage with us?" he asked, when Hibern stayed silent. "Or will you run?"

Fern's black eyes narrowed, the first time Kitty had seen her angry. "You are a disgrace and a mockery," she said. "I won't treat with you, so either begin your battle, or be gone."

Her voice was thin; Kitty wavered between admiration and dismay at her temerity. Even though, so far, the man had done nothing whatsoever that was even remotely threatening, Kitty felt danger as intensely as she had when Tdanerend had ordered her dragged off and shot.

"You are not yet worth my time," the man retorted, without any hint of anger at all.

And he vanished.

"Ugh," Fern exclaimed, and flopped down onto the dirty hearth. "Oh!"

Outside, the storm rumbled and the wind shrieked. Kitty crouched down, her knees watery with relief.

"What? I don't understand," Kitty said tentatively.

"That horrible name. He'll probably spread it all around, and—"

"What?"

Fern looked up, her mouth long with rueful humor. "Deheldegarthe. Means, oh, 'Battle Daughter,' but it was used in our history for heroines of stature, and before that, fighting queens." Her eyes turned toward the fire. Kitty saw twin flames reflect in them. "Hibern Deheldegarthe! I'll probably never hear the last of that. Fight my own battles! Phew! I put the no-growth spell on poor Stefan, so he won't age while I try to learn enough magic to give him sanity again... But use magic against my father? I won't... I wish..." Fern began, then stopped as she studied the leaping flames.

Her frown gradually smoothed out.

Kitty turned her own face toward the fire, enjoying the warmth. The flames wove upward in bright patterns that she could almost descry, almost, if she watched a little harder, a little longer...

Her thoughts seemed to dissolve in the bright flickering oranges and golds and yellows, a pleasant sort of dissolution that reminded her—reminded her—

A mental image appeared among the flames, gray eyes flecked with green, a steady, unblinking gaze that—

"Augh!" she yelled, ripping her focus away from that fire.

Fear burned through her, chased by the icy relief of a near escape. "Uhn!" She picked up Fern's cloak and flung it over the girl's head, then looked about wildly for something with which to put that fire out.

Fern let out a muffled exclamation, and clawed the garment away from her face. She stared at Kitty, her eyes wide, her hair ruffled. "What—oh, Kitty!" She gave a shuddering sigh. "That was a near one. *Thank* you."

Kitty said shakily, "What is it, a spell on that fire?" She had her back to it now. "I almost got caught, too, but it felt like the other day, when he did that with his eyes."

Hibern whirled her cloak about her shoulders. "Storm or not, we had better go." She stalked out onto the smooth, snowy ground.

But the storm had already abated considerably, as suddenly as it had come. That probably had been magic too, Kitty realized, and shuddered. The subtlety and effectiveness of such magic was nastier than all of Tdanerend's screaming and threats.

Hibern walked fast, her head low, her mouth compressed tightly. Kitty could feel her anger; Fern was only aware of her own fear, and how she tried to hide it from Kyale, who could do nothing to help.

֎CЯℰᏢ

The girls made rapid progress the rest of the way through the wooded parkland to the nearby estate where Collet's family lived in a long, rambling building that was not a castle. Again Fern used illusion to cloak herself and Kitty as they passed through an open gate in a high wall along which armed warriors in green and yellow livery patrolled.

The two girls avoided the main entrance, moving around through ordered gardens to the back, where Hibern knocked on a secluded glass door.

Almost at once a weedy, lively-faced fair-haired girl of about fourteen opened it, her welcoming grin broad. "Fern," she said softly. "And Princess Kyale! Welcome! We have waited all these weeks to thank you in person for rescuing Ndand."

Kitty looked blank, for she'd almost forgotten Ndand's existence—having only seen her for a very brief moment. Then she smiled. "Well, you know it was actually the Mearsieans who did that."

"King Leander, and the Mearsieans," Collet said, hands wide. "We know. You must convey our thanks personally to King Leander. For the rescue is proof that allying with you Lerorans was ever a good idea. Is she happy?"

"The Mearsieans sent a message to Leander. The horrible magic spells Tdanerend put on her are gone," Kitty reported, remembering what Leander had told her a few days after their arrival back from the water world. At the time Kitty had not been the least interested in Ndand, but at least she remembered what he'd said. "She is perfectly happy, doing something with music, according to the Mearsieans."

"We hope she can return home some day," Collet said. "We couldn't figure a way to get her free from her father's terrible spells, and you will always have our gratitude. Now, what brings you?"

"I've got Senrid Montredaun-An in my room," Fern said, and Collet's eyes rounded. "And here's what has happened..."

She told everything—except the encounters with the Norsundrian Detlev. Kitty half-listened to the familiar story, instead watching Collet's reactions.

It surprised her that anyone would ever think about Ndand. Were families really so loyal? Kitty wished she had some relatives, someone besides a stepbrother who was so busy all the time, and whom she really didn't understand. She remembered CJ and Faline talking together, laughing, even, on the water world, and sighed. If only she had a sister, or even a girl cousin!

"... it's possible, but I would have to talk to my mother first," Collet said, recalling Kitty's attention. "This is way too important for me to decide. Stay here until I come back. I'll send Micai in." She grinned as she dashed out.

And soon a six-year-old boy raced in, bringing a set of toy boats that he simply had to show Hibern. He chattered happily, and Kitty found herself sitting on the floor with Micai, putting some carved wooden warriors through an adventure. The toys were spread all about them, and Kitty's wild vocal variations for the imaginary characters made the boy laugh with delight. After a time Kitty was vaguely aware of the door opening, and a woman's hand beckoning to Fern, but since they didn't seem to need her, she turned her attention back to the story-game.

Collet slid in and crouched down, watching. Kitty adored having an audience; at first she felt a pang of discontent when Collet joined in, but her ideas were so much fun the three of them were soon engrossed, battling heroes against Norsundrians all round the room.

Kitty was disappointed when Fern returned and whispered, "We'd better go." When she looked up, the strain in Fern's eyes made the game vanish from her attention like her breath in the cold winter air.

Fern didn't talk on the long walk back.

Nothing terrible happened, though Fern kept watching, and listening, and even sniffing, her strides long, so long poor small Kitty had to trot to keep up. Not that she complained. Kitty felt so apprehensive that they couldn't get back fast enough, and the sight of Latvian's castle came as an intense relief.

From the shelter of the evergreens once again Fern cast illusion around them, and they walked in just long enough to get well within Latvian's wards. Then Hibern transferred them upstairs to her room.

Senrid woke up on their entrance. His cold was definitely in the soggy stage; he had a besorcelled handkerchief right beside him. But the fever was gone.

"Your nose is as red as a cherry," Kitty pointed out.

"What a surprise." Senrid looked up expectantly. "Hibern? Did you talk to your contact?"

"It will take a couple of days for everyone to meet and decide," Fern said. "I suspect those are days you need as well."

"And while you're thinking," Kitty put in, feeling that Senrid was having far too easy a time. "You can consider that business that we talked about—"

"Shut up," he said, and off he went into a coughing fit.

It sounded worse than ever, but Kitty's disgust turned to surprise when Fern stepped up and smacked him a couple times on the back.

Senrid looked surprised as well, then relieved. "Why did that work?"

"I don't know. I wish we could get a healer up here, but we can't risk it. All I know is, when coughs get soggy—and I've caught a few—that smack kills the tickle."

Senrid waved a hand in a circle, and blew his nose.

"Yeccch," Kitty said. "That is so disgusting—"

Fern touched her arm, and did the sign, and they both appeared in the upper room.

"No fair picking on invalids," Hibern said, smiling.

"If you knew what he's managed to do to *my* life," Kitty grumped. "Oh well. I think I'll read some more records. Which ones have girls having adventures? Preferably girls who are princesses?"

ഇരൻടഃ

Senrid woke up and found himself in darkness. He snapped up a zaplight, and in its weak blue glow lit a waiting candle. He saw the evening tray on the floor. The steeped leaf was no longer steaming, but he didn't care. He got up, relieved that he no longer felt as heavy as a horse.

Another day, and he'd be well enough to move.

He touched his waiting clothes on the chair, and then decided why not? A trip through the frame, and then he got dressed. He felt immeasurably better to be in his own clothes again, with his knives in place. He passed the nightgown through and hung it neatly on its hook, then prowled the circumference of the room, wondering if it would be considered a breach of hospitality to pull down one of Hibern's books to read. Their truce was friendly on the surface, but it remained that, a truce.

He thought of going up to the invisible room, remembered Kyale there, and decided his own company was much preferable.

But then the whoosh of displaced air made him step to the bed, and Hibern appeared.

"Ah, I hoped you'd be awake," she said, the candle flame long and golden in her black eyes. "Kitty is asleep. There is much we need to talk about."

She dropped into her wingchair, and he sat on the bed, wrinkling his nose at the whiff of stale sick-sweat that met his nose. He made a mental note to pull the bed apart and put the sheets and quilt through the frame before he slept next.

"What I said was true, but I didn't go into why, because these are Marloven concerns," she said, surprising him. "Kitty has no interest in the details anyway. So. I spoke with a key person—not Collet—who is going to contact some other key people. Their structure is a lot like the military hierarchies, with a person in charge of each region, to whom others report. What I was told was this. If the first person is willing to see you, then Kitty will be provided with that name. And likewise the second, and so on, each contact providing her with the name of the next. They will contact one another ahead of you. And then you will meet them, and answer their questions."

Senrid sighed. "I don't want her along."

"It sounds as if you already made that choice."

"What do you know about it?"

"Only what I've guessed: that Kitty won't go home until you provide her with something she wants."

Senrid blew his nose, then said, "It doesn't take much thinking to put together your contact. I already know that the regional assistant's wife is kin to your family, and also to my mother. I would guess she's the main link, through her daughter."

Hibern said, "And what do you think will happen if you try to force her knowledge from her?"

Senrid said impatiently, "I'm not forcing anything from anyone. I've known Collet's name since I investigated this place last summer, but I kept that to myself. I didn't really care about Faline, a foreigner, when I first heard about her, but I figured offering my uncle Faline would distract him from going after Marloven civilians—" He stopped, and shrugged. "Well, do you know what they were intending to do with this secret organization?"

"Oh, yes," Hibern said. "Though I just found it out. They were all waiting on the future, in default of a better plan. They expected you and me to marry, as Latvian and Tdanerend had pledged. And they were going to back me in a power play, when the time came. First against Tdanerend, and then...who knows?"

Senrid whistled soundlessly. "Power play? I take it that means, after they got rid of Tdanerend they'd help you get rid of me?"

Hibern opened her hand. "Not my plan, I repeat. Believe me, my pose of insanity was always to avoid marriage. I don't want to be married to any king."

Senrid felt anger and appreciation seesaw inside him, and humor tipped the balance into appreciation. "Typical Marloven plotting, eh?"

She turned both palms up. "Here's where it gets nasty. You had better know this: Faline Sherwood is an Yxubarec." She paused expectantly.

Senrid was about to exclaim "A what?" The words were shaped on his lips, but then he remembered reading about them.

He remembered what they could do.

And from there, it was a fast leap to Tdanerend's true intent: not just to get Latvian to develop loyalty spells on a convenient foreigner, but to wrench Faline's will to their command—after which she'd be ordered to take Senrid's shape, and then his place.

He drew a late breath, though for a long moment everything hurt: his heart, his ribs, even breathing.

Hibern had been watching, her mouth a line. "Yes," she said. "That, by the way, is the real reason my father and your uncle had their falling out. My father has his problems, most of which stem from him not quite seeing anyone but himself as real. The world is a potential magical experiment to him. But even he thought that going too far, and it woke him up to some of the worst things he's done in the name of experiments and learning. All at the Regent's behest."

Senrid whooshed out his breath. "Thank you for telling me."

"It was decided you ought to know. Though Faline, poor thing, hates people finding out her true nature. Now, to the next piece of bad news." She sat back, her expression wry. "That Detlev confronted Kitty and me today, and he made a verbal jab at me about those very plans. At the time I thought he meant I was supposed to be plotting against my father, but now I know what he really meant."

And she repeated the conversation, plus what had nearly happened.

Senrid heard her out, and grimaced. "This looks bad, though I believe the fellow has to be an idiot, or none of us would be here, right? I mean, why not just act?"

"All I know is that I take his implied threats very seriously," Hibern said, her voice betraying her tension. She looked up at her own walls, as if spies lurked behind the stones. Senrid knew that sensation, that there was no actual privacy— that even one's thoughts could be betrayed. "He knew about their plans. He knew my plans! I've never told anyone in this entire country. I really thought that if I was careful here, what I did when I visited distant mages would be perfectly safe, that I was anonymous. So maybe the reason why we're here is just what he said: he doesn't think we're worth his time. Yet."

Senrid mentally dismissed the Norsundrian's threat as so much hot air. Far more important to him were the problems right here at home. He said, "I've been debating whether I might use magic, after that Detlev so conveniently removed Tdanerend's wards off me."

"I wouldn't," she advised. "Not until you can get rid of whatever *he* might have warded you with." She sighed. "Well. I'm going away, soon's I get Collet's answer, to consult—" She hesitated, then said, in an even voice, "Tsauderei of Sarendan, and Erai-Yanya of Roth Drael."

Senrid said sardonically, "What do you think I'm going to do to them? I don't even know who they are."

"The ones who trained me, though there are others. There has to be a reason why Detlev of Norsunder, who can command armies whenever he wants them, found it worthwhile to sit around in an abandoned woodcutter's shack waiting for me today."

Back to him again? With an inward shrug Senrid said, "Testing? Like me the other day."

"For what? Why here? Why us? Is it because elsewhere in the world the dyra are on the move again, and world events might be drawing us in?"

"No one is drawing me anywhere," he said promptly, then frowned. "The what are on the move?"

She shook her head. "Never mind. As you say, you've enough to do here." She got to her feet.

The interview was over. The truce seemed to be intact.

He said, "Is there something I can read?"

She gave him a strange smile. "Feel free to read anything in this room." She hesitated, then got up, her fingers poised to make the sign that would take her up to the hidden chamber. "I started out learning black magic until I performed my first transfer, and found myself on the border of Sartor, and in danger of walking into the time-binding that held them for over a century. I soon learned that even the mage with the best intentions can't stay neutral, and continue with black magic."

Senrid had survived thus far by outthinking ambitious adults around him. And as for Norsunder, he believed most of the stories about them were only scare-stories. After all, if they were half as omniscient and all-powerful as the whispers had 'em, why weren't they more successful?

"Watch me," he said.

PART FIVE

ONE

Kitty enjoyed being in charge of the spies' names for two days.

She'd pledged to Hibern, before she and Senrid left, that she would not attempt again to force him into a trade of her promise for information.

It was an easy agreement to make. She had already privately resolved on the same thing, which meant that she felt obligated to remind him how annoying he was, otherwise she was Giving In. She'd also bolstered herself against any threats he might make against her by finding and hiding in her bodice what she thought of as her secret weapon, though she hadn't mentioned it to Hibern, because, well, just because, it was only borrowed, *not* stolen. Hibern was too friendly to Senrid—didn't seem to understand how rotten he was, so a princess has to look out for herself, doesn't she?

That was Kitty's reasoning, but her emotions veered between guilt and satisfaction that she had a secret weapon as they said their farewells to Hibern and she transferred them down to the snow outside the tower. They got away with the aid of Hibern's illusion spells, and found two waiting mounts where they'd been told they would. Collet's family had arranged for the horses, one of them with a training saddle. This was like saddle-pads used anywhere else, but with a strong canvas piece stitched in for a beginner to grab hold of.

Kitty mumbled in disgust to herself as she fumbled her way onto the mount, but after her long trip from Tannantaun to Crestel, she'd discovered that she could actually manage to stay on one of those dreadful creatures. If she had to do it again, it would be nice to have something to hang onto besides the animal's hair.

"All right," Senrid said, "where to?"

Kitty eyed him. He had a red nose, and the nasty cough, but otherwise he looked pretty much as usual—especially with his skinny frame covered in the overlong black cloak that he'd brought from Crestel. Time for a try that wouldn't be a trade-threat, it *wouldn't*.

"Wish you were well?"

"Yes." He looked impatient.

"Want to get rid of Tdanerend?"

"Yes."

"Wish I was dead and gone?"

A quick, reluctant grin. "Yes."

"Will-you-take-it-back?"

Senrid sighed. "Where. To."

"Are you asking or demanding?"

Senrid's horse plunged. It didn't throw him, and he didn't seem to mind the movement. When the animal was quiet again, except for the strange head-tossings, he said with that narrow-eyed stare she loathed so passionately, "I didn't ask you to be here. It was your choice to come along."

"If *you* hadn't ruined things at home—"

Senrid turned away, his whole body expressive of intense anger. He didn't speak—but he was coughing again, coughing hard, gasping for air, and Kitty got scared, and maneuvered her own horse to edge closer so she could lean over and sock him, hard, on the back.

Senrid whooped, coughed, and he held his breath. They both held their breath.

When it seemed to be over, he leaned an arm on the horse's neck, damp strands of loose hair hanging down on his sweat-beaded forehead. Kitty felt all her anger turn into apprehension. She cast a nervous glance around, but saw only white fields stretching away to the evergreen-dotted hillsides, blue with subtle shadows under the light gray sky.

Finally Senrid looked up, pale except for the red in his cheeks. "Where to?"

"Berdua."

"Long ride. " He wheezed.

She wanted to ask, *Will you make it?* but didn't want to seem to care.

"Let's go," he said.

ಬಂCR⅄ꝏ

He proved that he could make it. By the end of the first day, she was wondering if *she* would make it. As well the weather then turned bad, or (she was convinced) they would have ridden all night.

Their guise was as regional governor's messengers, and as such they had changes of fresh horses waiting at designated posting-houses. Kitty never did figure out the system. She didn't care. What concerned her was the cold, and her sore legs, and staying on during the long gallops.

They slept in a kind of military inn called a 'posting house', only for messengers and the like, not for warriors. It was scary enough, but Kitty didn't talk to anyone, and the other kids—boys and girls both, housed in a big, long attic dorm over the stable—didn't talk to her. They all retired early to bed, and everyone was up before dawn. Senrid before anyone of them, she noted sourly, struggling to wakefulness as the other kids bustled cheerfully about her.

Nobody talked about revolutions, or executions, or anything else like that. Mostly it was about horses. Horses, and food, and snow.

She got her stiff, aching legs to move, and resigned herself to another long, dull day.

While her spirits flagged, Senrid's soared.

It was good to be out in the wind again, riding fast. Walking would have worn him down, but he could ride forever. He was free, he was going to meet his people face to face for the first time, without his uncle's spies watching and ordering his behavior for his own good. Anticipation lent him strength.

He knew now that Keriam, the one officer he had always respected, was on his side, so much that he was now risking his own life on Senrid's behalf. Others might back him against the

Regent—motivated by a hope that they would eventually control the little boy-king—but Senrid knew Keriam too well. Had come to regard him as the most honest man in the kingdom. Keriam had trained him, had talked history with him, but had never suggested he take the throne. Nor had he given any hint of secret organizations. Or covert support.

The fact that this message reached him now meant that Keriam had decided, somehow, that Senrid had become worthy to take his father's place.

Somehow. What did it? Senrid thought as the horses crested a hill, and trotted past a long train of fodder-carrying wagons.

Senrid longed to talk to him, ask questions he'd never dared speak aloud hitherto.

He also longed to keep Keriam from Tdanerend's fangs, but knew that the man would stay there in the place of most danger, in order to monitor all that was happening.

ಬಂ(ೞ೬ಿ)ಡ

The end of the second day's riding brought them to Berdua— another walled town, all built of peachy gold stone and granite, with its ubiquitous guards. The stone was familiar enough, and the slight tilt to the roofs on hills, but in Vasande Leror walls had long since been knocked down in favor of gardens or vegetable plots, saving only their royal castle, and Leander planned to fix that as soon as he could justify the expense. These towns all looked war-like, and Kitty felt scared all over again, but Senrid got them past as messengers. Apparently kids, boys especially, were a common enough sight, riding back and forth across the country bearing communications from this citadel to that. It was good practice for those who wanted to attempt to get into the academy, whose admittance test selected for riding skills above all. War training was what you learned after you got there.

Inside the town, they threaded their way slowly along busy streets, for neither of them knew their way about, and a messenger ought to know. It was Kitty who dismounted and asked directions at an inn, which brought them finally to the home of a prosperous trader in honey and beeswax candles.

They rode round to the stable nearby that catered to businesses along that street, then walked back to the shop. Kitty marched in, sniffing in pleasure. The shop smelled wonderful. As he walked in close behind her, Senrid looked quickly about for a half-expected ambush.

No one was in sight. A girl their own age emerged from a back room. "May I help you?"

Kitty said, "Collet sent me."

The girl's gaze shifted immediately to Senrid, who stood under her silent, acute scrutiny. She then surveyed the only other people in the room, a pair of teenage prentices arguing in a far corner about which candles burned slower, and whispered, "This way."

They were soon established in a small upper room, into which half a dozen adults crowded.

Senrid's heart drummed against his ribs, which were sore from the coughing, but he met every assessing gaze with his own. This was the first time, ever, that he'd gotten to meet ordinary unknown Marlovens without his uncle or his spies. Before he'd been thrown off-world he'd been surrounded by Tdanerend's guards and toadies, and outside them, ringing the royal citadel in a vast perimeter, the rest of the guard, keeping a gulf between the rulers and those who were ruled.

No one spoke; they seemed to be waiting. A small boy appeared, bearing a tray from which wafted the aroma of fresh coffee, and a sigh escaped Senrid. The boy blushingly offered him a fine porcelain cup, which he accepted. The rest of the cups were passed to the other adults. Kyale, he was relieved to see, did not grimace or comment, though he had already heard plenty about how disgusting she found coffee. She had good enough manners when she wanted to bother.

Then the doorway darkened and an old woman came in, her face seamed and weather-beaten, her gray hair pulled high on the back of her head in the old-fashioned horsetail style. Like the light cavalry had worn a couple generations before, and apparently long, long before that.

She sat down before Senrid, in the front, the best seat, and the others arranged around her, ceding her the right.

"You've a look of your father," she said.

Senrid opened his hands.

"The plan is?" Her back was straight, her gaze unreadable.

"The plan is to march on Choreid Dhelerei. If no better date is set, at the first of the month. A circle around the capital, all people rising, too many for Tdanerend to order shot down. It's not my plan, but I agreed to it."

"What would you have done?"

"Go straight to the capital, find Keriam. Win him. The academy. Beyond that I hadn't planned, not until I knew who was with me and who not."

"Mph."

He felt sweat prickling his armpits. "I already have Gherdred's word that he won't oppose me, but he will not attack Marloven citizens, on anyone's orders. I don't want a civil war."

"So why do you want the throne?" she asked, her expression difficult to interpret.

"If Tdanerend had been a great king, I'd—" He stopped, gulped. Could he say it? Would it be true? But he'd grown up realizing that his uncle wasn't a good ruler, a conviction that had warped his own life into its present path. There had never been any question in his mind of not getting rid of Tdanerend and then ruling himself. He remembered Leander during the summer, the diffuse green gaze as he considered dropping all claims to power and going blithely off to travel. Senrid had thought him a liar, until he realized that Leander didn't lie.

He dismissed memory, and refocused his eyes on the old woman, who had not stopped watching him. "If my uncle had been a great ruler, then no one would listen to me," he said, and paused to blow his nose. No one moved, or spoke, or made any sign. The sound was ridiculously loud, and Senrid felt that inner flutter that presaged laughter. He tried to see what they saw, and decided with grim humor that he had to be about the worst looking excuse for a king in history—short, scrawny, with a red nose and voice that sounded after too short a time like the quack of a duck. "If he had been great, none of us would be **here** now."

The woman grunted. "You have the look of Indevan, **but** you have the quick tongue of Kendred."

Fast looks, a shifted shoe, whispers. Senrid felt surprise at the mention of his exiled uncle, the shadowy, mysterious Kendred who had made a last, spectacular ride cross-country just ahead of the old king's assassins. That had been when Senrid's own father was too small to remember, so of course he'd left no writings about his older brother. The old king had destroyed whatever existed; Senrid knew his name, and about that last ride, but little else.

So he said, experimentally, "Is that bad?"

And won a laugh. A single noise, almost like a bark. "He was quick-witted. Like you."

This told him nothing.

"And after?" she asked. "What then?"

They were all watching. It seemed none of them breathed. Mostly light-colored eyes under fair hair, people of all ages and degrees—except military. Though Senrid had his doubts about that old woman. He wished that he could see her hands, except she had them hidden in the wide sleeves of her dark blue woolen robe.

"And then," he said, "back to my father's laws."

Keep it simple, he'd decided back in Hibern's tower. They wanted Indevan's Law, and so did he. How to implement it, he as yet had not idea, but he was sure that the less he showed his ignorance about the actual work of governing, the better he'd sound.

She leaned forward. "So you would reinstate Indevan's Law? Over whom?"

Senrid closed his eyes. So wasn't going to escape after all! How had Indevan worded it in the one personal record Tdanerend hadn't found and destroyed? He had read it so many times, but was only recently beginning to understand a bit of it. "Over us all. *The only way to justice is for the continuity to be in the law, not in who holds power.* My father said that. Means the law holds for all, ruler on down."

Quick whispers. The woman made a slight sign, no more than a raise of her chin, and the watchers fell silent.

She grunted. "Some like things fine the way they are. What about them?"

He'd expected questions, but not this interrogation. He was tired, and the single sip of coffee after that long ride made him light-headed. He was tempted to say, as his grandfather would have said, *Then up against the wall with them*, but he didn't. "I don't know." It was out before he could consider.

"Then they'll tear you apart like a wolf pack with a rabbit."

Senrid's eyes itched. He wanted to rub them, but kept his hands motionless. *Don't show weakness.*

"I've been kept out of too much of current affairs to speak with any conviction," he said slowly. "By the time I realized I would have to take what I wanted, events got away from me."

Shifts, exchanged glances.

The old woman grunted again. "Looked bad enough, from a distance. Like you ran. And others maintain you will say anything if you think someone wants to hear it. But." She gestured, a flash of robe sleeve. "Commander Keriam says that such use of wits was your only weapon. To him you told the truth. Then, what you did over the mountain, that showed some promise. Something's missing, we know that much, but then we've known for some time now we weren't going to hear everything. Not from the Regent." She didn't wait for him to answer, instead saying, "So what do you do with those who resist going back to Indevan's Law?"

"Find out why. If I can. Some are going to compromise, some will leave. Some," he hesitated, thought of the worst of Tdanerend's toadies, and papers he'd been forced to sign. The ones who'd been given permission to slap him, beat him, humiliate him in front of others—all for his own good—who had enthusiastically carried out the Regent's interrogations, assassinations, tortures. Anger flared through him, and he said, "Some are walking dead."

And she gave a grunt of approval, sitting back, and putting her hands on her knees. A flash of old, seamed palms, with callus marks, the kind you got after years of work with sword and bow and spear. "There are indeed some who deserve the wall."

Murmurs—names. He caught a few. Two he knew, and loathed. A few he didn't.

"And supposing," she said, her voice lifting. Behind her there was instant silence. "Supposing you get us back to Indevan's Law. And then?"

"And then we go on."

"To?"

He opened his mouth to say it was a waste of time groping so far into the future, but then he remembered her hands, and realized what she meant. If he straightened out the army, then what would he do with them?

An army doesn't sit still. You keep it busy, or it will find ways to keep you busy, all his ancestors had agreed on that. Highly trained warriors, all clamoring for glory, for rank, have to make war.

The old woman said in a low voice, "I was with your grandfather, academy scrub to captain. We all would have fought and died at his side. Then. When he took the throne, we thought for a time that the Golden Age was back. For a time." Her lined mouth thinned. "He discovered too late you rein 'em or ride 'em. He rode. And couldn't stop."

Senrid thought of the wars his grandfather had initiated.

"Indevan's Law. Then?" she prompted.

And it all fell into place—Hibern's concerns, Tdanerend's mysterious rages. Detlev's sardonic smile.

The essence of strategy is to use what you can't control.

"And then we make ready for the big war," he said. "Norsunder is on the move."

It hit them all, he saw it. Only the old woman didn't stir or speak, but her eyes had gone so narrow they were almost shut, except he saw a tiny pinpoint of golden gleam under her eyelids, reflection from the candles up behind Senrid. Around her murmurs, glances, made it clear that the word *Norsunder* had been whispered, maybe not overtly, but in private.

"So you won't ally us with them," the old woman said.

"No."

"The *old* king said we Marlovens were born to ride under the Banner of the Damned," the woman said.

The *old* king. The tone of voice, the emphasis on *old*, made it clear whom she meant: his many-greats grandfather, the terrible warrior-mage who'd built an empire with his First Lancers, who had vanished straight into Norsunder with that entire force riding behind him, his personal banner at the head of a ghost force that had galloped—dark and bloody—through Marloven legends ever since. No one ever spoke his name aloud, lest he hear and come a-riding for more recruits; nobody used the old fox banner, ancient as it was.

They all knew he could come charging out of Norsunder, at the head of the First Lancers, again.

Senrid said cheerily, "Well, I wasn't." And sneezed.

It was inadvertent, but the anticlimax seemed to release them all from the grip of memory, or of the inexorable grip of the past.

They were all talking now, and the old woman leaned forward and struck his knee with her fist. "You'll do. You live through this, and bring it off, and we'll back you."

Instinct prompted him then. "And you. Will you come to Choreid Dhelerei?"

She cracked a laugh. "I'm too old to meddle with kings any more. But we shall see, boy, we shall see."

The others were talking now, earnest conversations on all sides. The interrogation was over.

He blurted, "Kendred. What was he like?"

She had been about to rise, and sat back again, considering. "He wanted power. Had courage. Your father had courage, accepted power. Tdanerend wants power, has no courage."

Senrid shook his head. "I don't see—"

The old woman turned her head, made a spitting motion, then said deliberately, "Kendred was a horse-turd."

There was no time to react. She moved out, her long robe swaying behind her. A nod here, and whispered word there, and she was gone.

Senrid sat back, his breath trickling out. His shirt was clammy with sweat, and his gut growled with hunger. He held onto the cold coffee cup with both hands, lest his fingers tremble. He hadn't even gotten to drink it.

But then the girl reappeared, and said, "There's food downstairs, if you've a mind."

Senrid got up and followed gratefully.

So did Kitty, who yawned and yawned again. Finally!

She had very quickly gotten bored with the political talk—the soft, urgent undervoices mentioning names and places she'd never heard of. She'd hoped to hear plenty of reviling against Tdanerend, and maybe some nasty plans for him, but was disappointed. Instead, that ugly old woman had yakked on and on at Senrid as if they would be stupid enough to believe what a liar would blab at them.

Well, they were Marlovens, and they deserved whatever happened to them.

She yawned again, hoping the dinner wouldn't be disgusting. The next town, she knew, was going to be another long ride away.

TWO

Before they left, a man drew Kitty aside and gave her not only the name, but instructions on how to find the next spy in the river town Chardaus.

She obediently committed them to memory, telling Senrid as soon as they were outside Berdua's walls.

It annoyed her considerably that except for the spy-name business, the Marlovens had exhibited no interest whatever in Princess Kyale Marlonen. She'd thought they would wonder at her presence, would treat her like, like what? Like a royal visitor? Like she was some kind of ambassador? Like she was *interesting*, at least? She had given up on anyone in this barbaric country treating her like a princess ought to be treated.

Now she was stuck riding through a miserable winter on an errand that had nothing to do with her, and danger could threaten any moment. But she couldn't leave and go home.

She pestered Senrid once or twice about the promise, but only because it annoyed him. She didn't expect him to give in, not any more, and anyway, would she go home if he did?

As they raced side-by-side westward toward Chardaus, she thought about what Arel's cousin had said. What was his name again? Oh, who cared. The important thing was Leander's message about giving Senrid whatever aid he could.

She hadn't really thought about that until she'd seen Hibern's reaction, when she told them about that interview. Hibern's expression had surprised Kitty. The message had obviously meant more than it seemed to, and whatever extra meaning it carried, Hibern had approved.

Leander was good at making his words say more than they seemed to. The rotten thing was, sometimes a person didn't figure out the extra meaning until later—when she couldn't really get mad at him about it.

When Kitty considered Hibern's reaction, she wondered if Leander had somehow guessed what had happened, and was sending Kitty herself a kind of message. Like he approved of what she'd done, and he wasn't angry about the magic, or that she'd left.

Or was that her imagination?

She stewed about it as they rode. What she wanted was to be able to tell Leander everything, and to have him tell her she'd done the right thing, and to hear him condemn Senrid for being a selfish idiot—though it was true that without Senrid's help, they'd probably both be dead. But why couldn't Senrid have rescued them all, without all the sneaking and the secrecy?

Kitty smiled sourly between her horse's hairy ears as they raced across the boring, white-covered plains south of Choreid Dhelerei. If *she* could have rescued everyone and looked like a hero, she wouldn't have thought twice about it.

Well, maybe she'd at least get a mention in Marloven records, if Senrid managed to pull them safely through this current mess.

As long as it never got any more dangerous, she decided finally, she didn't really mind being the person in charge of the names.

☙⟡❧

As the weeks slipped by, they rode from Chardaus to Zheirban, and then up toward the region called Eveneth (where they were to meet at a farmhouse), and then on to yet another town. It seemed miraculous that they were never chased.

Oh, they saw plenty of warriors galloping this way and that along the roads, and sometimes cross-country. But Senrid looked like another skinny light-haired kid, of which there were plenty. Nobody stopped them, or if they did, the messenger badge invariably got them the nod to pass on their way. Race on, rather.

Kitty noted sourly that nobody in Marloven Hess ever seemed to walk anywhere, or take carriages, like civilized people. They all rode, and what's more, they rode fast. Though she had no interest whatsoever in horses, she couldn't help but learn a bit about them—such as the fact that the ones everyone raved about all came from the Nelkereth plains, which were beyond Vasande Leror's own eastern border. Nobody lived there. People didn't settle there because of some old treaty. The Marlovens were the ones who'd had it forced on them, and they in turn enforced it lest their neighbors get grabby. In Vasande Leror Nelkereth horses, or cross-breeds, were common enough, but no one trained them like these Marlovens did, or rode with those minimal saddles, more like pads, and the merest halter just to hold reins, rather than heavy bridles and bits that were common other places. The horses here seemed almost different creatures.

And the Marlovens did not use the Nelkereth horses for work, only for riding. Other kinds did other jobs. The smell of horse was everywhere, horse and wool, for tunics and cloaks. Droppings were wanded in the cities, and along the roads, like at home, but here it was the military that seemed responsible. At home there was a guild.

Riding seemed a part of life in Marloven Hess, like rising at dawn, and scarcely ever stopping to eat. No wonder Senrid got sick, the way he'd stay up late yakking and babbling away to these idiots he'd never met, and would probably never see again, but oh no, would he ever sleep in? Huh! It was as if Tdanerend appeared with the cold winter sun each day, and they had to rise before it and gallop on.

At least, she thought when midway through the third week they started out right at dawn in order to get ahead of an approaching storm, she'd gotten used to riding.

಄ CŖŞ ಐ

While she brooded on these subjects, Senrid brooded on the same ones, but from his perspective.

He watched the gray clouds advancing from the west and wondered if the series of storms that had blasted through were a result of his spell earlier in the month, or if winter would have been harsh anyway.

He wouldn't let the weather slow him. He couldn't let it.

He sensed the spreading net of information going out, settling its protection over him; the patrols either ignored him, or if they had to stop, the questions were suspiciously few. But the new, uncertain alliance between the white-magic faction and a goodly portion of the kingdom's civilian population wasn't going to be able to protect him forever.

He knew Tdanerend had to be sitting on the throne in Choreid Dhelerei demanding daily reports, and ordering ridings out to investigate every reported sighting, faked sightings that his growing net of allies helpfully sent in.

And indeed, every day, from every corner of the kingdom, reports were relayed in of short, blond boys spotted riding about. Some days, up to fifteen separate sightings. Those reports with enough detail to investigate proved to be true enough, there *were* short blond boys riding about—but none of them were Senrid. Tdanerend, enraged and anxious, could fault no one for lack of cooperation: angry as he was, there was no way around the fact that the description of Senrid apparently fit seven out of ten boys in the kingdom.

What Senrid didn't know—and wished he could find out—was how much the military were cooperating, at least obliquely, by dutifully chasing down shadows and not pursuing those who cast them.

As he rode, he considered each conversation he'd had, wincing over his own lapses, and pondering what others said— and what they didn't say.

He still didn't know who that tough old woman was who'd faced him in Berdua, and he was desperate to get home and plunge into research. *Home.* Choreid Dhelerei would either be his home, or he'd be dead. He could never walk away and leave it behind, the way Leander had talked of leaving his land.

Instead, as his hands numbed on the reins of his new mount, and he fought against the intermittent cough, he thought about home. He'd probably keep his bedroom. Why not? But for a study, it made so much more sense to choose a room nearby, and what better room than that one downstairs, with its row of four tall windows looking westward across the academy and the plains beyond? That would be a work room, his own. No more the pretentious cavern down in the government wing, with its vaulted ceilings and frigid air and lack of natural light. It made reading old magic books needlessly difficult (glowglobes being 'weakness'); maybe that was another reason Tdanerend was a rotten mage.

The prospect of the pending march did not worry Senrid. All the signs were there, it would happen. The people, whatever their motivations—and he was learning a lot about that—were going to rise on the turn of the month, and converge on Choreid Dhelerei. And the light cavalry wouldn't ride them down. He suspected if they refused direct orders, the foot would also refuse.

What came after obsessed him because he couldn't really plan for it. He did not know what Tdanerend would do.

He did not know what he himself would do.

And he did not know if that souleater from Norsunder was lurking around—*We will continue our discourse when I choose*—or what he would do.

Senrid hadn't performed any magic, not even the smallest zaplight or illusion, but he took scant comfort from the idea that that man couldn't trace him through magic. Ordinary mages couldn't trace him. Despite his bluster to Hibern, he sensed that this Detlev was an order of magnitude different, and who knew what he could or couldn't do—or why. Again, he longed desperately to be at home, researching this new threat. Despite the verbal engagements with the people he'd been meeting, being away from home, from magic and research and messengers, made him feel blinded.

∞Cₔᴈᵒᴄᴈ

"But you appear to have promised a houseful of trades-people that you would provide for a civilian judiciary."

The man smiled, his voice urbane and not at all accusatory, but Senrid gritted his teeth.

"I didn't promise."

"Your words as reported have implied it," was the prompt, gentle answer.

The prosperous-looking farmers and traders crowded into the tavern's upper room stayed silent, impossible to read. The spokesman—so many of them had not offered names, and Senrid had not asked—continued to peel an apple, the little gold knife steady in his fingers.

Senrid looked down at his own hands. It had been easy to say that he'd consider what sounded so reasonable, but on further consideration he knew that such a promise would anger the Jarls. They sat in judgment over civilian as well as regional military matters, except in capital cases. He knew that. It was one of the few concrete facts he had been able to learn about governmental process, if only by accident, when Tdanerend had presided over a jurisdiction question several years before, and he'd made Senrid sit on the great throne and corroborate his judgment.   But some civilians maintained that the Jarls knew only military matters, not those of land or trade, and therefore they ought to be heard and judged by peers.

What other words of his had been misreported? That his conversations were being spread from mouth to ear he'd seen the evidence of already—questions following on answers he'd given previously. Fast as he and Kitty had been, word, it appeared, traveled faster.

"I didn't promise," he repeated. "I said it sounded reasonable. Obviously it's a question to raise at Convocation. See how the Jarls feel."

"They will dislike it immensely," the man answered. In his fingers the long peel curled, like a red ribbon, down from the fruit. "Surely you must comprehend."

From elsewhere in the tavern wafted the smells of food. Under the smell of stale ale in this room, Senrid whiffed fresh bread and some kind of peppery fish sauce. His insides gnawed, reminding him that he hadn't eaten since early morning, and that had been a few hasty bites, interrupted by...

He couldn't remember. Couldn't think past the noise from the common room below: the clinks of cutlery and dishes, and occasional shouts of laughter from local people who either didn't know what was going on, or didn't care.

Senrid realized his attention had splintered, and he refocused. The man who'd been observing him looked amused.

He finished peeling the apple, then said, "No one... appreciates, let us say, their powers summarily being curtailed." Dark eyes lifted from the knife to Senrid's own gaze.

The instructive tone was polite enough, but Senrid knew an insult when he heard it. For a king he was a sure, easy target—a short kid who had no weapons, no strength, and no personal guard to ensure his prestige. For a red-glaring moment he wished he did have a full complement of armed guards at his back, and he felt a jab of understanding, for the first time, of Tdanerend's tendency to use violence to beat down dissent.

I can't, he thought. *Even if I ever get the throne back if I send minions to muzzle beasts like this one, then I show that the minions are where the real power lies. And so people will court the minions. I have to be smarter, and quicker, than the beasts, until I get stronger.*

What to answer? There was no answer, not yet. "I'll remember your words," he said evenly. "And you." And hoped his tone was as ambiguous as he meant it to be.

Humor narrowed the man's eyes for about a heartbeat, and then he bit into his apple, stood and left, his finely made but anonymous wool robe swinging. Regional governor? Assistant? Local landowner? Senrid did not know who he was—and forced himself not to ask.

That interview was over, but others lingered to assault Senrid with questions, most of which required only that he say, "I'll look into that," or, "Yes, I agree." Last to be listened to were grievances against Tdanerend—all of them justified—and a few complaints about other guilds, or the army, or the local Jarl, and then he was alone with Kitty, who yawned fiercely as she sauntered in from an adjacent room.

"That man in the black robe was a fathead," she said, scowling over her shoulder. "He treated you like a little boy. If he'd treated *me* like a little—"

Senrid cut in tiredly, "Where to?"

"Nowhere," Kitty stated, crossing her arms. "No, I've given up on asking for that stupid promise back, because I know you're too selfish and rock-headed to care what happens to other people, but I *do* care about being hungry and tired, and if you drop down sick again from not eating enough, then I'll be alone in this nasty, rotten stinkpot of a kingdom. So I will tell you *after* we go somewhere. To eat. And rest."

From habit Senrid ignored all the bluster and took the point. He remembered from the map that the posting house for regional runners was a fairly short ride away.

"All right. We'll eat. Then ride."

Kitty put her nose in the air and marched out before him, because she couldn't hide her expression of relief that she'd gotten half her demand.

They remounted their tired horses, who showed a brief revival of energy after unseen hands had tended them and fed them while the kids were in the tavern.

The snowdrifts were very high, and progress was slow. It was nearly sunset when they reached the posting house. Senrid was surprised to see from the brown, churned snow that this particular spot—otherwise fairly isolated—had seen plenty of traffic that day. Recent, from the crisp edges of the hoof prints.

Instantly wary, he watched for signs of betrayal as they rode to the stable doors and dismounted. No assault team was stationed round the court, though: the stable was full of horses.

The only person they saw was a tall girl who came out to collect their mounts. Senrid flashed the badge, got a puzzled look and then a quick nod and grin, and inside they trod, tired, cold, and hungry, Senrid relaxing by degrees when the only sounds they heard were the high chatter of kid voices. No rumble of adults.

Heat, the smells of food and the sense of too many people in a close building thickened the air. They entered the long, plain mess that was common to all the posting houses—

and a whisper riffled through the huge gathering of kids, and then silence. An expectant silence, a tense one.

All the faces turned their way. In the back, Senrid saw their stablehand. She grinned and waved.

So the word had caught up with the kid population, huh? At least, the kids who lived and worked on the perimeter of the military, not quite civilian, not quite with the prestige of the real warriors or academy boys: the runners, wanders, stable-hands, yearling-trainers, and the like. Senrid considered the waiting faces. This confrontation was inevitable—he should have foreseen it. He wished it could have happened after food and rest, and not before.

Kitty repressed a groan. Were they *ever* going to be able to eat? It looked like Senrid was in for yet another meeting, this time with kids. Kitty looked them over, saw a mixture of liveries and civilian dress. She'd never seen so many Marloven kids in one place before. Except for Fern and Collet, the ones she'd met so far had either ignored her or been too shy to talk.

A girl at one of the front tables said, "Are you in truth the king?"

Kitty glanced from the girl to Senrid, who really did look pretty much like most of the other kids there, except he wasn't wearing anyone's livery. He still had on the old tunic of Leander's, shirt, trousers, riding boots, and the cloak he'd been wearing all along, like she wore the same gown and her sturdiest winter mocs. He had no sword, and folds of his handkerchief stuck out of one of his pockets.

Senrid said, "Yes."

The girl exchanged looks with two or three other girls, then said, "Will there be changes, if you depose the Regent?"

Senrid said, "If you mean academy trials, yes. No more boy-bar. Merit only. If I can get the Jarls to agree." He flashed that nasty smile. "And I intend to. Even if might take a couple of years."

Buzzing round the room. Most of the girls were pleased, but not all the boys. Stupid twit Jarls, Kitty thought narrowly— not that she would ever want to go to their stupid academy and learn how to be a disgusting Marloven villain. But these girls ought to get their chance if they wanted it.

Senrid watched the mixed reaction, and breathed slowly. He sensed what was coming next.

A boy stood up in the back. "Regent said you avoided academy-trial. You were too weak."

"Wrong," Senrid said. "He kept me away."

More looks. Kids were direct. After days of adults' oblique insults, and disbelief, and testing, and skepticism, it was almost a relief to deal with the blunt black-and-white judgment of peers.

"So let's see what you can do," another boy called—one who didn't stand up.

"All right," Senrid said, and blew his nose so it wouldn't run in the middle of the fight they were all here to witness.

If it was a sword challenge, then he was going to have to talk fast, because otherwise he'd be completely humiliated. He didn't have a sword, but a few here did. If only—

A tall, strong-looking kid was surreptitiously nudged and urged by fierce whisperings. He got to his feet, and walked, in silence, between the long tables. He wore Waldevan stable livery. And no sword.

Senrid slid off his cloak, slung it over a chair, but it slipped to the floor. Heard an hoarse whisper, "He's a runt!"

Senrid felt the ready energy that anger always provides, and he smiled up at the volunteer. "What's your choice?"

The kid looked awkward. "You choose."

Senrid said, "I'd as soon no one gets gutted, so—" He flicked out his knives. Whispers, then silence. He set them on an empty chair in a corner. Next the tunic, which he folded and laid over the back of the chair. Standing there in his shirt and trousers, he said, "Hands." And held his out.

The tall boy had a dagger in his riding boot. He pulled it free, and tossed it on top of Senrid's two, then carefully folded his livery tunic and laid it over Senrid's.

Senrid was peripherally aware of Kyale picking up his cloak and moving back. The two boys circled one another, Senrid assessing the way Keriam had trained him. By the time the kid made his first move, he knew he had won; Keriam's training was first-rate, it was what the best of the academy boys

got, and this boy was mostly untrained, obviously used to
relying on size and strength alone.

Senrid also sensed that thumping the kid right off would
be a humiliation that would make him an enemy. He was going
to have to win it—somehow—with finesse.

Kitty watched, feeling vaguely sick. Of course she didn't
care what happened to Senrid—*after* she got safely home. Until
then, she'd as soon not see him killed by some idiot much bigger
and heavier.

But how to stop this creepy fight? Not one of the kids
watching showed the least sign of interfering. Kitty slid her
sweaty fingers over her bodice, where she kept her secret
weapon. Not that it was the least use here. But it made her feel
stronger; she backed up quickly as the boys circled near.

Then the big one reached, took hold of Senrid's arm—
and before Kitty could pull in enough breath to yell a warning
the boys turned into a blur of arms and legs. Wham! They hit
the wooden floor, grunting and rolling, and then—to her
surprise—Senrid ended up on top.

But only for a moment. One of his coughing fits hit him,
hard, and he rolled backward. His head hit the floor with a thok!

Half-a-dozen kids started up *then*, when the fight was
over. A lot of good that would do, or were they all hiding the
fact that they were cowards? Not one of them even tried to stop
that fight, she thought in disgust.

It was Senrid's antagonist who extended a hand and
pulled Senrid up. He bent down and whispered something to
Senrid, who grinned and shrugged. Then they both laughed—
and Senrid coughed one last time, blew his nose, and sneezed, as
they both tucked in their shirts and pulled their tunics back on.

Kitty scanned the watching faces, saw approval, smiles,
and furtive, uncertain glances, so she stated in her best princess
manner, "Can we *finally* get something to eat?"

They all looked at her—and laughed!

Senrid felt the release of tension, and laughed as well,
but in relief. The crowd parted, and Kitty marched, nose in the
air, toward the cooks' table to get her plate and load it. Senrid
moved more slowly, hedged about with kids, all talking at once.

That's what Kyale should have been, he thought hazily. He was very near the last of his energy, but he knew there'd be no more tests that day. Kitty had a rare sense of timing—a player's sense of timing. Certainly unconscious. She lived her life playing roles, without even knowing it.

She should have been a play actor, he thought. Then he shook his head and dismissed the matter from his mind as questions and comments rained around him.

THREE

The first of the month dawned clear, cold, and frosty, snow glistening with a whiteness hard on the eyes.

Senrid and Kitty were already up when the sun rose. Kitty kept her complaints to herself, thinking: *This is the end. Soon I can go home.* She was tired from so many late nights and early mornings, and from so many missed meals. But she didn't complain about that either, because she had always gone off to sleep hearing the sound of Senrid's voice as he talked, talked, talked, and when she woke up, it was inevitably to find him long since dressed and busy either talking some more, or inspecting horses, or some other idiot thing. The only time he seemed to notice meals was when she insisted on them, and so she began insisting more than once a day.

But now—she hoped—this mess would soon be over.

She wrapped her cloak more tightly about her, resolving when she got home to put it, and her gown, in the fire first thing. She was thoroughly sick of them both, and wanted no reminders of her miserable stay in Marloven Hess.

At least she was alive.

But that might change.

Fear fluttered inside her as she peeked into the narrow hallway and saw Senrid talking to a tall man whose bearing reminded her of the warriors, though he was dressed like a farmer. Kitty paused, looking at the man's profile: was he familiar? Then she shrugged. Most of these Marlovens were light-haired, with that short haricut that made them all look alike.

Kitty stopped in the doorway of the inn where they'd spent the night, and watched people riding and walking by. Walking! Crunch, crunch, their steps cracked the ice from the night's snowfall-and-freeze; soon the road was mushy and slushy brown.

Still the people kept going, more of them than she'd have thought. They all seemed to be going southwards, toward Choreid Dhelerei.

Absolutely amazing.

She heard Senrid's fast step. For a moment he stood next to her, his breath clouding as he looked out at the crowds. Though people surrounded them, for that moment they were alone. No one waiting to talk to Senrid, or to whisper a message to Kitty. Though it had long since been unneeded, the spies had stuck to the plan, and Kitty had been the one to name each new destination.

Senrid said, "This is it. You want to go home? I'll risk a transfer if you want to risk where you might end up transferred to."

Kitty thought of Tdanerend and his creepy mirror ward, and then she thought of being home and not knowing what would happen.

She shook her head.

"I'm going to a military camp," Senrid said.

Kitty's mind reeled. Warriors! Didn't Tdanerend command them? How could Senrid dare go among them?

"If they turn out to be rotters, will you use your magic then?" she asked.

Senrid gave her one of those obnoxious grins. "So you want to see the end?"

"I've seen everything else," she said. "And endured everything else." She rubbed her backside. *And besides...* No, better not to even hint about what she'd done, she thought, surreptitiously touching her bodice. She wasn't so sure it was right—but a person had to protect herself, hadn't she?

Senrid laughed—not at all a mean laugh. It made him cough, but the cough was no longer the terrible one of the month before, and he looked like his old self. "I didn't think you'd stick it out."

She frowned, trying to find the insult, then realized that it was a sort of compliment—the only one she was ever likely to get. She folded her arms and snorted.

"I didn't think *you'd* make it," she countered. *"Or* me! But here we are, and I do want to see Tdanerend's sour face when you give him the boot."

Senrid grinned. "Then let's go." He jumped down the steps two at a time, and headed for the stable, his steps quick despite the ice.

Kitty scrambled to keep up. Soon they were on horses yet again, really good horses. Of late, when they did manage to sleep, Senrid had gotten the best rooms offered, not just a rolled mattress in a corner. And those rare meals were all served on fine porcelain—better than that at home—with silver spoons and knives. They'd gotten the best horses. People's attitudes had changed, though Kitty couldn't precisely pin down when it had changed—or why.

Thinking happily in anticipation of the next meal, she guided her mount behind his, and they rode not into the streets to join the marchers, but along a back route that was nearly empty of trades-people.

Soon they passed the town walls, riding fast adjacent to the great stream of people heading for the capital. Fresh white snow stretched out like a quilt over the land, bright and glittery. The ice was too thin to make them slip; the horses' hooves crunched as they cantered westward.

As always, Senrid seemed to know exactly where he was going. Kitty was glad to follow.

Senrid, meanwhile, searched constantly for landmarks. He'd never been able to tour the kingdom before. He'd mapped it several times, and that image of neatly drawn hills, forests, towns, villages, and rivers superimposed over his vision as they moved swiftly cross-country.

Three times they crossed roads of people all heading southwards. None of them spared the two kids a glance. Senrid contemplated how so much of the perceived power of kingship was in trappings. Had he been riding decked out in military dress-tunic (or in full war gear), with banner-bearing outriders, and a column of personal guards at his back, everyone would have known: *there rides a king.*

And he pictured them laughing at the undersized, baby-faced figure in the middle.

Self-mockery was his mood when at last they topped the rise above a feeder to the river Zheirban: the Rheid. They were now directly north of the capital, though as yet it could not be seen. A half bell's hard ride through the rolling hills, and he'd be there.

They were spotted long before they reached the camp. Senrid hadn't seen the scouting perimeter—as was right.

The camp was huge to Kitty's eyes, a city of bleached-canvas tents adjacent to what seemed to be endless horse picket-lines. The Marlovens stopped moving about when Kyale and Senrid rode in. Kitty shrank into her cloak, distrusting immediately the sight of so many Marloven warriors. Ugly memories of the invasion thundered through her head, and she wished she'd accepted Senrid's offer to go home.

But as they rode inside the tent-city she realized that this huge camp was not just for adults, there were kids all around too. Well, boys, at least. Lots and lots of them, from her own age to older than Leander, all dressed in gray, all of them busy with jobs. Some tended horses, others were oiling snapvine bowstrings, and many of them ran back and forth carrying messages.

They all stopped and stared. Then, as Senrid rode by, they did that salute thing she'd seen so much of lately, hand to heart. A very few of the older boys smiled, or made subtle signs, which Senrid returned.

They ignored Kitty. Fine. Better that than attack.

All in all she decided that she was glad she'd had the foresight to come prepared, and she hugged tightly to her the secret she'd kept hidden under her bodice.

But then they stopped right in the middle of the camp, before the central tent, and a plainly dressed warrior emerged. Kitty recognized his grayish dark hair as he laid hand to heart, a deliberate salute that made Senrid flush dull red.

Kitty stared in surprise as Senrid flung himself off his horse and ran forward, yelling, "Keriam!"

The man stepped back into the door of the tent, and Kitty almost missed his laugh, and the quiet voice—meant for only one person's ears—saying, "Well done, Curly."

"Curly?" Kitty repeated from the opening into the tent.

Senrid's head jerked round, and Kitty gave a yelp of sheer joy when she saw the embarrassment in his face.

Senrid groaned, *wishing* he'd hidden that reaction to the old nickname. Now he knew he'd be hearing it every time she opened her mouth.

Oh well. It did bring back good memories from the days when his father was alive.

Keriam had coffee waiting on a camp table, and a hot meal. Senrid ate ravenously; Kitty looked into the bowl, and was surprised to see the exact same sludgy soup that she'd been given as a prisoner in the tower back in Crestel what seemed a million years ago. Well, it made sense to cook this stuff for a lot of people who are under orders and so can't complain about the food, she decided as she dug in.

Keriam, meanwhile, leaned toward Senrid, eying him anxiously. "I'd heard that you were ill," Keriam said. "I see that it was no exaggeration."

Senrid flicked his hands outward. "Fine now." Joy rippled through him; only Kyale's presence kept him from babbling like a fool. "What happened?"

"Orders came down," Keriam said, "to find and kill you. And so the time for decision had come, obey or be foresworn, and we left."

Senrid felt the joy dissipate, and the grip of reality squeeze his insides. "Gherdred?"

"Out riding the perimeter round the city. The entire eastern wing. West is all down south at Darchelde Forest, under Jarl Waldevan's command."

"Darchelde! Why?" Senrid exclaimed.

"I don't know that."

"No one's set foot in it for centuries. Is it still blasted from magic? Is the old Montredaun-An castle even standing?"

"Can't answer any of it. All I can tell you is, that was their orders."

Senrid got up, feeling restless, realized the tent was too small to pace in, and he sat down again. "Something's going on."

Keriam nodded soberly. "Something big enough that he's sent half the foot down there as well."

"Then who's protecting him in Choreid Dhelerei?"

"His personal guard. They all know it's stay with him or die, after the excesses they've enjoyed over the last few years."

"Not all," Senrid said. "Not all of them."

Keriam looked grim. "They chose personal allegiance. The consequences are theirs."

Senrid said, "I have to talk to him. We can't have a bloodbath."

Keriam's face was difficult to read at any time, but Senrid thought he saw the approval he'd longed for his entire life. "Then we had better ride, hadn't we?"

Kitty groaned with artistic fervor. "Didn't we just get off those horses?"

If the Marlovens even heard her, it was more than she knew.

Keriam stepped to the front of his tent and said something-or-other to someone-or-other, and shortly thereafter she heard a horn blaring a fall of notes that sounded kind of stirring. When she peeked out, she saw everyone scrambling about in orderly haste, belting on weapons, pulling on helms, collapsing tents that were swiftly rolled and stashed in wagons. The boys fetched horses from those enormous picket lines at the other end of the camp as other boys wanded the ground where they'd been; Kitty saw the brief glitter and flash of magic as the droppings vanished.

Some of those boys she'd seen earlier surrounded Senrid, and they talked and laughed, Senrid looking like a little kid again, as he had last summer.

Then they all mounted and lined up in less time than it took for Kitty to get her cats found and fed, at home.

If anyone had asked her, she would have preferred to be with the kids. Even though they were only boys, and Marlovens at that, at least they were more or less her age. But nobody did ask, and instead there she was, riding next to Senrid, followed by

Keriam, who had all those medals on again, a gold and black hilted dagger at his waist, and a curve-tipped sword in a saddle sheath—those were the visible weapons—and behind him adults with banners and enough steel to arm the entire kingdom of Vasande Leror, Kitty thought sourly: men, women, and children. Two weapons apiece.

Senrid looked over once, his gaze distracted. Kitty said, "They don't have enough extra swords for you to get one too, Curly?"

He looked pained—but not angry-pained. It was the on-the-verge-of-laughter pained, which disappointed her. "Guess not," he said. Then he grinned. "Why, you want one?"

"Oh, of course," Kitty said, trowelling on the sarcasm. "Tdanerend will take one look at me and run flapping and squawking back to the chicken roost. And afterwards I'll give everyone lessons."

Senrid snorted, but it was an absent snort; his thoughts were already galloping ahead. As usual. She rolled her eyes and sighed.

And so they came at last to the city. The gates were barred, the walls suspiciously empty.

Keriam made some kind of motion to one of the young messengers riding near him, and the kid raised a trumpet and played one of those falls of triplets.

The riders halted then reformed into two long lines, the horses dancing and whuffing and shaking combed and clean manes. The low hills all around the city were dotted with folk, some lined up in neat columns, others not.

"Look there. Atop North Tower," Keriam said, and handed a spyglass over to Senrid.

"He's spotted you and me," Senrid said. "I can tell, just by the way he's standing. Phew," he added with a nervous laugh. "I'm glad I'm not there to hear what he's got to be saying!"

Senrid—nervous? Kitty decided it was time to take out her secret weapon. She slid her hand under the laced bodice, and pulled out one of Fern's magic books. Borrowed only—of course. Kitty would *never* steal. But Hibern had gone somewhere else, so it wasn't as if she would be using this book, and anyway Kitty really had felt a lot better about riding in the midst of Marloven Hess with some of Fern's magic with her—though it had turned out she couldn't read any of it.

But if Tdanerend saw her, he wouldn't know that.

She grinned, imagining Tdanerend watching her—in horror—as she flipped pages.

"Did Hibern give you that?" Senrid asked, as though nothing else was happening.

Kitty's cheeks burned. "I planned on taking it back. It was to keep me safe. Just in case. I thought it might fool your uncle into thinking we had a bunch of wards and spells on our side."

Senrid's mouth curled into that sarcastic look that made her want to kick him clean off his horse, but before she could say anything he turned back to scanning through the spyglass. Then he stiffened. "That has to be—" He smacked the spyglass closed. "He's got one of those damned Norsundrians up there! Kyale. You can go right ahead and fool him now."

And without asking, he grabbed her wrist and did the transport spell.

Kitty found herself moments later standing high above the city of Choreid Dhelerei, on the tallest tower of the royal castle. Her stomach lurched; a sharp, cold wind hit her face.

The wind made tears sting her eyes, and she blinked, still holding Fern's book up, as if she were about to read a spell, as Senrid talked in a fast, low undervoice to his uncle, telling him who was where and what they were ready to do.

The three were now alone, Kitty saw, but that was scant relief, for Tdanerend looked like a madman. His face was an ugly dark red, his eyes bloodshot with rage and probably with even worse lack of sleep than she and Senrid had experienced.

Senrid, too, was shocked at the haggardness of his uncle's face.

Tdanerend gave vent to vicious expletives, ending with, "You betrayed me, you—"

Senrid cut through the invective. "You betrayed yourself." He felt stirrings of pity, but was not going to show any. Not after coming this far, after what he'd heard, after what he'd endured. "Uncle, it's time for me to take my father's place." He indicated the people massed below. "They agree."

Senrid saw immediately that it was the wrong thing to say—but then to Tdanerend's perspective anything Senrid said, except for *I surrender*, would have been wrong. The amassed people below, the cavalry riding round the city walls—not at his command, but despite it, all were effective enough proof that he'd lost.

Thoughts streamed through Senrid's mind, cold and clear as the harsh winter wind: what it must have been like to be raised as the replacement, the threat, the brother whose value would only be measured by Indevan's disgrace. But Indevan had not made Kendred's mistakes, had not been disgraced, and one day he turned his back when the two were alone, a gesture maybe not of trust, but of release.

Of release. Senrid now saw why he couldn't kill Leander that day during summer, because it was too much like what had happened in his own family.

I would have become Tdanerend.

While he was thinking, time passed, though he was unaware. Tdanerend stared down into his face, saw the marks of recovery from illness in the fine bones emerging from Senrid's once round cheeks. The determination setting his jaw, the mouth and eyes that were so very much like Indevan's.

The boy had been alone after that confrontation in the Crestel castle—Tdanerend knew that. So how had he managed to raise all these people and send them against the rightful king? *I am the rightful king—I am! I have done the work for years—*

They are all traitors!

But you couldn't kill an entire kingdom—oh yes you could—

Tdanerend made a strangled noise of inarticulate rage, raised his hands and vanished, leaving Senrid alone with Leander's silly stepsister, there on the city wall.

FOUR

Kitty sat on the polished black-marble steps below the awe-inspiring Marloven throne, her chin on her hands, her eyes burning with exhaustion, and thought about how weird life was.

Nobody else was in that huge room. She was alone. Who would ever have thought she'd sit there, of all places, bored and tired and hungry?

But she needed to rest her feet before she went spelunking through any more of this endless nightmare of a castle, searching for Senrid.

Events had gone so quickly! She was trying to figure them out, from the time she'd turned to Senrid and said, "It's over! He's gone! You won!"

"No," he'd said back to her, absent, his spyglass already up at his eye. "No, it's not over, he's made a retreat. Listen! I've got to get downstairs before that mob smashes their way in and burns down the city looking for Uncle's toadies to hack apart." He'd frowned at her, then added, "Toadies who might come looking for me to hack apart. And you, if you're here. Time for you to go back. Tell Keriam to get his people on patrol, lock down the city, and to send the civs back home."

Before she could protest, he'd transferred her!

Suddenly there she was, standing in the snow in front of Keriam's horse, where she fell down because of that nasty transfer magic. But she gave the message, and someone else thought to lead her horse to her or she'd probably still be out there wandering around.

No, she thought, laughing to herself. It wasn't a message, it was Senrid's first command as king. And *she'd* been his...his herald?

Uhnnn. She rubbed her eyes, her mind filled with visions from that afternoon. The crashing of weapons against shields, the cheers echoing back and forth across frozen fields. And then they were all in motion—all of them except her. People swarmed around her as she rode slowly toward the city gates: warriors dashing this way and that, knots of people riding forward and veering, or riding away, or marching grimly along the churned-up road. They all seemed to know what to do, or at least where they were going—all except her.

She'd made her way through the gates, proceeding even more slowly as warriors galloped about, weapons drawn. The sun was setting; shadows made the streets more frightening than ever. A couple times she heard distant shouts, and the clang and crash of weapons, and her horse shied as Kitty tried to find another route. Three times she saw fresh bloodstains, twice in streets, and once right near the gate to the royal castle.

But she'd ridden in anyway. Where else had she to go?

Because the castle was huge, and no servants were about, she'd dismounted and let the horse go wherever it wanted to while she wandered grand hallways, all of which apparently led to this throne room.

And here she sat, for what seemed forever.

She sighed, feeling stiff and tired and sore. If only she could figure out where Senrid might be. She was afraid to go into the plainer halls lest she stumble onto that prison area, and they stick her in one of those millions of cells and forget about her. But she was so tired, and so hungry!

Just as she was thinking that a young man dashed in, his tunic splattered with mud. "Who are you? Where are the runners?" he asked hoarsely.

"I dunno," Kitty said, ignoring his first question. She'd resigned herself to the fact that nobody in this barbaric kingdom had the slightest interest in Princess Kyale Marlonen of Vasande Leror.

"Commanders Gherdred or Keriam?"

Kitty spread her hands. The man frowned and dashed out—but with a shadow. He knew his way about, and if he was looking for Keriam, he might find Senrid there as well. And if he did, so would she.

The man strode down torchlit side-halls for a surprisingly short distance, Kitty speeding behind. He paused before a carved wooden door with guards at either side.

"Ambred of the West Wing to see either Gherdred or Keriam," the man said to the guards, his voice echoing in the vaulted hallway.

The door was opened, light slanted out. Kitty ghosted up behind as the man dashed inside. The guard almost shut the door in her face, and then—an obvious afterthought—let her in.

Several older men stood in a semi-circle, all of them glittering with swords, and medals, and all the rank things. In their midst Senrid sat on the floor cross-legged, chin on his hands, elbows on knees, staring at a huge map he'd unrolled before him. Behind him, in a huge fireplace, a blaze gave off light and heat, and she realized that in addition to being hungry she was cold.

All turned when the messenger strode in, his heels loud in the quiet room.

He saluted, and said to one of the men, "Ambred, West Wing, ordered by Commander Waldeven to report directly to you: the Norsundrians are massing on the southern border."

Senrid said before anyone could speak, "Which end of the border? Darchelde? Or Methden?"

"Darchelde."

Senrid scrambled to his feet. "I've got to go."

Keriam said, "Senrid, if—"

Senrid said impatiently, "I'll wager anything he went to Darchelde to hide out. He's too angry to think. Yesterday he was ordering our own people to fight each other. If the Norsundrians are there, it means he's in contact when them. If they offer him a command he'd hand off his soul for the chance to march against us and win, and then we're all finished— including him. I've got to stop him from turning the entire western cavalry and foot over to Norsunder!"

Shock tightened faces, bodies, widened eyes.   And nobody gainsaid him.

He seemed to see Kitty for the first time. "You got that book of Fern's?"

She nodded.

"We might need it as a bluff."   Two hasty steps; he paused only to grab his tunic and cloak. Then he was right next to her, and again the nasty visceral smear of a transfer.

৵ি৪৪ৈ৩

The transfer brought them into thorough darkness.   Both of them smelled the sharp scents of decaying wood and old leaves on the frigid air.

Aware of Kyale's quick, frightened breathing next to him, Senrid squeezed her wrist warningly as he listened.

Nothing.

So he risked his first magic, and snapped up a fairly strong zaplight. Its blue glow revealed ugly, twisted trees and blasted growth of the magic-poisoned forest of Darchelde.

"This is bad," Senrid said in an undertone as he pulled on his tunic. Then he slung his cloak round him. "Worse than I thought. The old front gates were here—nothing left."

Kitty shuddered, grabbing hold of a warped, rough tree branch while she fought vertigo. "Where is this place?"

"Family's old lair," Senrid said grimly. "From before we took the throne back. At least there isn't much snow on the ground. Come on."

"Took the throne back," Kitty repeated. "I suppose your family didn't inherit it?"

Senrid said, "Ever since the days of the first empire every change has been bloody. My family was no exception."

"Yeccch." Kitty's exclamation was soft, but no less heartfelt.

"He'll be holed up in the castle, if there's anything left of it," Senrid said. "Ah. There it is."

The trees had grown right up to cracked, mossy walls. Kitty looked up, saw the uneven roofline etched against the clear night sky. "No guards?"

"What's left of his personal guard will be inside. Most of them are dead. They never even knew he left, and I couldn't stop—" He paused, shook his head. "Well, anyway, I'll bet he sent some of them ahead to make the place ready as a fallback, which means they're all inside plotting away. Come on, let's get in there before the Norsundrians do."

But he didn't lead the way toward the crumbled front gate. Kitty followed, stumbling over unseen tree roots and stones as they made their way slowly to one side. Senrid kept pausing and looking intently about, but he didn't make his light any brighter.

He knew the floor plan of the old place—he'd studied it out of curiosity when he'd read the records of the last Montredaun-Ans to live there, for it had been used as a kind of glorified prison for recalcitrant princes a few generations back. He'd wondered if he might some day be incarcerated there.

"Since you're the new king—I mean, you will be—are you going to change your name?" Kitty asked.

Senrid paused in his search and stared at her. "Why ever should I?"

"Because—" She thought about all the changes she'd seen in him, and then thought of the things that hadn't changed, and from there it was easy to think of all the things she didn't understand. "Because you're a fathead."

When in doubt, resort to insult. Those are safe enough.

Senrid snorted. "What are you hinting at, Pluquerta?"

That you really are a white but you don't know it, she thought, but she'd never, ever, never-never-never say it, because she knew he'd do something horrid not to spite her, but to convince himself.

"That I hope you're not next on Norsunder's list," she muttered. "What's a Pluquerta?"

"Old Language. Means a short, loud, wretch. I looked it up just for you!"

Kitty had to laugh in spite of the awful situation. Then she said, "Senrid, we've come this far. Why won't you take that promise back?"

"Because that's not what you were hinting at." He nudged her. "This way."

The doorway he'd sought was nearly overgrown with a particularly nasty prickle-bush of some sort. They squeezed past it, and into a dank-smelling hallway. The blue light showed mosses and fungi on what had once been surprisingly fine tiling.

"Will things be all right back in Choreid Dhelerei?" she asked.

"Yes. Keriam will keep the city locked down. The problem isn't there, it's here." He sighed softly. "At least I have Keriam. I feared all this past month he'd be killed—that Tdanerend would find him out, and he'd be the first against the wall. Because he was the only one I trusted, ever since my father died."

Kitty opened her mouth—and something weird with glowing eyes and sharp teeth exploded from the web-hung darkness and ratcheted past them.

Kitty began to shriek, but Senrid thumped her in the gut, and when her breath whooshed out, he clamped a dusty-smelling hand over her mouth.

"No sound."

She shook her head.

He lifted his hand away, and she whimpered, "I can't go any farther."

"So you'll go in that forest alone?"

"N-no..."

"It's not far. Where's that stubborn, obnoxious brat I relied on? I need you to bluff Tdanerend into thinking we've got—" Senrid faltered.

"What? What is it?" Kitty looked around fearfully.

His voice hardened. "Nothing."

He thought: *Erdrael*. And he saw it then, he was trapped between two sides. He wondered what Hibern had been told, when she dashed off to consult her powerful white mages. Did *she* know who had been watching him?

At least Norsunder was unequivocal about the cost of their aid. The white magic powers might not *say* they owned you if they helped, but he was sure that they'd also demand allegiance, couched in sweet-sounding words like *honor, duty, obligation*. The records were full of reports of their self-serving platitudes in the treaties they'd forced on his ancestors. Talk about hypocrisy!

Angrily he shoved past hanging webs and mossy, rotting hangings, and led the short way up a narrow curving stair to a gallery above a huge firelit room. He motioned Kitty down. They crawled forward on their hands and knees, peering through the carved stone railing.

What they saw was a massive fireplace—big enough to ride a horse into. It opened onto the mighty room, its floor slate. At the fireplace end was a long stone table, the legs carved in stylized angles and curves resembling great raptor feet. Senrid and Kyale both felt, on seeing the reddish outline of those claws and the carved stone feathers sweeping back to support the table, as if they'd been cast back in time.

It was only a momentary reaction, because they then saw the three men, all rendered small by the size of the room, and the table, and the long shadows stretching out from the fire to blend into the darkness beyond.

Tdanerend stood directly before the fire, talking, a dark silhouette except for his gesturing hands, their tendons fire-outlined. Another man leaned against the table, maps rolled under his arm. The third stood before both, his aspect attentive, hand on his sword hilt. Kyale frowned, trying to hear the voices, but all she could make out were the sibilants.

Senrid nudged her. "We're too late," he breathed.

Kitty heard the slow, deliberate ring of heels on stone, and from the shadows emerged a man whose form was shrouded in a sweeping black cloak; firelight emphasized the hard bones of his face. It was Detlev.

Tdanerend and his two liegemen fell silent.

Detlev's voice carried clearly. "Tdanerend Montredaun-An, your lack of resolution has nearly lost you a kingdom. You do want to reign, do you not?"

"Reign," Senrid repeated, barely audible. "Not rule. Does he hear that?"

"Of course I want my kingdom." Tdanerend's voice was loud and harsh, much louder than the Norsundrian's, but it didn't carry the undertone of command. It was defensive, angry—impotent.

"Then join us. Of your own free will. The benefits of the alliance will have you back on your throne by tomorrow."

"How do I know you'll leave me here as king? That's what I want, what I always wanted. I don't want anything else, and I've heard what happens to those you take."

"You will stay. We need someone of ours here, especially now. But as for your kingship, there is the little matter of your nephew."

"He can be dealt with tomorrow."

"Why wait when it can be done much more successfully tonight?"

The Norsundrian turned his head and looked up at the balcony; both kids could see in the fire's glow the amusement narrowing the light hazel eyes.

Kitty felt her throat constrict. Senrid lifted a fist and pounded it lightly on the stone. "Damn, damn, damn." Then he breathed into her ear, "It's a trap. Stay here."

He stood up, swung his legs over the stone railing, and jumped. Kitty, her cheek pressed against the stone floor of the balcony, heard his heels hit the stone, and then his characteristic quick walk.

"Uncle Tdanerend, don't be a fool. We can settle our own problems without his kind. We don't need outsiders, who have their own objectives." His voice sharpened with dislike, but Kitty heard how high his voice was, how boyish.

Senrid heard it as well, wincing inwardly.

"I heard what you were going to do," Tdanerend snarled. "Put me on trial. Trial! I'd rather be shot. Was it revenge for not trying your little white-magic friends?"

"It's not revenge," Senrid exclaimed. "I wanted to tell you, but you wouldn't listen. It's Indevan's Law. People want it. My father was right, I know he was right—that a king can't be above the law, or we'll never get past bloodbaths. Never."

The Norsundrian said, "Do you find this boy entertaining, Tdanerend? I do. But weak, I'm afraid, very weak. Surely this isn't your influence?"

Tdanerend's frenzied gaze wrenched between Senrid and Detlev, his teeth showing in a rictus of fury, the fire's reflection leaping in his wide eyes.

"You can put me on trial," Senrid offered. "Jarls as judges—and the regional Commanders. The king has to obey the law too—"

"The only law," Detlev said, "is power."

Senrid's voice sharpened, high and trembling, "You're full of—"

The Norsundrian laughed.

Senrid shut his mouth, knowing that to give in to his own temper was to lose; Detlev glanced over his shoulder at the balcony and added, "Come on down, little girl! Haven't we met before? Join us. Entertain us as well."

Senrid sucked in his breath. So they really could read minds, these Norsundrians? He'd been so sure it was nothing but some kind of trick to make them seem omniscient.

Kitty yelled from the balcony, "I prefer the company up here. It's less stinky."

The Norsundrian made a casual gesture, and black magic snapped, making Senrid's hairs lift and his nose sting. Kitty stood before them, Fern's book clutched to her, her hair briefly lifting, as though lightning had struck nearby. She staggered, then began screaming insults, until the Norsundrian reached out with casual strength and slapped her across the face.

She wind-milled backward, smashing into the table and almost dropping her book.

Tdanerend never gave her a second glance.

The Norsundrian turned to Senrid. "Despite your weakness, you occasionally show a glimmer of potential. Yield now, and save yourself what will seem endless distress."

"Get lost."

"You're a coward?"

It took Senrid by surprise. He looked up, startled, and met the firelit gaze that seemed green now, green as spring and compelling as distant music once heard and barely remembered.

Images flitted through his mind: his mother, a barely perceived presence, her voice rising and falling in song, the words... The words... Wasn't there danger?

In horror Kitty saw Senrid's expression going blank and inward, and she knew what to do. Sucking in her breath, she shoved herself away from the table and smacked Senrid squarely from behind, with all her strength. They both tumbled onto the stone floor.

Senrid rolled free and up in a single move, his vision swimming dizzily; Kitty wrestled with her skirts, then scrambled to her feet.

They were too late.

Tdanerend had already been caught.

A trap within a trap. Despair made Senrid feel sick.

Detlev murmured to Tdanerend in a low voice, and although Senrid screamed, "Uncle!" he never moved, his gaze stayed transfixed.

From the shadows more gray-coated figures emerged, and flanked the two kids before Senrid could try knocking his uncle over to break the power of that gaze. Detlev stepped forward and traced a sign with his forefinger on Tdanerend's temple, and then turned those cold hazel eyes Senrid's way.

"Your uncle," he said, "had little to offer. He will serve, for a time, as a puppet on your throne while we are busy elsewhere."

Tdanerend did not react—he sat there, his focus distant, his face more relaxed than Senrid remembered having seen it in years. Had he any will left? *Probably not, and he'll never know it*, Senrid thought, his throat constricting.

Detlev smiled. "Your turn is next, and for you it will not be so easy."

He made a gesture, and the silent guards gripped their arms and marched the kids out of the hall into the dark winter night.

FIVE

Senrid and Kyale were held outside for a short time.

No one spoke. Senrid didn't dare try a transfer—not with those iron-grip mitts on him, because either the spell would destroy him or the Norsundrians would go right along.

Anger, regret, fear, even sorrow—unexpected and unwelcome—battled inside his mind, making it even harder to think against the exhaustion of the long day.

Kitty waited in numb terror, her cheek throbbing from where that terrible man had smacked her. Then she remembered something Faline had said, and scrubbed her hand over her cheek, flung the invisible villain-cooties down onto the snow, and stomped them as best she could despite the grip on one of her arms.

Senrid gave a soft laugh, his breath clouding. "That," he said, "you have to have gotten from the Mearsieans."

Before Kitty could answer Detlev emerged, a threatening silhouette in the weak blue starlight. He murmured some magic spells; Senrid felt a pang shoot through his temples, and knew that he'd been warded. Not clumsy wards, like Tdanerend's, but the real thing. Detlev seemed to feel no reaction to having performed strong magic. He immediately executed the transfer.

Emergence was followed by more terror: had they shifted to the temporal base that Norsunder had reputedly established south of Sartor?

No. The smells were too much like home. Senrid didn't recognize the hill they were on, nor the shadowy landscape below, but he knew instinctively that he was in Marloven Hess.

No one spoke. The two kids were marched a short distance. Senrid realized they were in the midst of a camp. He and Kyale were thrust inside an empty tent before Senrid could get a good look around.

Kitty turned on him. "Get us out!"

"I can't." Senrid sat on the ground, which was cold, but not wet. "He warded me."

Kitty fought against terrible fear, and anger, and hopelessness. "You *idiot*. You made me come along—"

"Shut up," Senrid said wearily. "If I'd known it was a trap I wouldn't have come either. I thought we could brandish Hibern's book under my uncle's nose, and lie about a network of white mages all ready to wipe us both out. Anything to get him to..."

"To what?" Kitty asked. "Were you really going to put him on trial?"

"Didn't you listen to anything this past two weeks?"

"No." She was unapologetic. "It was boring, and had nothing to do with me."

"It still doesn't," he shot back.

"I don't care. I want to know."

Senrid sighed. "If he'd agreed to it, yes. Trial. Indevan's Law. I'd abide by it too—we all would."

Kitty sighed. "Is that why that awful man, the one with the gold knife, was so nasty a week or two ago? He said something about the frailty of youth when he was walking away. I don't think he knew I was listening."

"Oh, he did, all right. Probably why he said it." Senrid pulled his knees up to his chin and wrapped his arms around his legs. Tiredness seemed to settle on his mind like a fog. "A lot of them think I'd obey the laws because I'm not strong enough to be the law, that I'm just a kid and don't know any better, and at first I wondered about it myself. But I don't think I'll change. I don't believe I'll change. What I do think—believe—is that if people—the common people, not the privileged—see everyone treated the same under the same law, then they'll come to expect it. The biggest fight will be against the regional commanders, the Jarls, the ones who ruled like petty kings and Tdanerend winked at their excesses as long as they paid him lip service. Well, and sent him muscle for his stupid war plans."

Kitty listened to the headlong words, hearing one in two and comprehending fewer than that. What she listened for, she didn't hear: what he'd planned to do about Tdanerend.

"So if Uncle Icky didn't agree to the trial?"

"I don't know. Sometimes, when I was angry, I envisioned having him shot. But other times I, well, felt pity." Senrid grimaced in the dark. "Hoped he'd just leave. After all, Kendred never came back. For all we know he's dead—either that or training horses somewhere, though I doubt that one."

"That Detlev monster probably got him a long time ago," Kitty said sourly. "So how was that a trap? I don't get it."

Senrid hesitated, thinking of ears listening. Why else had they been put together? Unless the Norsundrians simply didn't care what a couple of kids said to one another.

But if that was true, why had Detlev lured his uncle down to Darchelde except to get them both alone? Because Senrid was sure of it now, sure that Tdanerend had been slated for that spell ever since he'd first listened to the empty promises of the Norsundrians.

'We will continue this discourse...' I think the real trap was for me. Not for my brains and certainly not for my brawn, but because the army was no longer loyal to Tdanerend, they were divided—and then they shifted their loyalty to me.

He really was king, now. A king with a force poised not to become Norsundrians, but to fight them—unless he himself ordered them to change sides.

And this soul-rotted scum wanted him to make that decision with his own mind and will intact.

Anger and a desperate desire to win free made him restless, but the tent was too small to prowl round, so he forced himself to sit still. Besides, he was tired. And cold.

He said to Kitty, "Oh, it doesn't matter. How about we get some rest. Tomorrow will be grim enough without our facing it tired."

"No thanks to you," she huffed, settling down. "Curly!"

He laughed—or tried to, but he felt that sick flutter inside that could so easily turn into a wail of fear, and clenched his jaw.

Moments later he heard her breathing go deep. He tried to compose himself to sleep, but his mind kept racing from memory to memory, conversation to conversation, and back through time and experience to his reading.

He fell asleep trying to remember his father's voice. But all he heard was his uncle's.

ॐCRॐ

Dawn arrived, gray, bleak, and bitterly cold. Senrid's head ached, his gut tightened with fear—and with his determination not to show that fear.

The tent-flap was unceremoniously yanked open, and the kids pulled out. Kyale struggled. A mistake. Senrid saw her thrust ahead of him down the forest path, and the helmed and armed guard shoving her along seemed deliberately to choose rough shrubs and low branches. Just the type of pointless, petty cruelty you'd expect of Norsundrian low-rankers.

The big blades' torture would be more exquisite.

Poor Kyale was a disheveled, wet mess, her face crossed with red scratches, when they halted on a cliff.

Detlev awaited them, dressed in the unmarked gray of Norsunder, his long black cloak sweeping out over the cliff edge, flagged by the wind. Senrid looked from that observant hazel gaze, the slight smile, down to the two armies in the valley below, one camped, one already armed and in formation, and horror seized him. Why weren't the Marlovens ready? Magic had probably hidden the Norsundrians until the last moment.

But where had all the Norsundrians come from? Senrid could not believe the effort in magic and logistics. Was there some other reason for that force to be in the area?

"Senrid," Detlev said, breaking the desperate stream of his thoughts. "This is the lesson in real politics I had in mind. Observe. And learn."

Kitty's fear twisted into terror at the white-lipped sickness in Senrid's face as he stared down. She forced herself to look downward as well. The lines on the left were still and ready—the Marlovens on the right scrambled into place.

"What?" She nudged Senrid, realized he was trembling. "What?"

"We're at the border, and my army has been taken by surprise. They're going to defend the kingdom against the invaders." He stopped, this throat tightened. When he spoke again his voice was rough. "If I don't command them to change sides—to let the Norsundrians in—it'll be a slaughter." The last few words were high with anguish.

She looked down again. Once she would have been glad, fiercely so, to see Marlovens mowed down like barley at harvest time, but now her only emotion was dread.

As the group on the cliff watched in silence, the wet, cold winter wind fingering hair and clothing, below in the valley the front lines met, and the brownish white snow soon was dyed scarlet.

The Norsundrians advanced, killing all before them. There were too many, and they moved like they'd drilled for centuries.

Senrid turned his head into his shoulder, one hand gripping a barren tree branch. "I won't do it," he said between clenched teeth.

"Will not watch?" Detlev asked, sounding detached, amused. "Haven't the stomach for it after all?" His smile disappeared. "You have only to say the word, and I'll halt it."

Senrid gritted his teeth. "You lie."

"Do you not believe me?" Detlev continued. "I'm afraid it's your gamble, for I tell the truth when it suits me. Right now I have no interest in any of them below. It's you I want, which is why I arranged this demonstration of the effects of power. You seem to have lost sight of its meaning in recent weeks as you tangled yourself up in white-magic illusions of obligation and 'honor'." His voice scathed the last word.

Below, a horse screamed; the sound carried upwards on the frigid wind.

"There is only one law," Detlev said. "And that is force."

A horn blared. The cavalry were riding, hard, to the rescue. But there was no chance to feel pride in their speed, the mettlesome horses dashing over the snow, the silvery helms

gleaming and their horsetails streaming in the wind, because—
suddenly—before they even could even raise their bows to aim
at the Norsundrian front lines—they too began to fall. Illusion-
cloaked crossbowmen rippled into view on the wings of the
battle, where they had been lying in wait.

The calm, unemotional voice continued inexorably. "I
want your surrender. Now. No magic tricks, no easy will-
binding spell to take away the awareness of choice. Of your
own free will, and forever. Only then will I stop the slaughter of
your people, King Senrid."

Kyale pressed her knuckles against her mouth lest she
scream. Senrid's breathing was fast, but he did not look away.

Detlev drawled out his words now, the sneer like a
whiplash, "You prate of protection, but I observe you are willing
to trade their lives for yours." And then, his voice hard,
deliberate: "All of them, Senrid. Every one. As dead men
they're coming soulbound straight to me to use or spend as I
wish, and you're making the choice for them."

Senrid recoiled, his head snapping sideways as if he'd
been slapped. Then his chest heaved, and Kitty's horror
increased when she saw the sheen of tears in his eyes, but then
he threw back his head and cried in anguish and despair,
"*Erdrael!*"

Light coruscated, blinding them.

Kitty tried to rub the sparkles from her vision.

When she took her hand away, she and Senrid and a girl
their age, who seemed made of sunglow, were alone.

All around them the wind had stopped, and motion, and
time. Detlev and his guards were either invisible, or gone.

Senrid angrily dashed his wrist across his eyes. "It's a
cheat," he said fiercely, his voice unsteady, husky with grief.
"It's all a lie. You own me now, is that it? Instead of them?"

"Free will, Senrid," Erdrael said. Her voice echoed like
the peal of a bell. "You had to see the difference. If you had
chosen them, it would have been your last choice. Ever. Detlev
told you that much of the truth. You chose my help, and you
have the rest of your life—and after. This is as much as I can
give you."

"Free will," Senrid repeated, his tone making the words a mockery.

Erdrael said, her smile sad, "You'll face hard choices again, and again, and again. That is the nature of life. But right now you are free to make them."

"Who sent you?" Senrid demanded. "What is your price?"

But then he blinked, or both kids blinked, and sound, and motion, and time were restored.

Erdrael was gone. So was Detlev.

They were alone on the cliff.

Kyale breathed in a shaky breath. "Was that an *angel?*" Of course it was! Where was Detlev? Had the angel chased him off? She became lost in her own surmises, relieved and joyful and apprehensive; she shivered in the wintry wind, but it was a shiver of release.

Senrid's attention remained riveted below, where the battle had turned, for the Norsundrians did not seem to see their enemies any more. The glitter of magic winkled from horizon to horizon, the gray forces were drawn to the south, and then away into a sudden squall of snow, and they vanished.

The horns summoning the Marlovens echoed up the rock-face, and Senrid watched as the remainder of the western wing of the light cavalry massed again, and the foot reformed, except for those detailed to see to the fallen.

They were safe. And Senrid was able at last to look away.

Kitty stood, head down, her arms wrapped tightly about her under her cloak.

Detlev was still gone. And so—Senrid felt certain—were his wards.

Senrid touched Kyale's arm, and transferred them back to Choreid Dhelerei.

They appeared in his room.

"You summoned an angel," Kyale said, as though stunned.

"It wasn't," Senrid responded wearily, scrubbing a shaky wrist across his eyes. The glitter of tears was gone, though his eyes were marked with tension and tiredness. "Just some illusory image, made by some white mage's trickery. Here, give me Hibern's book. I'll return it."

Kyale shook her head as she handed Senrid the book. "It *was*. Llhei told me about angels, immortal beings from outside of time, but *good*. She never lied."

He shrugged. "Believe what you want."

"Well, whatever it was, at least she kicked out that stinker of a Norsundrian. You won." She sighed, a long, dramatic sigh. "So—after all that—"

"Yes," he said. "I rescind the promise. It doesn't matter any more." And before she could speak, he sent her home—he could see the destination as well as his own room.

⊷⟨Ⱨ⟩⊶

She found herself standing in Crestel-castle's courtyard outside the double doors. She was *home!*

As soon as she could get her legs to work she ran inside, crying, laughing, stumbling up the stairs. She wanted to see everyone, to tell them everything, except she was apprehensive that Leander might still be angry—and so she intended to rid herself of every vestige of Marloven Hess before she faced him.

She sped down the hall toward her room, glad to find it empty. But her door was a little ajar. Odd—unless someone was cleaning it against her return.

Satisfied that that had to be the explanation, she pushed the door open and started in, then caught a flicker above the edge of her vision.

She looked up, saw a wide, shallow baking pan teeter— she opened her mouth—to meet a face full of flour!

"Welcome home, o White Princess!" came Leander's chortle from behind.

"Ptui! Bleh! Yuk!"

"Hibern sent a message that you might be on the way back—that it was all over. So I set up a ward for your return, and arranged this little surprise—"

"Arrgh!" she yelled, but it was fake anger, and as she chased Leander down the hall, his laughter sounded as happy as hers.

SIX

Senrid was alone at last, without his silver-haired, self-appointed conscience. Kyale would blab his actions to anyone who would listen. What did that foolish promise matter any more? She'd tell them all that he'd called on an angel—if there even was such a thing—to rescue him. After that, the fact that he'd sentimentally helped an enemy escape would seem like mere caprice.

He was only alone for a few moments.

Footsteps alerted him to the fact that Tdanerend had put wards on his room. Of course. Well, those could be removed—if he survived whatever was coming next.

The door banged open, and there was Keriam.

"Senrid! You're alive!" The man ran in, his face looking younger than it had for a couple of years. He laughed aloud, stopped, stood straight, and then with deliberate care thumped his fist to his heart—then to his forehead.

His fist, not his palm. The formal salute for a newly crowned king.

"Not yet," Senrid whispered, finding that his voice was gone. "Not yet." His vision blurred again, but this time they were not the tears of grief, of shame and despair, but of happiness.

He wiped his sleeve across his eyes, drew in a shaky breath, and said, "We're rid of them. But I'm not convinced it's for long. Detlev left, taking his men. We did not defeat them. If anything—" His voice suspended again, and he forced the words out, roughly. "If anything, we would have gone down in defeat under their steel."

"Tell me."

Senrid did, in quick words; his emotions steadied as he gave detailed observations on the battle. He referred to Erdrael merely as a mage's illusion. Keriam did not question it. He knew nothing of magic.

At the end, Keriam rubbed his chin. "Defeat, maybe, but not surrender. I think Waldevan would have struck his banner first. If he wavered, I know Jarend of Methden would have struck his own banner before surrendering to them."

They both fell silent, contemplating what that meant: Marloven warriors who saw their banner struck down by their own side were thus required to either fight to the death or to suicide; at least then they would escape the magic binding their souls to Norsunder.

"I would have joined them if possible," Senrid said. "And it may come to it yet. We will have to see to our defenses, as soon as we can."

Keriam looked at the distraught young face before him, the tense, intelligent brow. Senrid's mind was already racing ahead, as he'd seen so many times, but at last the boy was not confined to circumventing his uncle's fear-driven pettiness. He could, at last, take command. He had the will and the brains— but not the training.

It seemed he was going to get that through necessity rather than practice.

Keriam said, "This crisis will unite us faster than anything else. Shall I summon the captains and commanders for general reports?"

"Do that. I have to get busy and write down all the promises I made," Senrid said. "I don't even know who I made them to—and I didn't dare write anything down—but one thing for certain, they know who I am. And they'll remember. So I'd better be ready for 'em."

Keriam saluted again, and left swiftly.

ಬೌಲ್ಬೊಞ

Morning turned into afternoon without Senrid noticing.   At
some point someone brought in food. Senrid was glad to see it,
and paused long enough to thank the person, but when he
remembered to eat—after a long rumble from his stomach—the
food had gone cold.

He ate it anyway, and got right back to work; first he
wrote down everything he'd been keeping in his head from his
conversations with his people, and then he read the papers he'd
found in the conference chamber off the throne room. When he
was done he looked up, surprised to discover the sun had already
set.

He picked up Hibern's book and carried it and his pile of
papers downstairs to the room he'd chosen to be his study, and
cast them on the table.

Before he could reconsider, he forced himself to go to his
uncle's rooms. If the servants had destroyed it, he supposed he
couldn't blame them, but would it mean they were beyond
control? Would there be riots now?

Was he, in fact, a weak little boy unable to control a
kingdom?

The Regent's rooms, next to the closed suite that had
belonged to King Indevan, were guarded by two of Keriam's
men.

Senrid slipped in, and spoke the word to ignite the magic
torches, which shed flickering reddish light on a quiet room.
Senrid stared around, frowning at the faint but sharp scent of
fear-sweat on the still air. Had Tdanerend forgotten to use his
cleaning frame? No. Senrid turned around slowly. No, the
smell was too faint for that, too ubiquitous, as if it had sunk into
the plaster on the walls. His uncle had lived in fear for years, and
it had worsened recently. The room reeked of it, not only in the
physical realm, but Senrid sensed it in spirit.

He surveyed the room. Everything was neat. In the
wardrobe hung uniforms, boots set below. Senrid crossed to the
table beside the wardrobe, and laid his hand on the carved chest
there. He lifted it, and saw, precisely organized, most of the
ancient medals belonging to the family. Tdanerend's symbols of

the greatness he'd craved. Senrid shut his eyes, pictured the archive room, and transferred the chest down there.

The rest of this stuff I'll have burned, he thought. *If Tdanerend returns, he'll have to start all over again.*

He passed beyond, to his uncle's private workroom, where he knew he'd find the papers of import. The papers in the conference chamber had turned out to be merely finished decrees, and copies of general commands to the army. Here, Senrid hoped to find notes on half-finished projects, especially in magic. He had not forgotten Hibern's sickening revelation about that cheerful Faline Sherwood being an Yxubarec—a shape-changer. His uncle had intended to get rid of him, all right, there was no doubt about it now.

The old anger and urgency seized him. With quick fingers he sorted over the papers lying on the desk, glancing at each and making two piles. One, worthless stuff, he would burn; the rest, he'd read more slowly.

He was kneeling at the cold fireplace, striking a spark against the pile of papers laid on the stones when a scratch at the door recalled his attention.

"Yes?"

A servant came in—one of his own. The man smiled a grim sort of smile, tired as he was, and said, "There is a visitor to see you, Senrid-Harvaldar."

Harvaldar, the Marloven word for crowned king. The man had enjoyed saying that. Senrid felt it, and his face reddened.

The fire caught. He saw it take good hold of the papers. They turned brown, withered, fell into ash before he straightened up, retucking the other pile more securely under his armpit. "Where?"

"Throne room."

All the way at the other end of the castle. Senrid repressed the instinctual fear with impatient determination. He could not hide. It was now his castle, his kingdom, and he must be seen.

So he began to walk down silent halls, past the enormous raptors and running horses, the doors that had opened and closed on so many of his ancestors, sometimes for violent purpose.

Shall I post guards outside my doors, to prevent surprises? No. Runners, yes. Not guards. I won't start living like Tdanerend.

He turned a corner and nearly stumbled over a party of servants busy scrubbing at walls and the slate floor, where several of Tdanerend's spies had made their last stand. All the servants scrambled up, or back, fists to hearts.

Fists to hearts. Senrid grinned, walking on, faster and faster, as everyone he encountered, from officers and guards to servants—all of them, without exception, saluted.

Elation bloomed behind his ribs and he began to run. He knew smiling faces could conceal violent intentions; he knew his work was only beginning, that danger had not disappeared, it had only receded.

But still he ran. He ran despite tiredness, and hunger, despite worries, he felt light as a bird, the bloom inside blossoming in his heart as joy, and laughter streamed behind him.

He ran downstairs, crossing from the residence wing to the governmental wing, and as he passed the big offices—some empty, some with scribes and academy boy messengers who stood in the doorways, curious, perhaps wondering what to do now that the great business of organizing a vast army was suspended. He flicked a salute and again they responded. Some with quick, inadvertent grins.

He stopped, panting, outside the throne room, where two guards had taken up their accustomed position. On whose orders? Probably Keriam's. Senrid passed through the doors, wondering if he was about to face an armed host, but in the vast, cold, eternally torchlit throne room there was only one figure, a tall thin girl with long dark hair. She was staring up at the great screaming eagle banner over the throne.

She turned at the sound of Senrid's step echoing up the vaulted walls.

"Senrid. You succeeded." She studied him gravely.

"Hibern!" He paused, some of his joy diminishing. "So your mages *have* been spying on me, then?"

She snorted. "I got a warning tracer from home. Latvian is busy destroying a lot of papers. Tsauderei, I assure you, probably thinks about affairs at this end of the continent about once a decade—if that."

"And the other mages?" Senrid persisted.

Hibern's brows lifted. "Are you suddenly seeing white spies, like your uncle saw conspirators?"

Senrid compressed his lips against a hot retort, then said only, "Come upstairs."

Back through the hallways, where they encountered more cleaning parties. Hibern frowned. It was obvious enough what had happened here.

They did not speak until they reached the room Senrid had chosen for his study. Someone had lit a lamp. He looked around and shut the door. "That was not on my orders," he said, jerking his chin over his shoulder. "In fact I tried to stop it, but I was already too late by the time my uncle retreated to the castle wall, and then transferred away. I think they'd been planning their own coups a long time, and when he lost control a couple days ago, they acted. Apparently they had quite a time with my uncle's pet torturer," he added bleakly. "Which no one told me about until it was all over."

Hibern drew in a long breath. "That, too, seems to be traditional with our people." She gave a wry smile. "Do you know how long it took for certain of the mages to trust me before they'd teach me?"

"Oh, I can imagine." Senrid thought of the Mearsieans and their unvarnished opinion of him, then grimaced. "And you insist no one is spying on me? Who would it be but one of your busybody mages?"

Hibern sat down in the single chair. "Tell me what makes you think someone is watching you. I still think that business off world was accidental. Your magic reached a human world-portal and propelled you through."

Senrid shook his head. "I'd go for that if afterward we'd all gotten propelled together right back home. But someone put me with those Mearsiean boys, someone sent Leander and Kyale home, and I presume the Mearsieans and Autumn as well. And 713 just vanished. I hope to somewhere he wanted to be. He couldn't have come home again, not and survive a day."

Hibern shook her head. "It's possible that they all thought their destinations—"

"I thought myself into East Arland, a place I've never spent the space of two breaths thinking about before, landing myself with a pair of boys I'd never met?"

Hibern lifted her hands. "I would say that the fact they were Mearsieans might be some connection—surely Faline mentioned them—but I know it's weak. There's something you're leaving out. Has to be. You don't seem to like it, either," she added, giving him one of her acute scrutinies. "But you may as well tell me, if you want my opinion on whether or not you have been interfered with by the people who have trained me."

Senrid's lip curled. "Kyale will be blabbing all over about her cursed 'angel'. Here's the truth." And he gave her an exact accounting of what happened there far away with the Mearsiean boys, and then on the cliff with Detlev.

Hibern's eyes widened, but she did not interrupt.

"Well?" he said finally, and perched on a table. "What do you think? White trickery? *Don't* try that angel business on me."

Hibern shrugged. "I think it foolish to deny that there are realms between that of matter and that of the spirit, just because we, abiding in the world of matter, cannot perceive everything. If there are angels—and they do consistently show up in the rare record—they must be a being an order of magnitude outside our understanding—"

Senrid snorted. "I think it's poetic foolery, all of it. The stories about angels all go on far too much about powers of goodness. If only I could believe that! Of course there are vast powers outside—or inside—the universe, but good? That they make and play with worlds like children play with polished rocks, that I can believe. Innate good? No such thing." He waved a hand dismissively. "Easier to believe the 'Erdrael' image was a ghost. Ghosts turn up far more consistently in records. Even some of my own ancestors saw ghosts."

Hibern looked at his angry face, his tense hands, and decided the subject was one he would have to explore on his own. "I don't think Erdrael was an angel, or a ghost. From anything I've ever read ghosts don't speak, or even hear when they are spoken to."

"Right."

"So, illusion, then, but who made it, and why? No one that I know would do anything like that—and for that matter, roughly the same time you were facing Detlev on that cliff, there was a conference going on at Tsauderei's, about some—some issues recently arisen in Sartor." Hibern frowned. "All the most powerful mages I know of were there. They couldn't have been running an illusion that complicated at the same time, and at this distance."

Senrid sensed that the 'issues' were fairly sizable, but he knew he wasn't going to hear about them. And in any case, he had enough to think about at home.

"Well, if you don't think one of your white-magic mages was being busy on my behalf, then I'll have to look elsewhere. No Great Power of Good is on my side, that much I'm sure of. Here's what I really think I saw: my kingdom and I were briefly pulled into the edge of a much larger battle, on a fantastic scale that takes centuries to prepare for, involving powers confined to this world."

"Yes," Hibern said. "I can agree with that."

Shock, excitement, worry, and challenge zinged through Senrid.

"What I don't know is *why*."

"I don't know either." Hibern turned her palms up. "So what will you do now?"

"Defend us. If I can. Learn what my uncle had been keeping secret about day-to-day government, as soon as I can. Keep the promises I made."

She smiled. "That does sound like you'll be busy." She rubbed her knuckles over the table lightly, saw her book lying there, and picked it up. "I suspected Kyale might have taken that, though why she would want to learn to magically bind stone vaulting and reinforce furnishing joints is beyond me."

"She seems to have had an idea she could brandish it under Tdanerend's nose and make him quail in fear."

Hibern sighed. But she said nothing derogatory about Kyale—and Senrid, mindful of how much the girl had gone through on his behalf, didn't either.

"So what about my father?" Hibern asked at last, her dark eyes serious.

Senrid said, "Hands off. But it has to be both ways."

"I take it I'm supposed to carry this threat to him?"

Senrid waved impatiently. "Of course not. I'll confront him myself. I want him to see me face to face. I'll leave him alone if he leaves me alone. And I'll explain that leaving me alone means leaving my kingdom alone."

She turned her palm up then got to her feet. "I have to return. Is there anything you would like my help with?"

"Please," Senrid said. "Find out where Ndand is, if you can. Or at least find out if she's really free of my uncle's spells, and if she's happy. If she doesn't want to come home, well, maybe she's better off elsewhere. I don't believe for a moment things are going to settle into a peaceful Golden Age here."

"No," Hibern said, and sighed. "I'll do that. And I'll bring you any news I think you should know. How's that?" He opened his hands—she touched fingers to heart—then transferred out.

Cold air stirred around the room, and Senrid was alone again, thinking over what she'd said—and what she'd kept to herself. What he'd learned was that he hadn't enough power to fight any great mages, white or Norsundrian.

And beyond that, the first question he had to face was: Would Detlev have stopped the slaughter if he'd surrendered?

He looked down at his hands. His fingers shook, a delayed reaction from what he'd been forced to watch on the southern cliff. He felt sick inside—and was still tired and hungry—but he had to think it out before he planned his next action, planned tomorrow, planned next week. And, if he lived, next month. Could he have stood there and watched them all die, had there been no Erdrael?

For that matter, would Detlev have waited for it to happen? Why didn't he strike Senrid down, or muscle him off to their base? Why did it have to be so agonizing?

A lesson in real politics.

He thought of the dead. Each was a person, someone's brother, or son, or father, who'd woken up that morning eager, or determined, or bored, or tired, or maybe even sick. Live Marlovens, his own people, smashed beyond life so easily, without regret. He made an inner vow that no matter what happened, he would never surrender to Detlev. Never would he even treat with Norsunder, no matter what they offered in supposed alliance. If Detlev had designed that exercise in cruelty to terrify him into submission, it had had the opposite effect.

He would stay free of Norsunder, even if it finally meant allying with the white mages.

Having decided that, he looked up at the four windows letting in the weak moonlight, and from the windows he took in the rest of the room. There he'd put his desk. And over there the bookshelves, and another shelf for maps.

He paced it out, finding the chore calming to the spirit.

When he was done, he had it all organized in his mind. The room, and his first orders.

He had to get reports from Gherdred and Keriam on where his army was.

He had to countermand some of his uncle's recent orders, and begin examining the laws his uncle had been making in his name...treasury...the academy...the rank system...trade?

The unending stream of plans, demands, compromises, questions, needs, wants of the last two weeks closed in on him, but he was used to thinking ahead and ordering his actions in terms of strongest need first.

Senrid stopped at his window and looked out at the jumble of roofs that housed the academy—where boys like him lived and learned.

He thought of Hibern, then, her wit and strength of will. CJ Sherwood, loudmouthed and opinionated but undoubtedly courageous. Collet's quiet skills. Faline's cheery capability, Autumn's amazing magic. Even Kyale, annoying as she was, had shown unexpected qualities. Crazy to keep girls out, it was the equivalent of denying his kingdom half its strength.

So the academy would soon be full of girls and boys his own age, learning as he was learning.

He smiled. Part of kingship was to be ready.
He—and Marloven Hess—would get ready together.

✺ The End ✺

‍ Author Note ‍

I adopted myself into Clair's gang by internally changing my
first name when I was eight years old.

Senrid's story was written just after I turned fifteen, in early
summer, 1966. This story fits into the middle of a series of
stories about kids in Sartorias-deles who find themselves mixed
up in world events. Some of them eventually discover abilities
lost for centuries.

If you'd like to know more about the timeline, stories, and
world, visit my website at:

http://www.sff.net/people/sherwood/writing/longproject.html

Breinigsville, PA USA
23 September 2009
224644BV00001B/14/A